THE ROUGH ROAD

BY
WILLIAM J. LOCKE

AUTHOR OF "THE RED PLANET," "THE WONDERFUL YEAR,"
"JAFFERY," "THE BELOVED VAGABOND," ETC.

I0563605

WILDSIDE PRESS

www.wildsidebooks.com

THE ROUGH ROAD

THE ROUGH ROAD

CHAPTER I

THIS is the story of Doggie Trevor. It tells of his doings and of a girl in England and a girl in France. Chiefly it is concerned with the influence that enabled him to win through the War. Doggie Trevor did not get the Victoria Cross. He got no cross of distinction whatever. He did not even attain the sorrowful glory of a little white cross above his grave in the Western Front. Doggie was no hero of romance, ancient or modern. But he went through with it and is alive to tell the tale.

The brutal of his acquaintance gave him the name of "Doggie" years before the War was ever thought of, because he had been brought up from babyhood like a toy Pom. The almost freak offspring of elderly parents, he had the rough world against him from birth. His father died before he had cut a tooth. His mother was old enough to be his grandmother. She had the intense maternal instinct and the brain, such as it is, of an earwig. She wrapped Doggie — his real name was James Marmaduke — in cotton-wool and kept him so until he was almost a grown man. Doggie had never a chance. She brought him up like a toy Pom until he was twenty-one — and then she died. Doggie, being comfortably off, continued the maternal tradition and kept on bringing himself up like a toy Pom. He did not know what else to do. Then, when he was six-and-twenty, he found himself at the edge of the world gazing in timorous

7

starkness down into the abyss of the Great War.
Something kicked him over the brink and sent him
sprawling into the thick of it.

That the world knows little of its greatest men
is a commonplace among silly aphorisms. With
far more justice it may be stated that of its least
men the world knows nothing and cares less. Yet
the Doggies of the War who on the cry of "Havoc!"
have been let loose, much to their own and everybody else's stupefaction, deserve the passing tribute
sometimes, poor fellows, of a sigh, sometimes of a
smile, often of a cheer. Very few of them — very
few, at any rate, of the English Doggies — have
tucked their little tails between their legs and run
away. Once a brawny humourist wrote to Doggie
Trevor "*Sursum cauda.*" Doggie happened to be
at the time in a water-logged front trench in Flanders
and the writer basking in the mild sunshine of
Simla with his Territorial Regiment. Doggie,
bidden by the Hedonist of circumstance to up with
his tail, felt like a scorpion.

Such feelings, however, will be more adequately
dealt with hereafter. For the moment it is only
essential to obtain a general view of the type to
which Trevor belonged.

If there is one spot in England where the present
is the past, where the future is still more of the
past, where the past wraps you and enfolds you in
the dreamy mist of Gothic things, where the lazy
meadows sloping riverward deny the passage of the
centuries, where the very clouds are secular, it is
the cathedral town of Durdlebury. No factory
chimneys defile with their smoke its calm air, or
defy its august and heaven-searching spires. No
rabble of factory hands shocks its few and sedate
streets. Divine Providence, according to the de-
vout, and the crass stupidity of the local authorities seventy years ago, according to progressive

minds, turned the main line of railway twenty miles from the sacred spot. So that to this year of grace it is the very devil of a business to find out, from Bradshaw, how to get to Durdlebury, and, having found, to get there. As for getting away, God help you! But who ever wanted to get away from Durdlebury, except the Bishop? In pre-motor days he used to grumble tremendously and threaten the House of Lords with Railway Bills and try to blackmail the Government with dark hints of resignation, and so he lived and threatened and made his wearisome diocesan round of visits and died. But now he has his episcopal motor-car, which has deprived him of his grievances.

In the Close of Durdlebury, greenswarded, silent, sentinelled by immemorial elms that guard the dignified Gothic dwellings of the cathedral dignitaries, was James Marmaduke Trevor born. His father, a man of private fortune, was Canon of Durdlebury. For many years he lived in the most commodious canonical house in the Close with his sisters Sophia and Sarah. In the course of time a new Dean, Dr. Conover, was appointed to Durdlebury, and, restless innovator that he was, underpinned the North Transept and split up Canon Trevor's home by marrying Sophia. Then Sarah, bitten by the madness, committed abrupt matrimony with the Rev. Vernon Manningtree, Rector of Durdlebury. Canon Trevor, many years older than his sisters, remained for some months in bewildered loneliness, until one day he found himself standing in front of the Cathedral altar with Miss Mathilda Jessup, while the Bishop pronounced over them words diabolically strange yet ecclesiastically familiar. Miss Jessup, thus transformed into Mrs. Trevor, was a mature and comfortable maiden lady of ample means, the only and orphan daughter of a late Bishop of Durdlebury. Never had there been such a marrying and giving in marriage in the Cathedral circle. Children were born in Decanal, Rectorial, and Canonical homes. First a son to the Manningtrees, whom they named Oliver. Then a daughter to the Conovers. Then a son, named James Marmaduke, after the late Bishop Jessup, was born to the Trevors. The profane say that Canon Trevor, a profound patristic theologian and an enthusiastic palaeontologist, couldn't make head or tail of it all, and, unable to decide whether James Marmaduke should be attributed to the Tertullian or the Neolithic period, expired in an agony of dubiety. At any rate the poor man died. The widow, of necessity, moved from the Close, in order to make way for the new Canon, and betook herself with her babe to Denby Hall, the comfortable house on the outskirts of the town in which she had dwelt before her marriage.

The saturated essence of Durdelbury ran in Marmaduke's blood: an honourable essence, a proud essence; an essence of all that is statically beautuful and dignified in English life; but an essence which, without admixture of wilder and more fluid elements, is apt to run thick and clog the arteries. Marmaduke was coddled from his birth. The Dean, then a breezy, energetic man, protested. Sarah Manningtree protested. But when the Dean's eldest-born died of diphtheria, Mrs. Trevor, in her heart, set down the death as a judgement on Sophia for criminal carelessness; and when young Oliver Manningtree grew up to be an intolerable young Turk and savage, she looked on Marmaduke, and, thanking heaven that he was not as other boys were, enfolded him more than ever beneath her motherly wing. When Oliver went to school in the town and tore his clothes and rolled in mud and punched other boys' heads, Marmaduke remained at home under the educational charge of a governess. Oliver,

lean and lanky and swift-eyed, swaggered through
the streets unattended from the first day they sent
him to a neighbouring kindergarten. As the months
and years of his childish life passed, he grew more and
more independent and vagabond. He swore blood
brotherhood with a butcher-boy and, unknown to
his pious parents, became the leader of a ferocious
gang of pirates. Marmaduke, on the other hand,
was never allowed to cross the road without feminine escort. Oliver had the profoundest contempt
for Marmaduke. Being two years older, he kicked
him whenever he had a chance. Marmaduke
loathed him. Marmaduke shrank into Miss Gunter
the governess's skirts whenever he saw him. Mrs.
Trevor therefore regarded Oliver as the youthful
incarnation of Beelzebub, and quarrelled bitterly
with her sister-in-law.

One day Oliver, with three or four of his piratical
friends, met Marmaduke and Miss Gunter and a
little toy terrier in the High Street. The toy
terrier was attached by a lead to Miss Gunter on
the one side, Marmaduke by a hand on the other.
Oliver straddled rudely across the path.

"Hallo! Look at the two little doggies!" he
cried. He snapped his fingers at the terrier. "Come
along, Tiny!" The terrier yapped. Oliver grinned
and turned to Marmaduke. "Come along, Fido,
dear little doggie."

"You're a nasty, rude, horrid boy, and I shall tell
your mother," declared Miss Gunter, indignantly.

But Oliver and his pirates laughed with the truculence befitting their vocation, and bowing with
ironical politeness, let their victim depart to the
parody of a popular song: "Good-bye, Doggie,
we shall miss you."

From that day onwards Marmaduke was known
as "Doggie" throughout all Durdlebury, save to
his mother and Miss Gunter. The Dean himself

grew to think of him as "Doggie." People to
this day call him Doggie without any notion of the
origin of the name.

To preserve him from persecution Mrs. Trevor
jealously guarded him from association with other
boys. He neither learned nor played any boyish
games. In defiance of the doctor, whom she regarded as a member of the brutal anti-Marmaduke
League, Mrs. Trevor proclaimed Marmaduke's delicacy of constitution. He must not go out into the
rain lest he should get damp, nor into the hot sunshine lest he should perspire. She kept him like
a precious plant in a carefully warmed conservatory.
Doggie, used to it from birth, looked on it as his
natural environment. Under feminine guidance
and tuition he embroidered and painted screens
and played the piano and the mandolin, and read
Miss Charlotte Yonge and learned history from the
late Mrs. Markman. Without doubt his life was
a happy one. All that he asked for was seques-
tration from Oliver and his associates.

Now and then the cousins were forced to meet —
at occasional children's parties, for instance. A
little daughter, Peggy, had been born in the Deanery,
replacing the lost first-born, and festivals, to which
came the extreme youth of Durdlebury, were given
in her honour. She liked Marmaduke, who was
five years her senior, because he was gentle and
clean and wore such beautiful clothes and brushed
his hair so nicely; whereas she detested Oliver, who,
even at an afternoon party, looked as if he had just
come out of a rabbit-hole. Besides, Marmaduke
danced beautifully; Oliver couldn't and wouldn't,
disdaining such effeminate sports. His great joy
was to put out a sly leg and send Doggie and his
partner sprawling. Once the Dean caught him at
it and called him a horrid little beast, and threatened
him with neck and crop expulsion if he ever did

it again. Doggie, who had picked himself up and listened to the rebuke, said:

"I'm very glad to hear you talk to him like that, Uncle. I think his behaviour is perfectly detestable."

The Dean's lips twitched and he turned away abruptly. Oliver glared at Doggie.

"Oh, my holy Aunt!" he whispered hoarsely. "Just you wait till I get you alone!"

Oliver got him alone, an hour later, in a passage, having lain in ambush for him, and, after a few busy moments, contemplated a bruised and bleeding Doggie blubbering in a corner.

"Do you think my behaviour is detestable now?"

"Yes," whimpered Doggie.

"I've a good mind to go on licking you until you say 'no,'" said Oliver.

"You're a great big bully," said Doggie.

Oliver reflected. He did not like to be called a bully. "Look here," said he. "I'll stick my right arm down inside the back of my trousers and fight you with my left."

"I don't want to fight, I can't fight," cried Doggie.

Oliver put his hands in his pockets.

"Will you come and play Kiss-in-the-Ring, then?" he asked sarcastically.

"No," replied Doggie.

"Well, don't say I haven't made you generous offers," said Oliver, and stalked away.

It was all very well for the Rev. Vernon Manningtree, when discussing this incident with the Dean, to dismiss Doggie with a contemptuous shrug and call him a little worm without any spirit. The unfortunate Doggie remained a human soul with a human destiny before him. As to his lack of spirit.

"Where," said the Dean, a man of wider sympathies, "do you suppose he could get any from?

Look at his parentage. Look at his upbringing by that idiot woman."

"If he belonged to me I'd drown him," said the Rector.

"If I had my way with Oliver," said the Dean, "I'd skin him alive."

"I'm afraid he's a young devil," said the Rector, not without paternal pride. "But he has the makings of a man."

"So has Marmaduke," replied the Dean.

"Bosh!" said Mr. Manningtree.

When Oliver went to Rugby happier days than ever dawned for Marmaduke. There were only the holidays to fear. But as time went on the haughty contempt of Oliver, the public school-boy, for the home-bred Doggie forbade him to notice the little creature's existence; so that even the holidays lost their gloomy menace and became like the normal halcyontide. Meanwhile Doggie grew up. When he reached the age of fourteen the Dean, by strenuous endeavour, rescued him from the unavailing tuition of Miss Gunter. But school for Marmaduke Mrs. Trevor would not hear of. It was brutal of Edward — the Dean — to suggest such a thing. Marmaduke — so sensitive and delicate — school would kill him. It would undo all the results of her unceasing care. It would make him coarse and vulgar like other horrid boys. She would sooner see him dead at her feet than at a public school. It was true that he ought to have the education of a gentleman. She did not need Edward to point out her duty. She would engage a private tutor.

"All right. I'll get you one," said the Dean.

The Master of his old college at Cambridge sent him an excellent youth who had just taken his degree — a second class in the Classical Tripos —

an all-round athlete and a gentleman. The first
thing he did was to take Marmaduke on the lazy
river that flowed through the Durdlebury meadows,
thereby endangering his life, wofully blistering his
hands, and making him ache all over his poor little
body. After a quarter of an hour's interview with
Mrs. Trevor, the indignant young man threw up
his post and departed.

Mrs. Trevor determined to select a tutor herself.
A scholastic agency sent her a dozen candidates.
She went to London and interviewed them all. A
woman, even of the most limited intelligence, in-
variably knows what she wants, and invariably
gets it. Mrs. Trevor got Phineas McPhail, M.A.
Glasgow, B.A. Oxford (Third Class Mathematical
Greats), reading for Holy Orders.

"I was training for the ministry in the Free Kirk
of Scotland," said he, "when I gradually became
aware of the error of my ways, until I saw that
there could only be salvation in the episcopal form
of Church government. As the daughter of a
bishop, Mrs. Trevor, you will appreciate my conscientious position. An open scholarship and the
remainder of my little patrimony enabled me to
get my Oxford degree. You would have no objec-
tion to my continuing my theological studies
while I undertake the education of your son?"

Phineas McPhail pleased Mrs. Trevor. He had
what she called a rugged, honest Scotch face, with
a very big nose in the middle of it, and little grey
eyes overhung by brown and shaggy eyebrows.
He spoke with the mere captivating suggestion of
an accent. The son of decayed, proud, and now
extinct gentlefolk, he presented personal testimonials
of an unexceptionable quality.

Phineas McPhail took to Doggie and Durdlebury
as a duck to water. He read for Holy Orders for
seven years. When the question of his ordination

arose, he would declare impressively that his sacred duty was the making of Marmaduke into a scholar and a Christian. That duty accomplished, he would begin to think of himself. Mrs. Trevor accounted him the most devoted and selfless friend that woman ever had. He saw eye to eye with her in every detail of Marmaduke's upbringing. He certainly taught the boy, who was naturally intelligent, a great deal, and repaired the terrible gaps in Miss Gunter's system of education. McPhail had started life with many eager curiosities, under the impulse of which he had amassed considerable knowledge of a superficial kind which, lolling in an armchair with a pipe in his mouth, he found easy to impart. To the credit side of Mrs. Trevor's queer account it may be put that she did not object to smoking. The late Canon smoked incessantly. Perhaps the odour of tobacco was the only keen memory of her honeymoon and brief married life.

During his seven years of soft living Phineas McPhail scientifically developed an original taste for whisky. He seethed himself in it as the ancients seethed a kid in its mother's milk. He had the art to do himself to perfection. Mrs. Trevor beheld in him the mellowest and blandest of men. Never had she the slightest suspicion of evil courses. To such a pitch of cunning in the observance of the proprieties had he arrived, that the very servants knew not of his doings. It was only later — after Mrs. Trevor's death — when a surveyor was called in by Marmaduke to put the old house in order, that a disused well at the back of the house was found to be half filled with thousands of whisky bottles secretly thrown in by Phineas McPhail.

The Dean and Mr. Manningtree, although ignorant of McPhail's habits, agreed in calling him a lazy hound and a parasite on their fond sister-in-law. And they were right. But Mrs. Trevor

turned a deaf ear to their slanders. They were
unworthy to be called Christian men, let alone
ministers of the Gospel. Were it not for the sacred
associations of her father and her husband, she
would never enter the Cathedral again. Mr. Mc-
Phail was exactly the kind of tutor that Marmaduke needed. Mr. McPhail did not encourage
him to play rough games, or take long walks, or
row on the river, because he appreciated his constitutional delicacy. He was the only man in the
world during her unhappy widowhood who understood Marmaduke. He was a treasure beyond
price.

When Doggie was sixteen, fate, fortune, chance,
or whatever you like to call it, did him a good turn.
It made his mother ill and sent him away with her
to foreign health resorts. Doggie and McPhail
travelled luxuriously, lived in luxurious hotels, and
visited in luxurious ease various picture galleries
and monuments of historic or aesthetic interest.
The boy, artistically inclined and guided by the
idle yet well-informed Phineas, profited greatly.
Phineas sought profit to them both in other ways.

"Mrs. Trevor," said he, "don't you think it a
sinful shame for Marmaduke to waste his time over
Latin and Mathematics, and such things as he can
learn at home, instead of taking advantage of his
residence in a foreign country to perfect himself in the
idiomatic and conversational use of the language?"

Mrs. Trevor, as usual, agreed. So thenceforward,
whenever they were abroad, which was for three or
four months of each year, Phineas revelled in sheer
idleness, nicotine, and the skilful consumption of
alcohol, while highly paid professors taught Marmaduke, and incidentally himself, French and
Italian.

Of the world, however, and of the facts, grim or
seductive, of life, Doggie learned little. Whether

by force of some streak of honesty, whether through sheer laziness, whether through canny self-interest, Phineas McPhail conspired with Mrs. Trevor to keep Doggie in darkest ignorance.   His reading was selected like that of a young girl in a convent: he was taken only to the most innocent of plays; foreign theatres, casinos, and such like wells of delectable depravity existed almost beyond his ken.   Until he was twenty it never occurred to him to sit up after his mother had gone to bed.   Of strange goddesses he knew nothing. His mother saw to that.   He had a mild affection for his cousin Peggy, which his mother encouraged.   She allowed him to smoke cigarettes, drink fine claret, the remains of the cellar of her father the Bishop, a connoisseur, and crême de menthe.   And until she died, that was all poor Doggie knew of the lustiness of life.

Mrs. Trevor died, and Doggie, as soon as he had recovered from the intensity of his grief, looked out upon a lonely world.   Phineas, like Mrs. Micawber, swore he would never desert him.   In the perils of Polar exploration or the comforts of Denby Hall, he would find Phineas McPhail ever by his side. The first half dozen or so of these declarations consoled Doggie tremendously.   He dreaded the Church swallowing up his only protector and leaving him defenceless.   Conscientiously, however, he said:

"I don't want your affection for me to stand in your way, sir."

"'Sir'?" cried Phineas.   "Is it not practicable for us to do away with the old relations of master and pupil and become as brothers?   You are now a man and independent.   Let us be Pylades and Orestes.   Let us share and share alike.   Let us be Marmaduke and Phineas."

Doggie was touched by such devotion.   "But

your ambitions to take Holy Orders which you have sacrificed for my sake?"

"I think it may be argued," said Phineas, "that the really beautiful life is delight in continued sacrifice. Besides, my dear boy, I am not quite so sure as I was when I was young, that by confining oneself within the narrow limits of a sacerdotal profession, one can retain all one's wider sympathies both with human infirmity and the gladder things of existence."

"You're a true friend, Phineas," said Doggie.

"I am," replied Phineas.

It was just after this that Doggie wrote him a cheque for a thousand pounds on account of a vaguely indicated year's salary.

If Phineas had maintained the wily caution which he had exercised for the past seven years, all might have been well. But there came a time when unneedfully he declared once more that he would never desert Marmaduke, and declaring it hiccoughed so horribly and stared so glassily, that Doggie feared he might be ill. He had just lurched into Doggie's own peacock-blue and ivory sitting-room when he was mournfully playing the piano.

"You're unwell, Phineas. Let me get you something."

"You're right, laddie," Phineas agreed, his legs giving way alarmingly so that he collapsed on a brocade-covered couch. "It's a touch of the sun, which I would give you to understand," he continued with a self-preservatory flash, for it was an overcast day in June, "is often magnified in power when it is behind a cloud. A wee drop of whisky is what I require for a complete recovery."

Doggie ran into the dining-room and returned with a decanter of whisky, glass and siphon — an adjunct to the sideboard since Mrs. Trevor's death. Phineas filled half the tumbler with spirit, tossed

it off, smiled fantastically, tried to rise, and rolled
upon the carpet. Doggie, frightened, rang the bell.
Peddle, the old butler, appeared.

"Mr. McPhail is ill. I can't think what can be
the matter with him."

Peddle looked at the happy Phineas with the
eyes of experience.

"If you will allow me to say so, sir," said he, "the
gentleman is dead drunk."

And that was the beginning of the end of Phineas.
He lost grip of himself. He became the scarlet
scandal of Durdlebury and the terror of Doggie's
life. The Dean came to the rescue of a grateful
nephew. A swift attack of delirium tremens
crowned and ended Phineas McPhail's Durdlebury
career.

"My boy," said the Dean on the day of Phineas's
expulsion, "I don't want to rub it in unduly, but
I've warned your poor mother for years, and you
for months, against this bone-idle, worthless fellow.
Neither of you would listen to me. But you see
that I was right. Perhaps now you may be more
inclined to take my advice."

"Yes, Uncle," replied Doggie, submissively.

The Dean, a comfortable, florid man in the early
sixties, took up his parable and expounded it for
three-quarters of an hour. If ever young man heard
that which was earnestly meant for his welfare,
Doggie heard it from his Very Reverend uncle's
lips.

"And now, my dear boy," said the Dean by way
of peroration, "you cannot but understand that it
is your bounden duty to apply yourself to some
serious purpose in life."

"I do," said Doggie. "I've been thinking over
it for a long time. I'm going to gather material
for a history of wall-papers."

CHAPTER II

THENCEFORWARD Doggie, like the late Mr. Matthew Arnold's fellow millions, lived alone. He did not complain. There was little to complain about. He owned a pleasant old house set in fifteen acres of grounds. He had an income of three thousand pounds a year. Old Peddle, the butler, and his wife, the housekeeper, saved him from domestic cares. Rising late and retiring early, like the good King of Yvetot, he cheated the hours that might have proved weary. His meals, his toilet, his music, his wall-papers, his drawing and embroidering—specimens of the last he exhibited with great success at various shows held by Arts and Crafts Guilds and such like high and artistic fellowships — his sweet peas, his chrysanthemums, his postage stamps, his dilettante reading and his mild social engagements, filled most satisfyingly the hours not claimed by slumber. Now and then appointments with his tailor summoned him to London. He stayed at the same mildewed old family hotel in the neighbourhood of Bond Street at which his mother and his grandfather the Bishop, had stayed for uncountable years. There he would lunch and dine stodgily in musty state. In the evenings he would go to the plays discussed in the less giddy of Durdlebury ecclesiastical circles. The play over, it never occurred to him to do otherwise than drive decorously back to Sturrock's Hotel. Suppers at the Carlton or the Savoy were outside his sphere of thought or opportunity. His only acquaintance in London were vague elderly female friends of his mother,

who invited him to chilly semi-suburban teas, and
entertained him with tepid reminiscence and criticism of their divers places of worship. The days
in London thus passed drearily, and Doggie was
always glad to get home again.

In Durdlebury he began to feel himself appreciated. The sleepy society of the place accepted
him as a young man of unquestionable birth and
irreproachable morals. He could play the piano,
the harp, the viola, the flute, and the clarionette,
and sing a very true mild tenor. As secretary of
the Durdlebury Musical Association, he filled an
important position in the town. Dr. Flint —
Joshua Flint, Mus. Doc., organist of the Cathedral,
scattered broadcast golden opinions of Doggie.
There was once a concert of old English music
which the dramatic critics of the great newspapers
attended — and one of them mentioned Doggie
— "Mr. Marmuduke Trevor, who played the viol
da gamba as to the manner born." Doggie cut
out the notice, framed it, and stuck it up in his
peacock-and-ivory sitting-room.

Besides music, Doggie had other social accomplish-
ments. He could dance. He could escort young
ladies home of nights. Not a dragon in Durdlebury would not have trusted Doggie with untold
daughters. With women, old and young, he had
no shynesses. He had been bred among them,
understood their purely feminine interests, and
instinctively took their point of view. On his
visits to London he could be entrusted with com-
missions. He could choose the exact shade of silk
for a drawing-room sofa cushion, and had an un-
erring taste in the selection of wedding presents.
Young men other than budding ecclesiastical dignitaries were rare in Durdlebury, and Doggie had
little to fear from the competition of coarser masculine natures. In a word, Doggie was popular.

Although of no mean or revengeful nature, he was human enough to feel a little malicious satisfaction when it was proved to Durdlebury that Oliver had gone to the devil. His Aunt Sarah, Mrs. Manningtree, had died midway in the Phineas McPhail period; Mr. Manningtree a year or so later had accepted a living in the North of England and died when Doggie was about four-and-twenty. Meanwhile Oliver, who had been withdrawn young from Rugby, where he had been a thorn in the side of the authorities, and had been pinned like a cockchafer to a desk in a family counting-house in Lothbury, E. C., had broken loose, quarrelled with his father, gone off with paternal malediction and a maternal heritage of a thousand pounds to California, and was lost to the family ken. When a man does not write to his family, what explanation can there be save that he is ashamed to do so? Oliver was ashamed of himself. He had taken to desperate courses. He was an outlaw. He had gone to the devil. His name was rarely mentioned in Durdlebury — to Marmaduke Trevor's very great and catlike satisfaction. Only to the Dean's ripe and kindly wisdom was his name not utterly anathema.

"My dear," said he once to his wife, who was deploring her nephew's character and fate, — "I have hopes of Oliver even yet. A man must have something of the devil in him if he wants to drive the devil out."

Mrs. Conover was shocked.

"My dear Edward!" she cried.

"My dear Sophia," said he with a twinkle in his mild blue eyes that had puzzled her from the day when he first put a decorous arm around her waist. "My dear Sophia, if you knew what a ding-dong scrap of fiends went on inside me before I could bring myself to vow to be a virtuous milk-and-water parson, your hair, which is as long and beautiful as ever, would stand up straight on end."

Mrs. Conover sighed.

"I give you up."

"It's too late," said the Dean.

The Manningtrees, father and mother and son, were gone. Doggie bore the triple loss with equanimity. Then Peggy Conover, hitherto under the eclipse of boarding-schools, finishing schools, and foreign travel, swam, at the age of twenty, within his orbit. When first they met after a year's absence she very gracefully withered the symptoms of the cousinly kiss, to which they had been accustomed all their lives, by stretching out a long, frank, and defensive arm. Perhaps, if she had allowed the salute, there would have been an end of the matter. But there came the phenomenon which, unless she was a minx of craft and subtlety, she did not anticipate: for the first time in his life he was possessed of a crazy desire to kiss her. Doggie fell in love. It was not a wild, consuming passion. He slept well, he ate well, and he played the flute without a sigh causing him to blow discordantly into the holes of the instrument. Peggy vowing that she would not marry a parson, he had no rivals. He knew not even the pinpricks of jealousy. Peggy liked him. At first she delighted in him as in a new and animated toy. She could pull strings and the figure worked amazingly and amusingly. He proved himself to be a useful toy, too. He was at her beck all day long. He ran on errands, he fetched and carried. Peggy realised blissfully that she owned him. He haunted the Deanery.

One evening after dinner the Dean said:

"I am going to play the heavy father. How are things between you and Peggy?"

Marmaduke, taken unawares, reddened violently. He murmured that he didn't know.

"You ought to," said the Dean. "When a young man converts himself into a girl's shadow, even although he is her cousin and has been brought up with her from childhood, people begin to gossip. They gossip even within the august precincts of a stately cathedral."

"I'm very sorry," said Marmaduke. "I've had the very best intentions."

The Dean smiled. "What were they?"

"To make her like me a little," replied Marmaduke. Then, feeling that the Dean was kindly disposed, he blurted out awkwardly: "I hoped that one day I might ask her to marry me."

"That's what I wanted to know," said the Dean. "You haven't done it yet?"

"No," said Marmuduke.

"Why don't you?"

"It seems taking such a liberty," replied Marmaduke.

The Dean laughed. "Well, I'm not going to do it for you. My chief desire is to regularise the present situation. I can't have you two running about together all day and every day. If you like to ask Peggy, you have my permission and her mother's."

"Thank you, Uncle Edward," said Marmaduke.

"Let us join the ladies," said the Dean.

In the drawing-room the Dean exchanged glances with his wife. She saw that he had done as he had been bidden. Marmaduke was not an ideal husband for a brisk, pleasure-loving, modern young woman. But where was another husband to come from? Peggy had banned the Church. Marmaduke was wealthy, sound in health, and free from vice. It was obvious to maternal eyes that he was in love with Peggy. According to the Dean, if he wasn't, he oughtn't to be forever at her heels. The young woman herself seemed to take considerable pleasure

in his company. If she cared nothing for him, she
was acting in a reprehensible manner. So the Dean
had been deputed to sound Marmaduke.

Half an hour later the young people were left
alone. First the Dean went to his study. Then
Mrs. Conover departed to write letters. Marmaduke, advancing across the room from the door which
he had opened, met Peggy's mocking eyes as she
stood on the hearthrug with her hands behind her
back. Doggie felt very uncomfortable. Never had
he said a word to her in betrayal of his feelings. He
had a vague idea that propriety required a young
man to get through some wooing before asking a
girl to marry him. To ask first and woo afterwards
seemed putting the cart before the horse. But
how to woo that remarkably cool and collected
young person standing there, passed his wit.

"Well," she said. "The dear old birds seem very
fussy to-night. What's the matter?" And as he
said nothing, but stood confused with his hands
in his pockets, she went on. "You too seem rather
ruffled. Look at your hair."

Doggie, turning to a mirror, perceived that an
agitated hand had disturbed the symmetry of his
sleek, black hair, brushed without a parting away
from the forehead over his head. Hastily he
smoothed down the cockatoo-like crest.

"I've been talking to your father, Peggy."

"Have you really?" she said with a laugh.

Marmaduke summoned his courage.

"He told me I might ask you to marry me," he
said.

"Do you want to?"

"Of course I do," he declared.

"Then why not do it?"

But before he could answer, she clapped her
hands on his shoulders and shook him and laughed
out loud.

"Oh, you dear, silly old thing! What a way to propose to a girl!"

"I've never done such a thing before," said Doggie, as soon as he was released.

She resumed her attitude on the hearthrug.

"I'm in no great hurry to be married. Are you?"

He said, "I don't know. I've never thought of it. Just whenever you like."

"All right," she returned calmly. "Let it be a year hence. Meanwhile we can be engaged. It'll please the dear old birds. I know all the tabbies in the town have been mewing about us. Now they can mew about somebody else."

"That's awfully good of you, Peggy," said Marmaduke. "I'll go up to town to-morrow and get you the jolliest ring you ever saw."

She sketched him a curtsey. "That's one thing, at any rate, I can trust you in — your taste in jewellery."

He moved nearer to her. "I suppose you know, Peggy dear, I've been awfully fond of you for quite a long time."

"The feeling is more or less reciprocated," she replied lightly. Then, "You can kiss me if you like. I assure you it's quite usual."

He kissed her somewhat shyly on the lips.

She whispered: "I do think I care for you, old thing." Marmaduke replied sententiously: "You have made me a very happy man." Then they sat down side by side on the sofa, and for all Peggy's mocking audacity, they could find nothing in particular to say to each other.

"Let us play patience," she said at last.

And when Mrs. Conover appeared a while later, she found them poring over the cards in a state of unruffled calm. Peggy looked up, smiled and nodded.

"We've fixed it up, Mummy; but we're not going to be married for a year."

Doggie went home that evening in a tepid glow.
It contented him.   He thought himself the luckiest
of mortals.   A young man with more passion or
imagination might have deplored the lack of romance in the betrothal.   He might have desired
on the part of the maiden either more shyness,
delicacy, and elusiveness or more resonant emotion.
The finer tendrils of his being might have shivered,
ready to shrivel, as at a touch of frost, in the cool,
ironical atmosphere which the girl had created
around her.   But Doggie was not such a young
man.   Such passions as heredity had endowed
him with had been drugged by training.   No tales
of immortal love had ever fired his blood.   Once,
somewhere abroad, the unprincipled McPhail found
him reading *Manon Lescaut* — he had bought a
cheap copy haphazard, — and taking the delectable
volume out of his hands, asked him what he thought
of it.

"It's like reading about a lunatic," replied the
bewildered Doggie.   "Do such people as Des Grieux
exist?"

"Ay, laddie," replied McPhail, greatly relieved.
"Your acumen has pierced to the root of the matter.
They do exist, but nowadays we put them into
asylums.   We must excuse the author for living in
the psychological obscurity of the eighteenth century.   It's just a silly, rotten book."

"I'm glad you're of the same opinion as myself,"
said Doggie, and thought no more of the absurd
but deathless pair of lovers.   The unprincipled
McPhail, not without pawky humour, immediately
gave him *Paul et Virginie*, which Doggie, after
reading it, thought the truest and most beautiful
story in the world.   Even in later years, when his
intelligence had ripened and his sphere of reading
expanded, he looked upon the passion of a Romeo
or an Othello as a conventional peg on which the

poet hung his imagery, but having no more relation to real life as it is lived by human beings than the blood-lust of the half-man, half-bull Minotaur, or the uncomfortable riding conversation of the Valkyrie.

So Doggie Trevor went home perfectly contented with himself, with Peggy Conover, with his Uncle and Aunt, of whom hitherto he had been just a little bit afraid, with Fortune, with Fate, with his house, with his peacock-and-ivory room, with a great clump of type script and a mass of coloured proof-prints which represented a third of his projected history of wall-papers, with his feather-bed, with Goliath, his almost microscopic Belgium griffon, with a set of Nile-green silk underwear that had just come from his outfitters in London, with his new Rolls-Royce car and his new chauffeur Briggins — (parenthetically it may be remarked that a seven-hour excursion in this vehicle, youth in the back seat and Briggins at the helm, all ordained by Peggy, had been the final cause of the evening's explanations) — with the starry heavens above, with the well-ordered earth beneath them, and with all human beings on the earth, including Germans, Turks, Infidels and Heretics — all save one: and that, as he learned from a letter delivered by the last post, was from a callous, heartless London manicurist who, giving no reasons, regretted that she would be unable to pay her usual weekly visit to Durdlebury on the morrow. Of all days in the year: just when it was essential that he should look his best!

"What the deuce am I going to do?" he cried pitching the letter into the waste-paper basket.

He sat down to the piano in the peacock-and-ivory room and tried to play the nasty, crumpled roseleaf of a manicurist out of his mind. Suddenly he remembered, with a kind of shock, that he had pledged himself to go up to London the next day to buy an engagement ring. So, after all, the manicurist's defection did not matter. All was again well with the world.

Then he went to bed and slept the sleep of the just and perfect man living the just and perfect life in a just and perfect universe.

And the date of this happening was the fifteenth day of July in the year of grace one thousand nine hundred and fourteen.

CHAPTER III

THE shadow cast by the great apse of the Cathedral slanted over the end of the Deanery garden, leaving the house in the blaze of the afternoon sun, and divided the old red-brick wall into a vivid contrast of tones. The peace of centuries brooded over the place. No outside convulsions could ever cause a flutter of her calm wings. As it was thirty years ago, when the Dean first came to Durdlebury, as it was three hundred, six hundred years ago, so it was now; and so it would be hundreds of years hence as long as that majestic pile housing the Spirit of God should last.

Thus thought, thus, in some such words, proclaimed the Dean, sitting in the shade, with his hands clasped behind his head. Tea was over. Mrs. Conover; thin and faded, still sat by the little table, wondering whether she might now blow out the lamp beneath the silver kettle. Sir Archibald Bruce, a neighbouring landowner, and his wife had come, bringing their daughter Dorothy to play tennis. The game had already started on the court some little distance off — the players being Dorothy, Peggy, and a couple of athletic, flannel-clad parsons. Marmaduke Trevor reposed on a chair under the lee of Lady Bruce. He looked very cool and spick and span in a grey cashmere suit, grey shirt, socks and tie, and grey swede shoes. He had a weak, good-looking little face and a little black moustache turned up to the ends. He was discoursing to his neighbour on Palestrina.

The Dean's proclamation had been elicited by some remark of Sir Archibald.

"I wonder how you have stuck it for so long," said the latter. He had been a soldier in his youth and an explorer, and had shot big game.

"I haven't your genius, my dear Bruce, for making myself uncomfortable," replied the Dean.

"You were energetic enough when you first came here," said Sir Archibald. "We all thought you a desperate fellow who was going to rebuild the Cathedral, turn the Close into industrial dwellings, and generally play the deuce."

The Dean sighed pleasantly. He had snowy hair and a genial, florid, clean-shaven face.

"I was appointed very young, — six and thirty, — and I thought I could fight against the centuries. As the years went on I found I couldn't. The grey changelessness of things got hold of me, incorporated me into them. When I die — for I hope I shan't have to resign through doddering senility — my body will be buried there," — he jerked his head slightly towards the Cathedral — "and my dust will become part and parcel of the fabric — like that of many of my predecessors."

"That's all very well," said Sir Archibald, "but they ought to have caught you before this petrifaction set in, and made you a bishop."

It was somewhat of an old argument, for the two were intimates. The Dean smiled and shook his head.

"You know I declined —"

"After you had become petrified."

"Perhaps so. It is not a place where ambitions can attain a riotous growth."

"I call it a rotten place," said the elderly worldling. "I wouldn't live in it myself for twenty thousand a year."

"Lots like you said the same in crusading times — Sir Guy de Chevenix, for instance, who was the Lord, perhaps, of your very manor, and an amazing fire-eater — but — see the gentle irony of it — there his bones lie, at peace for ever, in the rotten place, with his effigy over them cross-legged, and his dog at his feet, and his wife by his side. I think he must sometimes look out of Heaven's gate down on the Cathedral and feel glad, grateful — perhaps a bit wistful — if the attribution of wistfulness, which implies regret, to a spirit in Paradise doesn't savour of heresy —"

"I'm going to be cremated," interrupted Sir Archibald, twirling his white moustache.

The Dean smiled and did not take up the cue. The talk died. It was a drowsy day. The Dean went off into a little reverie. Perhaps his old friend's reproach was just. Dean of a great cathedral at thirty-six, he had the world of dioceses at his feet. Had he used to the full the brilliant talents with which he started? He had been a good Dean, a capable, business-like Dean. There was not a stone of the Cathedral that he did not know and cherish. Under his care the stability of every part of the precious fabric had been assured for a hundred years. Its financial position, desperate on his appointment, was now sound. He had come into a scene of petty discords and jealousies; for many years there had been a no more united chapter in any cathedral Close in England. As an administrator he had been a success. The devotion of his life to the Cathedral had its roots deep in spiritual things. For the greater glory of God had the vast edifice been erected, and for the greater glory of God had he, its guardian, reverently seen to its preservation and perfect appointment. Would he have served God better by pursuing the ambitions of youth? He could have had his bishopric: but he knew that the choice lay between him and Chanways, a flaming spirit, eager for power, who hadn't the sacred charge of a cathedral, and he declined. And now Chanways was a force in the church and the country, and was making things hum. If he, Conover, after fifteen years of Durdlebury, had accepted, he would have lost the power to make things hum. He would have made a very ordinary, painstaking bishop, and his successor at Durdlebury might possibly have regarded that timeworn wonder of spiritual beauty merely as a steppingstone to higher sacerdotal things. Such a man, he considered, having once come under the holy glamour of the Cathedral, would have been guilty of the Unforgivable Sin. He had therefore saved two unfortunate situations.

"You are quite an intelligent man, Bruce," he said with a sudden whimsicality, "but I don't think you would ever understand."

The set of tennis being over, Peggy, flushed and triumphant, rushed into the party in the shade.

"Mr. Petherbridge and I have won — 6–3," she announced. The old gentlemen smiled and murmured their congratulations. She swung to the tea-table some paces away, and plucked Marmaduke by the sleeve, interrupting him in the middle of an argument. He rose politely.

"Come and play."

"My dear," he said, "I'm such a duffer at games."

"Never mind. You'll learn in time."

He drew out a grey silk handkerchief as if ready to perspire at the first thought of it. "Tennis makes one so dreadfully hot," said he.

Peggy tapped the point of her foot irritably, but she laughed as she turned to Lady Bruce.

"What's the good of being engaged to a man if he can't play tennis with you?"

"There are other things in life besides tennis, my dear," replied Lady Bruce.

The girl flushed, but being aware that a pert answer turneth away pleasant invitations, said nothing. She nodded and went off to her game, and informing Mr. Petherbridge that Lady Bruce was a platitudinous old tabby, flirted with him up to the nice limits of his parsonical dignity. But Marmaduke did not mind.

"Games are childish and somewhat barbaric. Don't you think so, Lady Bruce?"

"Most young people seem fond of them," replied the lady. "Exercise keeps them in health."

"It all depends," he argued. "Often they get exceedingly hot, then they sit about and catch their death of cold."

"That's very true," said Lady Bruce. "It's what I'm always telling Sir Archibald about golf. Only last week he caught a severe chill in that very way. I had to rub his chest with camphorated oil."

"Just as my poor dear mother used to do to me," said Marmaduke.

There followed a conversation on ailments and their treatment in which Mrs. Conover joined. Marmaduke was quite happy. He knew that the two elderly ladies admired the soundness of his views and talked to him as to one of themselves.

"I'm sure, my dear Marmaduke, you're very wise to take care of yourself," said Lady Bruce, "especially now, when you have the responsibilities of married life before you."

Marmaduke curled himself up comfortably in his chair. If he had been a cat, he would have purred. The old butler, grown as grey in the service of the Deanery as the Cathedral itself — he had been page and footman to Dr. Conover's predecessor, — removed the tea-things and brought out a tray of glasses and lemonade with ice clinking refreshingly against the sides of the jug. When the game was over the players came and drank and sat about the lawn. The shadow of the apse had spread over the garden to the steps of the porch.

Anyone looking over the garden wall would have beheld a scene typical of the heart of England — a scene of peace, ease, and perfectly ordered comfort. The two well-built young men, one a minor canon, the other a curate, lounging in their flannels, clever-faced, honest-eyed, could have been bred nowhere but in English public schools and at Oxford or Cambridge. The two elderly ladies were of the fine flower of Provincial England; the two old men, so different outwardly, one burly, florid, exquisitely ecclesiastical, the other thin, nervous, soldierly, each was an expression of high English tradition. The two young girls, unerringly correct and dainty for all their modern abandonment of attitude, pretty, flushed of cheek, frank of glance, were two of a hundred thousand flowers of girlhood that could have been picked that afternoon in lazy English gardens. And Marmaduke's impeccable grey costume struck a harmonizing English note of Bond Street and the Burlington Arcade. The scent of the roses massed in delicate splendour against the wall, and breathing now that the cool shade had fallen on them, crept through the still air to the flying buttresses and the window mullions and traceries and the pinnacles of the great English cathedral. And in the midst of the shaven lawn gleamed the old cut-glass jug on its silver tray.

Someone did look over the wall and survey the scene: a man, apparently supporting himself with tense, straightened arms on the coping; a man with a lean, bronzed, clean-shaven face, wearing an old soft felt hat at a swaggering angle; a man with a smile on his face and a humorous twinkle in his eyes. By chance he had leisure to survey the scene for some time unobserved. At last he shouted:

"Hello! Have none of you ever moved for the last ten years?"

At the summons everyone was startled. The

young men scrambled to their feet. The Dean rose and glared at the intruder, who sprang over the wall, recklessly broke through the rose-bushes and advanced with outstretched hand to meet him.

"Hello, Uncle Edward!"

"Goodness gracious me!" cried the Dean, "it's Oliver!"

"Right first time," said the young man, gripping him by the hand. "You're not looking a day older. And Aunt Sophia —" he strode up to Mrs. Conover and kissed her. "Do you know," he went on, holding her at arms' length and looking round at the astonished company, "the last time I saw you all you were doing just the same? I peeped over the wall just before I went away, just such a summer afternoon as this, and you were all sitting round drinking the same old lemonade out of the same old jug — and, Lady Bruce, you were here, and you, Sir Archibald" — he shook hands with them rapidly. "You haven't changed a bit. And you — good Lord! Is this Peggy?" He put his hand on the Dean's shoulder and pointed at the girl.

"That's Peggy," said the Dean.

"You're the only thing that's grown. I used to gallop with you on my shoulders all round the lawn. I suppose you remember? How do you do?"

And without waiting for an answer he kissed her soundly. It was all done with whirlwind suddenness. The tempestuous young man had scattered every-one's wits. All stared at him.

Releasing Peggy, "My holy Aunt!" he cried. "There's another of 'em. It's Doggie! You were in the old picture, and I'm blessed if you weren't wearing the same beautiful grey suit. How do, Doggie?"

He gripped Doggie's hand. Doggie's lips grew white.

"I'm glad to welcome you back, Oliver," he said. "But I would have you to know that my name is Marmaduke."

"Sooner be called Doggie myself, old chap," said Oliver.

He stepped back, smiling at them all, a handsome, devil-may-care fellow, tall, tough, and supple, his hands in the pockets of a sun-stained, double-breasted blue jacket.

"We're indeed glad to see you, my dear fellow," said the Dean, recovering equanimity, "but what have you been doing all this time, and where on earth have you come from?"

"I've just come from the South Seas. Arrived in London last evening. This morning I thought I'd come and look you up."

"But if you had let us know you were coming, we should have met you at the station with the car. Where's your luggage?"

He jerked a hand. "In the road. My man's sitting on it. Oh, don't worry about him," he cried airily to the protesting Dean. "He's well trained. He'll go on sitting on it all night."

"You've brought a man — a valet?" asked Peggy.

"It seems so."

"Then you must be getting on."

"I don't think he turns you out very well," said Doggie.

"You must really let one of the servants see about your things, Oliver," said Mrs. Conover, moving towards the porch. "What will people say?"

He strode after her and kissed her. "Oh, you dear old Durdelbury Aunt! Now I know I'm in England again. I haven't heard those words for years!"

Mrs. Conover's hospitable intentions were anticipated by the old butler, who advanced to meet them with the news that Sir Archibald's car had been brought round. As soon as he recognized Oliver he started back, mouth agape.

"Yes, it's me all right, Burford," laughed Oliver. "How did I get here? I dropped from the moon."

He shook hands with Burford, of whose life he had been the plague during his childhood, proclaimed him as hardy and unchanging as a gargoyle, and instructed him where to find man and luggage.

The Bruces and the two clerical tennis players departed. Marmaduke was for taking his leave, too. All his old loathing of Oliver had suddenly returned. His cousin stood for everything he detested, — swagger, arrogance, self-assurance. He hated the shabby rakishness of his attire, the self-assertive aquiline beak of a nose which he had inherited from his father, the Rector. He dreaded his aggressive masculinity. He had come back with the same insulting speech on his lips. His finger-nails were dreadful. Marmaduke desired as little as possible of his odious company. But his Aunt Sophia cried out, "You'll surely dine with us to-night, Marmaduke, to celebrate Oliver's return?"

And Oliver chimed in, "Do. And don't worry about changing. I can't. I've no evening togs. My old ones fell to bits when I was trying to put them on, on board the steamer, and I had to chuck 'em overboard. They turned up a shark who went for 'em. So don't you worry, Doggie, old chap. You look as pretty as paint as you are. Doesn't he, Peggy?"

Peggy, with a slight flush on her cheek, came to the rescue and linked her arm in Marmaduke's.

"You haven't had time to learn everything yet, Oliver; but I think you ought to know that we are engaged."

"Holy Gee! Is that so? My compliments."

He swept them a low bow. "God bless you, my children."

"Of course he'll stay to dinner," said Peggy. And she looked at Oliver as who should say "Touch him at your peril. He belongs to me."

So Doggie had to yield. Mrs. Conover went into the house to arrange for Oliver's comfort, and the others strolled round the garden.

"Well, my boy," said the Dean, "so you're back in the old country."

"Turned up again like a bad penny."

The Dean's kindly face clouded. "I hope you'll soon be able to find something to do."

"It's money I want, not work," said Oliver.

"Ah!" said the Dean, in a tone so thoughtful as just to suggest a lack of sympathy.

Oliver looked over his shoulder — the Dean and himself were preceding Marmaduke and Peggy on the trim gravel path. "Do you care to lend me a few thousands, Doggie?"

"Certainly not," replied Marmaduke.

"There's family affection for you, Uncle Edward! I've come half way round the earth to see him and — say, will you lend me a fiver?"

"If you need it," said Marmaduke in a dignified way, "I shall be very happy to advance you five pounds."

Oliver brought the little party to a halt and burst into laughter.

"I believe you good people think I've come back broke to the world. The black sheep returned like a wolf to the fold. Only Peggy drew a correct inference from the valet — wait till you see him! As Peggy said, I've been getting on." He laid a light hand on the Dean's shoulder. "While all you folks in Durdlebury, especially my dear Doggie, for the last ten years have been durdling, I've been doing. I've not come all this way to tap relations for five-pound notes. I'm swaggering into the City of London for Capital — with a great big C."

Marmaduke twirled his little moustache. "You've taken to company promoting," he remarked acidly.

"I have. And a damn — I beg your pardon, Uncle Edward — we poor Pacific Islanders lisp in damns for want of deans to hold us up — and a jolly good company too. We — that's I and another man — that's all the company as yet — two's company, you know — own a trading-fleet."

"You own ships!" cried Peggy.

"Rather. Own 'em, sail 'em, navigate 'em, stoke 'em, clean out the boilers, sit on the safety valves when we want to make speed, do every old thing —"

"And what do you trade in?" asked the Dean.

"Copra, *bêche de mer*, mother of pearl —"

"Mother of pearl! How awfully romantic!" cried Peggy.

"We've got a fishery. At any rate, the concession. To work it properly we require capital. That's why I'm here — to turn the concern into a limited company."

"And where is this wonderful place?" asked the Dean.

"Huaheine."

"What a beautiful word!"

"Isn't it?" said Oliver. "Like the sigh of a girl in her sleep."

The old Dean shot a swift glance at his nephew; then took his arm and walked on, and looked at the vast mass of the Cathedral and at the quiet English garden in its evening shadow.

"Copra, *bêche de mer*, mother of pearl, Huaheine," he murmured. "And these strange foreign things are the commonplaces of your life!"

Peggy and Marmaduke lagged behind a little. She pressed his arm.

"I'm so glad you're staying for dinner. I shouldn't like to think you were running away from him."

"I was only afraid of losing my temper and making a scene," replied Doggie with dignity.

"His manners are odious," said Peggy. "You leave him to me."

Suddenly the Dean, taking a turn that brought him into view of the porch, stopped short.

"Goodness gracious!" he cried, "who in the world is that?"

He pointed to a curious object slouching across the lawn; a short, hirsute man wearing a sailor's jersey, and smoking a stump of a blackened pipe. His tousled head was bare; he had very long arms and great powerful hands protruded at the end of long sinewy wrists from inadequate sleeves. A pair of bright eyes shone out of his dark, shaggy face, like a Dandy Dinmont's. His nose was large and red. He rolled as he walked. Such a sight had never been seen before in the Deanery garden.

"That's my man. Peggy's valet," said Oliver, airily. "His name is Chipmunk. A beauty, isn't he?"

"Like master, like man," murmured Doggie.

Oliver's quick ears caught the words intended only for Peggy. He smiled brightly.

"If you knew what a compliment you were paying me, Doggie, you wouldn't have said such a thing."

The man, seeing the company stare at him, halted, took his pipe out of his mouth, and scratched his head.

"But — er — forgive me, my dear Oliver," said the Dean. "No doubt he is an excellent fellow — but don't you think he might smoke his pipe somewhere else?"

"Of course he might," said Oliver. "And he jolly well shall." He put his hand to his mouth, sea-fashion — they were about thirty yards apart — and shouted. "Here, you! What the eternal blazes are you doing here?"

"Please don't hurt the poor man's feelings," said the kindly Dean.

Oliver turned a blank look on his uncle. "His what? Ain't got any. Not that kind of feelings." He proceeded: "Now then, look lively! Clear out; skidoo!"

The valet touched his forehead in salute and "Where am I to go to, Cap'en?"

"Go to —"

Oliver checked himself in time and turned to the Dean.

"Where shall I tell him to go?" he asked sweetly.

"The kitchen garden would be the best place," replied the Dean.

"I think I'd better go and fix him up myself," said Oliver. "A little conversation in his own language might be beneficial."

"But isn't he English?" asked Peggy.

"Born and bred in Wapping," said Oliver.

He marched off across the lawn; and, could they have heard it, the friendly talk that he had with Chipmunk would have made the Saint and the Divines, and even the Crusader, Sir Guy de Chevenix, who were buried in the Cathedral, turn in their tombs.

Doggie, watching the disappearing Chipmunk, Oliver's knuckles in his neck, said: "I think it monstrous of Oliver to bring such a disreputable creature down here."

Said the Dean: "At any rate, it brings a certain excitement into our quiet surroundings."

"They must be having the time of their lives in the servants' hall," said Peggy.

CHAPTER IV

AFTER breakfast the next morning Doggie, attired in a green, shot-silk dressing-gown entered his own particular room and sat down to think. In its way it was a very beautiful room, — high, spacious, well proportioned, facing southeast. The wall-paper, which he had designed himself, was ivory white, with veinings of peacock blue. Into the ivory silk curtains were woven peacocks in full pride. The cushions were ivory and peacock-blue. The chairs, the writing table, the couch, the bookcases, were pure Sheraton and Hepplewhite. Vellum-bound books filled the cases — Doggie was very particular about his bindings. Delicate water-colours alone adorned the walls. On his neatly set out writing table lay an ivory set — inkstand, pen-tray, blotter and calendar. Bits of old embroidery harmonising with the peacock shades were spread here and there. A pretty collection of eighteenth-century Italian ivory statuettes were grouped about the room. A spinet inlaid with ebony and ivory formed a centre for the arrangement of many other musical instruments, a viol, mandolins gay with ribbons, a theorbo, flutes, and clarionettes. Through the curtains nearly drawn across an alcove could be guessed the modern monstrosity of a grand piano. One tall, closed cabinet was devoted to his collection of wall-papers. Another, open, to a collection of little dogs in china, porcelain, faïence,— thousands of them; he got them through dealers from all over the world. He had the finest collection in existence, and maintained a friendly and learned correspondence with the other collector, an elderly, disillusioned Russian Prince who lived somewhere near Nijni-Novgorod. On the spinet and on the writing table were great bowls of golden *rayon d'or* roses.

Doggie sat down to think. An unwonted frown creased his brow. Several problems distracted him. The morning sun streaming into the room disclosed, beyond doubt, discolorations, stains, and streaks on the wall-paper. It would have to be renewed. Already he had decided to design something to take its place. But last night Peggy had declared her intention to turn this abode of bachelor comfort into the drawing-room, and to hand over to his personal use some other apartment, possibly the present drawing-room, which received all the blaze and glare of the afternoon sun. What should he do? Live in the sordidness of discoloured wall-paper for another year, or go through the anxiety of artistic effort and manufacturer's stupidity and delay, to say nothing of the expense, only to have the whole thing scrapped before the wedding. Doggie had a foretaste of the dilemmas of matrimony. He had a gnawing suspicion that the trim and perfect life was difficult of attainment.

Then, meandering through this wilderness of dubiety, ran thoughts of Oliver. Everyone seemed to have gone crazy over the fellow. Uncle Edward and Aunt Sophia had hung on his lips while he lied unblushingly about his adventures. Even Peggy had listened open-eyed and open-mouthed when he had told a tale of shipwreck in the South Seas: how the schooner had been caught in some beastly wind, and the masts had been torn out and the rudder carried away, and how it had struck a reef, and how something had hit him on the head and he knew no more till he woke up on a beach and found that the unspeakable Chipmunk had swum with him for a week — or whatever the time was — until they got to land. If hulking, brainless dolts like Oliver, thought Doggie, like to fool around in schooners and typhoons, they must take the consequences. There was nothing to brag about. The higher man was the intellectual, the aesthetic, the artistic being. What did Oliver know of Lydian modes or Louis Treize decoration or Aztec clay dogs? Nothing. He couldn't even keep his socks from slopping about over his shoes. And there was Peggy all over the fellow, although before dinner she had said she couldn't bear the sight of him. Doggie was perturbed. On bidding him good-night she had kissed him in the most perfunctory manner — merely the cousinly peck of a dozen years ago — and had given no thought to the fact that he was driving home in an open car without an overcoat. He had felt distinctly chilly on his arrival and had taken a dose of ammoniated quinine. Was Peggy's indifference a sign that she had ceased to care for him? That she was attracted by the buccaneering Oliver?

Now suppose the engagement was broken off he would be free to do as he chose with the redecoration of the room. But suppose, as he sincerely and devoutly hoped, it wasn't? Dilemma on dilemma. Added to all this, Goliath, the miniature Belgian griffon, having probably overeaten himself, had complicated pains inside, and the callous vet. could or would not come round till the evening. In the meantime Goliath might die.

He was at this point of his reflections when, to his horror, he heard a familiar voice outside the door.

"All right, Peddle. Don't worry. I'll show myself in. Look after that man of mine. Quite easy. Give him some beer in a bucket and leave him to it."

Then the door burst open and Oliver, pipe in mouth and hat on one side, came into the room.

"Hallo, Doggie! Thought I'd look you up. Hope I'm not disturbing you."

"Not at all," said Doggie. "Do sit down."

But Oliver walked about and looked at things.

"I like your water-colours. Did you collect them yourself?"

"Yes."

"I congratulate you on your taste. This is a beauty. Who is it by?"

The appreciation brought Doggie at once to his side. Oliver the connoisseur was showing himself in a new and agreeable light. Doggie took him delightedly round the pictures, expounding their merits and their little histories. He found that Oliver, although unlearned, had a true sense of light and colour and tone. He was just beginning to like him, when the tactless fellow, stopping before the collection of little dogs, spoiled everything.

"My holy Aunt!" he cried — an objurgation which Doggie had abhorred from boyhood — and he doubled with laughter in his horrid schoolboy fashion. "My dear Doggie — is that your family? How many litters?"

"It's the finest collection of the kind in the world," replied Doggie, stiffly, "and is worth several thousand pounds."

Oliver heaved himself into a chair — that was Doggie's impression of his method of sitting down — a Sheraton chair with delicate arms and legs.

"Forgive me," he said, "but you're such a funny devil." Doggie gaped. The conception of himself as a funny devil was new. "Pictures and music I can understand. But what the deuce is the point of these damn little dogs?"

But Doggie was hurt. "It would be useless to try to explain," said he.

Oliver took off his hat and sent it skimming on to the couch.

"Look here, old chap," he said. "I seem to have put my foot into it again. I didn't mean to, really. Peggy gave me hell this morning for not treating you as a man and a brother, and I came round to try to put things right."

"It's very considerate of Peggy, I'm sure," said Marmaduke.

"Now, look here, old Doggie —"

"I told you when we first met yesterday that I vehemently object to being called Doggie."

"But why?" asked Oliver. "I've made enquiries and find that all your pals —"

"I haven't any pals, as you call them."

"Well, all our male contemporaries in the place who have the honour of your aquaintance — they all call you Doggie, and you don't seem to mind."

"I do mind," replied Marmaduke, angrily, "but as I avoid their company as much as possible, it doesn't very much matter."

Oliver stretched out his legs and put his hands behind his back — then wriggled to his feet. "What a beast of a chair! Anyhow," he went on, puffing at his pipe, "don't let us quarrel. I'll call you Marmaduke, if you like, when I can remember — it's a beast of a name — like the chair. I'm a rough sort of chap. I've had ten years' pretty tough training. I've slept on boards. I've slept in the open without a cent to hire a board. I've gone cold and I've gone hungry, and men have knocked me about and I've knocked men about — and I've lost the Durdlebury sense of social values. In the wilds if a man once gets the name, say, of Duck-Eyed Joe, it sticks to him, and he accepts it and answers to it and signs 'Duck-Eyed Joe' on an I. O. U. and honours the signature."

"But I'm not in the wilds," said Marmaduke,

"and haven't the slightest intention of ever leading the unnatural and frightful life you describe. So what you say doesn't apply to me."

"Quite so," replied Oliver. "That wasn't the moral of my discourse. The habit of mind engendered in the wilds applies to me. Just as I could never think of Duck-Eyed Joe as George Wilkinson, so you, James Marmaduke Trevor, will live imperishably in my mind as Doggie. I was making a sort of apology, old chap, for my habit of mind."

"If it is an apology," said Marmaduke.

Oliver, laughing, clapped him boisterously on the shoulder. "Oh, you solemn, comic cuss!" He strode to a rose-bowl and knocked the ashes of his pipe into the water — Doggie trembled lest he might next squirt tobacco juice over the ivory curtains. "You don't give a fellow a chance. Look here, tell me, as man to man, what are you going to do with your life? I don't mean it in the high-brow sense of people who live in unsuccessful plays and garden cities, but in the ordinary common-sense way of the world. Here you are, young, strong, educated, intelligent — "

"I'm not strong," said Doggie.

"Oh, shucks! A month's exercise would make you as strong as a mule. Here you are — what the blazes are you going to do with yourself?"

"I don't admit that you have any right to question me," said Doggie, lighting a cigarette.

"Peggy has given it to me. We had a heart to heart talk this morning, I assure you. She called me a swaggering, hectoring barbarian. So I told her what I'd do. I said I'd come here and squeak like a little mouse and eat out of your hand. I also said I'd take you out with me to the Islands and give you a taste for fresh air and salt water and exercise. I'll teach you how to sail a schooner and how to go about barefoot and swab decks. It's a life for a man, out there, I tell you. If you've nothing better to do than living here snug like a flea on a dog's back, until you get married, you'd better come."

Doggie smiled pityingly, but said politely, "Your offer is very kind, Oliver, but I don't think that kind of life would suit me."

"Oh, yes, it would," said Oliver. "It would make you healthy, wealthy, — if you took a fancy to put some money into the pearl fishery, — and wise. I'd show you the world, make a man of you, for Peggy's sake, and teach you how men talk to one another in a gale of wind."

The door opened and Peddle appeared.

"I beg your pardon, Mr. Oliver, but your man —"

"Yes? that about him? Is he misbehaving himself? Kissing the maids?"

"No, sir," said Peddle, "but none of them can get on with their work. He has drunk two quart jugs of beer and wants a third."

"Well, give it to him."

"I shouldn't like to see the man intoxicated, sir," said Peddle.

"You won't. No one has or ever will."

"He is also standing on his head, sir, in the middle of the kitchen table."

"It's his great parlour-trick. You just try to do it, Peddle — especially after two quarts of beer. He's showing his gratitude, poor chap, just like the juggler of Notre Dame in the story. And I'm sure everybody's enjoying themselves?"

"The maids are nearly in hysterics, sir."

"But they're quite happy?"

"Too happy, sir."

"Lord!" cried Oliver, "what a lot of stuffy owls you are! What do you want me to do? What would you like me to do, Doggie? It's your house."

"I don't know," said Doggie. "I've had nothing

to do with such people. Perhaps you might go
and speak to him."

"No, I won't do that. I tell you what, Peddle,"
said Oliver brightly. "You lure him out into the
stable yard with a great hunk of pie — he adores
pie — and tell him to sit there and eat it till I come.
Tell him I said so."

"I'll see what can be done, sir," said Peddle.

"I don't mean to be inhospitable," said Doggie,
after the butler had gone, "but why do you take
this extraordinary person about with you?"

"I wanted him to see Durdlebury and Durdlebury to see him. Do it good," replied Oliver.
"Now, what about my proposition? Out there of
course you'll be my guest. Put yourself in charge
of Chipmunk and me for eight months, and you'll
never regret it. What Chipmunk doesn't know
about ships and drink and hard living isn't knowledge. We'll let you down easy — treat you kindly
— word of honour."

Doggie, being a man of intelligence, realised that
Oliver's offer arose from a genuine desire to do him
some kind of service. But if a friendly bull out of
the fulness of its affection invited you to accompany
him to the meadow and eat grass, what could you
do but courteously decline the invitation? This is
what Doggie did. After a further attempt at
persuasion, Oliver grew impatient, and picking up
his hat, stuck it on the side of his head. He was a
simple-natured, impulsive man. Peggy's spirited
attack had caused him to realize that he had
treated Doggie with unprovoked rudeness; but
then Doggie was such a little worm. Suddenly the
great scheme for Doggie's regeneration had entered
his head, and generously he had rushed to begin to
put it into execution. The pair were his blood
relations, after all. He saw his way to doing them
a good turn. Peggy, with all her go, — exemplified

by the manner in which she had gone for him, —
was worth the trouble he proposed to take with
Doggie. It really was a handsome offer. Most
fellows would have jumped at the prospect of being
shown round the islands with an old hand who
knew the whole thing backwards, from company-
promoting to beach-combing. He had not expected such a point-blank, bland refusal. It made
him angry.

"I'm really most obliged to you, Oliver," said
Doggie, finally. "But our ideals are so entirely
different. You're primitive, you know. You seem
to find your happiness in defying the elements,
whereas I find mine in adopting the resources of
civilisation to circumvent them."

He smiled, pleased with his little epigram.

"Which means," said Oliver, "that you're afraid
to roughen your hands and spoil your complexion."

"If you like to put it that way — symbolically."

"Symbolically be hanged!" cried Oliver, losing
his temper. "You're an effeminate little rotter
and I'm through with you. Go on and wag your
tail and sit up and beg for biscuits —"

"Stop!" shouted Doggie, white with sudden
anger which shook him from head to foot. He
marched to the door, his green silk dressing-gown
flapping round his legs, and threw it wide open.
"This is my house. I'm sorry to have to ask you
to get out of it."

Oliver looked intently for a few seconds into the
flaming little dark eyes. Then he said gravely:

"I'm a beast to have said that. I take it all
back. Good-bye."

"Good day to you," said Doggie; and when the
door was shut he went and threw himself, shaken,
on the couch, hating Oliver and all his works more
than ever. Go about barefoot and swab decks!
It was Bedlam madness. Besides being dangerous

to health, it would be excruciating discomfort. And to be insulted for not grasping at such martyrdom. It was intolerable.

Doggie stayed away from the Deanery all that day. On the morrow he heard, to his relief, that Oliver had returned to London with the unedifying Chipmunk. He took Peggy for a drive in the Rolls-Royce, and told her of Oliver's high-handed methods. She sympathised. She said, however:

"Oliver's a rough diamond."

"He's one of Nature's non-gentlemen," said Doggie.

She laughed and patted his arm. "Clever lad!" she said.

So Doggie's wounded vanity was healed. He confided to her some of his difficulties as to the peacock-and-ivory room.

"Bear with the old paper for my sake," she said. "It's something you can do for me. In the meanwhile you and I can put our heads together and design a topping scheme of decoration. It's not too early to start in right now, for it'll take months and months to get the house just as we want it."

"You're the best girl in the world," said Doggie; "and the way you understand me is simply wonderful."

"Dear old thing," smiled Peggy; "you're no great conundrum."

Happiness once more settled on Doggie Trevor. For the next two or three days he and Peggy tackled the serious problem of the reorganization of Denby Hall. Peggy had the large ideas of a limited though acute brain stimulated by social ambitions. When she became mistress of Denby Hall, she intended to reverse the invisible boundary that included it in Durdlebury and excluded it from the County. It was to be County — of the fine, inner Arcanum of county — and only Durdlebury by the grace of

Peggy Trevor. No "durdling," as Oliver called it, for her. Denby Hall was going to be the very latest thing of September, 1915, when she proposed, the honeymoon concluded, to take smart and startling possession. Lots of Mrs. Trevor's rotten old stuffy furniture would have to go. Marmaduke would have to revolutionise his habits. As she would have all kinds of jolly people down to stay, additions must be made to the house. Within a week after her engagement she had devised all the improvements. Marmaduke's room, with a great bay thrown out, would be the drawing-room. The present drawing-room, nucleus of a new wing, would be a dancing-room, with parquet flooring; when not used for tangos and the fashionable negroid dances, it would be called the morning-room; beyond that there would be a billiard-room. Above this first floor there could easily be built a series of guest chambers. As for Marmaduke's library, or study, or den, any old room would do. There were a couple of bedrooms overlooking the stable-yard which, thrown into one, would do beautifully.

With feminine tact she dangled these splendours before Doggie's infatuated eyes, instinctively choosing the opportunity of his gratitude for soothing treatment. Doggie telegraphed for Sir Owen Julius, R. A., surveyor to the Cathedral, the only architect of his acquaintance. The great man sent his partner, plain John Fox, who undertook to prepare a design.

Mr. Fox came down to Durdlebury on the 28th of July. There had been a lot of silly talk in the newspapers about Austria and Serbia to which Doggie had given little heed. There was always trouble in the Balkan States. Recently they had gone to war. It had left Doggie quite cold. They were all "Merry Widow," irresponsible people. They dressed in queer uniforms and picturesque costumes, and thought themselves tremendously important, and were always squabbling among themselves and would go on doing it till the day of Doom. Now there was more fuss. He had read in the *Morning Post* that Sir Edward Grey had proposed a Conference of the Great Powers. Only sensible thing to do, thought Doggie. He dismissed the trivial matter from his mind. On the morning of the 29th he learned that Austria had declared war on Serbia. Still, what did it matter?

Doggie had held aloof from politics. He regarded them as somewhat vulgar. Conservative by caste, he had once, when the opportunity was almost forced on him, voted for the Conservative candidate of the constituency. European politics on the grand scale did not arouse his interest at all. England, save as the wise Mentor, had nothing to do with them. Still, if Russia fought, France would have to join her ally. It was not till he went to the Deanery that he began to contemplate the possiblity of a general European war. For the next day or two he read his newspapers very carefully.

On Saturday, the 1st of August, Oliver suddenly reappeared, proposing to stay over the Bank Holiday. He brought news and rumours of war from the great city. He had found money very tight, Capital with a big C impossible to obtain. Everyone told him to come back when the present European cloud had blown over. In the opinion of the judicious it would not blow over. There was going to be war, and England could not stay out of it. The Sunday morning papers confirmed all he said. Germany had declared war on Russia. France was involved. Would Great Britain come in, or for ever lose her honour?

That warm, beautiful Sunday afternoon they sat on the peaceful lawn under the shadow of the great

Cathedral. Burford brought out the tea-tray and Mrs. Conover poured out tea. Sir Archibald and Lady Bruce and their daughter Dorothy were there and Doggie, impeccable in dark purple. Nothing clouded the centuries-old serenity of the place. Yet they asked the question that was asked on every quiet lawn, every little scrap of shaded garden throughout the land that day: Would England go to war?

And if she came in, as come she must, what would be the result? All had premonitions of strange shifting of destinies. As it was yesterday so it was to-day in that gracious shrine of immutability. But everyone knew in his heart that as it was to-day so would it not be to-morrow. The very word "war" seemed as out of place as the suggestion of Hell in Paradise. Yet the throb of the War Drum came over the broad land of France and over the sea and half over England, and its echo fell upon the Deanery garden, flung by the flying buttresses and piers and towers of the grey Cathedral.

On the morning of Wednesday, the 5th of August, it thundered all over the Close. The ultimatum to Germany as to Belgium had expired the night before. We were at war.

"Thank God," said the Dean, at breakfast, "we needn't cast down our eyes and slink by when we meet a Frenchman."

CHAPTER V

THE first thing that brought the seriousness of the war home to Doggie was a letter from John Fox. John Fox, a Major in a Territorial Regiment, was mobilised. He regretted that he could not give his personal attention to the proposed alterations at Denby Hall. Should the plans be proceeded with in his absence from the office, or would Mr. Trevor care to wait till the end of the war, which, from the nature of things, could not last very long? Doggie trotted off to Peggy. She was greatly annoyed.

"What awful rot!" she cried. "Fox, a Major of Artillery! I'd just as soon trust you with a gun. Why doesn't he stick to his architecture?"

"He'd be shot or something, if he refused to go," said Doggie. "But why can't we turn it over to Sir Owen Julius?"

"That old archaeological fossil?"

Peggy, womanlike, forgot that they had approached him in the first place. "He'd never begin to understand what we want. Fox hinted as much. Now, Fox is modern and up-to-date and sympathetic. If I can't have Fox, I won't have Sir Owen. Why, he's older than Dad! He's decrepit. Can't we get another architect?"

"Do you think, dear," said Doggie, "that, in the circumstances it would be a nice thing to do?"

She flashed a glance at him. She had woven no young girl's romantic illusions around Marmaduke. Should necessity have arisen, she could have furnished you with a merciless analysis of his character. But in that analysis she would have frankly included

57

a very fine sense of honour. If he said a thing wasn't quite nice — well, it wasn't quite nice.

"I suppose it wouldn't," she admitted. "We shall have to wait. But it's a rotten nuisance all the same."

Hundreds of thousands of not very intelligent, but at the same time by no means unpatriotic people like Peggy, at the beginning of the war thought trivial disappointments "rotten nuisances." We had all waxed too fat during the opening years of the Twentieth Century, and, not having a spiritual ideal in God's universe, we were in danger of perishing from Fatty Degeneration of the Soul. As it was, it took a year or more of war to cure us.

It took Peggy quite a month to appreciate the meaning of the mobilisation of Major Fox, R. F. A. A Brigade of Territorial Artillery flowed over Durdlebury, and the sacred and sleepy meadows became a mass of guns and horse-lines and men in khaki, and waggons and dingy canvas tents — and the old, quiet streets were thick with unaccustomed soldiery. The Dean called on the Colonel and officers, and soon the house was full of eager young men holding the King's commission. Doggie admired their patriotism, but disliked their whole-hearted embodiment of the military spirit. They seemed to have no ideas beyond their new trade. The way they clanked about in their great boots and spurs got on his nerves. He dreaded also lest Peggy should be affected by the meretricious attraction of a uniform. There were fine, hefty fellows among the visitors at the Deanery, on whom Peggy looked with natural admiration. Doggie bitterly confided to Goliath that it was the "glamour of brawn." It never entered his head during those early days that all the brawn of all the manhood of the nation would be needed. We had our well organized Army and Navy, composed of peculiarly constituted men whose duty it was to fight; just as we had our well organised National Church, also composed of peculiarly constituted men, whose duty it was to preach. He regarded himself as remote from one as from the other.

Oliver, who had made a sort of peace with Doggie and remained at the Deanery, very quickly grew restless.

One day, walking with Peggy and Marmaduke in the garden, he said: "I wish I could get hold of that confounded fellow, Chipmunk!"

Partly through deference to the good Dean's delicately hinted distaste for that upsetter of decorous households, and partly to allow his follower to attend to his own domestic affairs, he had left Chipmunk in London. Fifteen years ago Chipmunk had parted from a wife somewhere in the neighbourhood of the East India Docks. Both being illiterate, neither had since communicated with the other. As he had left her earning good money in a factory, his fifteen years' separation had been relieved from anxiety as to her material welfare. A prudent, although a beer-loving man, he had amassed considerable savings, and it was the dual motive of sharing these with his wife and of protecting his patron from the ever-lurking perils of London, that had brought him across the seas. When Oliver had set him free in town, he was going in quest of his wife. But as he had forgotten the name of the street near the East India Docks where his wife lived, and the name of the factory in which she worked, the successful issue of the quest, in Oliver's opinion, seemed problematical. The simple Chipmunk, however, was quite sanguine. He would run into her all right. As soon as he had found her he would let the Captain know. Up to the present he had not communicated with the Captain. He could give the Captain no definite address, so the

Captain could not communicate with him. Chipmunk had disappeared into the unknown.

"Isn't he quite capable of taking care of himself?" asked Peggy.

"I'm not so sure," replied Oliver. "Besides, he's hanging me up. I'm kind of responsible for him, and I've got sixty pounds of his money. It's all I could do to persuade him not to stow the lot in his pocket, so as to divide it with Mrs. Chipmunk as soon as he saw her. I must find out what has become of the beggar before I move."

"I suppose," said Doggie, "you're anxious now to get back to the South Seas?"

Oliver stared at him. "No, sonny, not till the war's over."

"Why, you wouldn't be in any great danger out there, would you?"

Oliver laughed. "You're the funniest duck that ever was, Doggie. I'll never get to the end of you." And he strolled away.

"What does he mean?" asked the bewildered Doggie.

"I think," replied Peggy, smiling, "that he means he's going to fight."

"Oh," said Doggie. Then after a pause he added, "He's just the sort of chap for a soldier, isn't he?"

The next day Oliver's anxiety as to Chipmunk was relieved by the appearance of the man himself, incredibly dirty and dusty and thirsty. Having found no trace of his wife, and having been robbed of the money he carried about him, he had tramped to Durdlebury, where he reported himself to his master as if nothing out of the way had happened.

"You silly blighter," said Oliver. "Suppose I had let you go with your other sixty pounds, you would have been pretty well in the soup, wouldn't you?"

"Yes, Cap'en," said Chipmunk.

"And you're not going on any blethering idiot

wild goose chases after wives and such like truck again, are you?"

"No, Cap'en," said Chipmunk.

This was in the stable-yard, after Chipmunk had shaken some of the dust out of his hair and clothes and had eaten and drunk voraciously. He was now sitting on an upturned bucket and smoking his clay pipe with an air of solid content. Oliver, lean and supple, his hands in his pockets, looked humorously down upon him.

"And you've got to stick to me for the future, like a roseate leech."

"Yes, Cap'en."

"You're going to ride a horse."

"A wot?" roared Chipmunk.

"A thing on four legs that kicks like hell."

"Wotever for? I ain't never ridden no 'osses."

"You're going to learn, you unmilitary-looking, worm-eaten scab. You've got to be a ruddy soldier."

"Gorblime!" said Chipmunk. "That's the first I 'eard of it. A 'oss soldier? You're not kiddin' are you, Cap'en?"

"Certainly not."

"Gorblime! Who would ha' thought it?" Then he spat lustily and sucked at his pipe.

"You've nothing to say against it, have you?"

"No, Cap'en."

"All right. And look here, when we're in the army you must chuck calling me 'Cap'en.'"

"What shall I have to call yer? Gineral?" Chipmunk asked simply.

"Mate, Bill, Joe — any old name."

"Ker-ist!" said Chipmunk.

"Do you know why we're going to enlist?"

"Can't say as 'ow I does, Cap'en."

"You chuckle-headed swab! don't you know we're at war?"

"I did 'ear some talk about it in a pub one night," Chipmunk admitted. "'Oo are we fighting? Dutchmen or Dagoes?"

"Dutchmen."

Chipmunk spat in his horny hands, rubbed them together and smiled. As each individual hair on his face seemed to enter into the smile, the result was sinister.

"Do you remember that Dutchman at Samoa, Cap'en?"

Oliver smiled back. He remembered the hulking, truculent German merchant whom Chipmunk, having half strangled, threw into the sea. He also remembered the amount of accomplished lying he had to practise in order to save Chipmunk from the clutches of the law and get away with the schooner.

"We leave here to-morrow," said Oliver. "In the meanwhile you'll have to shave your ugly face."

For the first time Chipmunk was really staggered. He gaped at Oliver's retiring figure. Even his limited and timeworn vocabulary failed him. The desperate meaning of the war has flashed suddenly on millions of men in millions of different ways. This is the way in which it flashed on Chipmunk.

He sat on his bucket pondering over the awfulness of it, and sucking his pipe long after it had been smoked out. The Dean's car drove into the yard and the chauffeur, stripping off his coat, prepared to clean it down.

"Say, Guv'nor," said Chipmunk hoarsely, "what do you think of this 'ere war?"

"Same as most people," replied the chauffeur tersely. He shared in the general disapproval of Chipmunk.

"But see 'ere. Cap'en he tells me I must shave me face and be a 'oss-soldier. I never shaved me face in me life, and I dunno 'ow to do it, just as I dunno 'ow to ride a 'oss. I'm a sailorman, I am, and sailormen don't shave their faces and ride 'osses. That's why I arsked yer what yer thought of this 'ere war."

The chauffeur struggled into his jeans and adjusted them before replying.

"If you're a sailor, the place for you is the navy," he remarked in a superior manner. "As for the cavalry, the Cap'en, as you call him, ought to have more sense —"

Chipmunk rose and swung his long arms threateningly.

"Look 'ere, young feller, do you want to have your blinkin' 'ead knocked orf? Where the Cap'en goes, I goes, and don't you make any mistake about it!"

"I didn't say anything," the chauffeur expostulated.

"Then don't say it. See? Keep your blinkin' 'ead shut and mind your own business."

And, scowling fiercely and thrusting his empty pipe into his trousers pocket, Chipmunk rolled away.

A few hours later Oliver, entering his room to dress for dinner, found him standing in the light of the window laboriously fitting studs into a shirt. The devoted fellow having gone to report to his master, had found Burford engaged in his accustomed task of laying out his master's evening clothes — Oliver during his stay in London had provided himself with these necessaries. A jealous snarl had sent Burford flying. So intent was he on his work, that he did not hear Oliver enter. Oliver stood and watched him. Chipmunk was swearing wholesomely under his breath. Oliver saw him take up the tail of the shirt, spit on it and begin to rub something.

"Ker-ist!" said Chipmunk.

"What in the thundering blazes are you doing there?" cried Oliver.

Chipmunk turned.

"Oh, my God!" said Oliver.

Then he sank on a chair and laughed and laughed, and the more he looked at Chipmunk the more he laughed. And Chipmunk stood stolid, holding the shirt of the awful, wet, thumb-marked front. But it was not at the shirt that Oliver laughed.

"Good God!" he cried. "Were you born like that?"

For Chipmunk, having gone to the barber's was clean-shaven, and revealed himself as one of the most comically ugly of the sons of men.

"Never mind," said Oliver, after a while, "you've made the sacrifice for your country."

"And wot if I get the face-ache?"

"I'd get something that looked like a face before I'd talk of it," grinned Oliver.

At the family dinner-table, Doggie being present, he announced his intentions. It was the duty of every able-bodied man to fight for the Empire. Had not half a million just been called for? We should want a jolly sight more than that before we got through with it. Anyway he was off to-morrow.

"To-morrow?" echoed the Dean.

Burford, who was handing him potatoes, arched his eyebrows in alarm. He was fond of Oliver.

"With Chipmunk."

Burford uttered an unheard sigh of relief.

"We're going to enlist in King Edward's Horse. They're our kind. Overseas men. Lots of 'em what you dear good people would call bad eggs. There you make the mistake. Perhaps they mayn't be fresh enough raw for a dainty palate — but for cooking, good hard cooking, by Gosh! nothing can touch 'em."

"You talk of enlisting, dear," said Mrs. Conover. "Does that mean as a private soldier?"

"Yes — a trooper. Why not?"

"You're a gentleman, dear. And gentlemen in the Army are officers."

"Not now, my dear Sophia," said the Dean. "Gentlemen are crowding into the ranks. They are setting a noble example."

They argued it out in their gentle, old-fashioned way. The Dean quoted examples of sons of Family who had served as privates in the South African war.

"And that to this," said he, "is but an eddy to a maëlstrom."

"Come and join us, James Marmaduke," said Oliver across the table. "Chipmunk and me. Three 'sworn brothers to France.'"

Doggie smiled easily. "I'm afraid I can't undertake to swear a fraternal affection for Chipmunk. He and I would have neither habits nor ideals in common."

Oliver turned to Peggy. "I wish," said he, with rare restraint, "he wouldn't talk like a book on deportment."

"Marmaduke talks the language of civilisation," laughed Peggy. "He's not a savage like you."

"Don't you jolly well wish he was!" said Oliver.

Peggy flushed. "No, I don't!" she declared.

The Dean being called away on business immediately after dinner, the young men were left alone in the dining-room when the ladies had departed. Oliver poured himself out a glass of port and filled his pipe — an inelegant proceeding of which Doggie disapproved. A pipe alone was barbaric, a pipe with old port was criminal. He held his peace, however.

"James Marmaduke," said Oliver, after a while, "what are you going to do?" Much as Marmaduke disliked the name of "Doggie," he winced under the irony of the new appellation.

"I don't see that I'm called upon to do anything," he replied.

Oliver smoked and sipped his port. "I don't want to hurt your feelings any more," said he gravely, "though sometimes I'd like to scrag you — I suppose because you're so different from me. It was so when we were childern together. Now I've grown very fond of Peggy. Put on the right track, she might turn into a very fine woman."

"I don't think we need discuss Peggy, Oliver," said Marmaduke.

"I do. She is sticking to you very loyally." Oliver was a bit of an idealist. "The time may come when she'll be up the devil's own tree. She'll develop a patriotic conscience. If she sticks to you while you do nothing, she'll be miserable. If she chucks you, as she probably will, she'll be no happier. It's all up to you, James Doggie Marmaduke, old son. You'll have to gird up your loins and take sword and buckler and march away like the rest. I don't want Peggy to be unhappy. I want her to marry a man. That's why I proposed to take you out with me to Huaheine and try to make you one. But that's over. Now here's the real chance. Better take it sooner than later. You'll have to be a soldier, Doggie."

His pipe not drawing, he was preparing to dig it with the point of a dessert-knife when Doggie interposed hurriedly.

"For goodness' sake, don't do that! It makes cold shivers run down my back!"

Oliver looked at him oddly, put the extinct pipe in his dinner-jacket pocket and rose.

"A flaw in the dainty and divine ordering of things makes you shiver now, old Doggie. What will you do when you see a fellow digging out another fellow's intestines with the point of a bayonet? A bigger flaw there somehow!"

"Don't talk like that — you make me sick," said Doggie.

CHAPTER VI

DURING the next few months there happened terrible and marvellous things which are all set down in the myriad chronicles of the time; which shook the world and brought the unknown phenomenon of change into the Close of Durdlebury. Folks of strange habit and speech walked it in, and gazing at the Gothic splendour of the place, saw through the mist of autumn and the mist of tears not Durdlebury but Louvain. More than one of those grey houses flanking the Cathedral and sharing with it the continuity of its venerable life, was a house of mourning; not for loss in the inevitable and not unkindly way of human destiny as understood and accepted with long disciplined resignation — but for loss sudden, awful, devastating; for the gallant lad who had left it but a few weeks before, with a smile on his lips, and a new and dancing light of manhood in his eyes, now with those eyes unclosed and glazed staring at the pitiless Flanders sky. Not one of those houses but was linked with a battlefield. Beyond the memory of man the reader of the Litany had droned the accustomed invocation on behalf of the Sovereign and the Royal Family, the Bishops, Priests and Deacons, the Lords of the Council, and all prisoners and captives, and the congregation had lumped them all together in their responses with an undifferentiating convention of fervour. What had prisoners and captives, any more than the Lords of the Council, to do with their lives, their hearts, their personal emotions? But now —

Durdlebury men were known to be prisoners in German hands, and after "all prisoners and captives" there was a long and pregnant silence, in which was felt the reverberation of war against pier and vaulted arch and groined roof of the cathedral, which was broken too, now and then, by the stifled sob of a woman, before the choir came in with the response so new and significant in its appeal — "We beseech thee to hear us, O Lord!"

And in every home the knitting-needles of women clicked as they did throughout the length and breadth of the land. And the young men left shop and trade and counting house. And young parsons fretted and some obtained the Bishop's permission to become Army chaplains, and others, snapping their fingers (figuratively) under the Bishop's nose, threw their cassocks to the nettles and put on the full (though in modern times not very splendiferous) panoply of war. And in course of time the Brigade of Artillery rolled away and new troops took their place: and Marmaduke Trevor, Esquire, of Denby Hall, was called upon to billet a couple of officers and twenty men.

Doggie was both patriotic and polite. Having a fragment of the British Army in his house, he did his best to make them comfortable. By January he had no doubt that the Empire was in peril, that it was every man's duty to do his bit. He welcomed the newcomers with open arms, having unconsciously abandoned his attitude of superiority over mere brawn. Doggie saw the necessity of brawn. The more the better. It was every patriotic Englishman's duty to encourage brawn. If the two officers had allowed him, he would have fed his billeted men every two hours on prime beefsteaks and Burgundy. He threw himself heart and soul into the reorganisation of his household. Officers and men found themselves in clover. The officers had champagne every night for dinner. They thought Doggie a capital fellow.

"My dear chap," they would say, "you're spoiling us. I don't say we don't like it and aren't grateful. We jolly well are. But we're supposed to rough it — to lead the simple life — what? You're doing us too well."

"Impossible!" Doggie would reply, filling up the speaker's glass. "Don't I know what we owe to you fellows? In what other way can a helpless, delicate crock like myself show his gratitude and in some sort of little way serve his country?"

When the sympathetic and wine-filled guest would ask what was the nature of his malady, he would tap his chest vaguely and reply:

"Constitutional. I've never been able to do things like other fellows. The least thing bowls me out."

"Damn hard lines — especially just now."

"Yes, isn't it?" Doggie would answer. And once he found himself adding, "I'm fed up with doing nothing."

Here can be noted a distinct stage in Doggie's development. He realised the brutality of fact. When great German guns were yawning open-mouthed at you, it was no use saying "Take the nasty, horrid things away. I don't like them." They wouldn't go unless you took other big guns and fired at them. And more guns were required than could be manned by the peculiarly constituted fellows who made up the artillery of the original British Army. New fellows not at all warlike, peaceful citizens who had never killed a cat in anger, were being driven by patriotism and by conscience to man them. Against Blood and Iron now supreme, the superior, aesthetic, and artistic being was of no avail. You might lament the fall in relative values of collections of wall-papers and little clay dogs, as much as you liked; but you could not deny the fall; they had gone down with something of an ignoble "wallop." Doggie began to set a high value on guns and rifles and such like deadly-engines and to enquire petulantly why the Government were not providing them at greater numbers and at greater speed. On his periodic visits to London he wandered round by Trafalgar Square and Whitehall, to see for himself how the recruiting was going on. At the Deanery he joined in ardent discussions of the campaign in Flanders. On the walls of his peacock and ivory room were maps stuck all over with little pins. When he told the young officer that he was wearied of inaction, he spoke the truth. He began to feel mightily aggrieved against Providence for keeping him outside this tremendous national League of Youth. He never questioned his physical incapacity. It was as real a fact as the German guns. He went about pitying himself and seeking pity.

The months passed. The regiment moved away from Durdlebury, and Doggie was left alone in Denby Hall. He felt solitary and restless. News came from Oliver that he had been offered and had accepted an infantry commission, and that Chipmunk, having none of the special qualities of a "'oss soldier," had, by certain skilful wire-pullings, been transfered to his regiment and had once more become his devoted servant. "A month of this sort of thing," he wrote, "would make our dear old Doggie sit up." Doggie sighed. If only he had been blessed with Oliver's constitution!

One morning Briggins, his chauffeur, announced that he could stick it no longer and was going to join up. Then Doggie remembered a talk he had had with one of the young officers who had expressed astonishment at his not being able to drive a car. "I shouldn't have the nerve," he had replied.

"My nerves are all wrong — and I shouldn't have the strength to change tyres and things." . . . If his chauffeur went, he would find it very difficult to get another. Who would drive the Rolls-Royce.

"Why not learn to drive yourself, sir?" said Briggins. "Not the Rolls-Royce. I would put it up or get rid of it, if I were you. If you engage a second-rate man, as you'll have to, who isn't used to this make of car, he'll do it in for you pretty quick. Get a smaller one in its place and drive it yourself. I'll undertake to teach you enough before I go."

So Doggie, following Briggins's advice, took lessons and, to his amazement, found that he did not die of nervous collapse when a dog crossed the road in front of the car, and that the fitting of detachable wheels did not require the strength of a Hercules. The first time he took Peggy out in the two-seater, he swelled with pride.

"I'm so glad to see you can do something!" she said.

Although she was kind and as mildly affectionate as ever, he had noticed of late a curious reserve in her manner. Conversation did not flow easily. There seemed to be something at the back of her mind. She had fits of abstraction from which, when rallied, she roused herself with an effort.

"It's the war," she would declare. "It's affecting everybody that way."

Gradually Doggie began to realise that she spoke truly. Most people of his acquaintance, when he was by, seemed to be thus afflicted. The lack of interest they manifested in his delicacy of constitution was almost impolite. At last he received an anonymous letter, "For little Doggie Trevor from the girls of Durdlebury," enclosing a white feather.

The cruelty of it broke Doggie down. He sat in his ivory and peacock room and nearly wept.

Then he plucked up courage and went to Peggy. She was rather white about the lips as she listened.

"I'm sorry," she said, "but I expected something of the sort to happen."

"It's brutal and unjust."

"Yes, it's brutal," she admitted, coldly.

"I thought you, at any rate, would sympathise with me," he cried.

She turned on him. "And what about me? Who sympathises with me? Do you ever give a moment's thought to what I've had to go through the last few months?"

"I don't quite know what you mean," he stammered.

"I should have thought it was obvious. You can't be such an innocent babe as to suppose people don't talk about you. They don't talk to you because they don't like to be rude. They send you white feathers instead. But they talk to me. 'Why isn't Marmaduke in khaki?' 'Why isn't Doggie fighting?' 'I wonder how you can allow him to slack about like that!'—I've had a pretty rough time fighting your battles, I can tell you, amd I deserve some credit. I want sympathy just as much as you do."

"My dear," said Doggie, feeling very much humiliated, "I never knew. I never thought. I do see now the unpleasant position you've been in. People are brutes. But," he added eagerly, "you told them the real reason?"

"What's that?" she asked, looking at him with cold eyes.

Then Doggie knew that the wide world was against him. "I'm not fit. I've no constitution. I'm an impossibility."

"You thought you had nerves until you learned to drive the car. Then you discovered that you hadn't. You fancy you've a weak heart. Perhaps

if you learned to walk thirty miles a day, you would
discover you hadn't that either. And so with the
rest of it."

"This is very painful," he said, going to the
window and staring out. "Very painful. You
are of the same opinion as the young women who
sent me that abominable thing."

She had been on the strain for a long while and
something inside her had snapped. At his woe-
begone attitude she relented, however, and came
up and touched his shoulder.

"A girl wants to feel some pride in the man
she's going to marry. It's horrible to have to be
always defending him — especially when she's not
sure she's telling the truth in his defence."

He swung round horrified. "Do you think I'm
shaming so as to get out of serving in the army?"

"Not consciously. Unconsciously I think you
are. What does your doctor say?"

Doggie was taken aback. He had no doctor.
He had not consulted one for years, having no
cause for medical advice. The old family physician
who had attended his mother in her last illness
and had prescribed Gregory powders for him as a
child, had retired from Durdlebury long ago. There
was only one person living familiar with his constitution, and that was himself. He made confession of the surprising fact. Peggy made a little
gesture.

"That proves it. I don't believe you have anything wrong with you. The nerves business made
me sceptical. This is straight talking. It's horrid,
I know. But it's best to get through with it once
and for all."

Some men would have taken deep offence and,
consigning Peggy to the devil, have walked out of
the room. But Doggie, a conscientious, even
though a futile human being, was gnawed for the

first time by the suspicion that Peggy might possibly be right. He desired to act honourably.

"I'll do," said he, "whatever you think proper."

Peggy was swift to smite the malleable iron. To use the conventional phrase might give an incorrect impression of redhot martial ardour on the part of Doggie.

"Good," she said, with the first smile of the day. "I'll hold you to it. But it will be an honourable bargain. Get Dr. Murdock to overhaul you thoroughly with a view to the army. If he passes you, take a commission. Dad says he can easily get you one through his old friend General Gadsby at the War Office. If he doesn't, and you're unfit, I'll stick to you through thick and thin, and make the young women of Durdlebury wish they'd never been born."

She put out her hand. Doggie took it.

"Very well," said he, "I agree."

She laughed and ran to the door.

"Where are you going?"

"To the telephone — to ring up Dr. Murdoch for an appointment."

"You're flabby," said Dr. Murdoch, the next morning, to an anxious Doggie in pink pyjamas; "but that's merely a matter of unused muscles. Physical training will set it right in no time. Otherwise, my dear Trevor, you're in splendid health. I was afraid your family history might be against you — the child of elderly parents, and so forth. But nothing of the sort. Not only are you a first class life for an insurance company, but you're a first class life for the Army — and that's saying a good deal. There's not a flaw in your whole constitution."

He put away his stethoscope and smiled at Doggie, who regarded him blankly as the Pronouncer of a

Doom. He went on to prescribe a course of physical exercises, so many miles a day walking, such and such back-breaking and contortional performances in his bath-room, if possible a skilfully graduated career in a gymnasium — but his words fell on the ears of a Doggie in a dream; and when he had ended, Doggie said:

"I'm afraid, Doctor, you'll have to write all that out for me."

"With pleasure," smiled the Doctor, and gripped him by the hand. And seeing Doggie wince, he said heartily: "Ah! I'll soon set that right for you. I'll get you something — an india-rubber contrivance to practise with for half an hour a day, and you'll develop a hand like a gorilla's."

Dr. Murdoch grinned his way, in his little car, to his next patient. Here was this young slacker, coddled from birth, absolutely horse-strong and utterly confounded at being told so. He grinned and chuckled so much that he nearly killed his most valuable old lady patient, who was crossing the roadway in the High Street.

But Doggie crept out of bed and put on a violet dressing-gown that clashed horribly with his pink pyjamas, and wandered like a man in a nightmare to his breakfast. But he could not eat. He swallowed a cup of coffee and sought refuge in his own room. He was frightened. Horribly frightened, caught in a net from which there was no escape, not the tiniest break of a mesh. He had given his word — and in justice to Doggie be it said that he held his word sacred — he had given his word to join the Army if he should be passed by Murdoch. He had been passed — more than passed. He would have to join. He would have to fight. He would have to live in a muddy trench, sleep in mud, eat in mud, plough through mud, in the midst of falling shells and other instruments of

death. And he would be an officer, with all kinds
of strange and vulgar men under him, men like
Chipmunk, for instance, whom he would never
understand. He was almost physically sick with
apprehension. He realised that he had never
commanded a man in his life. He had been mor-
tally afraid of Briggins, his late chauffeur. He
had heard that men at the front lived on some
solid horror called bully-beef dug out of tins, and
some liquid horror called cocoa also drunk out of
tins; that men kept on their clothes, even their
boots, for weeks at a time; that rats ran over them
while they tried to sleep; that lice, hitherto associated in his mind with the most revolting type of
tramp, out there made no distinction of persons.
They were the common lot of the lowest Tommy
and the finest gentleman.

And then the fighting. The noise of the horrid
guns. The disgusting sights of men shattered to
bloody bits. The horrible stench. The terror of
having one's face shot half away and being an
object of revolt and horror to all beholders for the
rest of life. Death. Feverishly he ruffled his
comely hair. Death. He was surprised that the
contemplation of it did not freeze the blood in his
veins. Yes. He put it clearly before him. He
had given his word to Peggy that he would go and
expose himself to Death. Death. What did it
mean? He had been brought up in orthodox,
Church of England Christianity. His flaccid mind
had never questioned the truth of its dogmas. He
believed, in a general sort of way, that good people
went to Heaven and bad people went to Hell.
His conscience was clear. He had never done any
harm to anybody. As far as he knew, he had broken
none of the Ten Commandments. In a technical
sense he was a miserable sinner, and so proclaimed
himself once a week. But though, perhaps, he

had done nothing in his life to merit eternal bliss
in Paradise, yet, on the other hand, he had committed no action which would justify a kindly and
just Creator in consigning him to the eternal flames
of Hell. Somehow the thought of Death did not
worry him. It faded from his mind, being far less
terrible than life under prospective conditions.
Discomfort, hunger, thirst, cold, fatigue, pain, above
all the terror of his fellows — these were the soul-
racking anticipations of this new life into which it
was a matter of honour for him to plunge. And
to an essential gentleman like Doggie a matter of
honour was a matter of life. And so, dressed in
his pink pyjamas and violet dressing-gown, amid
the peacock blue and ivory hangings of his boudoir
room, and stared at by the countless unsympathetic eyes of his little china dogs, Doggie Trevor
passed through his first Gethsemane.

His decision was greeted with joy at the Deanery.
Peggy threw her arms round his neck and gave
him the very first real kiss he had ever received.
It revived him considerably. His Aunt Sophia also
embraced him. The Dean shook him warmly by
the hand, and talked eloquent patriotism. Doggie
already felt a hero. He left the house in a glow,
but the drive home in the two-seater was cold,
and the pitch dark night presaged other nights of
mercilessness in the future; and when Doggie sat
alone by his fire, sipping the hot milk which Peddle
presented him on a silver tray, the doubts and fears
of the morning racked him again. An ignoble
possibility occurred to him. Murdoch might be
wrong. Murdoch might be prejudiced by local
gossip. Would it not be better to go up to London
and obtain the opinion of a first-class man to whom
he was unknown? There was also another alternative. Flight. He might go to America, and do

nothing. To the South of France and help in some
sort of way with hospitals for French and wounded.
He caught himself up short as these thoughts passed
through his mind, and he shuddered. He took up
the glass of hot milk and put it down again. Milk?
No. He needed something stronger. A glance
in a mirror showed him his sleek hair tousled into
an upstanding wig. In a kind of horror of himself
he went to the dining-room and for the first time
in his life drank a stiff whisky and soda for the sake
of the stimulant. Reaction came. He felt a man
once more. Rather suicide at once than such dam-
nable dishonour. According to the directions which
the Dean, a man of affairs, had given him, he sat
down and wrote his application to the War Office
for a commission. Then — unique adventure! —
he stole out of the barred and bolted house, without
thought of hat and overcoat (let the traducers of
alcohol mark it well), ran down the drive and posted
the letter in the box some few yards beyond his
entrance gates.

The Dean had already posted his letter to his
old friend General Gadsby at the War Office.

So the die was cast. The Rubicon was crossed.
The bridges were burnt. The irrevocable step
was taken. Dr. Murdoch turned up the next
morning with his prescription for physical training.
And then Doggie trained assiduously, monotonously, wearily. He grew appalled by the sense-
lessness of this apparently unnecessary exertion.
Now and then Peggy accompanied him on his
prescribed walks; but the charm of her company
was discounted by the glaring superiority of her
powers of endurance. When he was aching with
fatigue, she pressed along as fresh as Atalanta at
the beginning of her race. When they parted by
the Deanery door, she would stand flushed, radiant
in her youth and health, and say:

"We've had a topping walk, old dear. Now isn't it a glorious thing to feel oneself alive?"

But poor Doggie of the flabby muscles felt half dead.

The fateful letter burdening Doggie with the King's commission arrived a few weeks later: a second lieutenancy in a Fusilier battalion of the New Army. Dates and instructions were given. The impress of the Royal Arms at the head of the paper, with its grotesque, perky lion and unicorn, conveyed to Doggie a sense of the grip of some uncanny power. The type-written words scarcely mattered. The impress fascinated him. There was no getting away from it. Those two pawing beasts held him in their clutch. They headed a Death Warrant from which there was no appeal.

Doggie put his house in order, dismissed with bounty those of his servants who would be no longer needed, and kept the Peddles, husband and wife, to look after his interests. On his last night at home he went wistfully through the familiar place, the drawing-room sacred to his mother's memory, the dining-room so solid in its half-century of comfort, his own peacock and ivory room so intensely himself, so expressive of his every taste, every mood, every emotion. Those strange, old-world musical instruments — he could play them all with the touch or breath of a master and a lover. The old Italian theorbo. He took it up. How few to-day knew its melodious secret! He looked around. All these daintinesses and prettinesses had a meaning. They signified the magical little beauties of life — things which asserted a range of spiritual truths, none the less real and consolatory because vice and crime and ugliness and misery and war co-existed in ghastly fact on other facets of the planet Earth. The sweetness here expressed was as essential to the world's spiritual life as the sweet elements of foodstuffs to its physical life. To the getting together of all these articles of beauty he had devoted the years of his youth . . . And — another point of view — was he not the guardian by inheritance — in other words, by Divine Providence — of this beautiful English home, the trustee of English comfort, of the sacred traditions of sweet English life that had made England the only country, the only country, he thought, that could call itself a Country and not a Compromise, in the world?

And he was going to leave it all. All that it meant in beauty and dignity and ease of life. For what? For horror and filthiness and ugliness, for everything against which his beautiful peacock and ivory room protested. Doggie's last night at Denby Hall was a troubled one.

Aunt Sophia and Peggy accompanied him to London and stayed with him at his stuffy little hotel off Bond Street, while Doggie got his kitt together. They bought everything in every West End shop that any salesman assured them was essential for active service. Swords, revolvers, field-glasses, pocket-knives (for Gargantuan pockets), compasses, mess-tins, cooking-batteries, sleeping-bags, waterproofs, boots innumerable, toilet accessories, drinking cups, thermos flasks, field stationery cases, periscopes, tinted glasses, Gieve waistcoats, colera belts, portable medicine cases, ear-plugs, tin-openers, cork-screws, notebooks, pencils, luminous watches, electric torches, pins, housewives, patent seat walking-sticks — everything that the man of commercial instincts had devised for the prosecution of the war.

The amount of warlike equipment with which Doggie, with the aid of his Aunt Sophia and Peggy, encumbered the narrow little passages of Sturrock's Hotel must have weighed about a ton.

At last Doggie's uniforms, several suits, came home. He had devoted enormous care to their fit. Attired in one he looked beautiful. Peggy decreed a dinner at the Carlton. She and Doggie alone. Her mother could get some stuffy old relation to spend the evening with her at Sturrock's. She wanted Doggie all to herself, so as to realise the dream of many disgusting and humiliating months. And as she swept through the palm court and up the broad stairs and wound through the crowded tables of the restaurant with the khakiclad Doggie by her side, she felt proud and uplifted. Here was her soldier whom she had made. Her very own man in khaki.

"Dear old thing," she whispered, pressing his arm as they trekked to their table. "Don't you feel glorious? Don't you feel as if you could face the universe?"

Peggy drank one glass of the quart of champagne. Doggie drank the rest. On getting into bed he wondered why this unprecedented quantity of wine had not affected his sobriety. Its only effect had been to stifle thought. He went to bed and slept happily, for Peggy's parting kiss had been such as would conduce to any young man's felicity.

The next morning Aunt Sophia and Peggy saw him off to his depôt, with his ton of luggage. He leaned out of the carriage window and exchanged hand kisses with Peggy until the curve of the line cut her off. Then he settled down in his corner with the *Morning Post*. But he could not concentrate his attention on the morning news. This strange costume in which he was clothed seemed unreal, monstrous, no longer the natty dress in which he had been proud to prink the night before, but a nightmare, Nessus-like investiture, signifying some abominable, burning doom.

The train swept him into a world that was upside down.

CHAPTER VII

THOSE were proud days for Peggy. She went about Durdlebury with her head in the air, and her step was as martial as though she herself wore the King's uniform, and she regarded the other girls of the town with a defiant eye. If only she could discover, she thought, the sender of the abominable feather! In Timpany's drapery establishment she raked the girls at the counter with a searching glance. At the Cathedral services she studied the demure faces of her contemporaries. Now that Doggie was a soldier she held the anonymous exploit to be cowardly and brutal. What did people know of the thousand and one reasons that kept eligible young men out of the army? What had they known of Marmaduke? As soon as the illusion of his life had been dispelled, he had marched away with as gallant a tread as anybody; and though Doggie had kept to himself his shrinkings and his terrors, she knew that what to the average hardily bred young man was a gay adventure, was to him an ordeal of considerable difficulty. She longed for his first leave so that she could parade him before the town, in the event of there being a lurking sceptic who still refused to believe that he had joined the army.

Conspicuous in the drawing-room, framed in silver, stood a large, full-length photograph of Doggie in his new uniform.

She wrote to him daily, chronicling the little doings of the town, at times reviling it for its dulness. Dad, on numberless committees, was scarcely ever in the house, except for hurried meals. Most of the pleasant young clergy had gone. Many of the girls had gone too; Dorothy Bruce to be a probationer in a V. A. D. hospital. If Durdlebury were not such a rotten, out-of-the-world place, the infirmary would be full of wounded soldiers and she could do her turn at nursing. As things were, she could only knit socks for Tommies and a silk khaki tie for her own boy. But when everybody was doing their bit, these occupations were not enough to prevent her feeling a little slacker. He would have to do the patriotic work for both of them, tell her all about himself, and let her share everything with him in imagination. She also expressed her affection for him in shy and slangy terms.

Doggie wrote regularly. His letters were as shy and conveyed less information. The work was hard, the hours long, his accommodation Spartan. They were in huts on Salisbury Plain. Sometimes he confessed himself too tired to write more than a few lines. He had a bad cold in the head. He was better. They had inoculated him against typhoid and had allowed him two or three slack days. The first time he had unaccountably fainted; but he had seen some of the men do the same, and the doctor had assured him that it had nothing to do with cowardice. He had gone for a route march and had returned a dusty lump of fatigue. But after having shaken the dust out of his moustache — Doggie had a playful turn of phrase now and then — and drunk a quart of shandy gaff, he had felt refreshed. Then it rained hard and they were all but washed out of the huts. It was a very strange life — one which he never dreamed could have existed. "Fancy me," he wrote, "glad to sleep on a drenched bed!" There was the riding school. Why hadn't he learned to ride as a boy? He had been told that the horse was a noble animal

and the friend of man. He was afraid he would
return to his dear Peggy with many of his young
illusions shattered. The horse was the most ignoble,
malevolent beast that ever walked, except the
Sergeant-Major in the riding school. Peggy was
filled with admiration for his philosophic endurance
of hardships. It was real courage. His letters
contained simple statements of fact, but not a word
of complaint. On the other hand, they were not
ebullient with joy; but then, Peggy reflected, there
was not much to be joyous about in a ramshackle
hut on Salisbury Plain. "Dear old thing," she
would write, "although you don't grouse, I know
you must be having a pretty thin time. But
you're bucking up splendidly, and when you get
your leave I'll do a girl's very d——dest (Don't
be shocked, I'm sure you're learning far worse
language in the army) to make it up to you." Her
heart was very full of him.

Then there came a time when his letters grew
rarer and shorter. At last they ceased altogether.
After a week's waiting she sent an anxious telegram.
The answer came back. "Quite well. Will write
soon." She waited. He did not write. One evening an unstamped envelope addressed to her in a
feminine hand which she recognised as that of
Marmaduke's anonymous correspondent, was found
in the Deanery letter-box. The envelope enclosed
a copy of a cutting from the "Gazette" of the
morning paper, and a sentence was underlined and
adorned with exclamation marks at the sides.

"*R. Fusiliers. Tempy 2nd Lieutenant J. M.
Trevor resigns his commission.*"

The Colonel dealt with him as gently as he could
in that final interview. He put his hand in a
fatherly way on Doggie's shoulder and bade him
not take it too much to heart. He had done his
best; but he was not cut out for an officer. These

were merciless times. In matters of life and death we could not afford weak links in the chain. Soldiers in high command, with great reputations, had already been scrapped. In Doggie's case there was no personal discredit. He had always conducted himself like a gentleman and a man of honour, but he had not the qualities necessary for the commanding of men. He must send in his resignation.

"But what can I do, sir?" asked Doggie in a choking voice. "I am disgraced forever."

The Colonel reflected for a moment. He knew that Doggie's life had been a little hell on earth from the first day he had joined. He was very sorry for the poor little Toy Pom in his pack of hounds. It was scarcely the Toy Pom's fault that he had failed. But the Great Hunt could have no use for Toy Poms. At last he took a sheet of regimental notepaper and wrote:

"DEAR TREVOR,

"*I am full of admiration for the plucky way in which you have striven to overcome your physical disabilities, and I am only too sorry that they should have compelled the resignation of your commission and your severance from the regiment.*
Yours sincerely,
L. G. CAIRD,
Lt. Col."

He handed it to Doggie.

"That's all I can do for you, my poor boy," said he.

"Thank you, sir," said Doggie.

Doggie took a room at the Savoy Hotel, and sat there most of the day, the pulp of a man. He had gone to the Savoy, not daring to show his face at the familiar Sturrock's. At the Savoy he was but a number unknown, unquestioned. He wore civilian clothes. Such of his uniforms and martial paraphernalia as he had been allowed to retain in

camp — for one can't house a ton of kit in a hut —
he had given to his batman. His one desire now was
to escape from the eyes of his fellow men. He
felt that he bore upon him the stigma of his disgrace, obvious to any casual glance. He was the
man who had been turned out of the army as a
hopeless incompetent. Even worse than the slacker
— for ·the slacker might have latent the qualities
that he lacked. Even at the best and brightest,
he could only be mistaken for a slacker, once more
the likely recipient of white feathers from any damsel
patriotically indiscreet. The colonel's letter brought
him little consolation. It is true that he carried
it about with him in his pocket-book; but the
gibing eyes of observers had not the X-ray power
to read it there. And he could not pin it on his
hat. Besides, he knew that the kindly Colonel
had stretched a point of veracity. No longer
could he take refuge in his cherished delicacy of
constitution. It would be a lie.

Peggy, in her softest and most pitying mood,
never guessed the nature of Doggie's ordeal. Those
letters so brave, sometimes so playful, had been
written with shaky hand, misty eyes, throbbing
head, despairing heart. Looking back, it seemed to
him one blurred dream of pain. His brother officers
were no worse than those in any other Kitchener
regiment. Indeed, the Colonel was immensely
proud of them and sang their praises to any fellow
dugout who would listen to him at the Naval and
Military Club. But how were a crowd of young
men trained in the rough and tumble of public
schools, universities, and sport, and now throbbing
under the stress of the new deadly game, to understand poor Doggie Trevor? They had no time to
take him seriously, save to curse him when he did
wrong, and in their leisure time he became naturally
a butt for their amusement.

"Surely I don't have to sleep in there?" he asked the subaltern who was taking him round on the day of his arrival in camp, and showed him his squalid little cubby-hole of a hut with its dirty boards, its cheap table and chair, its narrow, sleep-dispelling little bedstead.

"Yes it's a beastly hole isn't it? Until last month we were under canvas."

"Sleeping on the bare ground?"

"Wallowing in the mud like pigs, not one of us without a cold. Never had such a filthy time in my life."

Doggie looked about him helplessly while the comforter smiled grimly. Already his disconsolate attitude towards the dingy hutments of the camp and the layer of thick mud on his beautiful new boots had diverted his companion.

"Couldn't I have this furnished at my own expense? A carpet and a proper bed, and a few pictures —"

"I wouldn't try."

"Why not?"

"Some of it might get broken — not quite accidentally."

"But surely," gasped Doggie, "the soldiers would not be allowed to come in here and touch my furniture?"

"It seems," said the subaltern, after a bewildered stare, "that you have quite a lot to learn."

Doggie had. The subaltern reported a new kind of animal to the mess. The mess saw to it that Doggie should be crammed with information — but information wholly incorrect and misleading, which added to his many difficulties. When his ton of kit arrived he held an unwilling reception in the hut and found himself obliged to explain to gravely curious men the use for which the various articles were designed.

"This, I suppose, is a new type of gas-mask?"

No. It was a patent cooker. Doggie politely showed how it worked. He also demonstrated that a sleeping-bag was not a kit sack of a size unauthorised by the regulations, and that a huge steel-pointed walking-stick had nothing to do with agriculture.

He was very weary of his visitors by the time they had gone. The next day the Adjutant advised him to scrap the lot. So sorrowfully he sent back most of his purchases to London.

Then the Imp of Mischance brought as a visitor to the mess a sub from another regiment who belonged to Doggie's part of the country.

"Why — I'm blowed, if it isn't Doggie Trevor!" he exclaimed carelessly. "How d'ye do, Doggie?"

So thenceforward he was known in the regiment by the hated name.

There were rags, in which, as he was often the victim, he was forced to join. His fastidiousness loathed the coarse personal contact of arms and legs and bodies. His undeveloped strength could not cope with the muscle of his young brother barbarians. Aching with the day's fatigue, he would plead, to no avail, to be left alone. Compared with these feared and detested scraps, he considered, in after times, battles to be agreeable recreations.

Had he been otherwise competent, he might have won through the teasing and the ragging of the mess. No one disliked him. He was pleasant mannered, good-natured and appeared to bear no malice. True his ignorance not only of the ways of the army but of the ways of their old hearty world, was colossal, his mode of expression rather that of a precise old Church dignitary than of a sub in a regiment of Fusiliers, his habits, including a nervous shrinking from untidiness and dirt, those of a dear

old maid; but the mess thought, honestly, that he
could be knocked into their own social shape, and
in the process of knocking carried out their own
traditions. They might have succeeded if Doggie
had discovered any reserve source of pride from
which to draw. But Doggie was hopeless at his
work. The mechanism of a rifle filled him with
dismay. He could not help shutting his eyes before he pulled the trigger. Inured all his life to
lethargic action, he found the smart, crisp move-
ments of drill almost impossible to attain. The
Riding School was a terror and a torture. Every
second he deemed himself in imminent peril of
death. Said the Sergeant-Major:

"Now, Mr. Trevor, you're sitting on a 'orse and
not a 'olly-bush."

And Doggie would wish the horse and the Sergeant-Major in hell.

Again, what notion could poor Doggie have of
command? He had never raised his mild tenor
voice to damn anybody in his life. At first the
tone in which the officers ordered the men about
shocked him. So rough, so unmannerly, so unkind.
He could not understand the cheery lack of resentment with which the men obeyed. He could not
get into the way of military directness, could never
check the polite "Do you mind" that came instinctively to his lips. Now if you ask a private soldier
whether he minds doing a thing instead of telling
him to do it, his brain begins to get confused. As
one defaulter whose confusion of brain had led him
into trouble observed to his mates: "What can
you do with a blighter who's a cross between a
blinking Archbishop and a ruddy dicky-bird?"
What else save show in divers and ingenious ways
that they mocked at his authority? Doggie had
the nervous dread of the men that he had anticipated. During his training on parade words of

command stuck in his throat. When forced out, they grotesquely mixed themselves together.

The adjutant gave advice.

"Speak out, man. Bawl. You're dealing with soldiers at drill, not saying sweet nothings to old ladies in a drawing-room."

And Doggie tried. Doggie tried very hard. He was mortified by his own stupidity. Little points of drill and duty that the others of his own standing seemed to pick up at once, almost by instinct, he could only grasp after long and tedious toil. No one realised that his brain was stupefied by the awful and unaccustomed physical fatigue.

And then came the inevitable end.

So Doggie crept into the Savoy Hotel and hid himself there, wishing he were dead. It was some time before he could wire the terrible letter to Peggy. He did so on the day when he saw that his resignation was gazetted. He wrote after many anguished attempts:

"DEAR PEGGY,

"*I haven't written before about the dreadful thing that has happened, because I simply couldn't. I have resigned my commission. Not of my own free will, for, believe me, I would have gone through anything for your sake, to say nothing of the country and my own self-respect. To put it brutally, I have been thrown out for sheer incompetence.*

"*I neither hope, nor expect, nor want you to continue your engagement to a disgraced man. I release you from every obligation your pity and generosity may think binding. I want you to forget me and marry a man who can do the work of this new world.*

"*What I shall do I don't know. I have scarcely yet been able to think. Possibly I shall go abroad. At any rate I shan't return to Durdlebury. If women sent me white feathers before I joined, what would they send me now? It will always be my consolation to know that you once gave me your love, in spite of the pain of realising that I have forfeited it by my unworthiness.*

"Please tell Uncle Edward that I feel keenly his position, for he was responsible for getting me the commission through General Gadsby. Give my love to my Aunt if she will have it.

Yours always affectionately,
J. MARMADUKE TREVOR."

By return of post came the answer.

"DEAREST,

"We are all desperately disappointed. Perhaps we hurried on things too quickly, and tried you too high all at once. I ought to have known. Oh, my poor, dear boy, you must have had a dreadful time. Why didn't you tell me? The news in the gazette came upon me like a thunderbolt. I didn't know what to think. I'm afraid I thought the worst, the very worst — that you had got tired of it and resigned of your own accord. How was one to know? Your letter was almost a relief.

"In offering to release me from my engagement you are acting like the honourable gentleman you are. Of course I can understand your feelings. But I should be a little beast to accept right away like that. If there are any feathers about, I should deserve to have them stuck on to me with tar. Don't think of going abroad or doing anything foolish, dear, like that, till you have seen me — that is to say us, for Dad is bringing Mother and me up to town by the first train to-morrow. Dad feels sure that everything is not lost. He'll dig out General Gadsby and fix up something for you. In the meantime get us rooms at the Savoy, though Mother is worried as to whether it's a respectable place for Deans to stay at. But I know you wouldn't like

*to meet us at Sturrock's — otherwise you would have
been there yourself.   Meet our train.   All love from*
                                                            PEGGY."

Doggie engaged the rooms, but he did not meet
the train. He did not even stay in the hotel to
meet them. He could not meet them. He could
not meet the pity in their eyes. He read in Peggy's
note a desire to pet and soothe him and call him
"Poor little Doggie," and he writhed. He could
not even take up an heroic attitude and say to
Peggy: "When I have retrieved the past and can
bring you an unsullied reputation, I will return and
claim you. Till then farewell." There was no
retrieving the past. Other men might fail at first
and then make good; but he was not like them.
His was the fall of Humpty Dumpty. Final,
irretrievable.

He packed up his things in a fright and, leaving
no address at the Savoy, drove to the Russell Hotel
in Bloomsbury. But he wrote Peggy a letter "to
await arrival." If time had permitted he would
have sent a telegram, stating that he was off for
Tobolsk or Tierra del Fuego, and thereby prevented their useless journey; but they had already
started when he received Peggy's message.

Nothing could be done, he wrote, in effect, to
her, nothing in the way of redemption. He would
not put her father to the risk of any other such
humiliation. He had learned by the most bitter
experience that the men who counted now in the
world's respect and in woman's love were men of a
type to which, with all the goodwill in the world,
he could not make himself belong — he did not say
to which he wished he could belong with all the
agony and yearning of his soul. Peggy must forget him. The only thing he could do was to act
up to her generous estimate of him as an honour-

able gentleman. As such it was his duty to withdraw for ever from her life. His exact words, however, were: "You know how I have always hated slang, how it has jarred upon me, often to your amusement, when you have used it. But I have learned in the past months how expressive it may be. Through slang I've learned what I am. I am a born 'rotter.' A girl like you can't possibly love and marry a rotter. So the rotter, having a lingering sense of decency, makes his bow and exits — God knows where."

Peggy, red-eyed, adrift, rudderless on a frightening sea, called her father into her bedroom at the Savoy and showed him the letter. He drew out and adjusted his round tortoise-shell rimmed reading glasses, and read it.

"That's a miraculously new Doggie," said he.

Peggy clutched the edges of his coat.

"I've never heard you call him that before."

"It has never been worth while," said the Dean.

CHAPTER VIII

A T the Savoy, during the first stupefaction of his misery, Doggie had not noticed particularly the prevalence of khaki. At the Russell it dwelt insistent, like the mud on Salisbury Plain. Men that might have been the twin brethren of his late brother officers were everywhere, free, careless, efficient. The sight of them added the gnaw of envy to his heart-ache. Even in his bedroom he could hear the jingle of their spurs and their cheery voices as they clanked along the corridor. On the third day after his migration he took a bold step and moved into lodgings in Woburn Place. Here at least he could find quiet, untroubled by heartrending sights and sounds. He spent most of his time in dull reading and dispirited walking. For he could walk now — so much had his training done for him — and walk for many miles without fatigue. For all the enjoyment he got out of it, he might as well have marched round a prison yard. Indeed there were some who tramped the prison yards with keener zest. They were buoyed up with the hope of freedom, they could look forward to the ever-approaching day when they should be thrown once more into the glad whirl of life. But the miraculously new Doggie had no hope. He felt for ever imprisoned in his shame. His failure preyed on his mind.

He dallied with thoughts of suicide. Why hadn't he saved at any rate, his service revolver? Then he remembered the ugly habits of the unmanageable thing — how it always kicked its muzzle up in the air. Would he have been able even to shoot himself with it? And he smiled in self-derision. Drowning was not so difficult. Any fool could throw himself into the water. With a view to the inspection of a suitable spot, Doggie wandered idly, in the dusk of one evening, to Waterloo Bridge, and turning his back to the ceaseless traffic, leaned his elbows on the parapet and stared in front of him. A few lights already gleamed from Somerset House and the more dimly seen buildings of the Temple. The dome of St. Paul's loomed a dark shadow on a mist. The river stretched below very peaceful, very inviting. The parapet would be easy to climb. He did not know whether he could dive in the approved manner, hands joined over head. He had never learned to swim, let alone dive. At any rate he could fall off. In that art the Riding School had proved him a past-master. But the spot had its disadvantages. It was too public. Perhaps other bridges might afford more privacy. He would inspect them all. It would be something to do. There was no hurry. As he was not wanted in this world, so he had no assurance of being welcome in the next. He had a morbid vision of avatar after avatar being kicked from sphere to sphere.

At this point of his reflections he became aware of a presence by his side. He turned his head and found a soldier, an ordinary private, very close to him, also leaning on the parapet.

"I thought I wasn't mistaken in Mr. Marmaduke Trevor."

Doggie started away, on the point of flight, dreading the possible insolence of one of the men of his late regiment. But the voice of the speaker rang in his ears with a strange familiarity, and the great fleshy nose, the high cheekbones and the little grey eyes in the weather-beaten face suggested vaguely someone of the long ago. His dawning recognition amused the soldier.

"Yes, laddie. Ye're right. It's your old Phineas. Phineas McPhail, Esq., M.A., defunct. Now 33702 Private P. McPhail *redivivus*."

He warmly wrung the hand of the semi-bewildered Doggie, who murmured: "Very glad to meet you, I'm sure."

Phineas, gaunt and bony, took his arm.

"Would it not just be possible," he said, in his old half-pedantic, half-ironic intonation, "to find a locality less exposed to the roar of traffic and the rude jostling of pedestrians and the inclemency of the elements, in which we can enjoy the amenities of a little refined conversation?"

It was like a breath from the past. Doggie smiled.

"Which way are you going?"

"Your way, my dear Marmaduke, was ever mine, until I was swept, I thought for ever, out of your path by a torrential spate of whisky."

He laughed, as though it had been a playful freak of destiny. Doggie laughed too. But for the words he had addressed to hotel and lodging-house folk, he had spoken to no one for over a fortnight. The instinctive craving for companionship made Phineas suddenly welcome.

"Yes. Let us have a talk," said he. "Come to my rooms, if you have the time. There'll be some dinner."

"Will I come? Will I have dinner? Will I re-enter once more the Paradise of the affluent? Laddie, I will."

In the Strand they hailed a taxi and drove to Bloomsbury. On the way Phineas asked:

"You mention your rooms. Are you residing permanently in London?"

"Yes," said Doggie.

"And Durdlebury?"

"I'm not going back."

"London's a place full of temptations for those without experience," Phineas observed sagely.

"I've not noticed any," Doggie replied. On which Phineas laughed and slapped him on the knee.

"Man," said he, "when I first saw you I thought you had changed into a disillusioned misanthropist. But I'm wrong. You haven't changed a bit."

A few minutes later they reached Woburn Place. Doggie showed him into the sitting-room on the drawing-room floor. A fire was burning in the grate, for though it was only early autumn, the evening was cold. The table was set for Doggie's dinner. Phineas looked round him in surprise. The heterogeneous and tasteless furniture, the dreadful mid-Victorian prints on the walls — one was the "Return of the Guards from the Crimea," representing the landing from the troopship, repellent in its smug unreality, the coarse glass and well-used plate on the table, the crumpled napkin in a ring (for Marmaduke, who in his mother's house had never been taught to dream that a napkin could possibly be used for two consecutive meals!), the general air of slipshod Philistinism, — all came as a shock to Phineas, who had expected to find in Marmaduke's "rooms" a replica of the fastidious prettiness of the peacock and ivory room at Denby Hall. He scratched his head covered with a thick brown thatch.

"Laddie," said he gravely. "You must excuse me if I take a liberty; but I canna fit you into this environment."

Doggie looked about him also. "Seems funny, doesn't it?"

"It cannot be that you've come down in the world?"

"To bed-rock," said Doggie.

"No?" said Phineas, with an air of concern. "Man, I'm awful sorry. I know what the coming down feels like. And I, finding it not abhorrent to a sophisticated and well-trained conscience, and thinking you could well afford it, extracted a thousand pounds from your fortune. My dear lad, if Phineas McPhail could return the money —"

Doggie broke in with a laugh. "Pray don't distress yourself, Phineas. It's not a question of money. I've as much as ever I had. The last thing in the world I've had to think of has been money."

"Then what in the holy names of Thunder and Beauty," cried Phineas, throwing out one hand to an ancient saddle-bag sofa whose ends were covered by flimsy rags, and the other to the decayed ormolu clock on the mantelpiece, "what in the name of common sense are you doing in this awful, inelegant lodging-house?"

"I don't know," replied Doggie. "It's a fact," he continued after a pause. "The scheme of decoration is revolting to every aesthetic sense which I've spent my life in cultivating. Its futile pretentiousness is the rasping irritation of every hour. Yet here I am. Quite comfortable. And here I propose to stay."

Phineas McPhail, M.A., late of Glasgow and Cambridge, looked at Doggie with his keen little grey eyes beneath bent and bristling eyebrows. In the language of 33702 Private McPhail, he asked:

"What the blazes is it all about?"

"That's a long story," said Doggie, looking at his watch. "In the meantime I had better give some orders about dinner. And you would like to wash."

He threw open a wing of the folding doors, once in Georgian times separating drawing-room from withdrawing-room, and now separating living-room from bedroom, and switching on the light, invited McPhail to follow.

"I think you'll find everything you want," said he.

Phineas McPhail, left alone to his ablutions, again looked round, and he had more reason than ever to ask what it was all about. Marmaduke's bedroom at Denby Hall had been a dream of satin wood and dull blue silk. The furniture and hangings had been Mrs. Trevor's present to Marmaduke on his sixteenth birthday. He remembered how he had been bored to death by that stupendous ass of an old woman — for so he had characterised her — during the process of selection and installation. The present room, although far more luxurious than any that Phineas McPhail had slept in for years, formed a striking contrast with that remembered nest of effeminacy.

"I'll have to give it up," he said to himself. But just as he had put the finishing touches to his hair an idea occurred to him. He flung open the door.

"Laddie, I've got it. It's a woman."

But Doggie laughed and shook his head, and, leaving McPhail, took his turn in the bedroom. For the first time since his return to civil life he ceased for a few moments to brood over his troubles. McPhail's mystification amused him. McPhail's personality and address, viewed in the light of the past, were full of interest. Obviously he was a man who lived unashamed on low levels. Doggie wondered how he could have regarded him for years with a respect almost amounting to veneration. In a curious unformulated way Doggie felt that he had authority over this man so much older than himself, who had once been his master. It tickled into some kind of life his deadened self-esteem. Here, at last, was a man with whom he could converse on sure ground. The khaki uniform caused him no envy.

"The poet is not altogether incorrect," said McPhail, when they sat down to dinner, "in pointing out the sweet uses of adversity. If it had not been for the adversity of a wee bit operation, I should not now be on sick furlough. And if I had not been on furlough I shouldn't have the pleasure of this agreeable reconciliation. Here's to you, laddie, and to our lasting friendship." He sipped his claret. "It's not like the Lafitte in the old cellar — *Eheu fugaces anni et* — what the plague is the Latin for vintages? But 'twill serve." He drank again and smacked his lips. "It will even serve very satisfactorily. Good wine at a perfect temperature is not the daily drink of the British soldier."

"By the way," said Doggie, "you haven't told me why you became a soldier."

"A series of vicissitudes dating from the hour I left your house," said Phineas, "vicissitudes the recital of which would wring your heart, laddie, and make angels weep if their lachrymal glands were not too busily engaged by the horrors of war, culminated four months ago in an attack of fervid and penniless patriotism. No one seemed to want me except my country. She clamoured for me on every hoarding and every omnibus. A recruiting sergeant in Trafalgar Square tapped me on the arm and said, 'Young man, your country wants you.' Said I, with my Scottish caution, 'Can you take your affidavit that you got the information straight from the War Office?' 'I can,' said he. Then I threw myself on his bosom and bade him take me to her. That's how I became 33702 Private Phineas McPhail, A Company 10th Wessex Rangers, at the remuneration of one shilling and twopence per diem."

"Do you like it?" asked Doggie.

Phineas rubbed the side of his thick nose thoughtfully.

"There you come to the metaphysical conception of human happiness," he replied. "In itself it is a vile life. To a man of thirty-four —"

"Good Lord!" cried Doggie, "I always thought you were about fifty!"

"Your mother caught me young, laddie. To a man of thirty-four, a graduate of ancient and honourable universities and a whilom candidate for Holy Orders, it is a life that would seem to have no attraction whatever. The hours are absurd, the work distasteful and the mode of living repulsive. But strange to say, it fully contents me. The secret of happiness lies in the supple adaptability to conditions. When I found that it was necessary to perform ridiculous antics with my legs and arms, I entered into the comicality of the idea and performed them with an indulgent zest which soon won me the precious encomiums of my superiors in rank. When I found that the language of the canteen was not that of the pulpit or the drawing-room, I quickly acquired the new vocabulary and won the pleasant esteem of my equals. By means of this faculty of adaptability I can suck enjoyment out of everything. But, at the same time, mind you, keeping in reserve a little secret fount of pleasure."

"What do you call a little secret fount of pleasure?" asked Doggie.

"I'll give you an illustration — and if you're the man I consider you to be, you'll take a humorous view of my frankness. At present I adapt myself to a rough atmosphere of coarseness and lustiness in which nothing coarse or lusty I could do would produce the slightest ripple of a convulsion: but I have my store of a cultivated mind and cheap editions of the classics, my little secret fount of Castaly to drink from whenever I so please. On the other hand, when I had the honour of being responsible for your education, I adapted myself to a hothouse atmosphere in which Respectability and the concomitant virtues of Supineness and Sloth were cultivated like rare orchids, but in my bedroom I kept a secret fount which had its source in some good Scots distillery."

Whereupon he attacked his plateful of chicken with vehement gusto.

"You're a Hedonist, Phineas," said Doggie, after a thoughtful pause.

"Man," said Phineas, laying down his knife and fork, "you've just hit it. I am. I'm an accomplished Hedonist. An early recognition of the fact saved me from the Church."

"And the Church from you," said Doggie quietly.

Phineas shot a swift glance at him beneath his shaggy brown eyebrows.

"Ay," said he. "Though, mark you, if I had followed my original vocation, the Bench of Bishops could not have surpassed me in the unction in which I would have wallowed. If I had been born a bee in a desert, laddie, I would have sucked honey out of a dead camel."

With easy and picturesque cynicism, and in a Glasgow accent which had curiously broadened since this spell of oriental ease at Denby Hall, he developed his philosophy, illustrating it by incidents more or less reputable in his later career. At first, possessor of the ill-gotten thousand pounds and of considerable savings from a substantial salary, he had enjoyed the short wild riot of the Prodigal's life. Paris saw most of his money — the Paris which under his auspices Doggie never knew. Plentiful claret set his tongue wagging in Rabelaisian reminiscence. After Paris came husks.

Not bad husks if you know how to cook them.
Borrowed salt and pepper and a little stolen butter
worked wonders. But they were irritating to
the stomach. He lay on the floor, said he, and
yelled for fatted calf; but there was no soft-headed
parent to supply it. Phineas McPhail must be a
slave again and work for his living. Then came
private coaching, free lance journalism, hunting
for secretaryships: the commonplace story humorously told of the wastrel's decline; then a gor-
geous efflorescence in light green and gold as the
man outside a picture palace in Camberwell —
and lastly, the penniless patriot throwing himself
into the arms of his desirous country.

"Have you any whisky in the house, laddie?"
he asked after the dinner things had been taken
away.

"No," said Doggie. "But I could easily get
you some."

"Pray don't," said McPhail. "If you had, I
was going to ask you to be kind enough not to let
your excellent landlord, whom I recognize as a
butler of the old school, produce it. Butlers of
the old school are apt, like Peddle, to bring in a
maddening tray of decanters, syphons and glasses.
You may not believe me, but I haven't touched a
drop of whisky since I joined the army."

"Why?" asked Doggie.

McPhail looked at the long, carefully preserved
ash of one of Doggie's excellent cigars.

"It's all a part of the doctrine of adaptability.
In order to attain happiness in the army, the first
step is to avoid differences of opinion with the civil
and military police and non-commissioned officers,
and such like sycophantic myrmidons of authority.
Being a man of academic education, it is with difficulty that I agree with them when I'm sober. If
I were drunk, my bonnie laddie —" he waved a

hand — "well — I don't get drunk. And as I have no use for whisky as merely an agreeable beverage, I have struck whisky out of my hedonistic scheme of existence. But if you have any more of that pleasant claret —"

Doggie rang the bell and gave the order. The landlord brought in bottle and glasses.

"And now, my dear Marmaduke," said McPhail, after an appreciative sip, "now that I have told you the story of my life, may I without impertinent curiosity again ask you what you meant when you said you had come down to bed-rock?"

The sight of the man, smug, cynical, shameless, sprawling luxuriously on the sofa, with his tunic unbuttoned, filled him with sudden fury: such fury as Oliver's insult had aroused, such as had impelled him during a vicious rag in the mess to clutch a man's hair and almost pull it out by the roots.

"Yes, you may, and I'll tell you," he cried, starting to his feet. "I've reached the bed-rock of myself — the bed-rock of humiliation and disgrace. And it's all your fault. Instead of training me to be a man, you pandered to my poor mother's weaknesses and brought me up like a little toy dog — the infernal name still sticks to me wherever I go. You made a helpless fool of me, and let me go out a helpless fool into the world. And when you came across me I was thinking whether it wouldn't be best to throw myself over the parapet. A month ago you would have saluted me in the street and stood before me at attention when I spoke to you —"

"Eh? What's that, laddie?" interrupted Phineas, sitting up. "You've held a commission in the army?"

"Yes," said Doggie fiercely. "And I've been chucked. I've been thrown out as a hopeless rotter. And who is most to blame — you or I? It's you.

You've brought me to this infernal place. I'm here in hiding — hiding from my family and the decent folk I'm ashamed to meet. And it's all your fault, and now you have it!"

"Laddie, laddie," said Phineas reproachfully, "the facts of my being a guest beneath your roof and my humble military rank, render it difficult for me to make an appropriate reply."

Doggie's rage had spent itself. These rare fits were short-lived and left him somewhat unnerved.

"I'm sorry, Phineas. As you say, you're my guest. And as to your uniform, God knows I honour every man who wears it."

"That's taking things in the right spirit," Phineas conceded graciously, helping himself to another glass of wine. "And the right spirit is a great healer of differences. I'll not go so far as to deny that there is an element of justice in your apportionment of blame. There may, on various occasions, have been some small dereliction of duty. But you'll have been observing that in the recent exposition of my philosophy I have not laboured the point of duty to disproportionate exaggeration."

Doggie lit a cigarette. His fingers were still shaking. "I'm glad you own up. It's a sign of grace."

"Ay," said Phineas. "No man is altogether bad. In spite of everything I've always entertained a warm affection for you, laddie, and when I saw you staring at bogies round about the dome of St. Paul's cathedral, my heart went out to you. You didn't look over happy."

Doggie, always responsive to human kindness, was touched. He felt a note of sincerity in McPhail's tone. Perhaps he had judged him harshly, overlooking the plea in extenuation which McPhail had set up — that in every man there must be some saving remnant of goodness.

"I wasn't happy, Phineas," he said. "I was as miserable an outcast as could be found in London, and when a fellow's down and out, you must forgive him for speaking more bitterly than he ought."

"Don't I know, laddie? Don't I know?" said Phineas, sympathetically. He reached for the cigar-box. "Do you mind if I take another? Perhaps two — one to smoke afterwards in memory of this meeting. It is a long time since my lips touched a thing so gracious as a real Havana."

"Take a lot," said Doggie generously. "I don't really like cigars. I only bought them because I thought they might be stronger than cigarettes."

Phineas filled his pockets. "You can pay no greater compliment to a man's honesty of purpose," said he, "than by taking him at his word. And now," he continued when he had carefully lit the cigar he had first chosen, "let us review the entire situation. What about our good friends at Durdlebury? What about your uncle, the Very Reverend the Dean, against whom I bear no ill-will, though I do not say that his ultimate treatment of me was not over hasty — what about him? If you call upon me to put my almost fantastically variegated experience of life at your disposal and advise you in this crisis, so I must ask you to let me know the exact conditions in which you find yourself."

Doggie smiled once again, finding something diverting and yet stimulating in the calm assurance of Private McPhail.

"I'm not aware that I've asked you for advice, Phineas."

"The fact that you're not aware of many things that you do is no proof that you don't do them — and do them in a manner perfectly obvious to another party," replied Phineas, sententiously. "You're asking for advice and consolation from any friendly human creature to whom you're not ashamed to speak.   You've had an awful sorrowful time, laddie."

Doggie roamed about the room, with McPhail's little grey eyes fixed on him.   Yes, Phineas was right.   He would have given most of his possessions to be able, these later days, to pour out his tortured soul into sympathetic ears.   But shame had kept him, still kept him, would always keep him from the ears of those he loved.   Yes, Phineas had said the diabolically right thing.   He could not be ashamed to speak to Phineas.   And there was something good in Phineas which he had noticed with surprise.   How easy for him, in response to bitter accusation, to cast the blame on his mother?   He himself had given the opening.   How easy for him to point to his predecessor's short tenure of office and plead the alternative of carrying out Mrs. Trevor's theory of education or of resigning his position in favour of some sycophant even more time-serving?   But he had kept silent. . . .   Doggie stopped short and looked at Phineas with eyes dumbly questioning and quivering lips.

Phineas rose and put his hands on the boy's shoulders and said very gently:

"Tell me all about it, laddie."

Then Doggie broke down, and with a gush of unminded tears found expression for his stony despair.   His story took a long time in the telling; and Phineas interjecting an occasional sympathetic "Ay, ay!" and a delicately hinted question extracted from Doggie all there was to tell, from the outbreak of war to their meeting on Waterloo Bridge.

"And now," cried he, at last, a dismally tragic figure, his young face distorted and reddened, his sleek hair ruffled from the back into unsightly perpendicularities (an invariable sign of distracted

emotion) and his hands appealingly outstretched,
— "what the hell am I going to do?"

"Laddie," said Phineas, standing on the hearthrug, his hands on his hips, "if you had posed the
question in the polite language of the precincts of
Durdlebury Cathedral, I might have been at a
loss to reply. But the manly invocation of hell
shows me that your foot is already on the upward
path. If you had prefaced it by the adjective that
gives colour to all the aspirations of the British
Army, it would have been better. But I'm not
reproaching you, laddie. *Poco a poco.* It is enough.
It shows me you are not going to run away to a
neutral country and present the unedifying spectacle of a mangy little British lion at the mercy of a
menagerie of healthy hyenas and such like inferior
though truculent beasties."

"My God!" cried Doggie, "haven't I thought of
it till I'm half mad? It would be just as you say
— unendurable." He began to pace the room
again. "And I can't go to France. It would be
just the same as England. Everyone would be
looking white feathers at me. The only thing I can
do is to go out of the world. I'm not fit for it. Oh,
I don't mean suicide. I've not enough pluck.
That's off. But I could go and bury myself in
the wilderness somewhere, where no one would
ever find me."

"Laddie," said McPhail, "I misdoubt that you're
going to settle down in any wilderness. You
haven't the faculty of adaptability of which I have
spoken to-night at some length. And your heart
is young and not coated with the holy varnish of
callousness, which is a secret preparation known
only to those who have served a long apprenticeship in a severe school of egotism."

"That's all very well," cried Doggie, "but what
the —"

Phineas waved an interrupting hand. "You've got to go back, laddie. You've got to whip all the moral courage in you and go back to Durdle- . bury. The Dean, with his influence, and the letter you have shown me from your Colonel, can easily get you some honourable employment in either Service not so exacting as the one which you have recently found yourself unable to perform."

Doggie threw a newly-lighted cigarette into the fire and turned passionately on McPhail.

"I won't. You're talking drivelling rot. I can't. I'd sooner die than go back there with my tail be- tween my legs. I'd sooner enlist as a private soldier."

"Enlist?" said Phineas, and he drew himself up straight and gaunt. "Well, why not?"

"Enlist?" echoed Doggie in a dull tone.

"Have you never contemplated such a possibility?"

"Good God, no!" said Doggie.

"I have enlisted. And I am a man of ancient lineage as honourable, so as not to enter into un- productive argument, as yours. And I am a Master of Arts of the two Universities of Glasgow and Cam- bridge. Yet I fail to find anything dishonourable in my present estate as 33702 Private Phineas McPhail in the British Army."

Doggie seemed not to hear him. He stared at him wildly.

"Enlist?" he repeated. "As a Tommy?"

"Even as a Tommy," said Phineas. He glanced at the armolu clock. "It is past one. The re- spectable widow woman near the Elephant and Castle who has let me a bedroom, will be worn by anxiety as to my non-return. Marmaduke, my dear, dear laddie, I must leave you. If you will be lunching here twelve hours hence, nothing will give me greater pleasure than to join you. Laddie, do you think you could manage a fried sole and a sweetbread?"

"Enlist?" said Doggie, following him out to the front door in a dream.

He opened the door. Phineas shook hands.

"Fried sole and a sweetbread at one-thirty?"

"Of course, with pleasure," said Doggie.

Phineas fumbled in his pockets.

"It's a long cry to this time of night from Blooms-bury to the Elephant and Castle. You haven't the price of a taxi fare about you, laddie — two or three pounds —?"

Doggie drew from his patent notecase a sheaf of One Pound and Ten Shilling treasury notes and handed them over to McPhail's vulture clutch.

"Good-night, laddie!"

"Good-night."

Phineas strode away into the blackness. Doggie shut the front door and put up the chain and went back into his sitting-room. He wound his fingers in his hair.

"Enlist? My God!"

He lit a cigarette and after a few puffs flung it into the grate. He stared at the alternatives.

Flight, which was craven, — a lifetime of self-contempt. Durdlebury, which was impossible. Enlistment — ?

Yet what was a man incapable yet able-bodied, honourable though disgraced, to do?

His landlord found him at seven o'clock in the morning asleep in an armchair.

CHAPTER IX

AFTER a bath and a change and breakfast, Doggie went out for one of his solitary walks. At Durdlebury such a night as the last would have kept him in bed in a darkened room for most of the following day. But he had spent many far, far worse on Salisbury Plain, and the inexorable reveillé had dragged him out into the raw, dreadful morning, heedless of his headache and yearning for slumber, until at last the process of hardening had begun. To-day Doggie was as unfatigued a young man as walked the streets of London; a fact which his mind was too confusedly occupied to appreciate. Once more was he beset less by the perplexities of the future than by a sense of certain impending doom. For to Phineas McPhail's "Why not?" he had been able to give no answer. He could give no answer now, as he marched with swinging step, automatically, down Oxford Street and the Bayswater Road in the direction of Kensington Gardens. He could give no answer as he stood sightlessly staring at the Peter Pan statue.

A one-armed man in a khaki cap and hospital blue came and stood by his side and looked in a pleased yet puzzled way at the exquisite poem in marble. At last he spoke — in a rich Irish accent.

"I beg your pardon, sir, but could you be telling me the meaning of it, at all?"

Doggie awoke and smiled.

"Do you like it?"

"I do," said the soldier.

"It is about Peter Pan. A kind of Fairy Tale.

111

You can see the 'little people' peeping out — I think you call them so in Ireland."

"We do that," said the soldier.

So Doggie sketched the outline of the immortal story of the Boy Who Will Never Grow Old, and the Irishman listened with deep interest.

"Indeed," said he after a time, "it is good to come back to the true things after the things out there." He waved his one arm in the vague direction of the War.

"Why do you call them true things?" Doggie asked quickly.

They turned away and Doggie found himself sitting on a bench by the man's side.

"It's not me that can tell you that," said he, "and my wife and children in Galway."

"Were you there at the outbreak of war?"

He was. A Reservist called back to the colours after some years of retirement from the army. He had served in India and South Africa, a hard-bitten old soldier, proud of the traditions of the old Regiment. There were scarcely any of them left — and that was all that was left of him. He smiled cheerily. Doggie condoled with him on the loss of his arm.

"Ah sure," he replied. "And it might keep me out of a fight when I go into Ballinasloe."

"Who would you want to fight?" asked Doggie.

"The dirty Sinn Feiners that do be always shouting 'Freedom for Ireland and to hell with freedom for the rest of the world.' If I haven't lost my arm in a glorious cause, what have I lost it for? Can you tell me that?"

Doggie agreed that he had fought for the greater freedom of humanity and gave him a cigarette, and they went on talking. The Irishman had been in the retreat from Mons, the first battle of Ypres, and he had lost his arm in no battle at all; just a

stray shell over the road as they were marching
back to billets.   They discussed the war, the ethics
of it.   Doggie still wanted to know why the realities
of blood and mud and destruction were not the
true things.   Gradually he found that the Irishman meant that the true things were the spiritual,
undying things; that the grim realities would pass
away; that from these dead realities would arise
the noble ideals of the future which would be sym-
bolised in song and marble, that all he had endured
and sacrificed was but a part of the Great Sacrifice
we were making for the Freedom of the World.
Being a man roughly educated on a Galway farm
and in an infantry regiment, he had great difficulty
in co-ordinating his ideas, but he had a curious
power of vision that enabled him to pierce to the
heart of things, which he interpreted according to
his untrained sense of beauty.

They parted with expressions of mutual esteem.
Doggie struck across the gardens with a view to
returning home by Kensington High Street, Pic-
cadilly, and Shaftesbury Avenue. He strode along
with his thoughts filled with the Irish soldier. Here
was a man, mained for life and quite content that
it should be so, who had reckoned all the horrors
through which he had passed as externals unworthy
of the consideration of his unconquerable soul;
a man simple, unassuming, expansive only through
his Celtic temperament, which allowed him to
talk easily to a stranger before whom his English
or Scotch comrade would have been dumb and
gaping as an oyster, obviously brave, sincere and
loyal. Perhaps something even higher. Perhaps
in essence, the very highest. The Poet Warrior.
The term struck Doggie's brain with a thud, like
the explosive fusion of two elements.

During his walk to Kensington Gardens a poison-
ous current had run at the back of his mind.   Drift-

ing on it, might he not escape? Was he not of too
fine a porcelain to mingle with the coarse and common
pottery of the ranks? Was it necessary to go into
the thick of the coarse clay vessels, just to be shattered? It was easy for Phineas to proclaim that
he had found no derogation to his dignity as a man
of birth and a University graduate in identifying
himself with his fellow privates. Phineas had sys-
tematically brutalised himself into fitness for the
position. He had armed himself in brass — *aes
triplex.* He smiled at his own wit. But he, James
Marmaduke Trevor, who had lived his life as a clean
gentleman, was in a category apart.

Now, he found that his talk with the Irishman
had been an antidote to the poison. He felt
ashamed. Did he dare set himself up to be finer
clay than that common soldier? Spiritually, was he
even of clay as fine? In a Great Judgment of Souls
which of the twain would be among the Elect? The
ultra-refined Mr. Marmaduke Trevor of Denby Hall,
or the ignorant Poet Warrior of Ballinasloe? "Not
Doggie Trevor," he said between his teeth. And
he went home in a chastened spirit.

Phineas McPhail appeared punctually at half-
past one, and feasted succulently on fried sole and
sweetbread.

"Laddie," said he, "the man that can provide
such viands is a Thing of Beauty which, as the poet
says, is a Joy for ever. The light in his window is
a beacon to the hungry Tommy dragging himself
through the viscous wilderness of regulation stew."

"I'm afraid it won't be a beacon for very long,"
said Doggie.

"Eh?" queried Phineas sharply. "You'd surely
not be thinking of refusing an old friend a stray
meal?"

Doggie coloured at the coarseness of the misunderstanding. "How could I be such a brute?

There won't be a light in the window because I shan't be here. I'm going to enlist."

Phineas put his elbows on the table and regarded him earnestly.

"I would not take too seriously words spoken in the heat of midnight revelry, even though the revel was conducted on the genteelest principles. Have you thought of the matter in the cool and sober hours of the morning?"

"Yes."

"It's an unco' hard life, laddie."

"The one I'm leading is a harder," said Doggie. "I've made up my mind."

"Then I've one piece of advice to give you," said McPhail. "Sink the name of Marmaduke, which would only stimulate the ignorant ribaldry of the canteen, and adopt the name of James which your godfather and godmother, with miraculous foresight, considering their limitations in the matter of common sense, have given you."

"That's a good idea," said Doggie.

"Also it would tend to the obliteration of class prejudices if you gave up smoking Turkish cigarettes at ten shillings a hundred and arrived in your platoon as an amateur of 'Woodbines.'"

"I can't stand 'Woodbines,'" said Doggie.

"You can. The human organism is so constituted that it can stand the sweepings of the elephants' house in the Zoölogical Gardens. Try. This time it's only Woodbines."

Doggie took one from the crumpled paper packet which was handed to him, and lit it. He made a wry face, never before having smoked American tobacco.

"How do you like the flavour?" asked Phineas.

"I think I'd prefer the elephants' house," said Doggie, eying the thing with disgust.

"You'll find it the flavour of the whole British Army," said McPhail.

A few days later the Dean received a letter bearing the pencilled address of a camp on the South Coast, and written by 35792 p^vte James M. Trevor, A Company, 2/10 th Wessex Rangers.   It ran:

"I hope you won't think it heartless of me to have left you so long without news of me; but until lately I had the same reasons for remaining in seclusion as when I last wrote. Even now I'm not asking for sympathy or reconsideration of my failure or desire in any way to take advantage of the generosity of you all.

"I have enlisted in the 10th Wessex. Phineas McPhail, whom I met in London and whose character for good or evil I can better gauge now than formerly, is a private in the same battalion. I don't pretend to enjoy the life any more than I could enjoy living in a kraal of savages in Central Africa. But that is a matter of no account. I don't propose to return to Durdlebury till the end of the war. I left it as an officer and I'm not coming back as a private soldier. I enclose a cheque for £500. Perhaps Aunt Sophia will be so kind as to use the money — it ought to last some time — for the general upkeep, wages, etc., of Denby Hall. I feel sure she will not refuse me this favour. Give Peggy my love, and tell her I hope she will accept the two-seater as a parting gift. It will make me happier to know that she is driving it.

"I am keeping on as a pied à terre in London the Bloomsbury rooms in which I have been living, and I've written to Peddle to see about making them more comfortable. Please ask anybody who might care to write to address me as 'James M.' and not as 'Marmaduke.'"

The Dean read the letter — the family were at breakfast; then he took off his tortoise shell spectacles and wiped them.

"It's from Marmaduke at last," said he.   "He has carried out my prophecy and enlisted."

Peggy caught at her breath and shot out her hand for the letter, which she read eagerly and then passed over to her mother. Mrs. Conover began to cry.

"Oh, the poor boy! It will be worse than ever for him."

"It will," said Peggy. "But I think it splendid of him to try. How did he bring himself to do it?"

"Breed tells," said the Dean. "That's what everyone seems to have forgotten. He's a thoroughbred Doggie. There's the old French proverb. *Bon chien chasse de race.*"

Peggy looked at him gratefully. "You're very comforting," she said.

"We must knit him some socks," observed Mrs. Conover. "I hear those supplied to the army are very rough and ready."

"My dear," smiled the Dean, "Marmaduke's considerable income does not cease because his pay in the army is one and twopence a day; and I should think he would have the sense to provide himself with adequate underclothing. Also, judging from the account of your shopping orgy in London, he has already laid in a stock that would last out several Antarctic winters."

The Dean tapped his egg gently.

"Then what can we do for the poor boy?" asked his wife.

The Dean scooped the top of his egg off with a vicious thrust.

"We can cut out slanderous tongues," said he.

There had been much calumniating cackle in the little town; nay, more: cackle is of geese; there had been venom of the snakiest kind. The Deanery, father and mother and daughter, each in their several ways, had suffered greatly. It is hard to stand up against poisoned ridicule.

"My dear," continued the Dean, "it will be our business to smite the Philistines, hip and thigh.

The reasons which guided Marmaduke in the resignation of his commission are the concern of nobody. The fact remains that Mr. Marmaduke Trevor resigned his commission in order to —"

Peggy interrupted him with a smile. "'In order to' — isn't that a bit Jesuitical, Daddy?"

"I have a great respect for the Jesuits, my dear," said the Dean, holding out an impressive egg-spoon. "The fact remains, in the eyes of the world, as I remarked, that Mr. Marmaduke Trevor of Denby Hall, a man of fortune and high position in the county, resigned his commission in order, for reasons best known to himself, to serve his country more effectively in the humbler ranks of the army, and — my dear, this egg is far too full for war time —" with a hazardous plunge of his spoon he had made a yellow yelky horror of the egg-shell — "and I'm going to proclaim the fact far and wide and — indeed — rub it in."

"That'll be jolly decent of you, Daddy," said his daughter. "It will help a lot."

In the failure of Marmaduke to retain his commission the family honour had not been concerned. The boy had done his best. They blamed not him but the disastrous training that had unfitted him for the command of men. They reproached themselves for their haste in throwing him headlong into the fiercest element of the national struggle towards efficiency. They could have found an easier school, in which he could have learned to do his share creditably in the national work. Many young men of their acquaintance, far more capable then Marmaduke, were wearing the uniform of a less strenuous branch of the service. It had been a blunder, a failure, but without loss of honour. But when slanderous tongues attacked poor Doggie for running away with a yelp from a little hardship; when a story or two of Doggie's career in the regiment arrived in Durdlebury, highly flavoured in transit and more and more poisoned as it went from mouth to mouth; when a legend was spread abroad that he had bolted from Salisbury Plain and was run to earth in a Turkish bath in London, and was only saved from court-martial by family influence, then the family honour of the Conovers was wounded to its proud English depths. And they could say nothing. They had only Doggie's word to go upon; they accepted it unquestioningly, but they knew no details. Doggie had disappeared. Naturally they contradicted these evil rumours. The good folks of Durdlebury expected them to do so, and listened with well-bred incredulity. To the question "Where is he now and what is he going to do?" they could only answer, "We don't know." They were helpless.

Peggy had a bitter quarrel with one of her intimates, Nancy Murdoch, daughter of the doctor who had proclaimed the soundness of Marmaduke's constitution.

"He may have told you so, dear," said Nancy, "but how do you *know?*"

"Because whatever else he may be, he's not a liar," retorted Peggy.

Nancy gave the most delicate suspicion of a shrug to her pretty shoulders.

That was the beginning of it. Peggy, naturally combative, armed for the fight and defended Marmaduke.

"You talk as though you were still engaged to him," said Nancy.

"So I am," declared Peggy rashly.

"Then where's your engagement ring?"

"Where I choose to keep it."

The retort lacked originality and conviction.

"You can't send it back to him, because you don't know where he is. And what did Mrs. Con-

over mean by telling mother that Mr. Trevor had
broken off the engagement?"

"She never told her any such thing," cried Peggy
mendaciously. For Mrs. Conover had committed
the indiscretion under assurance of silence.

"Pardon me," said Nancy, much on her dignity.
"Of course I understand your denying it. It isn't
pleasant to be thrown over by any man — but by a
man like Doggie Trevor —"

"You're a spiteful beast, Nancy, and I'll never
speak to you again. You've neither womanly
decency nor Christian feeling." And Peggy marched
out of the doctor's house.

As a result of the quarrel, however, she resumed
the wearing of the ring, which she flaunted defiantly
with left hand deliberately ungloved. Hitherto
she had not been certain of the continuance of the
engagement. Marmaduke's repudiation was definite enough; but it had been dictated by his sensitive honour. It lay with her to agree or decline.
She had passed through wearisome days of doubt.
A physically sound fighting man sent about his
business as being unfit for war does not appear a
romantic figure in a girl's eyes. She was bitterly
disappointed with Doggie for the sudden withering
of her hopes. Had he fulfilled them she could have
loved him whole-heartedly after the simple way of
women; for her sex, exhilarated by the barbaric
convulsion of the land, clamoured for something
heroic, something, at least, intensely masculine,
in which she could find feminine exultation. She
also felt resentment at his flight from the Savoy, his
silence and practical disappearance. Although not
blaming him unjustly, she failed to realise the
spiritual piteousness of this plight. If the war
has done any thing in this country, it has saved
the young women of the gentler classes, at any
rate, from the abyss of sordid and cynical material-

ism. Hesitating to announce the rupture of the engagement, she allowed it to remain in a state of suspended animation, and as a symbolic act, ceased to wear the ring. Nancy's taunts had goaded her to a more heroic attitude. The first person to whom she showed the newly ringed hand was her mother.

"The engagement isn't off until I declare it's off. I'm going to play the game."

"You know best, dear," said the gentle Mrs. Conover. "But it's all very upsetting."

Then Doggie's letter brought comfort and gladness to the Deanery. It reassured them as to his fate. It healed the wounded family honour. It justified Peggy in playing the game.

She took the letter round to Dr. Murdoch's and thrust it into the hand of an astonished Nancy, with whom, since the quarrel, she had not been on speaking terms.

"This is in Marmaduke's handwriting. You recognise it. Just read the top line when I've folded it. 'I have enlisted in the 10th Wessex.' See?" She withdrew the letter. "Now, what could a man, let alone an honourable gentleman, do more? Say you're sorry for having said beastly things about him."

Nancy, who had regretted the loss of a lifelong friendship, professed her sorrow.

"The least you can do, then, is to go round and spread the news, and say you've seen the letter with your own eyes."

To several others, on a triumphant round of visits, did she show the vindicating sentence. Any soft young fool, she asserted, with the directness and not unattractive truculence of her generation, can get a commission and muddle through, but it took a man to enlist as a private soldier.

"Everybody recognises now, darling," said the reconciled Nancy, a few days later, "that Doggie

is a top-hole, splendid chap. But I think I ought
to tell you that you're all boring Durdlebury stiff."

Peggy laughed. It was good to be engaged to a
man no longer under a cloud.

"*It will all come right, dear old thing,*" *she wrote to
Doggie. "It's a cinch, as the Americans say. You'll
soon get used to it — especially if you can realise what
it means to me. 'Saving face' has been an awful
business. Now it's all over. Of course I'll accept
the two-seater. I've had lessons in driving since you
went away — I had thoughts of going out to France
to drive Y. M. C. A. cars, but that's off for the present.
I'll love the two-seater. Swank won't be the word.
But 'a parting gift' is all rot. The engagement stands
and all Durdlebury knows it . . .*" and so on, and
so on. She set herself out, honestly, loyally, to be
the kindest girl in the world to Doggie. Mrs.
Conover happened to come into the drawing-room
just as she was licking the stamp. She thumped it
on the envelope with her palm and, looking round
from the writing desk against the wall, showed
her mother a flushed and smiling face.

"If anybody says I'm not good — the goodest
thing the Cathedral has turned out for half-a-dozen
centuries, I'll tear her horrid eyes out from their
sockets!"

"My dear!" cried her horrified mother.

Doggie kept the letter unopened in his tunic
pocket until he could find solitude in which to read
it. After morning parade he wandered to the
deserted trench at the end of the camp, where the
stuffed sacks, representing German defenders, were
hung for bayonet practise. It was a noon of grey
mist through which the alignments of huts and tents
were barely vivible. Instinctively avoiding the
wet earth of the parados, he went round, and, tired
after the recent spell of physical drill, sat down

on the equally wet sandbags of the model parapet, a pathetic, lonely little khaki figure, isolated for the moment by the kindly mist from an uncomprehending world.

He read Peggy's letter several times. He recognised her goodness, her loyalty. The grateful tears even came to his eyes, and he brushed them away hurriedly with a swift look round. But his heart beat none the faster. A long-faded memory of childhood came back to him in regained colour. Some quarrel with Peggy. What it was all about he had entirely forgotten; but he remembered her little flushed face and her angry words: "Well, I'm a sport and you ain't!" He remembered also rebuking her priggishly for unintelligible language and mincing away. He read the letter again in the light of this flash of memory. The only difference between it and the childish speech lay in the fact that instead of a declaration of contrasts, she now uttered a declaration of similitudes. They were both "sports." There she was wrong Doggie shook his head. In her sense of the word he was not a "sport." A sport takes chances, plays the game with a smile on his lips. There was no smile on his. He loathed the game with a sickening, shivering loathing. He was engaged in it because a conglomeration of irresistible forces had driven him into the *mêlée*. It never occurred to Doggie that he was under orders of his own soul. This simple yet stupendous fact never occurred to Peggy.

He sat on the wet sandbags and thought and thought. Though he reproached himself for base ingratitude, the letter did not satisfy him. It left his heart cold. What he sought in it he did not know. It was something he could not find, something that was not there. The sea mist thickened around him. Peggy seemed very far away. . . . He was still engaged to her — for it would be monstrous to persist in his withdrawal. He must accept the situation which she decreed. He owed that to her loyalty. But how to continue the correspondence? It was hard enough to write from Salisbury Plain, from here it was well nigh impossible.

Thus was Doggie brought up against a New Problem. He struggled desperately to defer its solution.

CHAPTER X

THE regiments of the new armies have gathered into their rank and file a mixed crowd transcending the dreams of Democracy. At one end of the social scale are men of refined minds and gentle nurture, at the other creatures from the slums, with slum minds and morals, and between them the whole social gamut is run. Experience seems to show that neither of the extreme elements tends, in the one case to elevate, or, in the other, to debase the battalion. Leading the common life, sharing the common hardships, striving towards common ideals, they inevitably, irresistibly tend to merge themselves in the average. The highest in the scale sink, the lowest rise. The process, so far as the change of soul state is concerned, is infinitely more to the amelioration of the lowest than to the degradation of the highest. The one, also, is more real, the other more apparent. In the one case, it is merely the shuffling off of manners, of habits, of prejudices and the assuming of others horribly distasteful or humorously accepted according to temperament; in the other case, it is an enforced education. And all the congeries of human atoms that make up the battalion, learn new and precious lessons and acquire new virtues — patience, obedience, courage, endurance. . . . But from the point of view of a decorous tea-party in a cathedral town, the tone — or the standard of manners, or whatever you would like by way of definition of that vague and comforting word — the tone of the average is deplorably low. The hooligan may be kicked for excessive foulness; but the rider of the high horse is brutally dragged down into the mire. The curious part of it all is that, the gutter element being eliminated altogether, the corporate standard of the remaining majority is lower than the standard of each individual.

By developing a philosophical disquisition on some such lines did Phineas McPhail seek to initiate Doggie into the weird mysteries of the new social life. Doggie heard with his ears but thought in terms of Durdlebury tea-parties. Nowhere in the mass could he find the spiritual outlook of his Irish Poet Warrior. The individuals that may have had it kept it preciously to themselves. The outlook, as conveyed in speech, was grossly materialistic. From the language of the canteen he recoiled in disgust. He could not reconcile it with the nobler attributes of the users. It was in vain for Phineas to plead that he must accept the *lingua franca* of the British Army like all other things appertaining thereto. Doggie's stomach revolted against most of the other things. The disregard (from his point of view) of personal cleanliness universal in the ranks, filled him with dismay. Even on Salisbury Plain he had managed to get a little hot water for his morning tub. Here, save in the officers' quarters, curiously remote, inaccessible paradise! — there was not such a thing as a tub in the place, let alone hot water to fill it. The men never dreamed of such a thing as a tub. As a matter of fact, they were scrupulously clean according to the lights of the British Tommy; but the lights were not those of Marmaduke Trevor. He had learned the supreme wisdom of keeping lips closed on such matters and did not complain, but all his fastidiousness rebelled. He hated the sluice of head and shoulders with water from a bucket in the raw open air. His hands swelled, blistered, and cracked; and his nails, once so beautifully manicured, grew rich black rims, and all the icy water in the buckets would not remove the grime.

Now and then he went into the town and had a hot bath; but very few of the others ever seemed to think of such a thing. The habit of the British Army of going to bed in its day shirt and under-clothes was peculiarly repellent. Yet Doggie knew that to vary from the sacred ways of his fellow men was to bring disaster on his head.

Some of the men slept under canvas still. But Doggie, fortunately as he reckoned (for he had begun to appreciate fine shades in misery) was put with a dozen others in a ramshackle hut of which the woodwork had warped and let in the breezes above, below, and all round the sides. Doggie, though dismally cold, welcomed the air for obvious reasons. They were fortunate, too, in having straw palliasses — recently provided when it was discovered that sleeping on badly boarded floors with fierce draughts blowing upwards along human spines was strangely fatal to human bodies — but Doggie found his bed very hard lying. And it smelt sour and sickly. For nights, in spite of fatigue, he could not sleep. His mates sang and talked, and bandied jests and sarcasms of esoteric meaning. Some of the recruits from factories or farms satirised their officers for peculiarities common to their social caste, and gave grotesque imitations of their mode of speech. Doggie wondered but held his peace. The deadly stupidity and weariness of it all! And when the talk stopped and they settled to sleep, the snorings and mutterings and coughings began and kept poor Doggie awake most of the night. The irremediable, intimate propinquity with coarse humanity oppressed him. He would have given worlds to go out, even into the pouring rain, and walk about the camp or sleep under a hedge, so

long as he could be alone. And he would think
longingly of his satin-wood bedroom, with its
luxurious bed and lavender-scented sheets, and of
his beloved peacock and ivory room and its pictures
and exquisite furniture and the great fire roaring
up the chimney, and devise intricate tortures for
the Kaiser who had dragged him down to this
squalour.

The meals — the rough cooking, the primitive
service — the table manners of his companions,
offended his delicate senses. He missed napkins.
Never could he bring himself to wipe his mouth
with the back of his hand and the back of his hand
on the seat of his trousers. Nor could he watch with
equanimity an honest soul pick his teeth with his
little finger. But Doggie knew that acquiescence
was the way of happiness and protest the way of
woe.

At first he made few acquaintances beyond those
with whom he was intimately associated. It seemed
more politic to obey his instincts and remain unobtrusive in company and drift away inoffensively
when the chance occurred. One of the men with
whom he talked occasionally was a red-headed
little cockney by the name of Shendish. For some
reason or other — perhaps because his name conveyed a perfectly wrong suggestion of the Hebraic
— he was always called "Mo" Shendish.

"Don't yer wish yer was back, mate?" he asked
one day, having waited to speak till Doggie had
addressed and stamped a letter which he was writing
at the end of the canteen table.

"Where?" said Doggie.

"'Ome, sweet 'ome. In the family castle, where
gilded footmen 'ands sausage and mash about on
trays and quarts of beer all day long. I do."

"You're a lucky chap to have a castle," said
Doggie.

Mo Shendish grinned. He showed little yellow teeth beneath a little red moustache.

"I ain't 'alf got one," said he. "It's in Mare Street, Hackney. I wish I was there now."

He sighed, and in an abstracted way he took a half-smoked cigarette from behind his ear and relit it.

"What were yer before yer joined? Yer look like a clerk." He pronounced it as if it were spelt with a "u."

"Something of the sort," replied Doggie cautiously.

"One can always tell you eddicated blokes. Making your five quid a week easy, I suppose?"

"About that," said Doggie. "What were you?"

"I was making my thirty bob a week regular. I was in the fish business, I was. And now I'm serving my ruddy country at one and twopence a day. Funny life, ain't it?"

"I can't say it's very enjoyable," said Doggie.

"Not the same as sitting in a snug orfis all day with a pen in your lilywhite 'and, and going 'ome to your 'igh tea in a top 'at. What made you join up?"

"The force of circumstances," said Doggie.

"Same 'ere," said Mo; "only I couldn't put it into such fancy language. First my pals went out one after the other. Then the gels began to look saucy at me, and at last one particular bit of skirt what I'd been walking out with, took to promenading with a blighter in khaki. It'd have been silly of me to go and knock his 'ead off, so I enlisted. And it's all right now."

"Just the same sort of thing in my case," replied Doggie. "I'm glad things are right with the young lady."

"First class. She's straight, she is, and no mistake abaht it. She's a —"

He paused for a word to express the inexpressive she.

" —A paragon — a peach?" — Doggie corrected himself. Then, as the sudden frown of perplexed suspicion was swiftly replaced by a grin of content, he was struck by a bright idea.

"What's her name?"

"Aggie. What's yours?"

"Gladys," replied Doggie with miraculous readiness of invention.

"I've got her photograph," Shendish confided in a whisper, and laid his hand on his tunic pocket. Then he looked round at the half-filled canteen to see that he was unobserved. "You won't give me away if I show it yer, will yer?"

Doggie swore secrecy. The photograph of Aggie, an angular, square-browed damsel, who looked as though she could guide the most recalcitrant of fishmongers into the paths of duty, was produced and thrust into Doggie's hand. He inspected it with polite appreciation, while his red-headed friend regarded him with fatuous anxiety.

"Charming! charming!" said Doggie in his pleasantest way. "What's her colouring?"

"Fair hair and blue eyes," said Shendish.

The kindly question, half idle yet unconsciously tactful, was one of those human things which cost so little but are worth so much. It gave Doggie a friend for life.

"Mo," said he, a day or two later, "you're such a decent chap. Why do you use such abominable language?"

"Gawd knows," smiled Mo, unabashed. "I suppose it's friendly like." He wrinkled his brow in thought for an instant. "That's where I think you're making a mistake, old pal, if you don't mind my mentioning it. I know what yer are, but the others don't. You're not friendly enough. See what I mean? Supposin' you say as you would in a city restoorang when you're 'aving yer lunch,

'Will yer kindly pass me the salt?' — well, that's
stand-offish — they say 'Come off it!' But if
you look about and say, 'Where's the b...y salt?'
that's friendly. They understand. They chuck
it at you."

Said Doggie, "It's very — I mean b...y — difficult."

So he tried to be friendly; and if he met with no
great positive success, he at least escaped animosity.
In his spare time he mooned about by himself, shy,
disgusted, and miserable. Once, when a group of
men were kicking a football about, the ball rolled
his way. Instead of kicking it back to the expec-
tant players, he picked it up and advanced to the
nearest man and handed it to him politely.

"Thanks, mate," said the astonished man, "but
why didn't you kick it?"

He turned away without waiting for a reply.
Doggie had not kicked it because he had never
kicked a football in his life, and shrank from an
exhibition of incompetence.

At drills things were easier than on Salisbury
Plain, his actions being veiled in the obscurity of
squad or platoon or company. Many others besides
himself were cursed by sergeants and rated by sub-
alterns and drastically entreated by captains. He
had the consolation of community in suffering.
As a trembling officer he had been the only one,
the only one marked and labelled as a freak part,
the only one stuck in the eternal pillory. Here
were fools and incapables even more dull and in-
effective than he. A ploughboy fellow-recruit from
Dorsetshire, Pugsley by name, did not know right
from left, and having mastered the art of forming
fours, could not get into his brain the reverse process
of forming front. He wept under the lash of the
corporal's tongue, and to Doggie these tears were
healing dews of Heaven's distillation. By degrees

he learned the many arts of war as taught to the
private soldier in England. He could refrain from
shutting his eyes when he pressed the trigger of
his rifle, but to the end of his career his shooting
was erratic. He could perform with the weapon
the other tricks of precision. Unencumbered he
could march with the best. The torture of the
heavy pack nearly killed him; but in time, as his
muscles developed, he was able to slog along under
the burden. He even learned to dig. That was
the worst and most back-breaking art of all.

Now and then Phineas McPhail and himself
would get together and walk into the little seaside
town. It was out of the season, and there was little
to look at save the deserted shops and the squall-
fretted pier and the maidens of the place, who usually
were in company with lads in khaki. Sometimes
a girl alone would give Doggie an unmistakable
glance of shy invitation, for Doggie in his short
slight way was not a bad-looking fellow, carrying
himself well and wearing his uniform with instinctive grace. But the damsel ogled in vain.

On one such occasion Phineas burst into a guffaw.

"Why don't you talk to the poor body? She's
a respectable girl enough. Where's the harm?"

"Go 'square-pushing'?" said Doggie contemptuously, using the soldiers' slang for walking about
with a young woman. "No, thank you."

"And why not? I'm not counselling you, laddie,
to plunge into a course of sensual debauchery. But
a wee bit gossip with a pretty, innocent girl —"

"My dear, good chap," Doggie interrupted.
"what on earth should I have in common with her?"

"Youth."

"I feel as old as hell," said Doggie bitterly.

"You'll be feeling older soon," said Phineas,
"and able to look down on hell with feelings of
superiority."

Doggie walked on in silence for a few paces. Then he said:

"A thing I can't understand is this mania for picking up girls — just to walk about the streets with them. It's so inane. It's a disease."

"Did you ever consider," said Phineas, "how in a station less exalted than that which you used to adorn, the young of opposite sexes manage to meet, select and marry? Man, the British Army's going to be a grand education for you in sociology."

"Well, at any rate you don't suppose I'm going to select and marry out of the street?"

"You might do worse," said Phineas. Then, after a slight pause he asked: "Have you any news lately from Durdlebury?"

"Confound Durdlebury!" said Doggie.

Phineas checked him with one hand and waved the other towards a hostelry on the other side of the street. "If you will give me the money in advance, so as to evade the ungenerous spirit of the no-treating law, you can stand me a quart of ale at the Crown and Sceptre and join me in drinking to its confusion."

So they entered the saloon bar of the public house, and Doggie drank a glass of beer while Phineas swallowed a couple of pints. Two or three other soldiers were there, in whose artless talk McPhail joined lustily. Doggie, unobtrusive at the end of the bar, maintained a desultory and uncomfortable conversation with the barmaid, who was of the florid and hearty type, about the weather.

Some days later, McPhail again made allusion to Durdlebury. Doggie again confounded it.

"I don't want to hear of it or think of it," he exclaimed, in his nervous way, "until this filthy horror is over. They want me to get leave and go down and stay. They're making my life miserable with kindness. I wish they'd let me alone. They don't understand a little bit. I want to get through this thing alone, all by myself."

"I'm sorry I persuaded you to join a regiment in which you were inflicted with the disadvantage of my society," said Phineas.

Doggie threw out an impatient arm. "Oh, you don't count," said he.

A few minutes afterwards, repenting his brusqueness, he tried to explain to Phineas why he did not count. The others knew nothing about him. Phineas knew everything.

"And you know everything about Phineas," said McPhail, grimly. "Ay, ay, laddie," he sighed. "I ken it all. When you're in Tophet, a sympathetic Tophetuan with a wee drop of the milk of human kindness is more comfort than a radiant angel who showers down upon you from the celestial Fortnum and Mason's potted shrimps and caviare."

The sombreness cleared for a moment from Doggie's young brow.

"I never can make up my mind, Phineas," said he, "whether you're a very wise man or an awful fraud."

"Give me the benefit of the doubt, laddie," replied McPhail. "It's the grand theological principle of Christianity."

Time went on. The regiment was moved to the East Coast. On the journey a Zeppelin raid paralysed the railway service. Doggie spent the night under the lee of the bookstall at Waterloo Station. Men huddled up near him, their heads on their kit bags, slept and snored. Doggie almost wept with pain and cold and hatred of the Kaiser. On the East coast much the same life as on the South, save that the wind, as if Hun-sent, found its way more savagely to the skin.

Then suddenly came the news of a large draft for France, which included both McPhail and

Shendish. They went away on leave. The gladness with which he welcomed their return showed Doggie how great a part they played in his new life. In a day or two they would depart God knew whither, and he would be left in dreadful loneliness. Through him the two men, the sentimental Cockney fishmonger and the wastrel graduate of Glasgow and Cambridge, had become friends. He spent with them all his leisure time.

Then one of the silly tragi-comedies of life occurred. McPhail got drunk in the crowded bar of a little public house in the village. It was the last possible drink together of the draft and their pals. The draft was to entrain before daybreak on the morrow. It was a foolish, singing, shouting khaki throng. McPhail, who had borrowed ten pounds from Doggie, in order to see him through the hardships of the front, established himself close by the bar and was drinking whisky. He was also distributing surreptitious sixpences and shillings into eager hands which would convert them into alcohol for eager throats. Doggie, anxious, stood by his side. The spirit from which McPhail had for so long abstained, mounted to his unaccustomed brain. He began to hector, and, master of picturesque speech, he compelled an admiring audience. Doggie did not realise the extent of his drunkenness until, vaunting himself as a Scot and therefore the salt of the army, he picked a quarrel with a stolid Hampshire giant who professed to have no use for Phineas's fellow-countrymen. The men closed. Suddenly someone shouted from the doorway.

"Be quiet, you fools! The A. P. M.'s coming down the road,"

Now the Assistant Provost Marshal, if he heard hell's delight going on in a tavern, would naturally make an inquisitorial appearance. The combatants were separated. McPhail threw a shilling on the bar counter and demanded another whisky. He was about to lift the glass to his lips when Doggie, terrified as to what might happen, knocked the glass out of his hand.

"Don't be an ass," he cried.

Phineas was very drunk. He gazed at his old pupil, took off his cap and, stretching over the bar, hung it on the handle of a beer-pull; then, staggering back, he pointed an accusing finger.

"He has the audacity to call me an ass. Little blinking Marmaduke Doggie Trevor. Little Doggie Trevor whom I trained up from infancy in the way he shouldn't go —"

"Why Doggie Trevor?" someone shouted in enquiry.

"Never mind," replied Phineas with drunken impressiveness. "My old friend Marmaduke has spilled my whisky and called me an ass. I call him Doggie, little Doggie Trevor. You all bear witness he knocked the drink out of my mouth. I'll never forgive him. He doesn't like being called Doggie — and I've no — no pred'lex'n to be called an ass. I'll be thinking I'm going just to strangle him."

He struck out his bony claws towards the shrinking Doggie; but stout arms closed round him and a horny hand was clamped over his mouth, and they got him through the bar and the back parlour into the yard, where they pumped water on his head. And when the A. P. M. and his satellites passed by, the quiet of *The Whip in Hand* was the holy peace of a nunnery.

Doggie and Mo Shendish and a few other staunch souls got McPhail back to quarters without much trouble. On parting, the delinquent, semi-sobered, shook Doggie by the hand and smiled with an air of great affection.

"I've been verra drunk, laddie. And I've been angry with you for the first time in my life. But when you knocked the glass out of my hand I thought you were in danger of losing your good manners in the army. We'll have many a pow-wow together when you join me out there."

The matter would have drifted out of Doggie's mind as one of no importance, had not the detested appellation by which Phineas hailed him struck the imagination of his comrades. It filled a long-felt want, no nickname for Private J. M. Trevor having yet been invented. Doggie Trevor he was and Doggie Trevor he remained for the rest of his period of service. He resigned himself to the inevitable. The sting had gone out of the name through his comrades' ignorance of its origin. But he loathed it as much as ever; it sounded in his ears an ever-lasting reproach.

In spite of the ill turn done in drunkenness, Doggie missed McPhail. He missed Mo Shendish, his more constant companion, even more. Their place was in some degree taken, or rather usurped, for it was without Doggie's volition, by "Taffy" Jones, once clerk to a firm of outside bookmakers. As Doggie had never seen a race-course, had never made a bet, and was entirely ignorant of the names even of famous Derby winners, Taffy regarded him as an astonishing freak worth the attention of a student of human nature. He began to cultivate Doggie's virgin mind by aid of reminiscence, and of such racing news as was to be found in the *Sportsman*. He was a garrulous person and Doggie a good listener. To please him Doggie backed horses, through the old firm, for small sums. The fact of his being a man of large independent means both he and Phineas (to his credit) had kept a close secret, his clerkly origin divined and promulgated by Mo Shendish being unquestioningly accepted, so the bets proposed by Taffy were of a modest nature. Once he brought off a forty to one chance. Taffy rushed to him with the news, dancing with excitement. Doggie's stoical indifference to the winning of twenty pounds, a year's army pay, gave him cause for great wonder. As Doggie showed similar equanimity when he lost, Taffy put him down as a born sportsman. He began to admire him tremendously.

This friendship with Taffy is worth special record, for it was indirectly the cause of a little revolution in Doggie's regimental life. Taffy was an earnest though indifferent performer on the penny whistle. It was his constant companion, the solace of his leisure moments and one of the minor tortures of Doggie's existence. His version of the *Marseillaise* was peculiarly excruciating.

One day when Taffy was playing it with dreadful variations of his own to an admiring group in the Y. M. C. A. hut, Doggie, his nerves rasped to the raw by the false notes and maddening intervals, snatched it out of his hand and began to play himself. Hitherto, shrinking morbidly from any form of notoriety, he had shown no sign of musical accomplishment. But to-day the musicians' impulse was irresistible. He played the *Marseillaise* as no one there had heard it on penny whistle before. The hut recognised a master's touch, for Doggie was a fine executant musician. When he stopped there was a roar: "Go on!" Doggie went on. They kept him whistling till the hut was crowded.

Thenceforward he was penny-whistler, by excellence, to the battalion. He whistled himself into quite a useful popularity.

CHAPTER XI

"WE'RE all very proud of you, Marmaduke," said the Dean.

"I think you're just splendid," said Peggy. They were sitting in Doggie's rooms in Woburn Place, Doggie having been given his three days' leave before going to France. Once again Durdlebury had come to Doggie and not Doggie to Durdlebury. Aunt Sophia, however, somewhat ailing, had stayed at home.

Doggie stood awkwardly before them, conscious of swollen hands and broken nails, shapeless ammunition boots and ill-fitting slacks, morbidly conscious, too, of his original failure.

"You're about ten inches more round the chest than you were," said the Dean admiringly.

"And the picture of health," cried Peggy.

"For anyone who has a sound constitution," answered Doggie, "it is quite a healthy life."

"Now that you've got into the way, I'm sure you must really love it," said Peggy with an encouraging smile.

"It isn't so bad," he replied.

"What none of us can quite understand, my dear fellow," said the Dean, "is your shying at Durdlebury. As we have written you, everybody's singing your praises. Not a soul but would have given you a hearty welcome."

"Besides," Peggy chimed in, "you needn't have made an exhibition of yourself in the town if you didn't want to. The poor Peddles are woefully disappointed."

"There's a war going on. They must bear up —
like lots of other people," replied Doggie.

"He's becoming quite cynical," Peggy laughed.
"But, apart from the Peddles, there's your own
beautiful house waiting for you. It seems so funny
not to go to it, instead of moping in these fusty
lodgings."

"Perhaps," said Doggie quietly, "if I went there
I should never want to come back."

"There's something to be said from that point
of view," the Dean admitted. "A solution of
continuity is never quite without its dangers. Even
Oliver confessed as much."

"Oliver?"

"Yes, didn't Peggy tell you?"

"I didn't think Marmaduke would be interested,"
said Peggy quickly. "He and Oliver have never
been what you might call bosom friends."

"I shouldn't have minded about hearing of him,"
said Doggie. "Why should I? What's he doing?"

The Dean gave information. Oliver, now a captain, had come home on leave a month ago, and had
spent some of it at the Deanery. He had seen a good
deal of fighting, and had one or two narrow escapes.

"Was he keen to get back?" asked Doggie.

The Dean smiled. "I instanced his case in my
remarks on the dangers of the solution of continuity."

"Oh, rubbish, Daddy," cried his daughter, with a
flush. "Oliver is as keen as mustard." The Dean
made a little gesture of submission. She continued.
"He doesn't like the beastliness out there for its
own sake, any more than Marmaduke will. But
he simply loves his job. He has improved tremendously. Once he thought he was the only man
in the country who had seen Life stark naked, and
he put on frills accordingly. Now that he's just
one of a million who have been up against Life
stripped to its skeleton, he's a bit subdued."

"I'm glad of that," said Doggie.

The Dean, urbanely indulgent, joined his finger-tips together and smiled. "Peggy is right," said he, "although I don't wholly approve of her modern lack of reticence in metaphor. Oliver is coming out true gold from the fire. He's a capital fellow. And he spoke of you, my dear Marmaduke, in the kindest way in the world. He has a tremendous admiration for your pluck."

"That's awfully good of him, I'm sure," said Doggie.

Presently the Dean, good, tactful man, discovered that he must go out and have a prescription made up at a chemist's. That arch-Hun enemy the gout, against which he must never be unprepared. He would be back in time for dinner. The engaged couple were left alone.

"Well?" said Peggy.

"Well, dear?" said Doggie.

Her lips invited. He responded. She drew him to the saddle-bag sofa and they sat down side by side.

"I quite understand, dear old thing," she said. "I know the resignation and the rest of it hurt you awfully. It hurt me. But it's no use grousing over spilt milk. You've already mopped it all up. It's no disgrace to be a private. It's an honour. There are thousands of gentlemen in the ranks. Besides — you'll work your way up and they'll offer you another commission in no time."

"You're very good and sweet, dear," said Doggie, "to have such faith in me. But I've had a year —"

"A year!" cried Peggy. "Good Lord! so it is." She counted on her fingers. "Not quite. But eleven months. It's eleven months since I've seen you. Do you realise that? The war has put a stop to time. It is just one endless day."

"One awful, endless day," Doggie acquiesced

with a smile. "But I was saying — I've had a year, or an endless day of eleven months, in which to learn myself. And what I don't know about myself isn't knowledge."

Peggy interrupted with a laugh. "You must be a wonder. Dad's always preaching about self-knowledge. Tell me all about it."

Doggie shook his head, at the same time passing his hand over it in a familiar gesture. Then Peggy cried:

"I knew there was something wrong with you. Why didn't you tell me? You've had your hair cut — cut quite differently."

It was McPhail, careful godfather, who had taken him as a recruit to the regimental barber and prescribed a transformation from the sleek long hair brushed back over the head to a conventional military crop with a rudiment of a side parting. On the crown a few bristles stood up as if uncertain which way to go.

"It's advisable," Doggie replied, "for a Tommy's hair to be cut as short as possible. The Germans are sheared like convicts."

Peggy regarded him open-eyed and puzzle-browed. He enlightened her no further, but pursued the main proposition.

"I wouldn't take a commission," said he, "if the War Office went mad and sank on its knees and beat its head in the dust before me."

"In heaven's name, why not?"

"I've learned my place in the world," said Doggie.

Peggy shook him by the shoulder and turned on him her young, eager face.

"Your place in the world is that of a cultivated gentleman of old family, Marmaduke Trevor of Denby Hall."

"That was the funny old world," said he, "that stood on its legs — legs wide apart with its hands beneath the tails of its evening coat, in front of the drawing-room fire. The present world's standing on its head. Everything's upside down. It has no sort of use for Marmaduke Trevor of Denby Hall. No more use than for Goliath. By the way, how is the poor little beast getting on?"

Peggy laughed. "Oh, Goliath is perfectly assured of his position. He has got it rammed into his mind that he drives the two-seater." She returned to the attack. "Do you intend always to remain a private?"

"I do," said he. "Not even a corporal — not even a bombardier. You see, I've learned to be a private of sorts, and that satisfies my ambition."

"Well, I give it up," said Peggy. "Though why you wouldn't let Dad get you a nice cushy job is a thing I can't understand. For the life of me I can't."

"I've made my bed and I must lie on it," he said, quietly.

"I don't believe you've got such a thing as a bed."

Doggie smiled. "Oh, yes, a bed of a sort." Then noting her puzzled face, he said consolingly: "It'll all come right when the war's over."

"But when will that be? And who knows, my dear man, what may happen to you?"

"If I'm knocked out, I'm knocked out, and there's an end of it," replied Doggie philosophically.

She put her hand on his. "But what's to become of me?"

"We needn't cry over my corpse yet," said Doggie.

The Dean, after a while, returned with his bottle of medicine which he displayed with conscientious ostentation. They dined. Peggy again went over the ground of the possible commission.

"I'm afraid she has set her heart on it, my boy," said the Dean.

Peggy cried a little on parting. This time Doggie

was going, not to the fringe, but to the heart of the
Great Adventure. Into the thick of the carnage.
A year ago, she said through her tears, she would
have thought herself much more fitted for it than
Marmaduke.

"Perhaps you are still, dear," said Doggie, with
his patient smile.

He saw them to the taxi which was to take them
to the familiar Sturrocks's. Before getting in,
Peggy embraced him.

"Keep out of the way of shells and bullets as
much as you can."

The Dean blew his nose, God-blessed him, and
murmured something incoherent about fighting
for the glory of old England.

"Good luck," cried Peggy from the window.

She blew him a kiss. The taxi drove off and
Doggie went back into the house with leaden feet.
The meeting, which he had morbidly dreaded, had
brought him no comfort. It had not removed the
invisible barrier between Peggy and himself. But
Peggy seemed so unconscious of it that he began to,
wonder whether it only existed in his diseased
imagination. Though by his silences and reserves
he had given her cause for resentment and reproach,
her attitude was nothing less than angelic. He
sat down moodily in an armchair, his hands deep
in his trousers pockets and his legs stretched out.
The fault lay in himself, he argued. What was the
matter with him? He seemed to have lost all
human feeling, like the man with the stone heart in
the old legend. Otherwise why had he felt no prick
of jealousy at Peggy's admiring comprehension of
Oliver? Of course he loved her. Of course he
wanted to marry her when this nightmare was over.
That went without saying. But why couldn't he
look to the glowing future? A poet had called a
lover's mistress "the lode-star of his one desire."

That to him Peggy ought to be. Lode-star. One desire. The words confused him. He had no lode-star. His one desire was to be left alone. Without doubt he was suffering from some process of moral petrifaction.

Doggie was no psychologist. He had never acquired the habit of turning himself inside out and gloating over the horrid spectacle. All his life he had been a simple soul with simple motives and a simple though possibly selfish standard to measure them. But now his soul was knocked into a chaotic state of complexity, and his poor little standards were no manner of use. He saw himself as in a glass darkly, mystified by unknown change.

He rose, sighed, shook himself.

"I give it up," said he, and went to bed.

Doggie went to France: a France hitherto un-dreamed of either by him or by any young English-man; a France clean swept and garnished for war, a France, save for the ubiquitous English soldiery, of silent towns and empty villages and deserted roads; a France of smiling fields and sorrowful faces of women and drawn, patient faces of old men — and even then, the women and old men were rarely met by day, for they were at work on the land, solitary figures on the landscape, with vast spaces between them. In the quiet townships English street signs and placards conflicted with their sense of being in friendly provincial France, and gave the impression of foreign domination. For beyond that long, grim line of eternal thunder, away over there in the distance, which was called the Front, street signs and placards in yet another alien tongue also outraged the serene genius of French urban life. Yet our signs were a symbol of a mighty Empire's brotherhood and the dimmed eyes that beheld the *Place de la Fontaine* transformed into

"Holborn Circus" and the *Grande Rue* into "Pic-
cadilly," smiled, and the owners with eager courtesy
directed the stray Tommy to "Regent Street"
which they had known all their life as the *Rue
Feuillemaisnil* — a word which Tommy could not
remember, still less pronounce. It was as much
as Tommy could do to get hold of an approximation
to the name of the town. And besides these re-
namings, other inscriptions flamed about the streets;
alphabetical hieroglyphs in which the mystic letters
H. Q. most often appeared; "This way to the
Y. M. C. A. hut"; in many humble windows the
startling announcement, "Washing done here."
British motor lorries and ambulances crowding
the little *Place* and aligned along the avenues.
British faces, British voices, everywhere. The blue
uniform and blue helmet of a French soldier seemed
as incongruous though as welcome as in London.

And the straight, endless roads, so French with
their infinite border of poplars, their patient little
stones marking every hundred metres until the
tenth rose into the proud kilometre stone proclaim-
ing the distance to the next stately town, rang too
with the sound of British voices, and the tramp of
British feet and the clatter of British transport,
and the screech and whirr of cars, revealing as they
passed the flash of red and gold of the British staff.
Yet the finely cultivated land remained to show
that it was France; and the little whitewashed
villages; the curé in shovel hat and rusty cassock;
the children in blue or black blouses, who stared as
the British troops went by; the patient, elderly
Territorials in their old pre-war uniforms, guarding
unthreatened culverts or repairing the roads; the
helpful signs set up in happier days by the Touring
Club of France.

Into this strange anomaly of a land came Doggie
with his draft, still half stupefied by the remorse-

lessness of the stupendous machine in which he had been caught, in spite of his many months of training in England. He had loathed the East Coast camp. When he landed at Boulogne in the dark and pouring rain, and hunched his pack with the others who went off singing to the rest camp, he regretted East Anglia.

"Give us a turn on the whistle, Doggie," said a corporal.

"I was sea-sick into it and threw it overboard," he growled, stumbling over the rails of the quay.

"Oh, you holy young liar!" said the man next him.

But Doggie did not trouble to reply, his neighbour being only a private like himself.

Then the draft joined its unit. In his youth Doggie had often wondered at the meaning of the familiar inscription on every goods-van in France: "40 Hommes. 8 Chevaux." Now he ceased to wonder. He was one of the forty men. . . . At the rail-head he began to march and at last joined the remnant of his battalion. They had been through hard fighting and were now in billets.

Until he joined them, he had not realised the drain there had been on the reserves at home. Very many familiar faces of officers were missing. New men had taken their place. And very many of his old comrades had gone, some to Blighty, some West of that Island of Desire; and those who remained had the eyes of children who had passed through the Valley of the Shadow of Death.

McPhail and Mo Shendish had passed through unscathed. In the reconstruction of the regiment chance willed that the three of them found themselves in the same platoon of A Company. Doggie almost embraced them when they met.

"Laddie," said McPhail to him, as he was drinking a mahogany coloured liquid, that was known

by the name of tea, out of a tin mug, and eating a
hunk of bread and jam, "I don't know whether
or not I'm pleased to see you.   You were safer in
England.   Once I misspent many months of my
life in shielding you from the dangers of France.
But France is a much more dangerous place nowadays, and I can't help you.   You've come right into
the thick of it.   Just listen to the hell's delight
that's going on over yonder."

The easterly wind brought them the roar streaked
with stridence of the artillery duel in progress on
the nearest sector of the front.

They were sitting in the cellar entrance to a house
in a little town which had already been somewhat
mauled.   Just opposite was a shuttered house on
the ground floor of which had been a hatter and
hosier's shop, and there still swung bravely on an
iron rod the red brim of what once had been a monstrous red hat.   Next door, the façade of the upper
stories had been shelled away, and the naked interiors gave the impression of a pathetic doll's
house.   Women's garments still swung on pegs.
A cottage piano lurched forward drunkenly on
three legs, with the keyboard ripped open, the treble
notes on the ground, the bass incongruously in the
air.   In the attic, ironically secure, hung a cheap
German print of blowsy children feeding a pig.
The wide, flag-stoned street smelt sour.   At various
cavern doors sat groups of the billeted soldiers.
Now and then squads marched up and down,
monotonously clad in khaki and dun-coloured helmets.   Officers, some only recognisable by the
Sam Browne belt, others spruce and point-device,
passed by.   Here and there a shop was open, and
the elderly proprietor and his wife stood by the
doorway to get the afternoon air.   Women and
children straggled rarely through the streets.   The
Boche had left the little town alone for some time;

they had other things to do with their heavy guns;
and all the French population, save those whose
homes were reduced to nothingness, had remained.
They took no notice of the distant bombardment.
It had grown to be a phenomenon of nature like
the wind and the rain.

But to Doggie it was new — just as the sight of
the wrecked house opposite, with its sturdy, crown-
less hat-brim of a sign, was new. He listened, as
McPhail had bidden him, to the artillery duel with
an odd little spasm of his heart.

"What do you think of that, now?" asked McPhail
grandly, as if it was The Greatest Show on Earth,
run by him, the Proprietor.

"It's rather noisy," said Doggie, with a little
ironical twist of his lips that was growing habitual.
"Do they keep it up at night?"

"They do."

"I don't think it's fair to interfere with one's
sleep like that," said Doggie.

"You've got to adapt yourself to it," said McPhail
sagely. "No doubt you'll be remembering my
theory of adaptability. Through that I've made
myself into a very brave man. When I wanted to
run away — a very natural desire considering the
scrupulous attention I've always paid to my bodily
well-being — I reflected on the preposterous ob-
stacles put in the way of flight by a bowelless
military system, and adapted myself to the static
and dynamic conditions of the trenches."

"Gorblime!" said Mo Shendish, stretched out by
his side, "just listen to him!"

"I suppose you'll say you sucked 'honey out of
the shells,'" remarked Doggie.

"I'm no great hand at mixing metaphors —"

"What about drinks?" asked Mo.

"Nor drinks either," replied McPhail. "Both
are bad for the brain. But as to what you were

saying, laddie, I'll not deny that I've derived considerable interest and amusement from a bombardment. Yet it has its sad aspect." He paused for a moment or two. "Man," he continued, "what an awful waste of money!"

"I don't know what old Mac is jawing about," said Mo Shendish, "but you can take it from me he's a holy terror with the bayonet. One moment he's talking to a Boche through his hat, and the next the Boche is wriggling like a worm on a bent pin."

Mo winked at Phineas. The temptation to "tell the tale" to the new-comer was too strong.

Doggie grew very serious. "You've been killing men like that?"

"Thousands, laddie," replied Phineas, the picture of unboastful veracity. "And so has our iron-gutted — I would have said steel-inviscerated, but he wouldn't understand it — comrade by my side."

Mo Shendish, helmeted, browned, dried, toughened, a very different Mo from the pallid ferret whom Aggie had driven into the ranks of war, hunched himself up, his hands clasping his knees.

"I don't mind doing it, when you're so excited you don't know where you are," said he, "but I don't like thinking of it afterwards."

As a matter of fact he had only once got home with the bayonet, and the memory was very unpleasant.

"But you've just thought of it," said Phineas.

"It was you, not me," said Mo. "That makes all the difference."

"It's astonishing," Phineas remarked sententiously, "how many people not only refuse to catch pleasure as it flies, but spurn it when it sits up and begs at them. Laddie," he turned to Doggie, "the more one wallows in Hedonism, the more one realises its unplumbed depths."

A little girl of ten, neatly pig-tailed but piteously

shod, came near, and seemed to cast a child's envious eye on Doggie's bread and jam.

"Approach, my little one," Phineas cried in French words but with the accent of Sauchiehall Street. "If I gave you a franc, what would you do with it?"

"I should buy nourishment (*de la nourriture*) for *maman*."

"Lend me a franc, laddie," said McPhail, and when Doggie had slipped the coin into his palm, he addressed the child in unintelligible grandiloquence, and sent her on her way mystified but rejoicing. *Ces bons drôles d'Anglais!*

"Ah, laddie," cried Phineas, stretching himself out comfortably by the lintel of the door. "You've got to learn to savour the exquisite pleasure of a genuinely kindly act."

"Hold on!" cried Mo. "It was Doggie's money you were flinging about."

McPhail withered him with a glance.

"You're an unphilosophical ignoramus," said he.

CHAPTER XII

PERHAPS one of the greatest influences which transformed Doggie into a fairly efficient though undistinguished infantry-man was a morbid social terror of his officers. It saved him from many a guard-room, and from many a heart to heart talk wherein the zealous lieutenant gets to know his men. He lived in dread lest military delinquence or civil accomplishment should be the means of revealing the disgrace which bit like an acid into his soul. His undisguisable air of superior breeding could not fail to attract notice. Often his officers asked him what he was in civil life. His reply, "A clerk, sir," had to satisfy them. He had developed a curious self-protective faculty of shutting himself up like a hedgehog at the approach of danger. Once a breezy subaltern had selected him as his batman; but Doggie's agonised "It would be awfully good of you, sir, if you wouldn't mind not thinking of it," and the appeal in his eyes, established the freemasonry of caste and saved him from dreaded intimate relations.

"All right, if you'd rather not, Trevor," said the subaltern. "But why doesn't a chap like you try for a commission?"

"I'm much happier as I am, sir," replied Doggie, and that was the end of the matter.

But Phineas when he heard of it — it was on the East Coast — began: "If you still consider yourself too fine to clean another man's boots —"

Doggie, in one of his quick fits of anger, interrupted: "If you think I'm just a dirty little snob, if you don't understand why I begged to be let off, you're the thickest-headed fool in creation!"

"I'm nae that, laddie," replied Phineas, with his usual ironic submissiveness. "Haven't I kept your secret all this time?"

Thus it was Doggie's fixed idea to lose himself in the locust swarm, to be prominent neither for good nor evil, even in the little clot of fifty, outwardly, almost identical locusts that formed his platoon. It braced him to the performance of hideous tasks; it restrained him from display of superior intellectual power or artistic capability. The world upheaval had thrown him from his peacock and ivory room, with its finest collection on earth of little china dogs, into a horrible, fetid hole in the ground in Northern France. It had thrown not the average young Englishman of comfortable position who had toyed with aesthetic superficialities as an amusement, but a poor little by-product of cloistered life who had been brought up from babyhood to regard these things as the nervous texture of his very existence. He was wrapped from head to heel in fine net, to every tiny mesh of which he was acutely sensitive.

A hole in the ground in Northern France. The regiment, after its rest, moved on and took its turn in the trenches. Four days on; four days off. Four days on of misery inconceivable. Four days on, during which the officers watched the men with the unwavering vigilance of kindly cats.

"How are you getting along, Trevor?"

"Nicely, thank you, sir."

"Feet all right?"

"Yes, thank you, sir."

"Sure? If you want to grouse, grouse away. That's what I'm talking to you for."

"I'm perfectly happy, sir."

"Darn sight more than I am!" laughed the sub-altern and with a cheery nod in acknowledgment of Doggie's salute, splashed down the muddy trench.

But Doggie was chilled to the bone, and he had no feeling in his feet which were under six inches of water, and his woollen gloves, being wet through, were useless, and prevented his numbed hands from feeling the sandbags with which he and the rest of the platoon were repairing the parapet; for the Germans had just consecrated an hour's general hate to the vicinity of the trench, and its exquisite symmetry, the pride of the platoon commander, had been disturbed. There had also been a few ghastly casualties. A shell had fallen and burst in the traverse at the far end of the trench. Something that looked like half a man's head and a bit of shoulder had dropped just in front of the dug-out where Doggie and his section was sheltering. Doggie staring at it was violently sick. In a stupefied way he found himself mingling with others who were engaged in clearing up the horror. A murmur reached him that it was Taffy Jones who had then been dismembered. . . . The bombardment over, he had taken his place with the rest in the reparation of the parapet; and as he happened to be at an end of the line, the officer had spoken to him. If he had been suffering tortures unknown to Attila and unimagined by his successors, he would have answered just the same.

But he lamented Taffy's death to Phineas, who listened sympathetically. Such a cheery comrade, such a smart soldier, such a kindly soul.

"Not a black spot in him," said Doggie.

"A year ago, laddie," said McPhail, "what would have been your opinion of a bookmaker's clerk?"

"I know," replied Doggie. "But this isn't a year ago. Just look round."

He laughed somewhat hysterically, for the fate of Taffy had unstrung him for the time.   Phineas contemplated the length of deep, narrow ditch, with its planks half swimming on filthy liquid, its wire revetment holding up the oozing sides, the dingy parapet above which it was death to put one's head, the grey, free sky, the only thing free along that awful row of parallel ditches that stretched from the Belgian coast to Switzerland, the clay-covered, shapeless figures of men, their fellows, almost undistinguishable even by features from themselves.

"It has been borne upon me lately," said Phineas, "that patriotism is an amazing virtue."

Doggie drew a foot out of the mud so as to find a less precarious purchase higher up the slope.

"And I've been thinking, Phineas, whether it's really patriotism that has brought you and me into this — what can we call it? Dante's Inferno is child's play to it."

"Dante had no more imagination," said Phineas, "than a Free Kirk precentor in Kirkcudbright."

"But is it patriotism?" Doggie persisted.   "If I thought it was, I should be happier.   If we had orders to go over the top and attack and I could shout 'England for ever!' and lose myself just in the thick of it —"

"There's a brass hat coming down the trench," said Phineas, "and brass hats have no use for rhapsodical privates."

They stood to attention as the staff-officer passed by.   Then Doggie broke in impatiently:

"I wish to goodness you could understand what I'm trying to get at."

A smile illuminated the gaunt, unshaven, mud-caked face of Phineas McPhail.

"Laddie," said he, "let England as an abstraction fend for itself.   But you've a bonny English soul

within you, and for that you are fighting. And so
had poor Taffy Jones. And I have a bonny Scottish
thirst, the poignancy of which both of you have
been happily spared. I will leave you, laddie, to
seek in slumber a surcease from martyrdom."

After one of the spells in the trenches, the worst
he had experienced, A Company was marched into
new billets some miles below the lines, in the once
prosperous village of Frélus. They had slouched
along dead tired, drooping under their packs, sodden
with mud and sleeplessness, silent, with not a note of
a song among them — but at the entrance to the
village, quickened by a word or two of exhortation
from officers and sergeants, they pulled themselves
together and marched in, heads up, forward, in faultless step. The G. O. was jealous of the honour of
his men. He assumed that his predecessors in the
village had been a "rotten lot," and was determined
to show the inhabitants of Frélus what a crack
English regiment was really like. Frélus was an
unimportant, unheard of village; but the opinion
of a thousand Fréluses made up France's opinion
of the British Army. Doggie, although half stupefied with fatigue, responded to the sentiment,
like the rest. He was conscious of making part of
a gallant show. It was only when they halted and
stood easy that he lost count of things. The wide
main street of the village swam characterless before
his eyes. He followed, not directions, but directed
men, with a sheeplike instinct, and found himself
stumbling through an archway down a narrow path.
He had a dim consciousness of lurching sideways
and confusedly apologising to a woman who supported him back to equilibrium. Then the next
thing he saw was a barn full of fresh straw, and when
somebody pointed to a vacant strip, he fell down,
with many others, and went to sleep.

The reveille sounded a minute afterwards, though
a whole night had passed; and there was the blessed
clean water to wash in — he had long since ceased
to be fastidious in his ablutions — and there was
breakfast, sizzling bacon and bread and jam.   And
there, in front of the kitchen, aiding with hot water
for the tea, moved a slim girl, with dark, and as
Doggie thought, tragic eyes.

Kit inspection, feet inspection, all the duties of
the day and dinner were over.   Most of the men
returned to their billets to sleep.   Some, including
Doggie, wandered about the village, taking the air,
and visiting the little modest cafés and talking with
indifferent success, so far as the interchange of
articulate ideas was concerned, with shy children.
McPhail and Mo Shendish being among the sleepers,
Doggie mooned about by himself in his usual self-
effacing way.   There was little to interest him in
the long, straggling village.   He had passed through
a hundred such.   Low, whitewashed houses inter-
spersed with perky, balconied buildings, given over
to little shops on the ground floor, with here and
there a discreet iron gate shutting off the doctor's
or the attorney's villa, and bearing the oval plate
indicating the name and pursuit of the tenant;
with here and there, too, long, whitewashed walls
enclosing a dairy or a timber yard, stretched on each
side of the great high road, and the village gradually
dwindled away at each end into the gently undulat-
ing country.   There were just a bye lane or two, one
leading up to the little grey church and presbytery,
and another to the little cemetery with its trim paths
and black and white wooden crosses and wirework
pious offerings.   At open doors the British soldiers
lounged at ease, and in the dim interiors behind
them the forms of the women of the house, blue
aproned, moved to and fro.   The early afternoon

was warm, a westerly breeze deadened the sound of
the distant bombardment to an unheeded drone,
and a holy peace settled over the place.

Doggie, clean, refreshed, comfortably drowsy,
having explored the village, returned to his billet,
and looking at it from the opposite side of the way,
for the first time realised its nature. The lane into
which he had stumbled the night before ran under
an archway supporting some kind of overhead
chamber, and separated the dwelling house from a
a warehouse wall on which vast letters proclaimed the
fact that Veuve Morin et Fils carried on therein
the business of hay and corn dealers. Hence,
Doggie reflected, the fresh, deep straw on which
he and his fortunate comrades had wallowed.
The double gate under the archway was held back
by iron stancheons. The two-storied house looked
fairly large and comfortable. The front door stood
wide open, giving the view of a neat, stiff little hall
or living-room. An article of furniture caught his
idle eye. He crossed the road in order to have a
nearer view. It was a huge, polished mahogany
cask standing about four feet high, bound with
shining brass bands, such as he remembered having
seen once in Brittany. He advanced still closer,
and suddenly the slim, dark girl appeared and stood
in the doorway and looked frankly and somewhat
rebukingly into his inquisitive eyes. Doggie flushed
as one caught in an unmannerly act. A crying
fault of the British Army is that it prescribes for
the rank and file no form of polite recognition of the
existence of civilians. It is contrary to Army Order
to salute or to take off their caps. They can only
jerk their heads and grin, a gauche proceeding which
places them at a disadvantage with the fair sex.
Doggie, therefore, sketched a vague salutation
halfway between a salute and a bow, and began a
profuse apology. Mademoiselle must pardon his

curiosity, but as a lover of old things he had been struck by the beautiful *tonneau.*

An amused light came into her sombre eyes, and a smile flickered round her lips. Doggie noted instantly how pale she was, and how tiny, faint, little lines persisted at the corners of those lips, in spite of the smile.

"There is no reason for excuses, Monsieur," she said. "The door was open to the view of everybody."

"*Pourtant,*" said Doggie, "*c'était un peu mal élevé.*"

She laughed.- "Pardon. But it's droll. First to find an English soldier apologising for looking into a house, and then to find him talking French like a *poilu.*"

Doggie said, with a little touch of national jealousy and a reversion to Durdlebury punctilio: "I hope, Mademoiselle, you have always found the English soldier conduct himself like a gentleman."

"*Mais oui, mais oui!*" she cried. "They are all charming. *Ils sont doux comme des moutons.* But this is a question of delicacy — somewhat exaggerated."

"It's good of you, Mademoiselle, to forgive me," said Doggie.

By all the rules of polite intercourse, either Doggie should have made his bow and exit, or the maiden, exercising her prerogative, should have given him the opportunity of graceful withdrawal. But they remained where they were, the girl framed by the doorway, the lithe little figure in khaki and lichen-coloured helmet looking up to her from the foot of the two front steps.

At last he said in some embarrassment: "That's a very beautiful cask of yours."

She wavered for a few seconds. Then she said:

"You can enter, Monsieur, and examine it, if you like."

Mademoiselle was very amiable, said Doggie.

Mademoiselle moved aside and Doggie entered,
taking off his helmet and holding it under his arm
like an opera-hat.   There was nothing much to see
in the little vestibule-parlour: a stiff, tasselled
chair or two, a great old linen press, taking up most
of one side o: a wall, a cheap table covered with a
chenille tablecloth, and the resplendent old cask,
about which he lingered.   He mentioned Brittany.
Her tragic face lighted up again.   Monsieur was
right.   Her aunt, Madame Morin, was Breton,
and had brought the cask with her as part of
her dowry, together with the press and other
furniture.   Doggie alluded to the vastly lettered
inscription, "Veuve Morin et Fils."   Madame Morin
was, in a sense, his hostess?   And the son?

"Alas, Monsieur!"

And Doggie knew what that "alas!" meant.

"Where, Mademoiselle?"

"The Argonne."

"And Madame your aunt?"

She shrugged her thin though shapely shoulders.
"It nearly killed her.   She is a little old and an
invalid.   She has been in bed for the last three
weeks."

"Then what becomes of the business?"

"It is I, Monsieur, who am the business.   And I
know nothing about it."   She sighed.   Then with
her blue apron — otherwise she was dressed in
unrelieved black — she rubbed an imaginary speck
from the brass banding of the cask.   "This, I
suppose you know, was for the best brandy, Monsieur."

"And now?" he asked.

"A memory.   A sentiment.   A thing of beauty."

In a feminine way which he understood she herded
him to the door, by way of dismissal.   Durdlebury
helped him.   A tiny French village has as many
slanderous tongues as an English cathedral city.

He was preparing to take polite leave when she looked swiftly at him, and made the faintest gesture of a detaining hand.

"Now I remember. It was you who nearly fell into me last night, when you were entering through the gate."

The dim recollection came back — the firm woman's arm round him for the few tottering seconds.

"It seems I am always bound to be impolite, for I don't think I thanked you," smiled Doggie.

"You were at the end of your tether." Then very gently, "*Pauvre garçon!*"

"The *sales Boches* had kept us awake for four nights," said Doggie. "That was why."

"And you are rested now?"

He laughed. "Almost."

They were at the door. He looked out and drew back. A knot of men were gathered by the gate of the yard. Apparently she had seen them too, for a flush rose to her pale cheeks.

"Mademoiselle," said Doggie, "I should like to creep back to the barn and sleep. If I pass my comrades they'll want to detain me."

"That would be a pity," she said demurely. "Come this way, Monsieur."

She led him through a room and a passage to the kitchen. They shared a pleasurable sense of adventure and secrecy. At the kitchen door she paused and spoke to an old woman chopping up vegetables.

"Toinette, let Monsieur pass." To Doggie she said: "*Au revoir, Monsieur,*" and disappeared.

The old woman looked at him at first with disfavour. She did not hold with Tommies needlessly tramping over the clean flags of her kitchen. But Doggie's polite apology for disturbing her, and a youthful grace of manner — he still held his tin-hat under his arm — caused her features to relax.

"You are English?"

With a smile he indicated his uniform. "Why, yes, Madame."

"How comes it then that you speak French?"

"Because I have always loved your beautiful France, Madame."

"France — *ah! la pauvre France!*" She sighed, drew a wisp of what had been a cornet of snuff from her pocket, opened it, dipped in a tentative finger and thumb and, finding it empty, gazed at it with disappointment, sighed again, and with the methodical hopelessness of age folded it up into the neatest of little squares and thrust it back in her pocket. Then she went on with her vegetables.

Doggie took his leave and emerged into the yard.

He dozed pleasantly on the straw of the barn, but it was not the dead sleep of the night. Bits of his recent little adventure fitted into the semi-conscious intervals. He heard the girl's voice saying so gently: "*Pauvre garçon!*" and it was very comforting.

He was finally aroused by Phineas and Mo Shendish, who, having slept like tired dogs some distance off down the barn, now desired his company for a stroll round the village. Doggie good-naturedly assented. As they passed the house door he cast a quick glance. It was open, but the slim figure in black with the blue apron was not visible within. The shining cask, however, seemed to smile a friendly greeting.

"If you believed the London papers," said Phineas, "you'd think that the war-worn soldier coming from the trenches is met behind the lines with luxurious Turkish baths, comfortable warm canteens, and Picture Palaces and theatrical entertainments. Can you perceive here any of those amenities of modern warfare?"

They looked around them and admitted that they could not.

"Apparently," said Phineas, "the Colonel, good but limited man, has missed all the proper places, and dumps us in localities unrecognised by the London Press."

"'Put me on the pier at Brighton,'" sang Mo Shendish. "But I'd sooner have Margit or Yarmouth any day. Brighton's too toffish for whelks. My! and cockles! I wonder whether we shall ever eat 'em again." A far-away, dreamy look crept into his eyes.

"Does your young lady like cockles?" Doggie asked sympathetically.

"Aggie? Funny thing, I was just thinking of her. She fair dotes on 'em. We had a day at Southend just before the war —"

He launched into anecdote. His companions listened, Phineas ironically carrying out his theory of adaptability, Doggie with finer instinct. It appeared there had been an altercation over right of choice with an itinerant vendor in which, to Aggie's admiration, Mo had come off triumphant.

"You see," he explained, "being in the fish trade myself, I could spot the winners."

James Marmaduke Trevor of Denby Hall laughed and slapped him on the back, and said indulgently: "Good old Mo!"

At the little school-house they stopped to gossip with some of their friends who were billeted there, and they sang the praises of the Veuve Morin's barn.

"I wonder you don't have the house full of officers, if it's so wonderful," said someone.

An omniscient corporal, in the confidence of the Quarter Master, explained that the landlady being ill in bed and the place run by a young girl, the house had been purposely missed. Doggie drew a breath of relief at the news, and attributed Madame Morin's malady to the intervention of a kindly providence.

Somehow he did not fancy officers having the run of the house.

They strolled on and came to a forlorn little *Débit de Tabac*, showing in its small window some clay pipes and a few flyblown picture postcards. Now Doggie, in spite of his training in adversity, had never resigned himself to "Woodbines" and other such brands supplied to the British Army, and, Egyptian and Turkish being beyond his social pale, he had taken to smoking French Régie tobacco, of which he laid in a stock whenever he had the chance. So now he entered the shop, leaving Phineas and Mo outside. As they looked on French cigarettes with sturdy British contempt, they were not interested in Doggie's purchases. A wan girl of thirteen rose from behind the counter.

"*Vous désirez, Monsieur?*"

Doggie stated his desire. The girl was calculating the price of the packets before wrapping them up, when his eyes fell upon a neat little pile of *cornets* in a pigeon-hole at the back. They directly suggested to him one of the great luminous ideas of his life. It was only afterwards that he realised its effulgence. For the moment he was merely concerned with the needs of a poor old woman who had sighed lamentably over an empty paper of comfort.

"Do you sell snuff?"

"But yes, Monsieur."

"Give me some of the best quality."

"How much does Monsieur desire?"

"A lot," said Doggie.

And he bought a great package, enough to set the whole village sneezing to the end of the war, and peering round the tiny shop and espying in the recesses of a glass case a little olive-wood box, ornamented on the top with pansies and forget-me-nots, purchased that also. He had just paid when his companions put their heads in the doorway. Mo pointing waggishly to Doggie, warned the little girl against his depravity.

"Mauvy, mauvy!" said he.

"*Qu'est-ce qu'il dit?*" asked the child.

"He's the idiot of the regiment whom I have to look after and feed with pap," said Doggie, "and, being hungry, he is begging you not to detain me."

"*Mon Dieu!*" cried the child.

Doggie, always courteous, went out with a "*Bon soir, Mademoiselle,*" and joined his friends.

"What were you jabbering to her about?" Mo asked suspiciously.

Doggie gave him the literal translation of his speech. Phineas burst into loud laughter.

"Laddie," said he, "I've never heard you make a joke before. The idiot of the regiment and you're his keeper! Man, that's fine. What has come over you to-day?"

"If he'd a-said a thing like that in Mare Street, Hackney, I'd have knocked his blinking 'ead orf," declared Mo Shendish.

Doggie stopped and put his parcel-filled hands behind his back.

"Have a try now, Mo."

But Mo bade him fry his ugly face, and thus established harmony.

It was late that evening before Doggie could find an opportunity of slipping, unobserved, through the open door into the house kitchen dimly illuminated by an oil lamp.

"Madame," said he to Toinette, "I observed to-day that you had come to the end of your snuff. Will you permit an English soldier to give you some? Also a little box to keep it in?"

The old woman, spare, myriad-wrinkled beneath her peasant's coiffe, yet looking as if carved out of weather-beaten elm, glanced from the gift to the donor and from the donor to the gift.

"But, Monsieur — Monsieur — why?" she began quaveringly.

"You surely have someone — *là-bas* — over yonder?" said Doggie with a sweep of his hand.

"*Mais oui?* How did you know? My grandson, *Mon petiot* —"

"It is he, my comrade, who sends the snuff to the *grand'mère.*"

And Doggie bolted.

CHAPTER XIII

AT breakfast next morning Doggie searched the courtyard in vain for the slim figure of the girl. Yesterday she had stood just outside the kitchen door. To-day her office was usurped by a hefty cook with the sleeves of his grey shirt rolled up and his collar open, and vast and tight-hitched braces unromantically strapped all over him. Doggie felt a pang of disappointment, and abused the tea. Mo Shendish stared and asked what was wrong with it.

"Rotten," said Doggie.

"You can't expect yer slap-up City A. B. C. shops in France," said Mo.

Doggie, who was beginning to acquire a sense of rueful humour, smiled and was appeased.

It was only in the afternoon that he saw the girl again. She was standing in the doorway of the house, with her hand on her bosom, as though she had just come out to breathe fresh air, when Doggie and his two friends emerged from the yard. As their eyes met, she greeted him with her sad little smile. Emboldened, he stepped forward.

"*Bonjour, mademoiselle.*"

"*Bonjour, monsieur.*"

"I hope, madame, your aunt is better to-day."

She seemed to derive some dry amusement from his solicitude.

"Alas, no, monsieur."

"Was that why I had not the pleasure of seeing you this morning?"

"Where?"

"Yesterday you filled our tea-kettles."

167

"But, monsieur," she replied primly, "I am not the *vivandière* of the regiment."

"That's a pity," laughed Doggie.

Then he became aware of the adjacent forms and staring eyes of Phineas and Mo, who for the first time in their military career beheld him on easy terms with a strange and prepossessing young woman. After a second's thought he came to a diplomatic decision.

"Mademoiselle," said he in his best Durdlebury manner, "may I dare to present my two comrades, my best friends in the battalion, Monsieur McPhail, Monsieur Shendish?"

She made them each a little formal bow, and then somewhat maliciously, addressing McPhail, as the bigger and the elder of the two.

"I don't yet know the name of your friend."

Phineas put his great hand on Doggie's shoulder.

"James Marmaduke Trevor."

"Otherwise called Doggie, Miss," said Mo.

She made a little graceful gesture of non-comprehension.

"Non compree?" asked Mo.

"No, Monsieur."

Phineas explained in his rasping and consciously translated French.

"It is a nickname of the regiment. Doggie."

The flushed and embarrassed subject of the discussion saw her lips move silently to the word.

"But his name is Trevor. Monsieur Trevor," said Phineas.

She smiled again. And the strange thing about her smile was that it was a matter of her lips and rarely of her eyes, which always maintained the haunting sadness of their tragic depths.

"Monsieur Trevor," she repeated, imitatively. "And yours, Monsieur?"

"McPhail."

"McFêle; *c'est assez difficile.* And yours?"

Mo guessed. "Shendish," said he.

She repeated that also, whereat Mo grinned fatuously, showing his little yellow teeth beneath his scrubby red moustache.

"My friends call me Mo," said he.

She grasped his meaning. "Mo," she said; and she said it so funnily and softly, and with ever so little a touch of quizzicality, that the sentimental warrior roared with delight.

"You've got it right fust time, Miss."

From her two steps height of vantage, she looked down on the three upturned British faces — and her eyes went calmly from one to the other.

She turned to Doggie. "One would say, Monsieur, that you were the Three Musketeers."

"Possibly, Mademoiselle," laughed Doggie. He had not felt so light-hearted for many months. "But we lack a d'Artagnan."

"When you find him, bring him to me," said the girl.

"Mademoiselle," said Phineas gallantly, "we would not be such imbeciles."

At that moment the voice of Toinette came from within.

"Ma'amselle Jeanne! Ma'amselle Jeanne!"

"*Oui, oui, j'y viens,*" she cried. *Bon soir, Messieurs,*" and she was gone.

Doggie looked into the empty vestibule and smiled at the friendly brandy cask. Provided it is pronounced correctly so as to rhyme with the English "Anne," it is a very pretty name. Doggie thought she looked like Jeanne — a Jeanne d'Arc of this modern war.

"Yon's a very fascinating lassie," Phineas remarked soberly, as they started on their stroll. "Did you happen to observe that all the time she was talking so prettily she was looking at ghosts behind us?"

"Do you think so?" asked Doggie, startled.

"Man, I know it," replied Phineas.

"Ghosts be blowed!" cried Mo Shendish. "She's a bit of orl right, she is. What I call class. Doesn't chuck 'erself at yer 'ead, like some of 'em, and, on the other 'and, has none of yer blooming stand-orfishness. See what I mean?" He clutched them each by an arm — he was between them. "Look 'ere. How do you think I could pick up this blinking lingo — quick?"

"Make violent love to Toinette and ask her to teach you. There's nothing like it," said Doggie.

"Who's Toinette?"

"The nice old lady in the kitchen."

Mo flung his arm away. "Oh, go and boil yourself!" said he.

But the making of love to the old woman in the kitchen led to possibilities of which Mo Shendish never dreamed. They never dawned on Doggie until he found himself at it that evening.

It was dusk. The men were lounging and smoking about the courtyard. Doggie, who had long since exchanged poor Taffy Jones's imperfect penny whistle for a scientific musical instrument ordered from Bond Street, was playing, with his sensitive skill, the airs they loved. He had just finished "Annie Laurie" — "Man," Phineas used to declare, "when Doggie Trevor plays 'Annie Laurie,' he has the power to take your heart by the strings and drag it out through your eyes" — he had just come to the end of this popular and gizzard-piercing tune and received his meed of applause, when Toinette came out of the kitchen, two great zinc crocks in her hands, and crossed to the pump in the corner of the yard. Three or four would-be pumpers, among them Doggie, went to her aid.

"All right, mother, we'll see to it," said one of them.

So they pumped and filled the crocks, and one man got hold of one and Doggie hold of another, and they carried them to the kitchen steps.

"*Merci, Monsieur*," said Toinette to the first; and he went away with a friendly nod. But to Doggie she said "*Entrez, Monsieur*." And Monsieur carried the two crocks over the threshold and Toinette shut the door behind him. And there, sitting over some needlework in a corner of the kitchen by a lamp, sat Jeanne.

She looked up rather startled, frowned for the brief part of a second and regarded him enquiringly.

"I brought in Monsieur to show him the photograph of *mon petiot*, the comrade who sent me the snuff," explained Toinette, rummaging in a cupboard.

"May I stay and look at it?" asked Doggie, buttoning up his tunic.

"*Mais parfaitement, Monsieur*," said Jeanne. "It is Toinette's kitchen."

"*Bien sûr*," said the old woman, turning with the photograph, that of a solid young infantryman. Doggie made polite remarks. Toinette put on a pair of silver-rimmed spectacles and scanned the picture. Then she handed it to Jeanne.

"Don't you think there is a great deal of resemblance?"

Jeanne directed a comparing glance at Doggie and smiled.

"Like two little soldiers in a pod," she said.

Toinette talked of her *petiot* who was at St. Mihiel. It was far away, very far. She sighed as though he were fighting remote in the Caucasus.

Presently came the sharp ring of a bell. Jeanne put aside her work and rose.

"It is my aunt who has awakened."

But Toinette was already at the door. "I will go up, Ma'amselle Jeanne. Do not derange yourself."

She bustled away. Once more the pair found themselves alone together.

"If you don't continue your sewing, Mademoiselle," said Doggie, "I shall think that I am disturbing you, and must bid you good-night."

Jeanne sat down and resumed her work. A sensation more like laughter than anything else fluttered round Doggie's heart.

"*Voulez-vous vous asseoir, Monsieur — Trevor?*"

"*Vous êtes bien aimable, Mademoiselle Jeanne*," said Doggie, sitting down on a straight backed chair by the oil-cloth covered kitchen table which was between them.

"May I move the lamp slightly?" he asked, for it hid her from his view.

He moved it somewhat to her left. It threw shadows over her features, accentuating their appealing sadness. He watched her and thought of McPhail's words about the ghosts. He noted too, as the needle went in and out of the fabric, that her hands, though roughened by coarse work, were finely made, with long fingers and delicate wrists. He broke a silence that grew embarrassing.

"You seem to have suffered greatly, Mademoiselle Jeanne," he said softly.

Her lips quivered. "*Mais oui, Monsieur.*"

"Monsieur Trevor," he said.

She put her hands and needlework in her lap and looked at him full.

"And you too have suffered."

"I? Oh, no."

"But yes, I have seen too much of it not to know. I see in the eyes. Your two comrades to-day — they are good fellows — but they have not suffered. You are different."

"Not a bit," he declared. "We're just little indistinguishable bits of the conglomerate Tommy."

"And I, Monsieur, have the honour to say that you are different."

This was very flattering. More — it was sweet unction, grateful to many a bruise.

"How?" said he.

"You do not belong to their world. Your Tommies are wonderful in their kindness and chivalry — until I met them I had never seen an Englishman in my life — I had imbecile ideas — I thought they would be without manners —*un peu insultants*. I found I could walk among them, without fear, as if I were a princess. It is true."

"It is because you have the air of a princess," said Doggie; "a sad, little disguised princess of a fairy tale, who is recognised by all the wild boars and rabbits in the wood."

She glanced aside. "There isn't a woman in Frélus who is differently treated. I am only an ignorant girl, half bourgeoise, half peasant, Monsieur, but I have my woman's knowledge — and I know there is a difference between you and the others. You are a son of good family. It is evident. You have a delicacy of mind and of feeling. You were not born to be a soldier."

"Mademoiselle Jeanne," cried Doggie, "do I appear as bad as that? Do you take me for an *embusqué manqué?*"

Now an *embusqué* is a slacker who lies in the safe ambush of a soft job. And an *embusqué manqué* is a slacker who fortuitously has failed to win the fungus wreath of slackerdom.

She flushed deep red.

"*Je ne suis pas malhonnête, Monsieur.*"

Doggie spread himself elbow-wise over the table. The girl's visible register of moods was fascinating.

"Pardon, Mademoiselle Jeanne. You are quite right. But it's not a question of what I was born to be — but what I was trained to be. I wasn't trained to be a soldier. But I do my best."

She looked at him waveringly.

"Forgive me, Mademoiselle."

"But you flash out on the point of honour."

Doggie laughed. "Which shows that I have the essential of the soldier."

Doggie's manner was not without charm. She relented.

"You know very well what I mean," she said rebukingly. "And you don't deserve that I should tell it to you. It was my intention to say that you have sacrificed many things to make yourself a simple soldier."

"Only a few idle habits," said Doggie.

"You joined, like the rest, as a volunteer?"

"Of course."

"You abandoned everything to fight for your country?"

Under the spell of her dark eyes Doggie said, as he had said to Phineas after the going West of Taffy Jones, "I think, Mademoiselle Jeanne, it was rather to fight for my soul."

She resumed her sewing. "That's what I meant long ago," she remarked with the first draw of the needle. "No one could fight for his soul without passing through suffering." She went on sewing. Doggie, shrinking from a reply that might have sounded fatuous, remained silent; but he realised a wonderful faculty of comprehension in Jeanne.

After a while he said: "Where did you learn all your wisdom, Mademoiselle Jeanne?"

"At the convent, I suppose. My father gave me a good education."

"An English poet has said 'Knowledge comes, but wisdom lingers'" — Doggie had rather a fight to express the meaning exactly in French — "You don't gather wisdom in convents."

"It is true. Since then I have seen many things."

She stared across the room, not at Doggie, and he thought again of the ghosts.

"Tell me some of them, Mademoiselle Jeanne," he said in a low voice.

She shot a swift glance at him, and met his honest brown eyes.

"I saw my father killed in front of me," she said in a strange, harsh voice.

"My God!" said Doggie.

"It was on the Retreat. We lived in Cambrai, my father and mother and I. He was an *avoué*. When we heard the Germans were coming, father, somewhat of an invalid, decided to fly. He had heard of what they had already done in Belgium. We tried to go by train. *Pas moyen*. We took to the road, with many others. We could not get a horse — we had postponed our flight till too late. Only a hand cart with a few necessaries and precious things. And we walked until we nearly died of heat and dust and grief. For our hearts were very heavy, Monsieur. The roads, too, were full of the English in retreat. I shall not tell you what I saw of the wounded by the roadside. I sometimes see them now in my dreams. And we were helpless. We thought we would leave the main roads, and at last we got lost and found ourselves in a little wood. We sat down to rest and to eat. It was cool and pleasant, and I laughed, to cheer my parents, for they knew how I loved to eat under the freshness of the trees." She shivered. "I hope I shall never have to eat a meal in a wood again. We had scarcely begun when a body of cavalry with strange pointed helmets rode along the path and, seeing us, halted. My mother, half dead with terror, cried out, '*Mon Dieu, ce sont des Uhlans!*' The leader, I suppose an officer, called out something in German. My father replied. I do not understand German, so

I did not know and shall never know what they said. But my father protested in anger, and stood in front of the horse making gestures. And then the officer took out his revolver and shot him through the heart, and he fell dead. And the murderer turned his horse's head round and he laughed. He laughed, Monsieur."

"Damn him!" said Doggie, in English. "Damn him!"

He gazed deep into Jeanne's dark, tearless eyes. She continued in the same even voice:

"My mother became mad. She was a peasant, a Bretonne, where the blood is fierce, and she screamed and clung to the bridle of the horse. And he rode her down and the horse trampled on her. Then he pointed at me, who was supporting the body of my father, and three men dismounted. But suddenly he heard something, gave an order and the men mounted again, and they all rode away laughing and jeering, and the last man, in bad French, shouted at me a foul insult. And I was there, Monsieur Trevor, with my father dead and my mother stunned and bruised and bleeding."

Doggie, sensitive, quivered to the girl's tragedy. He said with tense face:

"God give me strength to kill every German I see!" She nodded slowly. "No German is a human being. If I were God, I would exterminate the accursed race like wolves."

"You are right," said Doggie. A short silence fell. He asked: "What happened then?"

"*Mon Dieu*, I almost forget. I was overwhelmed with grief and horror. Some hours afterwards a small body of English infantry came — many of them had bloodstained bandages. An officer, who spoke a little French, questioned me. I told him what had happened. He spoke with another officer, and because I recognised the word 'Uhlans,' I knew they

were anxious about the patrol. They asked me
the way to some place — I forget where. But I
was lost. They looked at a map. Meanwhile my
mother had recovered consciousness. I gave her a
little wine from the bottle we had opened for our
repast. I happened to look at the officer and saw
him pass his tongue over his cracked lips. All the
men had thrown themselves down by the side of the
road. I handed him the bottle and the little tin
cup. To my surprise he did not drink. He said
'Mademoiselle, this is war, and we are all in very
great peril. My men are dying of thirst, and if you
have any more of the wine, give it to them, and they
will do their utmost to conduct your mother and
yourself to a place of safety.' Alas! there were only
three bottles in our little *panier* of provisions. Naturally I gave it all — together with the food. He
called a sergeant, who took the provisions and dis-
tributed them, while I was tending my mother.
But I noticed that the two officers took neither bite
nor sup. It was only afterwards, Monsieur Trevor,
that I realised I had seen your great English gentlemen. . . . Then they dug a little grave, *à pointe des
baionnettes*, for my father. . . . It was soon
finished . . . the danger was grave . . . and some
soldiers took a rope and pulled the hand cart, with
my mother lying on top of our little possessions,
and I walked with them, until the whole of my life
was blotted out with fatigue. We got on to the
Route Nationale again and mingled again with the
Retreat. And in the night, as we were still marching, there was a halt. I went to my mother. She
was cold, Monsieur, cold and stiff. She was dead."

She paused tragically. After a few moments
she continued:

"I fainted. I do not know what happened till I
recovered consciousness at dawn. I found myself
wrapped in one of our blankets lying under the

handcart. It was the market square of a little town. And there were many — old men and women and children, refugees like me. I rose and found a paper — a leaf torn from a notebook — fixed to the handcart. It was from the officer, bidding me farewell. Military necessity forced him to go on with his men — but he had kept his word and brought me to a place of safety. . . . That is how I first met the English, Monsieur Trevor. They had carried me, I suppose, on the handcart, all night, they who were broken with weariness. I owe them my life and my reason."

"And your mother?"

"How should I know? *Elle est restée là-bas*," she replied simply.

She went on with her sewing. Doggie wondered how her hand could be so steady. There was a long silence. What words, save vain imprecations on the accursed race, were adequate? Presently her glance rested for a second or two on his sensitive face.

"Why do you not smoke, Monsieur Trevor?"

"May I?"

"Of course. It calms the nerves. I ought not to have saddened you with my griefs."

Doggie took out his pink packet and lit a cigarette.

"You are very understanding, Mademoiselle Jeanne. But it does a selfish man like me good to be saddened by a story like yours. I have not had much opportunity in my life of feeling for another's suffering. And since the war — I am *abruti*."

"You? Do you think if I had not found you *sympatique*, I should have told you all this?"

"You have paid me a great compliment, Mademoiselle Jeanne." Then, after a while he asked, "From the market square of the little town you found means to come here?"

"Alas, no!" she said, putting her work in her lap

again. "I made my way, with my *charrette* — it was easy — to our original destination, a little farm belonging to the eldest brother of my father. The Farm of La Folette. He lived there alone, a widower, with his farm servants. He had no children. We thought we were safe. Alas! news came that the Germans were always advancing. We had time to fly. All the farmhands fled, except Père Grigou, who loved him. But my uncle was obstinate. To a Frenchman the soil he possesses is his flesh and his blood. He would die rather than leave it. And my uncle had the murder of my father and mother on his brain. He told Père Grigou to take me away, but I stayed with him. It was Père Grigou who forced us to hide. That lasted two days. There was a well in the farm, and one night Père Grigou tied up my money and my mother's jewelry and my father's papers, *enfin*, all the precious things we had, in a packet of waterproof and sank it with a long string down the well so that the Germans could not find it. It was foolish, but he insisted. One day my uncle and Père Grigou went out of the little copse where we had been hiding, in order to reconnoitre, for he thought the Germans might be going away; and my uncle, who would not listen to me, took his gun. Presently I heard a shot — and then another. You can guess what it meant. And soon Père Grigou came, white and shaking with terror. '*Il en a tué un, et on l'a tué!*'"

"My God!" said Doggie again.

"It was terrible," she said. "But they were in their right."

"And then?"

"We lay hidden until it was dark — how they did not find us I don't know — and then we escaped across country. I thought of coming here to my Aunt Morin, which is not far from La Folette, but

I reflected that soon the Boches would be here also. And we went on. We got to a high road — and once more I was among troops and refugees. I met some kind folks in a carriage, a Monsieur and Madame Tarride, and they took me in. And so I got to Paris, where I had the hospitality of a friend of the Convent, who was married."

"And Père Grigou?"

"He insisted on going back to bury my uncle. Nothing could move him. He had not parted from him all his life. They were foster-brothers. Where he is now, who knows?" She paused, looked again at her ghosts, and continued: "That is all, Monsieur Trevor. The Germans passed through here and re-passed on their retreat, and, as soon as it was safe, I came to help my aunt, who was *souffrante*, and had lost her son. Also because I could not live on charity on my friend, for, *voyez-vous*, I was without a sou — all my money having been hidden in the well by Père Grigou."

Doggie leant his elbows on the table.

"And you have come through all that, Mademoiselle Jeanne, just as you are — ?"

"How, just as I am?"

"So gentle and kind and comprehending?"

Her cheek flushed. "I am not the only French-woman who has passed through such things and kept herself proud. But the struggle has been very hard."

Doggie rose and clenched his fists and rubbed his head from front to back in his old indecisive way, and began to swear incoherently in English. She smiled sadly.

"*Ah, mon pauvre ami!*"

He wheeled round: "Why do you call me '*mon pauvre ami?*'"

"Because I see that you would like to help me, and you can't."

"Jeanne," cried Doggie, bending half over the table which was between them.

She rose, too, startled, on quick defensive. He said, in reply to her glance:

"Why shouldn't I call you Jeanne?"

"You haven't the right."

"What if I gain it?"

"How?"

"I don't know," said Doggie.

The door burst suddenly open, and the anxious face of Mo Shendish appeared.

"'Ere, you silly cuckoo, don't yer know you're on guard to-night? You've just got about thirty seconds."

"Good Lord!" cried Doggie, "I forgot. *Bon soir, Mademoiselle. Service militaire,*" and he rushed out.

Mo lingered, with a grin, and jerked a backward thumb.

"If it weren't for old Mo, Miss, I don't know what would happen to our friend Doggie. I got to look after him like a baby, I 'ave. He's on to relieve guard, and if old Mac — that's McPhail —" she nodded recognition of the name — "and I hadn't remembered, Miss, he'd 'ave been in what yer might call a 'ole. Compree?"

"*Oui.* Yes," she said. "*Garde. Sentinelle.*"

"Sentinel. Sentry. Right."

"He — was — late," she said, picking out her few English words from memory.

"Yuss," grinned Mo.

"He — guard — house?"

"Bless you, Miss, you talk English as well as I do," cried the admiring Mo. "Yuss. When his turn comes, up and down in the street, by the gate." He saw her puzzled look. "Roo. Port," said he.

"*Ah, oui, je comprends,*" smiled Jeanne. "*Merci, Monsieur, et bon soir.*"

"Good night, Miss," said Mo.

Some time later, he disturbed Phineas, by whose side he slept, from his initial preparation for slumber.

"Mac! Is there any book I could learn this blinking lingo from?"

"Try Ezekiel," replied Phineas sleepily.

CHAPTER XIV

THE spell of night sentry duty had always been Doggie's black hour. To most of the other military routine he had grown hardened or deadened. In the depths of his heart he hated the life as much as ever. He had schooled himself to go through it with the dull fatalism of a convict. It was no use railing at inexorable laws, irremediable conditions. The only alternative to the acceptance of his position was military punishment, which was far worse — to say nothing of the outrage of his pride. It was pride that kept the little ironical smile on his lips while his nerves were almost breaking with strain. The first time he came under fire he was physically sick — not from fear, for he stood it better than most, keeping an eye on his captain whose function it was to show an unconcerned face — but from sheer nervous reaction against the hideous noise, the stench, the ghastly upheaval of the earth, the sight of mangled men. When the bombardment was over, if he had been alone, he would have sat down and cried. Never had he grown accustomed to the foulness of the trenches. The sounder his physical condition, the more did his delicately trained senses revolt. It was only when fierce animal cravings dulled these senses, that he could throw himself down anywhere and sleep, that he could swallow anything in the way of food or drink. The rats nearly drove him crazy. . . . Yet, what had once been to him a torture, the indecent, nerve-rasping publicity of the soldier's life, had now become a compensation. It was not so much in companionship, like his friendly intercourse with Phineas and Mo, that he found an anodyne, but in the consciousness of being magnetically affected by the crowd of his fellows. They offered him protection against himself. Whatever pangs of self-pity he felt, whatever wan little pleadings for the bit of fine porcelain compelled to a rough usage which vessels of coarser clay could disregard, came lingeringly into his mind, he dared not express them to a living soul around. On the contrary, he set himself assiduously to cultivate the earthenware habit of spirit; not to feel, not to think, only to endure. To a humorously incredulous Jeanne he proclaimed himself *abruti*. Finally, the ceaseless grind of the military machine left him little time to think.

But in the solitary sleepless hours of sentry duty there was nothing to do but think; nothing wherewith to while away the time but an orgy of introspection. First came the almost paralysing sense of responsibility. He must keep, not only awake, but alert to the slightest sound, the slightest movement. Lives of men depended on his vigilance. A man can't screw himself up to this beautifully emotional pitch for very long and be an efficient sentry. If he did, he would challenge mice and shoot at cloud-shadows and bring the deuce of a commotion about his ears. And this Doggie, who did not lack ordinary intelligence, realised. So he strove to think of other things. And the other things all focussed down upon his Doggie self. And he never knew what to make of his Doggie self at all. For he would curse the things that he once loved as being the cause of his inexpiable shame, and at the same time yearn for them with an agony of longing.

And he would force himself to think of Peggy and her unswerving loyalty. Of her weekly parcel of dainty food which had arrived that morning. Of the joy of Phineas and the disappointment of the unsophisticated Mo over the *pâté de foie gras*.   But his mind wandered back to his Doggie self and its humiliations and its needs and its yearnings.   He welcomed enemy flares and star-shells and excursions and alarms.   They kept him from thinking, enabled him to pass the time.   But in the dead, lonely, silent dark, the hours were like centuries. He dreaded them.

To-night they fled like minutes.   It was a pitch black night, spitting fine rain.   It was one of Doggie's private grievances that it invariably rained when he was on outpost duty.   One of Heaven's little ways of strafing him for Doggieism.   But to-night he did not heed it.   Often the passage of transport had been a distraction for which he had longed and which, when it came, was warmly welcome.   But to-night, during his spell, the roadway of the village was as still as death, and he loved the stillness and the blackness.   Once he had welcomed familiar approaching steps.   Now he resented them.

"Who goes there?"

"Rounds."

And the officer, recognised, flashing an electric torch, passed on.   The diminuendo of his footsteps was agreeable to Doggie's ear.   The rain dripped monotonously off his helmet on to his sodden shoulders, but Doggie did not mind.   Now and then he strained an eye upwards to that part of the living-house that was above the gateway.   Little streaks of light came downwards through the shutter slats. Now it required no great intellectual effort to surmise that the light proceeded, not from the bedroom of the invalid Madame Morin, who would naturally have the best bedroom situated in the comfortable main block of the house, but from that of somebody else.   Madame Morin was therefore ruled out.   So was Toinette — ridiculous to think of her keeping all-night vigil. There remained only Jeanne.

It was supremely silly of him to march with super-martiality of tread up the pavement; but then it is often the way of young men to do supremely silly things.

The next day was fuss and bustle, from the private soldier's point of view. They were marching back to the trenches that night, and a crack company must take over with flawless equipment and in flawless bodily health. In the afternoon Doggie had a breathing spell of leisure. He walked boldly into the kitchen.

"Madame," said he to Toinette, "I suppose you know that we are leaving to-night?"

The old woman sighed. "It is always like that. They come, they make friends, they go, and they never return."

"You mustn't make the little soldier weep, *grand'mère*," said Doggie.

"No. It is the *grand'mères* who weep," replied Toinette.

"I'll come back all right," said he. "Where is Mademoiselle Jeanne?"

"She is upstairs, Monsieur."

"If she had gone out, I should have been disappointed," smiled Doggie.

"You desire to see her, Monsieur?"

"To thank her before I go for her kindness to me."

The old face wrinkled into a smile.

"It was not then for the *beaux yeux* of the *grand'-mère* that you entered?"

"*Si, si!* Of course it was," he protested. "But one, nevertheless, must be polite to Mademoiselle."

"*Aïe! aïe!*" said the old woman, bustling out. "I'll call her."

Presently Jeanne came in alone, calm, cool, and

in her plain black dress, looking like a sweet Fate. From the top of her dark brown hair to her trim, stout shoes, she gave the impression of being exquisitely ordered, bodily and spiritually.

"It was good of you to come," he cried, and they shook hands instinctively, scarcely realising it was for the first time. But he was sensitive to the frank grip of her long and slender fingers.

"Toinette said you wished to see me."

"We are going to-night. I had to come and bid you *au revoir.*"

"Is the company returning?"

"So I hear the Quarter Master says. Are you glad?"

"Yes, I am glad. One doesn't like to lose friends."

"You regard me as a friend, Jeanne?"

"*Pour sûr,*" she replied simply.

"Then you don't mind my calling you Jeanne?" said he.

"What does it matter? There are graver questions at stake in the world."

She crossed the kitchen and opened the yard door which Doggie had closed behind him. Meeting a query in his glance, she said:

"I like the fresh air, and I don't like secrecy."

She leaned against the edge of the table, and Doggie emboldened, seated himself on the corner, by her side, and they looked out into the little flagged courtyard in which the men, some in grey shirtsleeves, some in tunics, were lounging about among the little piles of accoutrements and packs. Here and there a man was shaving by the aid of a little mirror supported on a handcart. Jests and laughter were flung in the quiet afternoon air. A little group were feeding pigeons which, at the sight of crumbs, had swarmed iridescent from the tall *colombier* in the far corner near the gabled barn. As Jeanne did not speak, at last Doggie bent forward and, looking into her eyes, found them moist with tears.

"What is the matter, Jeanne?" he asked in a low voice.

"The war, *mon ami*," she replied, turning her face towards him, "the haunting tragedy of the war. I don't know how to express what I mean. If all those brave fellows there went about with serious faces, I should not be affected. *Mais, voyez-vous, leur gaieté fait peur.*"

Their laughter frightened her. Doggie, with his quick responsiveness, understood. She had put into a phrase the haunting tragedy of the war. The eternal laughter of youth quenched in a gurgle of the throat.

He said admiringly: "You are a wonderful woman, Jeanne."

Her delicate shoulders moved, ever so little. "A woman? I suppose I am. The day before we fled from Cambrai it was my *jour de fête*. I was eighteen."

Doggie drew in his breath with a little gasp. He had thought she was older than he.

"I am twenty-seven," he said.

She looked at him calmly and critically. "Yes. Now I see. Until now I should have given you more. But the war ages people. Isn't it true?"

"I suppose so," said Doggie. Then he had a brilliant idea. "But when the war is over, we'll remain the same age for ever and ever."

"Do you think so?"

"I'm sure of it. We'll still both be in our twenties. Let us suppose the war puts ten years of experience and suffering, and what not, on to our lives. We'll only then be in our thirties — and nothing possibly can happen to make us grow any older. At seventy we shall still be thirty."

"You are consoling," she admitted. "But what

if the war had added thirty years to one's life?
What if I felt now an old woman of fifty? But
yes, it is quite true. I have the feelings and the
disregard of convention of a woman of fifty. If
there had been no war, do you think I could have
gone among an English army — *sans gêne* — like
an old matron? Do you think a *jeune fille française
bien élevée* could have talked to you alone as I have
done the past two days? Absurd. The explanation is the war."

Doggie laughed. " *Vive la guerre!* " said he.

"*Mais non!* Be serious. We must come to an
understanding."

In her preoccupation she forgot the rules laid
down for the guidance of *jeunes filles bien élevées*,
and unthinkingly perched herself full on the kitchen
table on the corner of which Doggie sat in a one-
legged way. Doggie gasped again. All her assumed
age fell from her like a garment. Youth proclaimed itself in her attitude and the supple lines
of her figure. She was but a girl after all, a girl
with a steadfast soul that had been tried in un-
utterable fires; but a girl appealing, desirable. He
felt mighty protective.

"An understanding? All right," said he.

"I don't want you to go away and think ill of me
— that I am one of those women — *les affranchies*,
I think they call them — who think themselves
above social laws. I am not. I am *bourgeoise* to
my finger-tips, and I reverence all the old maxims
and prejudices in which I was born. But conditions are different. It is just like the priests who
have been called into the ranks. To look at them
from the outside, you would never dream they were
priests — but their hearts and their souls are untouched."

She was so earnest, in her pathetic youthfulness,
to put herself right with him, so unlike the English

girls of his acquaintance, who would have taken this chance companionship as a matter of course, that his face lost the smile and became grave, and he met her sad eyes.

"That was very bravely said, Jeanne. To me you will be always the most wonderful woman I have ever known."

"What caused you to speak to me the first day?" she asked, after a pause.

"I explained to you — to apologise for staring rudely into your house."

"It was not because you said to yourself, 'Here is a pretty girl looking at me. I'll go and talk to her'?"

Doggie threw his leg over the corner of the table and stood on indignant feet.

"Jeanne! How could you —?" he cried.

She leaned back, her open palms on the table. The rare light came into her eyes.

"That's what I wanted to know. Now we understand each other, Monsieur Trevor."

"I wish you wouldn't call me Monsieur Trevor," said he.

"What else can I call you? I know no other name."

Now he had in his pocket a letter from Peggy, received that morning, beginning "My dearest Marmaduke." Peggy seemed far away and the name still further. He was deliberating whether he should say "*Appelez-moi James*" or "*Appelez-moi Jacques*," and inclining to the latter as being more picturesque and intimate, when she went on:

"*Tenez*, what is it your comrades call you? 'Doggie?'"

"Say that again."

"Dog-gie."

He had never dreamed that the hated appellation could sound so adorable. Well — no one except

his officers called him by any other name, and it
came with a visible charm from her lips.   It brought
about the most fascinating flash of the tips of her
white teeth.   He laughed.

"*A la guerre comme à la guerre.*   If you call me
that, you belong to the regiment.   And I promise
you it is a fine regiment."

"*Eh bien,* Monsieur Dog-gie —"

"There's no Monsieur about it," he declared,
very happily.   "Tommies are not *Messieurs.*"

"I know one who is," said Jeanne.

So they talked in a young and foolish way, and
Jeanne for a while forgot the tragedies that had
gone and the tragedies that might come; and Doggie
forgot both the peacock and ivory room and the
fetid hole into which he would have to creep when
the night's march was over.   They talked of simple
things.   Of Toinette, who had been with Aunt
Morin ever since she could remember.

"You have won her heart with your snuff."

"She has won mine with her discretion."

"Oh-h!" said Jeanne, shocked.

And so on and so forth, while they sat side by
side on the kitchen table, swinging their feet.   After
a while they drifted to graver questions.

"What will happen to you, Jeanne, if your aunt
dies?"

"*Mon Dieu!*" said Jeanne —

"But you will inherit the property, and the
business?"

"By no means."   Aunt Morin had still a son,
who was already very old.   He must be forty-six.
He had expatriated himself many years ago and was
in Madagascar.   The son who was killed was her
Benjamin, the child of her old age.   But all her
little fortune would go to the colonial Gaspard
whom Jeanne had never seen.

But the Farm of La Folette?

"It has been taken and retaken by Germans and French and English, *mon pauvre ami*, until there is no farm left. You ought to understand that."

It was a thing that Doggie most perfectly understood: a patch of hideous wilderness, of poisoned, shell-scarred, ditch-defiled, barren, loathsome earth.

And her other relations? Only an uncle, her father's youngest brother, a curé in Douai in enemy occupation. She had not heard of him since the flight from Cambrai.

"But what is going to become of you?"

"So long as one keeps a brave heart what does it matter? I am strong. I have a good enough education. I can earn my living. Oh, don't make any mistake. I have no pity for myself. Those who waste efforts in pitying themselves are not of the stuff to make France victorious."

"I am afraid I have done a lot of self-pitying, Jeanne."

"Don't do it any more," she said gently.

"I won't," said he.

"If you keep to the soul you have gained, you can't," said Jeanne.

"*Toujours la sagesse.*"

"You are laughing at me."

"God forbid," said Doggie.

Phineas and Mo came strolling towards the kitchen door.

"My two friends, to pay their visit of adieu," said he.

Jeanne slid from the table and welcomed the newcomers in her calm, dignified way. Once more Doggie found himself regarding her as his senior in age and wisdom and conduct of life. The pathetic girlishness which she had revealed to him had gone. The age-investing ghosts had returned.

Mo grinned, interjected a British army French word now and then, and manifested delight when

Jeanne understood. Phineas talked laboriously, endeavouring to expound his responsibility for Doggie's welfare. He had been his tutor. He used the word "*tuteur*."

"That's a guardian, you silly ass," cried Doggie. "He means '*instituteur*.' Go on. Or, rather, don't go on. The lady isn't interested."

"*Mais oui*," said Jeanne, catching at the last English word. "It interests me greatly."

"*Merci, Mademoiselle*," said Phineas, grandly. "I only wish to explain to you that while I live you need have no fear for Doggie. I will protect him with my body from shells, and promise to bring him safe back to you. And so will Monsieur Shendish."

"What's that?" asked Mo.

Phineas translated.

"*Oui, oui, oui!*" said Mo, nodding vigorously.

A spot of colour burned on Jeanne's pale cheek, and Doggie grew red under his tanned skin. He cursed Phineas below his breath, and exchanged a significant glance with Mo. Jeanne said in her even voice:

"I hope all the Three Musketeers will come back safe."

Mo extended a grimy hand. "Well, good-bye, Miss. McPhail here and I must be going."

She shook hands with both, wishing them *bonne chance*, and they strolled away. Doggie lingered.

"You mustn't mind what McPhail says. He's only an old imbecile."

"You have two comrades who love you. That is the principal thing."

"I think they do, each in his way. As for Mo —"

"Mo?" She laughed. "He is delicious."

"Well —" said he, reluctantly, after a pause, "good-bye, Jeanne."

"*Au revoir* — Dog-gie."

"If I shouldn't come back — I mean if we were billeted somewhere else — I should like to write to you."

"Well — Mademoiselle Boissière, chez Madame Morin, Frélus. That is the address."

"And will you write too?"

Without waiting for a reply, he scribbled what was necessary on a sheet torn from a notebook and gave it to her. Their hands met.

"*Au revoir*, Jeanne."

"*Au revoir*, Dog-gie. But I shall see you again to-night."

"Where?"

"It is my secret. *Bonne chance.*"

She smiled and turned to leave the kitchen. Doggie clattered into the yard.

"Been doin' a fine bit o' coartin', Doggie," said Private Appleyard from Taunton, who was sitting on a box near by and writing a letter on his knees.

"Not so much of your courting, Spud," replied Doggie cheerfully. "Who are you writing to? Your best girl?"

"I be writin' to my own lawful mizzus," replied Spud Appleyard.

"Then give her my love. Doggie Trevor's love," said Doggie, and marched away through the groups of men.

At the entrance to the barn he fell in with Phineas and Mo.

"Laddie," said the former, "although I meant it at the time as a testimony of my affection, I've been thinking that what I said to the young leddy may not have been over tactful."

"It was taking it too much for granted," explained Mo, "that you and her were sort of keeping company.

"You're a pair of idiots," said Doggie, sitting down between them, and taking out his pink packet of Caporal. "Have a cigarette?"

"Not if I wos dying of — Look 'ere," said Mo, with the light on his face of the earnest seeker after Truth. "If a chap ain't got no food, he's dying of 'unger. If he ain't got no drink, he's dying of thirst. What the 'ell is he dying of if he ain't got no tobakker?"

"Army Service Corps," said Phineas, pulling out his pipe.

It was dark when A Company marched away. Doggie had seen nothing more of Jeanne. He was just a little disappointed; for she had promised. He could not associate her with light words. Yet perhaps she had kept her promise. She had said "*Je vous verrais.*" She had not undertaken to exhibit herself to him. He derived comfort from the thought. There was, indeed, something delicate and subtle and enchanting in the notion. As on the previous day, the fine weather had changed with the night and a fine rain was falling. Doggie, an indistinguishable, pack-laden ant in the middle of the four abreast ribbon of similar pack-laden ants, tramped on, in silence, thinking his own thoughts. A regiment going back to the trenches in the night is, from the point of view of the pomp and circumstance of glorious war, a very lugubrious procession. The sight of it would have rather hurt an old-time poet. An experienced regiment has no lovely illusions. It knows what it is going to, and the knowledge makes it serious. It would much rather be in bed or on snug straw than plodding through the rain to four days and nights of eternal mud and stinking high explosive shell. It sets its teeth and is a very stern, silent, ugly conglomeration of men.

"——— (*The adjective*) night," growled Doggie's right hand neighbour.

"——— (*The adjective*)" Doggie responded, mechanically.

But to Doggie it was less "————" (*adjective as before*) than usual. Jeanne's denunciation of self-pity had struck deep. Compared with her calamities, half of which would have been the stock-in-trade of a Greek dramatist wherewith to wring tears from mankind for a couple of thousand years, what were his own piffling grievances? As for the "————" night, instead of a drizzle, he would have welcomed a waterspout. Something that really mattered. . . . Let the Heavens or the Hun rain molten lead. Something that would put him on an equality with Jeanne . . . Jeanne, with her dark, haunting eyes and mobile lips, and the slim, young figure and her splendid courage. A girl apart from the girls he had known, apart from the women he had known, the women whom he had imagined — and he had not imagined many — his training had atrophied such imaginings of youth. Jeanne. Again her name conjured up visions of the Great Jeanne of Domremy. If only he could have seen her once again!

At the north end of the village the road took a sharp twist, skirting a bit of rising ground. There was just a glimmer of a warning light which streamed athwart the turning ribbon of laden ants. And as Doggie wheeled through the dim ray, he heard a voice that rang out clear.

"*Bonne chance!*"

He looked up swiftly. Caught the shadow of a shadow. But it was enough. It was Jeanne. She had kept her promise. The men responded incoherently, waving their hands, and Doggie's shout of "*Merci!*" was lost. But though he knew, with a wonderful throbbing knowledge, that Jeanne's cry was meant for him alone, he was thrilled by his comrades' instant response to Jeanne's voice. Not a man but he knew that it was Jeanne. But no matter. The company paid homage to Jeanne.

Jeanne who had come out in the rain and the dark, and had waited, waited, to redeem her promise. *"C'est mon secret."*

He ploughed on. Left, right! Thud, thud! Left, right! Jeanne, Jeanne!

CHAPTER XV

I N the village of Frélus life went on as before.
The same men, though a different regiment,
filled its streets and its houses; for by what
signs could the inhabitants distinguish one horde
of English infantrymen from another? Once a
Highland battalion had been billeted on them,
and for the first day or so they derived some excitement from the novelty of the costume; the
historic Franco-Scottish tradition still lingered and
they welcomed the old allies of France with special
kindliness; but they found that the habits and
customs of the men in kilts were identical, in their
French eyes, with those of the men in trousers. It
is true the Scotch had bagpipes. The village turned
out to listen to them in whole-eyed and whole-eared
wonder. And the memory of the skirling music
remained indelible. Otherwise there was little difference. And when a Midland regiment succeeded
a South Coast regiment, where was the difference
at all? They might be the same men.

Jeanne, standing by the kitchen door, watching
the familiar scene in the courtyard, could scarcely
believe there had been a change. Now and again,
she caught herself wondering why she could not
pick out any one of her Three Musketeers. There
were two or three soldiers, as usual, helping Toinette
with her crocks at the well. There she was, herself,
moving among them, as courteously treated as
though she were a princess. Perhaps these men,
whom she heard had come from manufacturing
centres, were a trifle rougher in their manners than
her late guests; but the intention of civility and rude

chivalry was no less sincere. They came and asked for odds and ends very politely. To all intents and purposes they were the same set of men. Why was not Doggie among them? It seemed very strange.

After a while she made some sort of an acquaintance with a sergeant who had a few words of French and appeared anxious to improve his knowledge of the language. He explained that he had been a teacher in what corresponded to the French *Écoles Normales*. He came from Birmingham, which he gave her to understand was glorified Lille. She found him very earnest, very self-centred in his worship of efficiency. As he had striven for his class of boys, so now was he striving for his platoon of men. In a dogmatic way he expounded to her ideals severely practical. In their few casual conversations he interested her. The English, from the first terrible day of their association with her, had commanded her deep admiration. But until lately — in the most recent past — her sex, her national aloofness, and her ignorance of English, had restrained her from familiar talk with the British Army. But now she keenly desired to understand this strange, imperturbable, kindly race. She put many questions to the Sergeant — always at the kitchen door, in full view of the courtyard, for she never thought of admitting him into the house — and his answers, even when he managed to make himself intelligible, puzzled her exceedingly. One of his remarks led her to ask for what he was fighting, beyond his apparently fixed idea of the efficiency of the men under his control. What was the spiritual idea at the back of him?

"The democratisation of the world and the universal brotherhood of mankind."

"When the British Lion shall lie down with the German Lamb?"

He flashed a suspicious glance. Strenuous schoolmasters in primary schools have little time for the cultivation of a sense of humour.

"Something of the sort must be the ultimate result of the war."

"But in the meantime you have got to change the German wolf into the *petit mouton*. How are you going to do it?"

"By British efficiency. By proving to him that we are superior to him in every way. We'll teach him that it doesn't pay to be a wolf."

"And do you think he will like being transformed into a lamb, while you remain a lion?"

"I don't suppose so, but we'll give him his chance to try to become a lion, too."

Jeanne shook her head. "No, Monsieur, wolf he is and wolf he will remain. A wolf with venomous teeth. The civilised world must see that the teeth are always drawn."

"I'm speaking of fifty years hence," said the Sergeant.

"And I of three hundred years hence."

"You're mistaken, Mademoiselle."

Jeanne shook her head. "No. I'm not mistaken. Tell me. Why do you want to become brother to the Boche?"

"I'm not going to be his brother till the war is over," said the Sergeant stolidly. "At present I am devoting all my faculties to killing as many of him as I can."

She smiled. "Sufficient for the day is the good thereof. Go on killing them, Monsieur. The more you kill, the fewer there will be for your children and your grandchildren to lie down with."

She left him and tried to puzzle out his philosophy. For the ordinary French philosophy of the war is very simple. They have no high-falutin', altruistic ideas of improving the Boche. They don't care a tinker's curse what happens to the unholy brood

beyond the Rhine, so long as they are beaten, humiliated, subjected: so long as there is no chance of
their ever deflowering again with their brutality the
sacred soil of France. The French mind cannot con-
ceive the idea of this beautiful brotherhood; but,
on the contrary, rejects it as something loathsome,
something bordering on spiritual defilement. . . .

No; Jeanne could not accept the theory that we
were waging war for the ultimate chastening and
beatification of Germany. She preferred Doggie's
reason for fighting. For his soul. There was something which she could grip. And having gripped
it, it was something around which her imagination
could weave a web of noble fancy. After all, when
she came to think of it, every one of the allies must
be fighting for his soul. For his soul's sake had not
her father died? Although she knew no word of
German, it was obvious that the Uhlan officer had
murdered him because he had refused to betray
his country. And her uncle. To fight for his soul,
had he not gone out with this heroic but futile
sporting gun? And this pragmatical sergeant?
What else had led him from his schoolroom to the
battlefield? Why couldn't he be honest about it
like Doggie?

She missed Doggie. He ought to be there, as she
had often seen him unobserved, talking with his
friends or going about his military duties, or playing
the flageolet with the magical touch of the musician.
She knew far more of Doggie than he was aware of.
. . . And at night she prayed for the little English
soldier who was facing Death.

She had much time to think of him during the
hours when she sat by the bedside of Aunt Morin,
who talked incessantly of François-Marie who was
killed on the Argonne, and Gaspard who, as a
territorial, was no doubt defending Madagascar
from invasion. And it was pleasant to think of him

because he was a new distraction from tragical
memories. He seemed to lay the ghosts. . . . He
was different from all the Englishmen she had met.
The young officers who had helped her in her flight,
had very much the same charm of breeding, very
much the same intonation of voice: instinctively
she knew him to be of the same social caste: but
they, and the officers whom she saw about the street
and in the courtyard, when duty called them there,
had the military air of command. And this her
little English soldier had not. Of course he was
only a private, and privates are trained to obedience.
She knew that perfectly well. But why was he not
commanding instead of obeying? There was a
reason for it. She had seen it in his eyes. She
wished she had made him talk more about himself.
Perhaps she had been unsympathetic and selfish.
He assumed, she reflected, a certain *crânerie* with
his fellows — and *crânerie* is "swagger" bereft of
vulgarity — we have no word to connote its conception in a French mind — and she admired it;
but her swift intuition pierced the assumption.
She divined a world of hesitancies behind the Mus-
keteer swing of the shoulders. He was so gentle, so
sensitive, so quick to understand. And yet so
proud. And yet again so unconfessedly dependent.
Her woman's protective instinct responded to a
mute appeal.

"But, Ma'amselle Jeanne, you are wet through,
you are perished with cold. What folly have you
been committing?" Toinette scolded when she
returned after wishing Doggie the last "*bonne
chance.*"

"The folly of putting my Frenchwoman's heart
(*mon cœur de Française*) into the hands of a brave
little soldier to fight with him in the trenches."

"*Mon Dieu, Ma'amselle*, you had better go
straight to bed, and I will bring you a *bon tilleul*

which will calm your nerves and produce a good perspiration."

So Toinette put Jeanne to bed and administered the infallible infusion of lime-leaves, and Jeanne was never the worse for her adventure. But the next day she wondered a little why she had undertaken it. She had a vague idea that it paid a little debt of sympathy.

An evening or two afterwards, Jeanne was sewing in the kitchen when Toinette, sitting in the armchair by the extinct fire, fished out of her pocket the little olive-wood box with the pansies and forget-me-nots on the lid, and took a long pinch of snuff. She did it with somewhat of an air which caused Jeanne to smile.

"*Dites donc*, Toinette, you are insupportable with your snuff-box. One would say a Marquise of the old school."

"Ah, Ma'amselle Jeanne," said the old woman, "you must not laugh at me. I was just thinking that, if anything happened to the *petit Monsieur*, I couldn't have the heart to go on putting his snuff up my old nose."

"Nothing will happen to him," said Jeanne.

The old woman sighed and re-engulfed the snuff-box. "Who knows? From one minute to another who knows whether the little ones who are dear to us are alive or dead?"

"And this *petit Monsieur* is dear to you, Toinette?" Jeanne asked, in her even voice, without looking up from her sewing.

"Since he resembles my *petiot*."

"He will come back," said Jeanne.

"I hope so," said the old woman mournfully.

In spite of manifold duties, Jeanne found the days curiously long. She slept badly. The tramp of the sentry below her window over the archway brought her no sense of comfort, as it had done for months before the coming of Doggie. All the less did it produce the queer little thrill of happiness which was hers when, looking down through the shutter slats, she had identified in the darkness, on a change of guard, the little English soldier to whom she had spoken so intimately. And when he had challenged the Rounds, she had recognised his voice. . . . If she had obeyed an imbecile and unmaidenly impulse, she would have drawn open the shutter and revealed herself. But apart from maidenly shrinkings, familiarity with war had made her realise the sacred duties of a sentry, and she had remained in discreet seclusion, awake until his spell was over. But now the rhythmical beat of the heavy boots kept her from sleeping, and would have irritated her nerves intolerably had not her sound common-sense told her that the stout fellow who wore them was protecting her from the Hun, together with a million or so of his fellow-countrymen.

She found herself counting the days to Doggie's return.

"At last, it is to-morrow!" she said to Toinette.

"What is it to-morrow?" asked the old woman.

"The return of our regiment," replied Jeanne.

"That is good. We have a regiment now," said Toinette, ironically.

The Midland company marched away — as so many had marched away before; but Jeanne did not go to the little embankment at the turn of the road to wish anyone good luck. She stood at the house door, as she had always done, to watch them pass in the darkness; for there is always something in the sight of men going into battle which gives you a lump in the throat. For Jeanne it had almost grown into a religious practice.

The Sergeant had told her that the newcomers would arrive at dawn. She slept a little; awoke with a start as day began to break; dressed swiftly, and went downstairs to wait. And then her ear caught the rumble and the tramp of the approaching battalion. Presently transport rolled by, and squads of men, haggard in the grey light, bending double under their packs, staggered along to their billets. And then came a rusty crew, among whom she recognised McPhail's tall, gaunt figure. She stood by the gateway, bareheaded, in her black dress and blue apron, defying the sharp morning air, and watched them pass through. She saw Mo Shendish, his eyes on the heels of the man in front. She recognised nearly all. But the man she looked for was not there.

He could not have passed without her seeing him; but as soon as the gateway was clear, she ran into the courtyard and fled across it to cut off the men. There was no Doggie. Blank disappointment was succeeded by sudden terror.

Phineas saw her coming. He stumbled up to her, dropped his pack at her feet, and spread out both his hands. She lost sight of the horde of weary, clay-covered men around her. She cried:

"Where is he?"

"I don't know."

"He is dead?"

"No one knows."

"But you must know, you!" cried Jeanne, with a new fear in her eyes which Phineas could not bear to meet, "You promised to bring him back."

"It was not my fault," said Phineas. "He was out on patrol last night — no, the night before, this is morning — repairing barbed wire. I was not with him."

"*Mais, mon Dieu,* why not?"

"Because the duties of soldiers are arranged for them by their officers, Mademoiselle."

"It is true. Pardon. But continue."

"A party went out to repair wire. It was quite

dark. Suddenly a German rifle-shot gave the alarm. The enemy threw up star-shells and the front trenches on each side opened fire. The wiring party of course lay flat on the ground. One of them was wounded. When it was all over, — it didn't last long, — our men got back bringing the wounded man."

"He is severely wounded? Speak," cried Jeanne.

"The wounded man was not Doggie. Doggie went out with the patrol, but he did not come back. That's why I said no one knows where he is."

She stiffened. "He is lying out there. He is dead."

"Shendish and I and Corporal Wilson, over there, who was with the party, got permission to go out and search. We searched all round where the repairs had been going on. But we could not find him."

"*Merci!* I ought not to have reproached you," she said steadily. "*C'est un grand malheur.*"

"You are right. Life for me is no longer of much value."

She looked at him in her penetrating way.

"I believe you," she said. "For the moment, *au revoir*. You must be worn out with fatigue."

She left him and walked through the straggling men, who made respectful way for her. All knew of her friendship with Doggie Trevor, and all realised the nature of this interview. They liked Doggie because he was good-natured and plucky, and never complained and would play the whistle on march as long as breath enough remained in his body. As his uncle, the Dean, had said, breed told. In a curious, half-grudging way they recognised the fact. They laughed at his singular inefficiency in the multitudinous arts of the handy man, proficiency in which is expected from the modern private, but they knew that he would go on till he dropped. And knowing that, they saved him from many a

reprimand which his absurd efforts in the arts
aforesaid would have brought upon him. And now
that Doggie was gone, they deplored his loss. But
so many had gone. So many had been deplored.
Human nature is only capable of a certain amount
of deploring while retaining its sanity. The men
let the pale French girl, who was Doggie Trevor's
friend, pass by in respectful silence — and that for
them was their final tribute to Doggie Trevor.

Jeanne passed into the kitchen. Toinette drew
a sharp breath at the sight of her face.

"*Quoi? Il n'est pas là?*"

"No," said Jeanne. "He is wounded," It was
impossible to explain to Toinette.

"Badly?"

"They don't know."

"*Oh, là, là!*" sighed Toinette. "That always
happens. That is what I told you."

"We have no time to think of such things," said
Jeanne.

The regimental cooks came up for the hot water,
and soon the hungry, weary, nerve-racked men
were served with the morning meal. And Jeanne
stood in the courtyard in front of the kitchen door,
and helped with the filling of the tea-kettles, as
though no little English soldier called "Dog-gie"
had ever existed in the regiment.

The first pale shaft of sunlight fell upon the
kitchen side of the courtyard, and in it Jeanne stood
illuminated. It touched the shades of gold in her
dark brown hair, and lit up her pale face and great
unsmiling eyes. But her lips smiled valiantly.

"What do yer think, Mac," said Mo Shendish,
squatting on the flagstones "do you think she was
really sweet on him?"

"Man," replied Phineas, "all I know is that she
has added him to her collection of ghosts. It's not
an over braw company for a lassie to live with."

And then, soon afterwards, the trench-broken men stumbled into the barn to sleep, and all was quiet again, and Jeanne went about her daily tasks with the familiar hand of death once more closing icily around her heart.

CHAPTER XVI

THE sick room was very hot and Aunt Morin very querulous. Jeanne opened a window, but Aunt Morin complained of currents of air. Did Jeanne want to kill her? So Jeanne closed the window. The internal malady from which Aunt Morin suffered, and from which it was unlikely that she would recover, caused her considerable pain from time to time; and on these occasions she grew fractious and hard to bear with. The retired septuagenarian village doctor who had taken the modest practise of his son, now far away with the army, advised an operation. But Aunt Morin, with her peasant's prejudice, declined flatly. She knew what happened in those hospitals where they cut people up just for the pleasure of looking at their insides. She was not going to let a lot of butchers amuse themselves with her old carcase. *Oh, non!* When it pleased the *bon Dieu* to take her, she was ready: the *bon Dieu* required no assistance from *ces messieurs.* And even if she had consented, how to take her to Paris, and once there, how to get the operation performed, with all the hospitals full and all the surgeons at the front? The old doctor shrugged his shoulders and kept life in her as best he might.

To-day, in the close room, she told a long story of the doctor's neglect. The medicine he gave her was water and nothing else — water with nothing in it. And to ask people to pay for that! She would not pay. What would Jeanne advise?

"*Oui, ma tante,*" said Jeanne.

209

"*Oui, ma tante?* But you are not listening to what I say. At least one can be polite."

"I am listening, *ma tante.*"

"You should be grateful to those who lodge and nourish you."

"I am grateful, *ma tante,*" said Jeanne patiently.

Aunt Morin complained of being robbed on all sides. The doctor, Toinette, Jeanne, the English soldiers — the last the worst of all. Besides not paying sufficiently for what they had, they were so wasteful in the things they took for nothing. If they begged for a few faggots to make a fire, they walked away with the whole wood-stack. She knew them. But all soldiers were the same. They thought that, in time of war, civilians had no rights. One of these days she would get up and come downstairs and see for herself the robbery that was going on.

The windows were tightly sealed. The sunlight hurting Aunt Morin's eyes, the outside shutters were half closed. The room felt like a stuffy, over-heated, over-crowded sepulchre. An enormous oak press, part of her Breton dowry, took up most of the side of one wall. This, together with a great handsome *bahut*, a couple of tables, a stiff armchair, were all too big for the moderately-sized apartment. Coloured prints of sacred subjects, tilted at violent angles, seemed eager to occupy as much air space as possible. And in the middle of the floor sprawled the vast oaken bed, with its heavy green brocade curtains falling tentwise from a great tarnished gilt crown in the ceiling.

Jeanne said nothing. What was the good? She shifted the invalid's hot pillow and gave her a drink of tisane, moving about the over-furnished, airless room in her calm and efficient way. Her face showed no sign of trouble, but an iron band clamped her forehead above her burning eyes. She could perform her nurse's duties, but it was beyond her power to concentrate her mind on the sick woman's unending litany of grievances. Far away beyond that darkened room, beyond that fretful voice, she saw vividly a hot waste, hideous with holes and rusted wire and shapes of horror; and in the middle of it lay huddled up a little khaki-clad figure with the sun blazing fiercely in his unblinking eyes. And his very body was beyond the reach of man, even of the most lion-hearted.

"*Mais qu'as-tu, ma fille?*" asked Aunt Morin. "You do not speak. When people are ill they need to be amused."

"I am sorry, *ma tante*, but I am not feeling very well to-day. It will pass."

"I hope so. Young people have no business not to feel well. Otherwise what is the good of youth?"

"It is true," Jeanne assented.

But what, she thought, was indeed the good of youth, in these terrible days of war? Her own was but a panorama of death. . . . And now one more figure, this time one of youth, too, had joined it.

Toinette came in.

"Ma'amselle Jeanne, there are two English officers downstairs who wish to speak to you."

"What do they want?" Jeanne asked wearily.

"They do not say. They just ask for Ma'amselle Boissière."

"They never leave one in peace, *ces gens-là*," grumbled Aunt Morin. "If they want more concessions in price, do not let them frighten you. Go to Monsieur le Maire to have it arranged with justice. These people would eat the skin off your back. Remember, Jeanne."

"*Bien, ma tante*," said Jeanne.

She went downstairs, conscious of gripping herself in order to discuss with the officers whatever business of billeting was in hand. For she had dealt with all such matters since her arrival in Frélus. She reached the front door and saw a dusty car with a military chauffeur at the wheel, and two officers standing on the pavement at the foot of the steps. One she recognised as the commander of the company to which her billeted men belonged. The other was a stranger, a lieutenant, with a different badge on his cap. They were talking and laughing together, like old friends newly met, which, by one of the myriad coincidences of the war, was really the case. On the appearance of Jeanne, they drew themselves up and saluted politely.

"Mademoiselle Boissière?"

"*Oui, Monsieur.*" Then, "Will you enter, Messieurs?"

They entered the vestibule where the great cask gleamed in its polished mahogany and brass. She bade them be seated.

"Mademoiselle, Captain Willoughby here tells me that you had billeted here last week a soldier by the name of Trevor," said the stranger, in excellent French, taking out notebook and pencil.

Jeanne's lips grew white. She had not suspected their errand.

"*Oui, Monsieur.*"

"Did you have much talk with him?"

"Much, Monsieur."

"Pardon my indiscretion, Mademoiselle — it is military service, and I am an Intelligence Officer — but did you tell him about your private affairs?"

"Very intimately," said Jeanne.

The Intelligence officer made a note or two and smiled pleasantly — but Jeanne could have struck him for daring to smile. "You had every reason for thinking him a man of honour?"

"What's the good of asking her that, Smithers?" Captain Willoughby interrupted in English. "Haven't I given you my word? The man's a mysterious little devil, but any fool can see that he's a gentleman."

"What do you say?" Jeanne asked tensely.

"*Je parle Français très peu,*" replied Captain Willoughby with an air of regret.

Smithers explained. "Monsieur le Capitaine says that he guarantees the honesty of the soldier Trevor."

Jeanne flashed, rigid. "Who could doubt it, Monsieur? He was a gentleman, a *fils de famille*, of the English aristocracy."

"Excuse me for a moment," said Smithers.

He went out. Jeanne, uncomprehending, sat silent. Captain Willoughby, cursing an idiot education, composed in his head a polite French sentence concerning the weather, but before he had finished Smithers reappeared with a strange twisted packet in his hand. He held it out to Jeanne.

"Mademoiselle, do you recognise this?"

She looked at it dully for a moment; then suddenly sprang to her feet and clenched her hands and stared open-mouthed. She nodded. She could not speak. Her brain swam. They had come to her about Doggie who was dead, and they showed her Père Grigou's packet. What was the connection between the two?

Willoughby rose impulsively. "For God's sake, Smithers, let her down easy. She'll be fainting all over the place in a minute."

"If this is your property, Mademoiselle," said Smithers, laying the packet on the chenille covered table, "you have to thank your friend Trevor for restoring it to you."

She put up both hands to her reeling head.

"But he is dead, Monsieur!"

"Not a bit of it. He's just as much alive as you or I."

Jeanne swayed, tried to laugh, threw herself half

on a chair, half over the great cask, and broke down in a passion of tears.

The two men looked at each other uncomfortably.

"For exquisite tact," said Willoughby, "commend me to an Intelligence Man."

"But how the deuce was I to know?" Smithers muttered, with an injured air. "My instructions were to find out the truth of a cock-and-bull story — for that's what it seemed to come to. And a girl in billets — well — how was I to know what she was like?"

"Anyhow, here we've got hysterics," said Willoughby.

"But who told her the fellow was dead?"

"Why, his pals. I thought so myself. When a man's missing, where's one to suppose him to be — having supper at the Savoy?"

"Well, I give women up," said Smithers. "I thought she'd be glad."

"I believe you're a married man."

"Yes, of course."

"Well, I ain't," said Willoughby. And in a couple of strides he stood close to Jeanne. He laid a gentle hand on her heaving shoulders.

"*Pas tué! Soolmong blessé,*" he shouted.

She sprang, as it were, to attention, like a frightened recruit.

"He is wounded?"

"Not very seriously, Mademoiselle." Smithers casting an indignant glance at his superior officer's complacent smile, reassumed mastery of the situation. "A Boche sniper got him in the leg. It will put him out of service for a month or two. But there is no danger."

"*Grâce à Dieu!*" said Jeanne.

She leaned, for a while, against the cask, her hands behind her, looking away from the two men. And the two young men stood, somewhat embarrassed, looking away from her and from each other. At last she said, with an obvious striving for the even note in her voice:

"I ask your pardon, Messieurs, but sometimes sudden happiness is more overwhelming than misfortune. I am now quite at your service."

"My God! she's a wonder," murmured Willoughby, who was fair, unmarried and impressionable. "Go on with your dirty work."

Smithers, dark and lean — in civil life he had been concerned with the wine trade in Bordeaux — proceeded to carry out his instructions. He turned over a leaf in his notebook and poised a ready pencil.

"I must ask you, Mademoiselle, some formal questions."

"Perfectly, Monsieur," said Jeanne.

"Where was this packet when last you saw it?"

She made her statement, calmly.

"Can you tell me its contents?"

"Not all, Monsieur. I, as a young girl, was not in the full confidence of my parents. But I remember my uncle saying there were about twenty thousand francs in notes, some gold, I know not how much, some jewellery of my mother's — oh, a big handful! — rings — one a hoop of emeralds and diamonds — a brooch with a black pearl belonging to my great grandmother —"

"It is enough, Mademoiselle," said Smithers, jotting down notes. "Anything else besides money and jewellery?"

"There were papers of my father, share certificates, bonds, — *que sais-je, moi*? "

Captain Smithers opened the packet which had already been examined.

"You're a witness, Willoughby, to the identification of the property."

"No," said Willoughby. "I'm just a baby captain of infantry, and wonder why the brainy

Intelligence department doesn't hand the girl her belongings and decently clear out."

"I've got to make my report, Sir," said Smithers, stiffly.

So the schedule was produced and the notes were solemnly counted, twenty-one thousand five hundred francs, and the gold four hundred francs, and the jewels were identified, and the bonds, of which Jeanne knew nothing, were checked by a list in her father's handwriting, and Jeanne signed a paper with Smithers's fountain pen, and Willoughby witnessed her signature, and thus she entered into possession of her heritage.

The officers were about to depart, but Jeanne detained them.

"Messieurs, you must pardon me, but I am quite bewildered. As far as I can understand, Monsieur Trevor rescued the packet from the well at my uncle's farm of La Folette, and got wounded in doing so."

"That is quite so," said Smithers.

"But, Monsieur, they tell me he was with a party in front of his trench, mending wire. How did he reach the well of La Folette? I don't comprehend at all."

Smithers turned to Willoughby. "Yes. How the dickens did he know the exact spot to go for?"

"We had taken over a new sector and I was getting the topography right with a map. Trevor was near by doing nothing, and as he's a man of education, I asked him to help me. There was the site of the farm marked by name, and the ruined well away over to the left in No Man's Land. I remember the beggar calling out 'La Folette!' in a startled voice, and when I asked him what was the matter, he said 'Nothing, sir.'"

Smithers translated and continued: "You see, Mademoiselle, this is what happened as far as I am concerned. I am attached to the Lancashire Fusiliers. Our battalion is in the trenches about three miles further up the line than our friends. Well, just before dawn yesterday morning, a man rolled over the parapet into our trench, and promptly fainted. He had been wounded in the leg and was half dead from loss of blood. Under his tunic was this package. We identified him and his regiment, and fixed him up and took him to the dressing-station. But things looked very suspicious. Here was a man who did not belong to us with a little fortune in loot on his person. As soon as he was fit to be interrogated, the C. O. took him in hand. He told the C. O. about you and your story. He regarded the nearness of the well as something to do with Destiny, and resolved to get you back your property — if it was still there. The opportunity occurred when the wiring party was alarmed. He crept out to the ruins by the well, fished out the packet, and a sniper got him. He managed to get back to our lines, having lost his way a bit, and tumbled into our trench.''

"But he was in danger of death all the time," said Jeanne, losing the steadiness of her voice.

"He was. Every second. It was one of the most dare-devil, scatter-brained things I've ever heard of. And I've heard of many, Mademoiselle. The only pity is that, instead of being rewarded, he will be punished."

"Punished?" cried Jeanne.

"Not very severely," laughed Smithers. "Captain Willoughby will see to that. But reflect, Mademoiselle. His military duty was to remain with his comrades, not to go and risk his life to get your property. Anyhow, it is clear that he was not out for loot. . . . Of course they sent me here as Intelligence Officer, to get corroboration of his story." He paused for a moment. Then he added. "Mademoiselle, I must congratulate you on the restoration of your fortune and the possession of a very brave friend."

For the first time the red spots burned on Jeanne's pale face.

"*Je vous remercie infiniment, Monsieur.*"

"*Il sera* all right," said Willoughby.

The officers saluted and went their ways. Jeanne took up her packet and mounted to her little room in a dream. Then she sat down on her bed, the unopened packet by her side, and strove to realise it all. But the only articulate thought came to her in the words which she repeated over and over again:

"*Il a fait cela pour moi! Il a fait cela pour moi!*"

He had done that for her. It was incredible, fantastic, thrillingly true, like the fairy-tales of her childhood. The little, sensitive English soldier, whom his comrades protected, whom she herself in a feminine way longed to protect, had done this for her. In a shy, almost reverent way, she opened out the waterproof covering, as though to reassure herself of the reality of things. For the first time since she left Cambrai a smile came into her eyes, together with grateful tears.

"*Il a fait cela pour moi! Il a fait cela pour moi!*"

A while later she relieved Toinette's guard in the sick room.

"*Eh bien?* And the two officers," queried Aunt Morin after Toinette had gone. "They have stayed a long time. What did they want?"

Jeanne was young. She had eaten the bread of dependence which Aunt Morin, by reason of racial instinct and the stress of sorrow and infirmity had contrived to render very bitter. She could not repress an exultant note in her voice. Doggie, too, accounted for something, for much.

"They came to bring good news, *ma tante*. The

English have found all the money and the jewels and the share certificates that Père Grigou sunk in the well of La Folette."

"*Mon Dieu!* It is true?"

"*Oui, ma tante.*"

"And they have restored them to you?"

"Yes."

"It is extraordinary. It is truly extraordinary! At last these English seem to be good for something. And they found that and gave it to you without taking anything?"

"Without taking anything," said Jeanne.

Aunt Morin reflected for a few moments, then she stretched out a thin hand.

"*Ma petite Jeanne chérie*, you are rich now."

"I don't know exactly," replied Jeanne with a mingling of truth and caution. "I have enough for the present."

"How did it all happen?"

"It was part of a military operation," said Jeanne.

Perhaps later she might tell Aunt Morin about Doggie. But now the thing was too sacred. Aunt Morin would question, question maddeningly, until the rainbow of her fairy-tale was unwoven. The salient fact of the recovery of her fortune was enough for Aunt Morin. It was. The old woman of the pain-pinched features looked at her wistfully from sunken grey eyes.

"And now that you are rich, my little Jeanne, you will not leave the poor old aunt who loves you so much, to die alone?"

"*Ah, mais non! mais non! mais non!*" cried Jeanne indignantly. "What do you think I am made of?"

"Ah!" breathed Aunt Morin, comforted.

"Also," said Jeanne, in the matter-of-fact French way, "*si tu veux*, I will henceforward pay for my lodging and nourishment."

"You are very good, my little Jeanne," said Aunt

Morin. "That will be a great help, for *vois-tu*, we are
very poor."

"*Oui, ma tante*. It is the war."

"Ah, the war, the war, this awful war! One has
nothing left."

Jeanne smiled. Aunt Morin had a very comfortably invested fortune left, for the late Monsieur
Morin, corn, hay and seed merchant, had been a
very astute person. It would make little difference
to the comfort of Aunt Morin, or to the prospects of
Cousin Gaspard in Madagascar, whether the present
business of Veuve Morin et Fils went on or not.
Of this Aunt Morin, in lighter moods, had boasted
many times.

"Everyone must do what he can," said Jeanne.

"Perfectly," said Aunt Morin. "You are a
young girl who well understands things. And now
— it is not good for young people to stay in a sick
room — one needs the fresh air. *Va te distraire,
ma petite*. I am quite comfortable."

So Jeanne went out to distract a self already
distraught with great wonder, great pride, and
great fear.

He had done that for her. The wonder of it bewildered her, the pride of it thrilled her. But he
was wounded. Fear smothered her joy. They
had said there was no danger. But soldiers always
made light of wounds. It was their way in this
horrible war, in the intimate midst of which she had
her being. If a man was not dead, he was alive,
and thereby accounted lucky. In their gay op-
timism they had given him a month or two of absence from the regiment. But even in a month
or two — where would the regiment be? Far,
far away from Frélus. Would she ever see Doggie
again?

To distract herself she went down the village
street, bareheaded, and up the lane that led to the

little church. The church was empty, cool, and
smelt of the hillside. Before the tinsel-crowned,
mild-faced image of the Virgin were spread the poor
votive offerings of the village. And Jeanne sank
on her knees and bowed her head, and, without
special prayer or formula of devotion, gave herself
into the hands of the Mother of Sorrows.

She walked back comforted, vaguely conscious
of a strengthening of soul. In the vast cataclysm
of things her own hopes and fears and destiny
mattered very little. If she never saw Doggie
again, if Doggie recovered and returned to the war
and was killed, her own grief mattered very little.
She was but a stray straw and mattered very little.
But what mattered infinitely, what shone with an
immortal flame, though it were never so tiny, was
the Wonderful Spiritual Something that guided
Doggie through the jaws of death.

That evening she had a long talk in the kitchen
with Phineas. The news of Doggie's safety had
been given out by Willoughby, without any details.
Mo Shendish had leaped about her like a fox-terrier,
and she had laughed, with difficulty restraining her
tears. But to Phineas, alone, she told her whole
story. He listened in bewilderment. And the
greater his bewilderment, the worse his crude trans-
lations of English into French. She wound up a
long, eager speech by saying:

"He has done this for me. Why?"

"*Amour*," replied Phineas, bluntly.

"It is more than love," said Jeanne, thinking of
the Wonderful Spiritual Something.

"If you could understand English," said Phineas,
"I would enter into the metaphysics of the subject
with pleasure, but in French it is beyond me."

Jeanne smiled, and turned to the matter-of-fact.

"He will go to England now that he is wounded?"

"He's on the way now," said Phineas.

"Has he many friends there? I ask, because he talks so little of himself. He is so modest."

"Oh, many friends. You see, Mademoiselle," said Phineas, with a view to setting her mind at rest, "Doggie's an important person in his part of the country. He was brought up in luxury. I know because I lived with him as his tutor for seven years. His father and mother are dead and he could go on living in luxury now, if he liked."

"He is then rich — Doggie?"

"He has a fine house of his own in the country, with many servants and automobiles and — wait —" he made a swift arithmetical calculation, "and an income of eighty thousand francs a year."

"*Comment?*" cried Jeanne sharply, with a little frown.

Phineas McPhail was enjoying himself, basking in the sunshine of Doggie's wealth. Also, when conversation in French resolved itself into the statement of simple facts, he could get along famously. So the temptation of the glib phrase outran his discretion.

"Doggie has a fortune of about two million francs."

"*Il doit faire un beau mariage,*" said Jeanne, with stony calm.

Phineas suddenly became aware of pitfalls, and summoned his craft and astuteness and knowledge of affairs. He smiled, as he thought, encouragingly.

"The only *beau mariage* is with the person one loves."

"Not always, Monsieur," said Jeanne, who had watched the gathering of the sagacities with her deep eyes. "In any case —" she rose and held out her hand — "our friend will be well looked after in England."

"Like a prince," said Phineas.

He strode away greatly pleased with himself, and went and found Mo Shendish.

"Man," said he, "have you ever reflected that the dispensing of happiness is the cheapest form of human diversion?"

"What've you been doin' now?" asked Mo.

"I've just left a lassie tottering over with blissful dreams."

"Gorblime!" said Mo, "and to think that if I could sling the lingo, I might've done the same!"

But Phineas had knocked all the dreams out of Jeanne. The British happy-go-lucky ways of marriage are not those of the French *bourgeoisie*, and Jeanne had no notion of British happy-go-lucky ways. Phineas had knocked the dream out of Jeanne by kicking Doggie out of her sphere. And there was a girl in England in Doggie's sphere whom he was to marry. She knew it. A man does not gather his sagacities in order to answer crookedly a direct challenge, unless there is some necessity.

Well. She would never see Doggie again. He would pass out of her life. His destiny called him, if he survived the slaughter of the war, to the shadowy girl in England. Yet he had done *that* for her. For no other woman could he ever in this life do *that* again. It was past love. Her brain boggled at an elusive spiritual idea. She was very young, flung cleanly trained from the convent into the war's terrific tragedy, wherein maiden romantic fancies were scorched in the tender bud. Only her honest traditions of marriage remained. Of love she knew nothing. She leaped beyond it, seeking, seeking. She would never see him again. There she met the Absolute. But he had done *that* for her — that which, she knew not why, but she knew —he would do for no other woman. The Splendour of it would be her everlasting possession.

She undressed that night, proud, dry-eyed, heroical, and went to bed, and listened to the rhythmic tramp of the sentry across the gateway below her window, and suddenly a lump rose in her throat and she fell to crying miserably.

CHAPTER XVII

"HOW are you feeling, Trevor?"

"Nicely, thank you, Sister."

"Glad to be in Blighty again?"

Doggie smiled. "Good old Blighty!"

"Leg hurting you?"

"A bit, Sister," he replied with a little grimace.

"It's bound to be stiff after the long journey, but we'll soon fix it up for you."

"I'm sure you will," he said politely.

The nurse moved on. Doggie drew the cool, clean sheet around his shoulders, and gave himself up to the luxury of bed — real bed. The morning sunlight poured through the open windows, attended by a delicious odour which after a while he recognised as the scent of the sea. Where he was he had no notion. He had absorbed so much of Tommy's philosophy as not to care. He had arrived with a convoy the night before, after much travel in ambulances by land and sea. If he had been a walking case, he might have taken more interest in things; but the sniper's bullet in his thigh had touched the bone, and in spite of being carried most tenderly about like a baby, he had suffered great pain, and longed for nothing and thought of nothing but a permanent resting-place. Now, apparently, he had found one, and, looking about him, he felt peculiarly content. He seemed to have seen no cleaner, whiter, brighter place in the world than this airy ward swept by the sea-breezes. He counted seven beds besides his own. On a table running down the ward stood a vase of sweet-peas and a bowl of roses. He thought there was never in the world so clean and cool a figure as the grey-clad nurse in her spotless white apron, cuffs, and cap.

When she passed near him again, he summoned her. She came to his bedside.

"What do you call this particular region of fairyland?"

She stared at him for a moment, adjusting things in her mind; for his name and style were 35792 Private Trevor, J. M., but his voice and phrase were those of her own social class. Then she smiled and told him. The corner of fairyland was a private auxiliary hospital in a Lancashire seaside town.

"Lancashire," said Doggie, knitting his brow in a puzzled way, "but why have they sent me to Lancashire? I belong to a West country regiment, and all my friends are in the South."

"What's he grousing about, Sister?" suddenly asked the occupant of the next bed. "He's the sort of chap that doesn't know when he's in luck and when he isn't. I'm in the Duke of Cornwall's Light Infantry, I am, and when I was hit before, they sent me to a military hospital in Inverness. That'd teach you, my lad. This for me every time. You ought to have something to grouse at."

"I'm not grousing, you idiot!" said Doggie.

"'Ere — who's he calling an idjit?" cried the Duke of Cornwall's Light Infantryman, raising himself on his elbow.

The nurse intervened; explained that no one could be said to grumble at a hospital when he called it Fairyland. Trevor's question was that of one in search of information. He did not realise that in assigning men to the various hospitals in the United Kingdom, the authorities could not possibly take into account an individual man's local association.

"Oh, well, if it's only his blooming ignorance —"

"That's just it, mate," smiled Doggie. "My blooming ignorance."

"That's all right," said the nurse. "Now you're friends."

"He had no right to call me an idjit," said the Duke of Cornwall's Light Infantryman. He was an aggressive, red-visaged man with bristly, black hair and stubbly, black moustache.

"If you'll agree that he wasn't grousing, Penworthy, I'm sure Trevor will apologise for calling you an idiot."

And into the nurse's eyes crept the queer smile of the woman learned in the ways of children.

"Didn't I say he wasn't grousing? It was only his ignorance?"

Doggie responded. "I meant no offence, mate, in what I said."

The other growled an acceptance, whereupon the nurse smiled an ironic benediction and moved away.

"Where did you get it?" asked Penworthy.

Doggie gave the information, and, in his turn, made the polite counter enquiry. Penworthy's bit of shrapnel, which had broken a rib or two, had been acquired just north of Albert. When he left, he said, we were putting it over in great quantities.

"That's where the great push is going to be in a few days."

"Aren't you sorry you're out of it?"

"Me?" The Duke of Cornwall's Light Infantryman shook his head. "I take things as I finds 'em, and I finds this quite good enough."

So they chatted, and, in the soldier's way, became friends. Later the surgeon arrived, and probed Doggie's wound and hurt him exquisitely, so that the perspiration stood out on his forehead, and his jaws ached afterwards from his clenching of them.

While his leg was being dressed he reflected that, a couple of years ago, if anyone had inflicted a twentieth part of such torture on him he would have yelled the house down. He remembered, with an inward grin, the anguished precautions on which he had insisted whenever he sat down in the expensive London dentist's chair.

"It must have hurt like fun," said the nurse, busily engaged with the gauze dressing.

"It's all in the day's work," replied Doggie.

The nurse pinned the bandage and settled him comfortably in bed.

"No one will worry you till dinner time. You'd better try to have a sleep."

So Doggie nodded and smiled and curled up as best he could, and slept the heavy sleep of the tired young animal. It was only when he awoke, physically rested and comparatively free from pain, that his mind, hitherto confused, began to work clearly, to straighten out the three days' tangle. — Yes, just three days. A fact almost impossible to realise. Till now it had seemed an eternity.

He lay with his arms crossed under his head and stared at the blue sky. It seemed a soft, comforting, English sky. The ward was silent. Only two beds were occupied, one by a man asleep, the other by a man reading a novel. His other roommates, including his neighbour Penworthy, were so far convalescent as to be up and away, presumably by the life-giving sea, whose rhythmic murmur he could hear. For the first time since he awoke to find himself bandaged up in a strange dugout and surrounded by strange faces, did the chaos of his ideas resolve itself into anything like definite memories. Yet many of them were still vague.

He had been out there, with the wiring party, in the dark. He had been glad, he remembered, to escape from the prison of the trench into the

open air. He was having some difficulty with a
recalcitrant bit of wire that refused to come straight
and jabbed him diabolically in unexpected places,
when a shot rang out and German flares went up
and everybody lay flat on the ground, while bullets
spat about them. As he lay on his stomach, a
flare lit up the ruined well of the farm of La Folette.
And the well and his nose and his heels were in a
bee-line. The realisation of the fact was the in-
ception of a fascinating idea. He remembered that
quite clearly. Of course his discovery, two days
before, of the spot where Jeanne's fortune lay hidden,
when his senior subaltern, with map and periscope,
had called him into consultation, had set his heart
beating and his imagination working. But not till
that moment of stark opportunity had he dreamed
of the mad adventure which he undertook. There,
in front of him, at the very farthest five hundred
yards away, in bee-line with nose and heels — that
was the peculiar and particular arresting fact — lay
Jeanne's fortune. In thinking of it he lost count
of shots and star-shells and heard no orders and saw
no dim forms creeping back to the safety of the
trench. And then all was darkness and silence.

Doggie lay on his back and stared at the English
sky and wondered how he did it. His attitude was
that of a man who cannot reconcile his sober self
with the idiot hero of a drunken freak. And yet,
at the time, the journey to the ruined well seemed the
simplest thing in the world. The thought of Jeanne's
delight shone uppermost in his mind. . . . Oh!
he was forgetting the star, which hung low beneath
a canopy of cloud, the extreme point of the famous
feet, nose and well bee-line. He made for it, now
and then walking low, now and then crawling. He
did not mind his clothes and hands being torn by
the unseen refuse of No Man's Land. His chief
sensation was one of utter loneliness, mingled with

exultance at freedom. He did not remember feeling afraid: which was odd, because when the star-shells had gone up and the German trenches had opened fire on the wiring party, his blood had turned to water and his heart had sunk into his boots, and he had been deucedly frightened.

Heaven must have guided him straight to the well. He had known all along that he merely would have to stick his hand down to find the rope . . . and he felt no surprise when the rope actually came in contact with his groping fingers; no surprise when he pulled and pulled and fished up the packet. It had all been pre-ordained. That was the funny part of the business which Doggie now could not understand. But he remembered that when he had buttoned his tunic over the precious packet, he had been possessed of an insane desire to sing and dance. He repressed his desire to sing, but he leaped about and started to run. Then the star in which he trusted must have betrayed him. It must have shed upon him a ray just strong enough to make him a visible object; for, suddenly, *ping!* something hit him violently on the leg and bowled him over like a rabbit into a providential shell-hole. And there he lay quaking for a long time, while the lunacy of his adventure coarsely and unsentimentally revealed itself.

As to the rest, he was in a state of befogged memory. Only one incident in that endless, cruel crawl home remained as landmark in his mind. He had paused to take breath, almost ready to give up the impossible flight — it seemed as though he were dragging behind him a ton of red-hot iron — when he became conscious of a stench violent in his nostrils. He put out a hand. It encountered a horrible, once human, face, and his fingers touched a round, recognisable cap. Horror drove him away from the dead German and inspired him with

the strength of despair. . . . Then all was fog and
dark again until he recovered consciousness in the
strange dug-out.

There the doctor had said to him: "You must
have a cast-iron constitution, my lad."

The memory caused a flicker round his lips. It
wasn't everybody who could crawl on his belly
for nearly a quarter of a mile with a bullet through
his leg, and come up smiling at the end of it. A cast-
iron constitution! If he had only known it fifteen,
even ten years ago, what a different life he might
have led! The great disgrace would never have
come upon him.

And Jeanne? What of Jeanne? After he had
told his story, they had given him to understand
that an officer would be sent to Frélus to corroborate
it, and, if he found it true, that Jeanne would enter
into possession of her packet. And that was all he
knew; for they had bundled him out of the front
trenches as quickly as possible; and once out he
had become a case, a stretcher case, and although
he had been treated as a case, with almost super-
human tenderness, not a soul regarded him as
a human being with a personality or a history —
not even with a military history. And this same
military history had vaguely worried him all the
time, and now that he could think clearly, worried
him with a very definite worry. In leaving his
firing party he had been guilty of a crime. Every
misdemeanour in the army is termed a crime — from
murder to appearing buttonless on parade. Was it
desertion? If so, he might be shot. He had not
thought of that when he started on his quest. It had
seemed so simple to account for half an hour's absence
by saying that he had lost his way in the dark. But
now, that plausible excuse was invalid. . . .

Doggie thought terribly hard that quiet, sea-
scented morning. After all, it did not very much

matter what they did to him. Sticking him up
against a wall and shooting him was a remote
possibility; he was in the British and not the German
Army. Field punishments of unpleasant kinds
were only inflicted on people convicted of unpleasant
delinquencies. If he were a sergeant or a corporal
he doubtless would be broken. But such is the
fortunate position of a private, that he cannot be
degraded to an inferior rank. At the worst they
might give him cells when he recovered. Well,
he could stick it. It didn't matter. What really
mattered was Jeanne. Was she in undisputed
possession of her packet? When it was a question
of practical warfare, Doggie had blind faith in his
officers — a faith perhaps even more childlike than
that of his fellow-privates, for officers were the men
who had come through the ordeal in which he had
so lamentably failed; but when it came to admin-
istrative affairs, he was more critical. He had
suffered during his military career from more than
one subaltern on whose arid consciousness the brain-
wave never beat. He had never met even a field
officer before whom, in the realm of intellect, he had
stood in awe. If any one of those dimly envisaged
and still more dimly remembered officers of the
Lancashire Fusiliers had ordered him to stand on
his head on top of the parapet, he would have obeyed
in cheerful confidence; but he was not at all certain
that, in the effort to deliver the packet to Jeanne,
they would not make an unholy mess of things.
He saw stacks of dirty, yellowish bits of paper, with
A. F. No. something or the other, floating between
Frélus and the Lancashire Battalion H. Q. and the
Brigade H. Q. and the Divisional H. Q., and so on
through the majesty of G. H. Q. to the awful War
Office itself. In pessimistic mood he thought that
if Jeanne recovered her property within a year, she
would be lucky.

What a wonderful creature was Jeanne! He shut his eyes to the blue sky and pictured her as she stood in the light, on the ragged escarpment, with her garments beaten by wind and rain. And he remembered the weary thud, thud of railway and steamer, which had resolved itself, like the rhythmic tramp of feet that night, into the ceaseless refrain: "Jeanne! Jeanne!"

He opened his eyes again and frowned at the blue English sky. It had no business to proclaim simple serenity when his mind was in such a state of complex tangle. It was all very well to think of Jeanne, Jeanne, whom it was unlikely that Fate would ever allow him to see again, even supposing the war ended during his lifetime; but there was Peggy — Peggy, his future wife, who had stuck to him loyally through good and evil repute. Yes, there was Peggy — not the faintest shadow of doubt about it. Doggie kept on frowning at the blue sky. Blighty was a very desirable country, but in it you were compelled to think. And enforced thought was an infernal nuisance. The beastly trenches had their good points, after all. There you were not called upon to think of anything; the less you thought, the better for your job; you just ate your bully-beef and drank your tea and cursed whizz-bangs and killed a rat or two, and thanked God you were alive.

Now that he came to look at it in proper perspective, it wasn't at all a bad life. When had he been worried to death, as he was now? And there were his friends: the humorous, genial, deboshed, yet ever kindly Phineas; dear old Mo Shendish, whose material feet were hankering after the vulgar pavement of Mare Street, Hackney, but whose spiritual tread rang on golden floors dimly imagined by the Seer of Patmos; Barrett, the D. C. M., the miniature Hercules, who, according to legend, though, modestly, he would never own to it, seized

two Boches by the neck and knocked their heads together till they died, and who, musically inclined,
would sit at his, Doggie's, feet while he played on
his penny whistle all the sentimental tunes he had
ever heard of; Sergeant Ballinghall, a tower of a
man, a champion amateur heavy-weight boxer with
a voice compared with which a megaphone sounded
like a maiden's prayer, and a Bardolphian nose and
an eagle eye and the heart of a broody hen, who
had not only given him. boxing lessons, but had
pulled him through difficult places innumerable . . .
and scores of others. He wondered what they
were doing. He also was foolish enough to wonder
whether they missed him, forgetting for the moment
that if a regiment took seriously to "missing" their
comrades sent to Kingdom Come or Blighty, they
would be more like weeping willows than destroyers
of Huns.

All the same, he knew that he would always live
in the hearts of two or three of them, and the knowledge brought him considerable comfort. It was
strange to realise how the tentacles of his being
stretched out gropingly towards these (from the
old Durdlebury point of view) impossible friends.
They had grafted themselves on to his life. Or
was that a correct way of putting it? Had they
not, rather, all grafted themselves on to a common
stock of life, so that the one common sap ran through
all their veins?

It took him a long time to get this idea formulated,
fixed and accepted. But Doggie was not one to
boggle at the truth, as he saw it. And this was
the truth. He, James Marmaduke Trevor of Denby
Hall, was a Tommy of the Tommies. He had
lived the Tommy life intensely. He was living
it now. And the extraordinary part of it was that
he didn't want to be anything else but a Tommy.
From the social or gregarious point of view his life

for the past year had been one of unclouded happiness. The realisation of it, now that he was clearly sizing up the ramshackle thing which he called his existence, hit him like the butt-end of a rifle. Hardship, cold, hunger, fatigue, stench, rats, the dread of inefficiency — all these had been factors of misery which he could never eliminate from his soldier's equation; but such free, joyous, intimate companionship with real human beings he had never enjoyed since he was born. He longed to be back among them, doing the same old weary, dreary things, eating the same old Robinson Crusoe kind of food, crouching with them in the same old beastly hole in the ground, while the Boche let loose hell on the trench: Mo Shendish's grin and his "'Ere, get in aht of the rain," and his grip on his shoulder dragging him a few inches further into shelter, were a spiritual compensation transcending all physical discomfitures and perils.

"It's all dam' funny," he said half aloud.

But this was England, and although he was hedged about, protected and restricted by War Office Regulation Red Tape twisted round to the strength of steel cables, yet he was in command of telegraphs, of telephones and, in a secondary degree, of the railway system of the United Kingdom. He found himself deprecating the compulsory facilities of communication in the civilised world. The Deanery must be informed of his homecoming.

As soon as he could secure the services of a nurse he wrote out three telegrams: one addressed "Conover, the Deanery, Durdlebury"; one to Peddle at Denby Hall; and one to Jeanne. The one to Jeanne was the longest and was "Reply paid."

"This is going to cost a small fortune, young man," said the nurse.

Doggie smiled as he drew out a £1 treasury note from his soldier's pocket-book, the pathetic object containing a form of Will on the right hand flap, and on the left the directions for the making of the will, concluding with the world-famous typical signature of Thomas Atkins.

"It's a bust, Sister," said he. "I've been saving up for it for months."

Then, duty accomplished, he reconciled himself to the corner of Fairyland in which he had awoke that morning. Things must take their course, and while they were taking it, why worry? So long as they didn't commit the outrage of giving him bully-beef for dinner, the present coolness and comfort sufficed for his happiness.

CHAPTER XVIII

THE replies to the telegrams were satisfactory. Peggy, adjuring him to write a full account of himself, announced her intention of coming up to see him as soon as he could guarantee his fitness to receive visitors. Jeanne wired: "*Paquet reçu. Mille remerciements.*" The news cheered him exceedingly. It was worth a hole in the leg. Henceforward Jeanne would be independent of Aunt Morin, of whose generous affection, in spite of Jeanne's loyal reticence, he had formed but a poor opinion. Now the old lady could die whenever she liked, and so much the better for Jeanne. Jeanne would then be freed from the unhealthy sick room, from dreary little Frélus, and from enforced consorting with the riff-raff (namely, all other regiments except his own) of the British Army. Even as it was, he did not enjoy thinking of her as hail-fellow-well-met with his own fellow-privates — perhaps with the exception of Phineas and Mo, who were in a different position, having been formally admitted into a peculiar intimacy. Of course if Doggie had possessed a more analytical mind, he would have been greatly surprised to discover that these feelings arose from a healthy, barbaric sense of ownership of Jeanne; that Mo and Phineas were in a special position because they humbly recognised this fact of ownership and adopted a respectful attitude towards his property, and that of all other predatory men in uniform he was distrustful and jealous. But Doggie was a simple soul, and went through a great many elementary emotions, just as Monsieur

237

Jourdain spoke prose, *sans le savoir.* Without knowing it, he would have gone to the ends of the earth for Jeanne, have clubbed over the head any fellow savage who should seek to rob him of Jeanne. It did not occur to him that savage instinct had already sent him into the jaws of Death solely in order to establish his primitive man's ownership of Jeanne. When he came to reflect, in his Doggie-ish way, on the motives of his exploit, he was somewhat baffled. Jeanne, with her tragic face, and her tragic history, and her steadfast soul shining out of her eyes, was the most wonderful woman he had ever met. She personified the heroic womanhood of France. The foul invader had robbed her of her family and her patrimony. The dead were dead and could not be restored; but the material wealth, God — who else? — had given him this miraculous chance to recover; and he had recovered it. National pride helped to confuse issues. He, an Englishman, had saved this heroic daughter of France from poverty. . . .

If only he could have won back to his own trench, and, later, when the company returned to Frélus, he could have handed her the packet and seen the light come into those wonderful eyes!

Anyhow she had received it. She sent him a thousand thanks. How did she look, what did she say when she cut the string and undid the seals and found her little fortune?

Translate Jeanne into a princess, the dirty waterproof package into a golden casket, himself into a knight disguised as a Squire of low degree, and what more could you want for a first class fairytale? The idea struck Doggie at the moment of "lights out," and he laughed aloud.

"It doesn't take much to amuse some people," growled his neighbour, Penworthy.

"Sign of a happy disposition," said Doggie.

"What've you got to be happy about?"

"I was thinking how alive we are, and how dead you and I might be," said Doggie.

"Well, I don't think it funny thinking how one might be dead," replied Penworthy. "It gives me the creeps. It's all very well for you. You'll stump around for the rest of your life like a gentleman on a wooden leg. Chaps like you have all the luck; but as soon as I get out of this, I'll be passed fit for active service, . . . and not so much of your larfing at not being dead. See?"

"All right, mate," said Doggie. "Good-night."

Penworthy made no immediate reply; but presently he broke out:

"What d'you mean by talking like that? I'd hate being dead."

A voice from the far end of the room luridly requested that the conversation should cease. Silence reigned.

A letter from Jeanne. The envelope bore a French stamp with the Frélus postmark, and the address was in a bold feminine hand. From whom could it be but Jeanne? His heart gave a ridiculous leap, and he tore the envelope open as he had never torn open envelope of Peggy's. But at the first two words the leap seemed to be one in mid air, and his heart went down, down, down, like an aeroplane done in, and arrived with a hideous bump upon rocks.

"*Cher Monsieur.*"

Cher Monsieur from Jeanne — Jeanne who had called him "Dog-gie" in accents that had rendered adorable the once execrated syllables! *Cher Monsieur!*

And the following, in formal French — it might have been a convent exercise in composition — is what she said:

"*The military authorities have remitted into my possession the package which you so heroically rescued from the well of the farm of La Folette. It contains all that my father was able to save of his fortune, and on consultation with Maître Pépineau here, it appears that I have sufficient to live modestly for the rest of my life. For the marvellous devotion of you, Monsieur, an English gentleman, to the poor interest of an obscure young French girl, I can never be sufficiently grateful. There will never be a prayer of mine, until I die, in which you will not be mentioned. To me it will be always a symbolic act of your chivalrous England in the aid of my beloved France. That you have been wounded in this noble and selfless enterprise, is to me a subject both of pride and terrifying dismay. I am moved to the depths of my being. But I have been assured, and your telegram confirms the assurance, that your wound is not dangerous. If you had been killed while rendering me this wonderful service, or incapacitated so that you could no longer strike a blow for your country and mine, I should never have forgiven myself. I should have felt that I had robbed France of a heroic defender. I pray God that you may soon recover, and in fighting once more against our common enemy, you may win the glory that no English soldier can deserve more than you. Forgive me if I express badly the emotions which overwhelm me. It is impossible that we shall meet again. One of the few English novels I have tried to read à coups de dictionnaire, was 'Ships that Pass in the Night.' In spite of the great thing that you have done for me, it is inevitable that we should be such passing vessels. It is life. If, as I shall ceaselessly pray, you survive this terrible war, you will follow your destiny as an Englishman of high position and I that which God marks out for me.*

"*I ask you to accept again the expression of my imperishable gratitude. Adieu.*

JEANNE BOISSIÈRE.*"

The more often Doggie read this perfectly phrased epistle, the greater waxed his puzzledom. The gratitude was all there; more than enough. It was gratitude and nothing else. He had longed for a human story telling just how the thing had happened, just how Jeanne had felt. He had wanted her to say: "Get well soon and come back and I'll tell you all about it." But instead of that she dwelt on the difference of their social status, loftily announced that they would never meet again, and that they would follow different destinies, and bade him the *adieu* which in French is the final leave-taking. All of which to Doggie the unsophisticated would have seemed ridiculous, had it not been so tragic. He couldn't reconcile the beautiful letter, written in faultless handwriting and impeccable French, with the rain-swept girl on the escarpment. What did she mean? What had come over her?

But the ways of Jeannes are not the ways of Doggies. How was he to know of the boastings of Phineas McPhail, and the hopelessness with which they filled Jeanne's heart? How was he to know that she had sat up most of the night in her little room over the gateway, drafting and re-drafting this precious composition until, having reduced it to soul-devastating correctitude, and, with aching eyes and head, made a fair and faultless copy, she had once more cried herself into miserable slumber?

At once Doggie called for pad and pencil, and began to write:

"MY DEAR JEANNE. *I don't understand. What fly has stung you?* (Quelle mouche vous a piquée?) *Of course we shall meet again. Do you suppose I am going to let you go out of my life?*"

He sucked his pencil. Jeanne must be spoken to severely.

"*What rubbish are you talking about my social
position? My father was an English parson* (pasteur
anglais), *and yours a French lawyer. If I have a
little money of my own, so have you. And we are not
ships, and we have not passed in the night. And that
we should not meet again is not Life. It is absurdity.
We are going to meet as soon as wounds and war will
let me, and I am not your* 'Cher Monsieur,' *but your*
'Cher Dog-gie,' *and —*"

"Here is a letter for you, brought by hand," said
the nurse, bustling to his bedside.

It was from Peggy.

"Oh, Lord!" said Doggie.

Peggy was there. She had arrived from Durdlebury all alone, the night before, and was putting
up at an hotel. The venerable idiot with red crosses
and bits of tin all over her who seemed to run the
hospital, wouldn't let her in to see him till the regulation visiting hour of three o'clock. That she,
Peggy, was a Dean's daughter who had travelled
hundreds of miles to see the man she was engaged
to, did not seem to impress the venerable idiot in the
least. "*Till three o'clock, then. With love from
Peggy.*"

"The lady, I believe, is waiting for an answer,"
said the nurse.

"Oh, my hat!" said Doggie, below his breath.

To write the answer he had to strip from the
pad the page on which he had begun the letter to
Jeanne. He wrote: "*Dearest Peggy.*" Then the
pencil point's impress through the thin paper stared
at him. Almost every word was decipherable.
Recklessly he tore the pad in half and on a virgin
page scribbled his message to Peggy. The nurse
departed with it. He took up the flimsy sheet
containing his interrupted letter to Jeanne and
glanced at it in dismay. For the first time it struck

him that such words, to a girl even of the lowest intelligence, could only have one interpretation. Doggie said "Oh, Lord!" and "Oh, my hat!" and Oh all sorts of unprintable things that he had learned in the Army. And he put to himself the essential question: What the Hades was he playing at?

Obviously the first thing to do was to destroy the letter to Jeanne and the tell-tale impress. This he forthwith did. He tore the sheets into the tiniest fragments, stretched out his arm to put the handful on the table by the bed, missed his aim and dropped it on the floor. Whereby he incurred the just wrath of the hard-worked nurse.

Again he took up Jeanne's letter. After all, what was wrong with it? He must look at things from her point of view. What had really happened? Let him set out the facts judicially. They had struck up a day or two's friendship. She had told him, as she might have told any decent soul, her sad and romantic story. The English during the great retreat had rendered her unforgetable services. She was a girl of a generously responsive nature. She would pay her debt of gratitude to the English soldier. Her fine *vale* on the memorable night of rain was part payment of her debt to England. Yes. Let him get things in the right perspective. . . . She had made friends with him because he was one of the few private soldiers who could speak her language. It was but natural that she should tell him of the sunken packet. It was one of the most vital facts of her life. But just an outside fact: nothing to do with any shy, mysterious workings of her woman's soul. She might have told the story to any man in the company without derogation from her womanly dignity. And any man Jack of them, having Jeanne's confidence, having the knowledge of the situation of the ruined well, having the God-sent opportunity of recovering the treasure, would, of absolute certainty, have done exactly what he, Doggie, had done. Supposing Mo Shendish had been the privileged person, instead of himself. What, by way of thanks, could Jeanne have written? A letter practically identical.

Practically. A very comfortable sort of word; but Doggie's cultivated mind disliked it. It was a slovenly word, a make-shift for the hard broom of clean thought. This infernal "practically" begged the whole question. Jeanne would not have sentimentalised to Mo Shendish about ships passing in the night. No, she wouldn't, in spite of all his efforts to persuade himself that she would. Well, perhaps dear old Mo was a rough, uneducated sort of chap. He could not have established with Jeanne such delicate relations of friendship as exist between social equals. Obviously the finer shades of her letter would have varied according to the personality of the recipient. Jeanne and himself, owing to the abnormal conditions of war, had suddenly became very intimate friends. The war, as she imagined, must part them for ever. She bade him a touching and dignified farewell, and that was the end of the matter. It had all been an idyllic episode: beginning, middle and end; neatly rounded off; a thing done, and done with — except as a strange romantic memory. It was all over. As long as he remained in the Army, a condition for which, as a private soldier, he was not responsible, how could he see Jeanne again? By the time he re-joined, the regiment would be many miles away from Frélus. This, in her clear, steady way, she realised. Her letter must be final.

It had to be final. Was not Peggy coming at three o'clock?

Again Doggie thought, somewhat wistfully, of the old carefree, full physical life, and again he murmured: "It's all dam' funny!"

Peggy stood for a moment at the door scanning the ward; then, perceiving him, she marched down with defiant glance at nurses and blue-uniformed comrades and men in bed and other strangers, swung a chair and established herself by his bedside.

"You dear old thing, I couldn't bear to think of you lying here alone," she said with the hurry that seeks to cover shyness. "I had to come. Mother's gone *fut* and can't travel, and Dad's running all the parsons' shows in the district. Otherwise one of them would have come too."

"It's awfully good of you, Peggy," he said, with a smile, for fair and flushed, she was pleasant to look upon. "But it must have been a fiendish journey."

"Rotten!" said Peggy. "But that's a trifle. You're the all important thing. Tell me straight. You're not badly hurt, are you?"

"Lord, no," he replied cheerfully. "Just the fleshy part of the leg — a clean bullet wound. Bone touched; but they say I'll be fit quite soon."

"Sure? They're not going to cut off your leg or do anything horrid?"

He laughed. "Sure," said he.

"That's all right."

There was a pause. Now that they had met they seemed to have little to say. She looked around. Presently she remarked:

"Everything looks quite fresh and clean."

"It's perfect."

"Rather public, though," said Peggy.

"Publicity is the paradoxical condition of the private's life," laughed Doggie.

Another pause.

"Well, how are you feeling?"

"First rate," said Doggie. "It's nothing to fuss over. I hope to be out again in a month or two."

"Out where?"

"In France — with the regiment."

Peggy drew a little breath of astonishment and sat up on her chair. His surprising statement seemed to have broken up the atmosphere of restraint.

"Do you mean to say you *want* to go back to the trenches?"

Conscientious Doggie knitted his brows. A fervent "Yes" would proclaim him a modern Paladin eager to slay Huns. Now, as a patriotic Englishman, he loved Huns to be slain, but as the survivor of James Marmaduke Trevor, dilettante expert on the theorbo and the viol da gamba and owner of the peacock and ivory room in Denby Hall, to say nothing of the collector of little china dogs, he could not honestly declare that he enjoyed the various processes of slaying them.

"I can't explain," he replied after a while. "When I was out, I thought I hated every minute of it. Now I look back, I find I've had quite a good time. I've not once really been sick or sorry. For instance, I've often thought myself beastly miserable with wet and mud and east wind — but I've never had even a cold in the head. I never knew how good it was to feel fit. And there are other things. When I left Durdlebury, I hadn't a man friend in the world. Now I have a lot of wonderful pals who would go through Hell for one another — and, for me."

"Tommies?"

"Of course — Tommies."

"You mean gentlemen in the ranks?"

"Not a bit of it. Or yes. All are gentlemen in the ranks. All sorts and conditions of men. The man whom I honour and love more than anyone else, comes from a fish-shop in Hackney. That's the fascinating part of it. Do understand me,

Peggy," he continued, after a short silence, during which she regarded him almost uncomprehendingly. "I don't say I'm yearning to sleep in a filthy dug-out, or to wallow in the ground under shell-fire, or anything of that sort. That's beastly. There's only one other word for it, which begins with the same letter, and the superior kind of private doesn't use it in ladies' society. . . . But while I'm lying here, I wonder what all the other fellows are doing — they're such good chaps — real, true, clean men — out there you seem to get to essentials — all the rest is leather and prunella — and I want to be back among them again. Why should I be in clover while they're in choking dust — a lot of it composed of desiccated Boches?"

"How horrid!" cried Peggy with a little shiver.

"Of course it's horrid. But they've got to stick it, haven't they? And then there's another thing. Out there one hasn't any worries."

Peggy pricked up her ears. "Worries? What kind of worries?"

Doggie became conscious of indiscretion. He temporised.

"Oh, all kinds. Every man with a sort of trained intellect must have them. You remember James Stuart Mill's problem: 'which would you sooner be — a contented hog or a discontented philosopher?' At the front you have all the joys of the contented hog."

Instinctively he stretched out his hand for a cigarette. She bent forward, gripped a matchbox and lit the cigarette for him.

Doggie thanked her politely; but in a dim way he felt conscious of something lacking in her little act of helpfulness. It had been performed with the unsmiling perfunctoriness of the nurse; an act of duty not of tenderness. As she blew out the match, which she did with an odd air of deliberation, her face wore the same expression of hardness it had done on that memorable day when she had refused him her sympathy over the white feather incident.

"I can't understand your wanting to go back at all. Surely you've done your bit," she said.

"No one has done his bit who's alive and able to carry on," replied Doggie.

Peggy reflected. Yes. There was some truth in that. But she thought it rather hard lines on the wounded to be sent back as soon as they were patched up. Most of them hated the prospect. That was why she couldn't understand Doggie's desire.

"Anyhow, it's jolly noble of you, dear old thing," she declared with rather a spasmodic change of manner, "and I'm very proud of you."

"For God's sake, don't go imagining me a hero," cried Doggie in alarm; "for I'm not. I hate the fighting like poison. The only reason I don't run away is because I can't. It would be far more dangerous than standing still. It would mean an officer's bullet through my head at once."

"Any man who is wounded in the defence of his country is a hero," said Peggy, defiantly.

"Rot!" said Doggie.

"And all this time you haven't told me how you got it. How did you?"

Doggie squirmed. The inevitable and dreaded question had come at last.

"I just got sniped when I was out, at night, with a wiring party," he said hurriedly.

"But that's no description at all," she objected.

"I'm afraid it's all I can give," Doggie replied. Then, by way of salve to a sensitive conscience, he added: "There was nothing brave or heroic about it, at all — just a silly accident. It was as safe as tying up hollyhocks in a garden. Only an idiot

Boche let off his gun on spec and got me. Don't let us talk about it."

But Peggy was insistent. "I'm not such a fool as not to know what mending barbed wire at night means. And whatever you may say, you got wounded in the service of your country."

It was on Doggie's agitated lips to shout a true "I didn't!" For that was the devil of it. Had he been so wounded, he could have purred contentedly while accepting the genuine hero's meed of homage and consolation. But he had left his country's service to enter that of Jeanne. In her service he had been shot through the leg. He had no business to be wounded at all. Jeanne saw that very clearly. To have exposed himself to the risk of his exploit was contrary to all his country's interests. His wound had robbed her of a fighting man, not a particularly valuable warrior, but a soldier in the firing line all the same. If every man went off like that on private missions of his own and got properly potted, there would be the end of the army. It was horrible to be an interesting hero under false pretences.

Of course he might have been George-Washingtonian enough to shout: "I cannot tell a lie. I didn't." But that would have meant relating the whole story of Jeanne. And would Peggy have understood the story of Jeanne? Could Peggy, in her plain-sailing, breezy British way, have appreciated all the subtleties of his relations with Jeanne? She would ask pointed, probably barbed, questions about Jeanne. She would tear the whole romance to shreds. Jeanne stood too exquisite a symbol for him to permit the sacrilege of Peggy's ruthless vivisection. For vivisect she would, without shadow of doubt. His long and innocent familiarity with womankind in Durdlebury had led him instinctively to the conclusion formulated by one of the world's great cynics in his advice to a young man: "If you care for happiness, never speak to a woman about another woman."

Doggie felt uncomfortable as he looked into Peggy's clear blue eyes; not conscience-stricken at the realisation of himself as a scoundrelly Don Juan — that never entered his ingenuous mind; but he hated his enforced departure from veracity. The one virtue that had dragged the toy Pom successfully along the Rough Road of the soldier's life was his uncompromising attitude to Truth. It cost him a sharp struggle with his soul to reply to Peggy:—

"All right. Have it so if it pleases you, my dear. But it was an idiot fluke all the same."

"I wonder if you know how you've changed," she said, after a while.

"For better or worse?"

"The obvious thing to say would be 'for the better.' But I wonder. Do you mind if I'm frank?"

"Not a bit."

"There's something hard about you, Marmaduke."

Doggie wrinkled lips and brow in a curious smile. "I'll be frank too. You see, I've been living among men instead of a pack of old women."

"I suppose that's it," Peggy said thoughtfully.

"It's a dud sort of place, Durdlebury," said he.

"Dud?"

He laughed. "It never goes off."

"You used to say, in your letters, that you longed for it."

"Perhaps I do now — in a way. I don't know."

"I bet you'll settle down there, after the war, just as though nothing had happened."

"I wonder," said Doggie.

"Of course you will. Do you remember our plans for the reconstruction of Denby Hall, which were knocked on the head? All that'll have to be gone into again."

"That doesn't mean that we need curl ourselves up there forever like caterpillars in a cabbage."

She arched her eyebrows. "What would you like to do?"

"I think I'll want to go round and round the world till I'm dizzy."

At this amazing pronouncement from Marmaduke Trevor, Peggy gasped. It also astonished Doggie himself. He had not progressed so far on the road to self-emancipation as to dream of a rupture of his engagement. His marriage was as much a decree of destiny as had been his enlistment when he walked to Peter Pan's statue in Kensington Gardens. But the war had made the prospect a distant one. In the vague future he would marry and settle down. But now Peggy brought it into alarming nearness, thereby causing him considerable agitation. To go back to vegetation in Durdlebury, even with so desirable a companion cabbage as Peggy, just when he was beginning to conjecture what there might be of joy and thrill in life — the thought dismayed him; and the sudden dismay found expression in his rhetorical outburst.

"Oh, if you want to travel for a year or two, I'm all for it," cried Peggy. "I can't say I've seen much of the world. But we'll soon get sick of it and yearn for home. There'll be lots of things to do. We'll take up our position as county people — no more of the stuffy old women you're so down on — and you'll get into Parliament and sit on committees, and so on, and altogether we'll have a topping time."

Doggie had an odd sensation that a stranger spoke through Peggy's familiar lips. Well, perhaps, not a stranger, but a half-forgotten dead and gone acquaintance.

"Don't you think the war will change things — if it hasn't changed them already?"

"Not a bit," Peggy replied. "Dad's always talking learnedly about social reconstruction, whatever that means. But if people have got money and position and all that sort of thing, who's going to take it away from them? You don't suppose we're all going to turn socialists and pool the wealth of the country, and everybody's going to live in a garden-city and wear sandals and eat nuts?"

"Of course not," said Doggie.

"Well, how are people like ourselves going to feel any difference in what you call social conditions?"

Doggie lit another cigarette, chiefly in order to gain time for thought; but an odd instinct made him secure the matchbox before he picked out the cigarette. Superficially Peggy's proposition was incontrovertible. Unless there happened some social cataclysm involving a newly democratised world in ghastly chaos, which, after all, was a remote possibility, the externals of gentle life would undergo very slight modification. Yet there was something fundamentally wrong in Peggy's conception of post-war existence. Something wrong in essentials. Now, a critical attitude towards Peggy, whose presence was a proof of her splendid loyalty, seemed hateful. But there was something wrong, all the same. Something wrong in Peggy herself that put her into opposition. In one aspect, she was the pre-war Peggy, with her cut and dried little social ambitions, and her definite projects of attainment; but in another she was not. The pre-war Peggy had swiftly turned into the patriotic English girl who had hounded him into the army. He found himself face to face with an amorphous, characterless sort of Peggy whom he did not know. It was perplexing, baffling. Before he could formulate an idea, she went on:

"You silly old thing, what change is there likely to be? What change is there now, after all? There's a scarcity of men. Naturally. They're out fighting. But when they come home on leave, life goes on just the same as before — tennis parties, little dances, dinners. Of course, lots of people are hard hit. Did I tell you that Jack Pounceby was killed — the only son? The war's awful and dreadful, I know — but if we don't go through with it cheerfully, what's the good of us?"

"I think I'm pretty cheerful," said Doggie.

"Oh, you're not grousing and you're making the best of it. You're perfectly splendid. But you're philosophising such a lot over it. The only thing before us is to do in Germany, Prussian militarism, and so on, and then there'll be peace, and we'll all be happy again."

"Have you met many men who say that?" he asked.

"Heaps. Oliver was talking about it only the other day."

"Oliver?"

At his quick challenge he could not help noticing a little cloud, as of vexation, pass over her face.

"Yes, Oliver," she replied with an unnecessary air of defiance. "He has been over here on short leave. Went back a fortnight ago. He's as cheerful as cheerful can be. Jollier than ever he was. I took him out in the dear old two-seater, and he insisted on driving to show how they drove at the front — and it's only because the Almighty must have kept a special eye on a Dean's daughter that I'm here to tell the tale."

"You saw a lot of him, I suppose," said Doggie.

A flush rose on Peggy's cheek. "Of course. He was staying at the Deanery most of his time. I wrote to you about it. I've made a point of telling you everything. I even told you about the two-seater."

"So you did," said Doggie. "I remember."

He smiled. "Your description made me laugh. Oliver's a Major now, isn't he?"

"Yes. And just before he got his Majority they gave him the Military Cross."

"He must be an awful swell," said Doggie.

She replied with some heat. "He hasn't changed the least little bit in the world."

Doggie shook his head. "No one can go through it, really go through it, and come back the same."

"You don't insinuate that Oliver hasn't really gone through it?"

"Of course not, Peggy dear. They don't throw M. C.'s about like Iron Crosses. In order to get it Oliver must have looked into the jaws of Hell. They all do. But no man is the same afterwards. Oliver has what the French call *panache* —"

"What's *panache*?"

"The real heroic swagger — something spiritual about it. Oliver's not going to let you notice the change in him."

"We saw 'The Bing Boys' at the Alhambra, and he laughed as if such a thing as war had never been heard of."

"Naturally," said Doggie. "All that's part of the *panache*."

"You're talking through your hat, Marmaduke," she exclaimed with some irritation. "Oliver's a straight, clean, English soldier."

"I've been doing my best to tell you so," said Doggie.

"But you seem to be criticising him because he's concealing something behind what you call his *panache*."

"Not criticising, dear. Only stating. I think I'm more Oliverian than you."

"I'm not Oliverian," cried Peggy, with burning cheeks. "And I don't see why we should discuss him like this. All I said was that Oliver, who has made himself a distinguished man and will be even more distinguished, and, at any rate, knows what he's talking about, doesn't worry his head with social reconstruction and all that sort of rot. I've come here to talk about you, not about Oliver. Let us leave him out of the question."

"Willingly," said Doggie. "I never had any reason to love Oliver; but I must do him justice. I only wanted to show you that he must be a bigger man than you imagine."

"I'm glad to hear you say so," cried Peggy, with a flash of the eyes. "I hope it's true."

"The war's such a whacking big thing, you see," he said with a conciliatory smile. "No one can prophesy exactly what's going to come out of it. But the whole of human society . . . the world, the whole of civilisation is being stirred up like a Christmas pudding. The war's bound to change the trend of all human thought. There must be an entire rearrangement of social values."

"I'm sorrry, but I don't see it," said Peggy.

Doggie again wrinkled his brow and looked at her, and she returned his glance stonily.

"You think I'm mulish."

She had interpreted Doggie's thought, but he raised a hand in protest.

"No, no."

"Yes, yes. Every man looks at a woman like that when he thinks her a mule or an idiot. We get to learn it in our cradles. But in spite of your superior wisdom, I know I'm right. After the war there won't be a bit of change, really. A duke will be a duke and a costermonger a costermonger."

"These are extreme cases. The duke may remain a duke but he won't be such a little tin god on wheels. He'll find himself in the position of a democratic viscount. And the costermonger will rise to the political position of an important tradesman. But between the two there'll be any old sort of flux."

"Did you learn all this horrible, rank socialism in France?"

"Perhaps, but it seems so obvious."

"It's only because you've been living among Tommies, who've got these stupid ideas into their heads. If you had been living among your social equals —"

"In Durdlebury?"

She flashed rebellion. "Yes. In Durdlebury. Why not?"

"I'm afraid, Peggy dear," he said, with his patient, pleasant smile, "you are rather sheltered from the war in Durdlebury."

She cried out indignantly.

"Indeed we're not. The newspapers come to Durdlebury, don't they? And everybody's doing something. We have the war all around us. We've even succeeded in getting wounded soldiers in the Cottage Hospital. Nancy Murdoch is a V. A. D. and scrubs floors. Cissy James is driving a Y. M. C. A. motor car in Calais. Jane Brown-Gore is nursing in Salonika. We read all their letters. Personally I can't do much because mother has crocked up and I've got to run the Deanery. But I'm slaving from morning to night. Only last week I got up a concert for the wounded. Alone I did it — and it takes some doing in Durdlebury, now that you're away and the Musical Association has perished of inanition. Old Dr. Flint's no earthly good, since Tom, the eldest son, you remember, was killed in Mesopotamia. So I did it all, and it was a great success. We netted four hundred and seventy pounds. And whenever I can get a chance, I go round the hospital and talk and read to the men and write their letters, and hear of everything. I don't think you've any right to say we're out of touch with the war. In a sort of way I know as much about it as you do."

Doggie in some perplexity scratched his head, a thing which he would never have done at Durdlebury. With humorous intent he asked:

"Do you know as much as Oliver?"

"Oliver's a field officer," she replied tartly, and Doggie felt snubbed. "But I'm sure he agrees with everything I say." She paused and, in a different tone, went on: "Don't you think it's rather rotten to have this piffling argument when I've come all this long way to see you?"

"Forgive me, Peggy," he said penitently. "I appreciate your coming more than I can say."

She was not appeased. "And yet you don't give me credit for playing the game."

"What game?" he asked with a smile.

"Surely you ought to know."

He reached out his hand and took hers. "Am I worth it, Peggy?"

Her lips twitched and tears stood in her eyes.

"I don't know what you mean?"

"Neither do I, quite," he replied simply. "But it seems that I'm a Tommy through and through, and that I'll never get Tommy out of my soul."

"That's nothing to be ashamed of," she declared stoutly.

"Of course not. But it makes one see all sorts of things in a different light."

"Oh, don't worry your head about that," she said, with pathetic misunderstanding. "We'll put you all right as soon as we get you back to Durdlebury. I suppose you won't refuse to come this time."

"Yes; I'll come this time," said Doggie.

So he promised, and the talk drifted on to casual lines. She gave him the mild chronicle of the sleepy town, described plays which she had seen on her rare visits to London, sketched out a programme for his all too short visit to the Deanery.

"And in the meanwhile," she remarked, "try to get these morbid ideas out of your silly old head."

Time came for parting. She rose and shook hands.

"Don't think I've said anything in depreciation of Tommies. I understand them thoroughly. They're wonderful fellows. Good-bye, old boy. Get well soon."

She kissed her hand to him at the door and was gone.

It was now that Doggie began to hate himself. For all the time that Peggy had been running on, eager to convince him that his imputation of aloofness from the war was undeserved, the voice of one who, knowing its splendours and its terrors, had pierced to the heart of its mysteries, rang in his ears.

"*Leur gaieté fait peur.*"

CHAPTER XIX

THE X-rays showed the tiniest splinter of bone in Doggie's thigh. The surgeon fished it up and the clean wound healed rapidly. The gloomy Penworthy's prognostication had not come true. Doggie would not stump about at ease on a wooden leg; but in all probability would soon find himself back in the firing line — a prospect which brought great cheer to Penworthy. Also to Doggie. For, in spite of the charm of the pretty hospital, the health-giving sea air, the long rest for body and nerves life seemed flat and unprofitable.

He had written a gay, irreproachable letter to Jeanne, to which Jeanne, doubtless thinking it the last word of the episode, had not replied. Loyalty to Peggy forbade further thought of Jeanne. He must henceforward think of Peggy and her sturdy faithfulness as hard as he could. But the more he thought, the more remote did Peggy seem. Of course the publicity of the interview had invested it with a certain constraint, knocked out of it any approach to sentimentality or romance. They had not even kissed. They had spent most of the time arguing from different points of view. They had been near to quarrelling. It was outrageous of him to criticise her; yet how could he help it? The mere fact of striving to exalt her was a criticism.

Indeed they were far apart. Into the sensitive soul of Doggie the war in all its meaning had passed. The soul of Peggy had remained untouched. To her, in her sheltered corner of England, it was a ghastly accident, like a railway collision blocking the traffic on her favourite line. For the men of her own class who took part in it, it was a brave adventure; for the common soldier, a sad but patriotic necessity. If circumstances had allowed her to go forth into the war-world, as nurse or canteen helper at a London terminus, or motor driver in France, her horizon would have broadened. But the contact with realities into which her dilettante little war activities brought her, was too slight to make the deep impression. In her heart, as far as she revealed herself to Doggie, she resented the war because it interfered with her own definitely marked out scheme of existence. The war over, she would regard it politely as a thing that had never been, and would forthwith set to work upon her aforesaid interrupted plan. And towards a comprehension of this apparent serenity the perplexed mind of Doggie groped with ill success. All his old values had been kicked into higgledy-piggledy confusion. All hers remained steadfast.

So Doggie reflected with some grimness that there are rougher roads than those which lead to the trenches.

A letter from Phineas did not restore equanimity. It ran:

"My dear Laddie,

"Our unsophisticated friend, Mo, and myself are writing this letter together, and he bids me begin it by saying that he hopes it finds you as it leaves us at present, in a muck of dust and perspiration. Where we are now I must not tell, for (in the opinion of the Censor) you would reveal it to the Very Reverend the Dean of Durdlebury, who would naturally telegraph the information to the Kaiser. But the Division is far, far from the idyllic land of your dreams, and there is bloody fighting ahead of us. And though the hearts of Mo and me go out to you, laddie, and though we miss you sore, yet Mo says he's blistering glad you're

*out of it and safe in your perishing bed with a Blighty
one. And such, in more academic phraseology, are
the sentiments of your old friend Phineas.*

"*Ah, laddie! it was a bad day when we marched
from the old billets; for the word had gone round that
we weren't going back. I had taken the liberty of
telling the lassie ye ken of something about your private
position and your worldly affairs, of which it seems
you had left her entirely ignorant. Of course, with
my native Scottish caution, and my knowledge of
human nature gained in the academies of prosperity
and the ragged schools of adversity, I did not touch on
certain matters of a delicate nature. That is no business of mine. If there is discretion in this world in
which you can trust blindly, it is that of Phineas
McPhail. I just told her of Denby Hall and your
fortune, which I fairly accurately computed at a
couple of million francs. For I thought it was right
she should know that you weren't just a scallywag
private soldier like the rest of us. And I am bound
to say that the lassie was considerably impressed. In
further conversation I told her something of your early
life, and, though not over desirous of blackening my
character in her bonnie eyes, I let her know what kind
of an injudicious upbringing you had been compelled
to undergo. 'Il a été élevé,' said I, 'dans —' What
the blazes was the French for cotton-wool? The war
has a pernicious effect on one's memory — I sometimes even forget the elementary sensations of inebriety
— 'Dans la ouate,' she said. And I remembered
the word, 'Oui, dans la ouate,' said I. And she
looked at me, laddie, or, rather, through me, out of her
great, dark eyes — you mind the way she treats your
substance as a shadow and looks through it at the
shadows that to her are substances — and she said
below her breath — I don't think she meant me to hear
it — 'Et c'est lui qui a fait cela pour moi.'*

"*Mo, in his materialistic way, is clamorous that I*

*should tell you about the chicken; the which, being
symbolical, I proceed to do. It was our last day. She
invited us to lunch in the kitchen, and shut the door
so that none of the hungry varlets of the company should
stick in their unmannerly noses and whine for scraps.
And there, laddie, was an omelette and cutlets and a
chicken and a* fromage à la crème *such as in the days
of my vanity I have never eaten, cooked by the old
body whose soul you won with a pinch of snuff. The
poor lassie could scarcely eat; but Mo saw that there
was nothing left. The bones on his plate looked as if
a dog had been at them for a week. And there was
vintage Haut Sauterne which ran down one's throat
like scented gold. 'Man,' said I to Mo, 'if you lap
it up like that, you'll be as drunk as Noah.' So he
cast a frightened glance at Mademoiselle, and sipped
like a young lady at a christening party. Then she
brings out cherries and plums and peaches, and opens
a half bottle of champagne and fills all our glasses, and
Toinette had a glass; and she rises in the pale, dignified,
Greek tragedy way she has, and she makes a wee bit
speech. 'Messieurs,' she said, 'perhaps you may
wonder why I have invited you. But I think you
understand. It is the only way I had of sharing with
Doggie's friends the fortune that he had so heroically
brought me. It is but a little tribute of my gratitude
to Doggie. You are his friends and I wish well that
you would be mine —* très franchement, très loyale-
ment.' *She put out her hand and we shook it. And
old Mo said, 'Miss, I'd go to Hell for you!' Whereupon the little red spot you may have seen for yourself
came into her pale cheek, and a soft look like a flitting
moonbeam crept into her eyes. Laddie, if I'm waxing
too poetical, just consider that Mademoiselle Jeanne
Boissière is not the ordinary woman the British private
soldier is in the habit of consorting with. Then she
took up her glass. 'Je vais porter un toast — Vive
l'Angleterre!' And although a Scotsman, I drank*

it as if it applied to me.   And then she cried 'Vive la
France!'   *And old Toinette cried* 'Vive la France!'
*And they looked transfigured, and I fairly itched to
sing the Marseillaise, though I knew I couldn't.
Then she chinked glasses with us —*

"'Bonne chance, mes amis!'

"*And then she made a sign to the auld wife, who
added the few remaining drops to our glasses.* 'To
Doggie!' *said Mademoiselle.   We drank the toast,
laddie.   Old Mo began in his cracked voice,* 'For he's
a jolly good fellow.' *I kicked him and told him to
shut up.   But Mademoiselle said:*

"'*I've heard of that.   It is a ceremony.   I like it.
Continue.*'

"*So Mo and I held up our glasses and, in indifferent
song, proclaimed you what the Army, developing
certain rudimentary germs, has made you, and Mademoiselle too held up her glass and threw back her head
and joined us in the Hip, hip, hoorays.   It would have
done your heart good, laddie, to have been there to see.
But we did you proud.*

"*When we emerged from the festival, the prettiest
which, in the course of a variegated career, I have ever
attended, Mo says:*

"'*If I hadn't a gel at home* —'

"'*If you hadn't got a girl at home,*' *said I,* '*you'd
be the next damnedest fool in the army to Phineas
McPhail!*'

"*We marched out just before dusk, and there she
was by the front door; and though she stood proud and
upright, and smiled with her lips and blew us kisses
with both hands, to which the boys all responded with
a cheer, there were tears streaming down her cheeks —
and the tears, laddie, were not for Mo, or me, or anyone
of us ugly beggars that passed her by.*

"*I also have good news for you, in that I hear from
the thunderous, though excellent, Sergeant Ballinghall
there is a probability that when you rejoin, the C. O.*

*will be afflicted with a grievous lapse of memory, and
that he will be persuaded that you received your wound
during the attack on the wiring party.*

*"As I said before, laddie, we're all like the Scots
wha hae wi' Wallace bled, and are going to our gory
bed or to victory. Possibly both. But I will remain
steadfast to my philosophy, and if I am condemned to
the said sanguinolent couch, I will do my best to derive
from it the utmost enjoyment possible. All kinds of
poets and such like lusty loons have shed their last drop
of ink in the effort to describe the Pleasures of Life —
but it will be reserved for the disembodied spirit of
Phineas McPhail to write the great philosophic
Poem of the World's History, which will be entitled
'The Pleasures of Death.' While you're doing nothing,
laddie, you might bestir yourself and find an enlightened
Publisher, who would be willing to give me an ante-
mortem advance, in respect of royalties accruing to
my ghost.*

*"Mo, to whom I have read the last paragraph, says
he always knew that eddication affected the brain.
With which incontrovertible proposition and our joint
love, I now conclude this epistle.*

Yours, PHINEAS.*"*

"Of all the blazing imbeciles!" Doggie cried aloud.
Why the unprintable unprintableness couldn't
Phineas mind his own business? Why had he given
his silly accident of fortune away in this childish
manner? Why had he told Jeanne of his cotton-wool
upbringing? His feet, even that of his wounded leg,
tingled to kick Phineas. Of course Jeanne, knowing
him now to be such a gilded ass, would have nothing
more to do with him. It explained her letter. He
damned Phineas to all eternity, in terms compared
with which the curse of Saint Ernulphus enunciated
by the late Mr. Shandy was a fantastic benediction.
"If I had a dog, quoth my Uncle Toby, I would not

curse him so." But if Uncle Toby had heard Doggie of the Twentieth Century Armies, who also swore terribly in Flanders, for "dog" he would have substituted "rattlesnake" or "German officer."

Yet such is the quiddity of the English Tommy, that through this devastating anathema ran a streak of love which at the end turned the whole thing into forlorn derision. And as soon as he could laugh, he saw things in a clear light. Both of his two friends were, in their respective ways, in love with his wonderful Jeanne. Both of them were steel-true to him. It was just part of their loyalty to foment this impossible romance between Jeanne and himself. If the three of them were now at Frélus, the two idiots would be playing gooseberry with the smirking conscientiousness of a pair of schoolgirls. So Doggie forgave the indiscretion. After all, what did it matter?

It mattered, however, to this extent, that he read the letter over and over again until he knew it by heart, and could picture to himself every phase of the banquet and every fleeting look on Jeanne's face.

"All this," he declared at last, "is utterly ridiculous." And he tore up Phineas's letter and, during his convalescence, devoted himself to the study of European politics, a subject which he had scandalously neglected during his elegantly leisured youth.

The day of his discharge came in due course. A suit of khaki took the place of the hospital blue. He received his papers, the seven days' sick furlough, and his railway warrant, shook hands with nurses and comrades, and sped to Durdlebury in the third-class carriage of the Tommy.

Peggy, in the two-seater, was waiting for him in the station yard. He exchanged greetings from afar, grinned, waved a hand, and jumped in beside her.

"How jolly of you to meet me!"

"Where's your luggage?"

"Luggage?"

It seemed to be a new word.   He had not heard it for many months. He laughed.

"Haven't got any, thank God! If you knew what it was to hunch a horrible canvas sausage of kit about, you'd appreciate feeling free."

"It's a mercy you've got Peddle," said Peggy. "He has been at the Deanery fixing things up for you for the last two days."

"I wonder if I shall be able to live up to Peddle," said Doggie.

"Who's going to start the car?" she asked.

"Oh, Lord!" he cried, and bolted out and turned the crank. "I'm awfully sorry," he added, when, the engine running, he resumed his place. "I had forgotten all about these pretty things. Out there a car is a sacred chariot set apart for gods in brass hats, and the ordinary Tommy looks on them with awe and reverence."

"Can't you forget you're a Tommy for a few days?" she said, as soon as the car had cleared the station gates and was safely under way.

He noted a touch of irritation. "All right, Peggy dear," said he. "I'll do what I can."

"Oliver's here, with his man Chipmunk," she remarked, her eyes on the road.

"Oliver? On leave again? How has he managed it?"

"You'd better ask him," she replied tartly. "All I know is that he turned up yesterday, and he's staying with us. That's why I don't want you to ram the fact of your being a Tommy down everybody's throat."

He laughed at the queer little social problem that seemed to be worrying her. "I think you'll find blood is thicker than military etiquette. After all, Oliver's my first cousin. If he can't get on with me, he can get out." To change the conversation, he added after a pause: "The little car's running splendidly."

They swept through the familiar old-world streets, which, now that the early frenzy of mobilising Territorials and training of new Armies was over, had resumed more or less their pre-war appearance. The sleepy meadows by the river, once ground into black slush by guns and ammunition waggons and horses, were now green again and idle, and the troops once billeted on the citizens had marched Heaven knows whither — many to Heaven itself — or whatever Paradise is reserved for the great-hearted English fighting man who has given his life for England. Only here and there a stray soldier on leave, or one of the convalescents from the cottage hospital, struck an incongruous note of war. They drew up at the door of the Deanery under the shadow of the grey cathedral.

"Thank God that is out of reach of the Boche," said Doggie, regarding it with a new sense of its beauty and spiritual significance. "To think of it like Rheims or Arras — I've seen Arras — seen a shell burst among the still standing ruins. Oh, Peggy — " he gripped her arm —"you dear people haven't the remotest conception of what it all is — what France has suffered. Imagine this mass of wonder all one horrible stone pie, without a trace of what it once had been."

"I suppose we're jolly lucky," she replied.

The door was opened by the old butler, who had been on the alert for the arrival.

"You run in," said Peggy. "I'll take the car round to the yard."

So Doggie, with a smile and a word of greeting, entered the Deanery. His uncle appeared in the hall, florid, whitehaired, benevolent, and extended both hands to the home-come warrior.

"My dear boy, how glad I am to see you. Welcome back. And how's the wound? We've thought night and day of you. If I could have spared the time, I should have run up north, but I've not a minute to call my own. We're doing our share of war work here, my boy. Come into the drawing-room."

He put his hand affectionately on Doggie's arm and, opening the drawing-room door, pushed him in and stood, in his kind, courtly way, until the young man had passed the threshold. Mrs. Conover, feeble from illness, rose and kissed him, and gave him much the same greeting as her husband. Then a tall, lean figure in uniform, who had remained in the background by the fireplace, advanced with outstretched hand.

"Hello, old chap!"

Doggie took the hand in an honest grip.

"Hello, Oliver!"

"How goes it?"

"Splendid," said Doggie. "You all right?"

"Top hole," said Oliver. He clapped his cousin on the shoulder. "My hat! you do look fit." He turned to the Dean. "Uncle Edward, isn't he a hundred times the man he was?"

"I told you, my boy, you would see a difference," said the Dean.

Peggy ran in, having delivered over the two-seater to myrmidons.

"Now that the affecting meeting is over, let us have tea. Oliver, ring the bell."

The tea came. It appeared to Doggie, handing round the three-tiered silver cake-stand, that he had returned to some forgotten former incarnation. The delicate china cup in his hand seemed too frail for the material usages of life, and he feared lest he should break it with rough handling. Old habit, however, prevailed, and no one noticed his sense of awkwardness. The talk lay chiefly between Oliver and himself. They exchanged experiences as to dates and localities. They bandied about the names of places which will be inscribed in letters of blood in history for all time, as though they were popular golf-courses. Both had known Ypres, and Plug Street, and the famous wall at Arras where the British and German trenches were but five yards apart. Oliver's division had gone down to the Somme in July for the great push.

"I ought to be there now," said Oliver. "I feel a hulking slacker and fraud, being home on sick leave. But the M. O. said I had just escaped shell-shock by the skin of my nerves, and they packed me home for a fortnight to rest up — while the regiment, what there's left of it, went into reserve."

"Did you get badly cut up?" asked Doggie.

"Rather. We broke through all right. Then machine guns which we had overlooked, got us in the back. Luckily they were spotted in time, and done in by the artillery, or not a soul would have come back."

"My lot's down there now," said Doggie.

"You're well out of it, old chap," laughed Oliver.

For the first time in his life Doggie began really to like Oliver. The old-time, swashbuckling swagger had gone — the swagger of one who would say: "I am the only live man in this comatose crowd. I am the dare-devil buccaneer who defies the thunder and sleeps on boards while the rest of you are lying soft in feather-beds." His direct, cavalier way he still retained; but the Army, with the omnipotent might of its inherited traditions, had moulded him to its pattern; even as it had moulded Doggie. And Doggie, who had learned many of the lessons in human psychology which the Army teaches, knew that Oliver's genial, familiar talk was not all due to his appreciation of their social equality in the bosom of their own family, but that he would have treated much the same any Tommy into whose companionship he had been casually thrown. The Tommy would have said "Sir" very scrupulously, which on Doggie's part would have been an idiotic thing to do; but they would have got on famously together, bound by the freemasonry of fighting men who had cursed the same foe for the same reasons. So Oliver stood out before Doggie's eyes in a new light, that of the typical officer, trusted and beloved by his men, and his heart went out to him.

"I've brought Chipmunk over," said Oliver. "You remember the freak? The poor devil hasn't had a day's leave for a couple of years. Didn't want it. Why should he go and waste money in a country where he didn't know a human being? But this time I've fixed it up for him, and his leave is co-terminous with mine. He has been my servant all through. If they took him away from me, he'd be quite capable of strangling the C. O. He's a funny beggar."

"And what kind of a soldier?" the Dean asked politely.

"There's not a finer one in all the armies of the earth," said Oliver.

After much further talk the dressing gong boomed softly through the house.

"You've got the Green Room, Marmaduke," said Peggy. "The one with the Chippendale stuff you used to covet so much."

"I haven't got much to change into," laughed Doggie.

"You'll find Peddle up there waiting for you," she replied.

And when Doggie entered the Green Room, there he found Peddle, who welcomed him with tears of joy and a display of all the finikin luxuries of the toilet and adornment which he had left behind at

Denby Hall. There were pots of pomade and face-
cream, and nail polish; bottles of hair-wash and
tooth-wash; little boxes and brushes for the moustache; half-a-dozen gleaming razors; the array of
brushes and combs and manicure set in tortoise-
shell with his crest in silver; the bottles of scent
with spray attachments; the onyx bowl of bath
salts beside the hip-bath ready to be filled from the
ewers of hot and cold water — the Deanery, old-
fashioned house, had but one family bath-room;
the deep-purple, silk dressing-gown over the foot-
rail of the bed; the silk pyjamas in a lighter shade
spread out over the pillow; the silk underwear and
soft-fronted shirt fitted with his ruby and diamond
sleeve-links, hung up before the fire to air; the
dinner jacket suit laid out on the glass-topped
Chippendale table, with black tie and delicate
handkerchief; the silk socks carefully tucked inside
out, the glossy pumps with the silver shoe-horn
laid across them.

"My God! Peddle," cried Doggie, scratching his
closely cropped head. "What the devil's all this?"

Peddle, grey, bent, uncomprehending, regarded
him blankly.

"All what, sir?"

"I only want to wash my hands," said Doggie.

"But aren't you going to dress for dinner, sir?"

"A private soldier's not allowed to wear mufti,
Peddle. They'd dock me of a week's pay if they
found out."

"Who's to find out, sir?"

"There's Mr. Oliver — he's a major."

"Lord, Mr. Marmaduke, I don't think he'd mind.
Miss Peggy gave me my orders, sir, and I think you
can leave things to her."

"All right, Peddle," he laughed. "If it's Miss
Peggy's decree, I'll change. I've got all I want."

"Are you sure you can manage, sir?" Peddle

asked anxiously, for time was when Doggie couldn't
stick his legs into his trousers unless Peddle held
them out for him.

"Quite," said Doggie.

"It seems rather roughing it here, Mr. Marmaduke,
after what you've been accustomed to at the Hall."

"That's so," said Doggie. "And it's martyrdom
compared with what it is in the trenches. There
we always have a Major-General to lace up our
boots, and a Field-Marshal's always hovering round
to light our cigarettes."

Peddle, who had never known him to jest, or his
father before him, went out in a muddled frame of
mind, leaving Doggie to struggle into his dress
trousers as best he might.

CHAPTER XX

WHEN Doggie, in dinner suit, went down-stairs, he found Peggy alone in the draw-ing room. She gave him the kiss of one accustomed to kiss him from childhood, and sat. down again on the fender-stool.

"Now you look more like a Christian gentleman," she laughed. "Confess. It's much more comfort-able than your wretched private's uniform."

"I'm not quite so sure," he said, somewhat ruefully, indicating his dinner jacket tightly con-stricted beneath the arms. "Already I've had to slit my waistcoat down the back. Poor old Peddle will have an apopleptic fit when he sees it. I've grown a bit since these elegant rags were made for me."

"*Il faut souffrir pour être beau*," said Peggy.

"If my being *beau* pleases you, Peggy, I'll suffer gladly. I've been in tighter places." He threw himself down in the corner of the sofa and joggled up and down like a child. "After all," he said, "it's jolly to sit on something squashy again, and to see a pretty girl in a pretty frock."

"I'm glad you like this frock."

"New?"

She nodded. "Dad said it was too much of a Vanity Fair of a vanity for war-time. You don't think so, do you?"

"It's charming," said Doggie. "A treat for tired eyes."

"That's just what I told Dad. What's the good of women dressing in sacks tied round the middle with a bit of string? When men come home from.

the front, they want to see their womenfolk looking pretty and dainty. That's what they've come over for. It's part of the cure. It's the first time you've been a real dear, Marmaduke. 'A treat for tired eyes.' I'll rub it into Dad hard."

Oliver came in — in khaki. Doggie jumped up and pointed to him.

"Look here, Peggy. It's the guard-room for me."

Oliver laughed. "Where the dinner kit I bought when I came home is now, God only can tell." He turned to Peggy. "I did change, you know."

"That's the pull of being a beastly Major," said Doggie. "They have heaps of suits. On the march, there are motor lorries full of them. It's the scandal of the army. The wretched Tommy has but one suit to his name. That's why, sir, I've taken the liberty of appearing before you in outgrown mufti."

"All right, my man," said Oliver. "We'll hush it up and say no more about it."

Then the Dean and Mrs. Conover entered, and soon they went in to dinner. It was for Doggie the most pleasant of meals. He had the superbly healthy man's whole-hearted or whole-stomached appreciation of unaccustomed good food|and drink: so much so, that when the Dean, after agonies of thwarted mastication, said gently to his wife: "My dear, don't you think you might speak a word in season to Peck" — Peck being the butcher — "and, forbid him, under the Defence of the Realm Act, if you like, to deliver to us in the evening as lamb that which was in the morning a lusty sheep?" he stared at the good old man as though he were Vitellius in person. Tough? It was like milk-fatted baby. He was already devouring, like Oliver, his second helping. Then the Dean, pledging him and Oliver in champagne, apologised: "I'm sorry, my dear boys, the 1904 has run out and there's no more to be got.   But the 1906, though not having the quality, is quite drinkable."

Drinkable!   It was laughing, dancing joy that went down his throat.

So much for gross delights.   There were others — finer.   The charm to the eye of the table with its exquisite napery and china and glass and silver and flowers.   The almost intoxicating atmosphere of peace and gentle living.   The full, loving welcome shining from the eye of the kind old Dean, his uncle by marriage, and of the faded, delicate lady, his own flesh and blood, his mother's sister.   And Peggy, pretty, flushed, bright-eyed, radiant in her new dress.   And there was Oliver. . . .

Most of all he appreciated Oliver's comrade-like attitude.   It was a recognition of him as a man and a soldier.   In the course of dinner talk Oliver said: —

"J. M. T. and I have looked Death in the face many a time — and really he's a poor raw-head and bloody-bones sort of Bogey;   don't you think so, old chap?"

"It all depends on whether you've got a funk-hole handy," he replied.

But that was mere lightness of speech.   Oliver's inclusion of him in his remark shook him to the depths of his sensitive nature.   The man who despises the petty feelings and frailties of mankind is doomed to remain in awful ignorance of that which is of beauty and pathos in the lives of his fellow-creatures.   After all, what did it matter what Oliver thought of him?   Who was Oliver?   His cousin — accident of birth — the black sheep of the family; now a Major in a different regiment and a different division.   What was Oliver to him or he to Oliver?   He had "made good" in the eyes of one whose judgment had been forged keen and absolute by heroic sorrows.   What did anyone else matter?

But to Doggie the supreme joy of the evening was the knowledge that he had made good in the eyes of Oliver. Oliver wore on his tunic the white mauve and white ribbon of the Military Cross. Honour where honour was due. But he, Doggie, had been wounded (no matter how), and Oliver frankly put them both on the same plane of achievement, thus wiping away, with generous hand, all hated memories of the past.

When the ladies had left the room, history repeated itself, in that the Dean was called away on business and the cousins were left alone together over their wine. Said Doggie:

"Do you remember the last time we sat at this table?"

"Perfectly," replied Oliver, holding up a glass of the old Deanery port to the light. "You were horrified at my attempting to clean out my pipe with a dessert knife."

Doggie laughed. "After all, it was a filthy thing to do."

"I quite agree with you. Since then I've learned manners."

"You also made me squirm at the idea of scooping out Boches' insides with bayonets."

"And you've learned not to squirm, so we're quits."

"You thought me a rotten ass in those days, didn't you?"

Oliver looked at him squarely.

"I don't think it would hurt you now if I said that I did." He laughed, stretched himself on his chair, thrusting both hands into his trouser pockets. "In many ways, it's a jolly good old war, you know — for those that pull through. It has taught us both a lot, Marmaduke."

Doggie wrinkled his forehead in his half humorous way.

"I wish it would teach people not to call me by that damn silly name."

"I have always abominated it, as you may have observed," said Oliver. "But in our present polite relations, old chap, what else is there?"

"You ought to know —"

Oliver stared at him. "You don't mean —?"

"Yes, I do."

"But you used to loathe it, and I went on calling you Doggie because I knew you loathed it. I never dreamed of using it now."

"I can't help it," replied Doggie. "The name got into the army and has stuck to me right through, and now those I love and trust most in the world and who love and trust me, call me 'Doggie,' and I don't seem to be able to answer to any other name. So, although I'm only a Tommy and you're a devil of a swell of a second in command, yet if you want to be friendly — well —"

Oliver leaned forward quickly. "Of course I want to be friends, Doggie, old chap. As for Major and private — when you pass me in the street you've damn well got to salute me, and that's all there is to it — but otherwise it's all rot. And now we've got to the heart-to-heart stage, don't you think you're a bit of a fool?"

"I know it," said Doggie cheerfully. "The Army has drummed that into me, at any rate."

"I mean in staying in the ranks. Why don't you apply for the Cadet Corps and so get through to a commission again?"

Doggie's brow grew dark. "I had all that out with Peggy long ago — when things were perhaps somewhat different with me. I was sore all over. I dare say you can understand. But now there are other reasons, much stronger reasons. The only real happiness I've had in my life has been as a Tommy. I'm not talking through my hat. The only real friends I've ever made in my life are Tommies. I've found real things as a Tommy, and I'm not going to start all over again to find them in another capacity."

"You wouldn't have to start all over again," Oliver objected.

"Oh, yes, I should. Don't run away with the idea that I've been turned by a miracle into a brawny hero. I ain't anything of the sort. To have to lead men into action would be a holy terror. The old dread of seeking new paths still acts, you see. I'm the same Doggie that wouldn't go out to Huaheine with you. Only now I'm a private and I'm used to it. I love it, and I'm not going to change to the end of the whole gory business. Of course Peggy doesn't like it," he added after a sip of wine. "But I can't help that. It's a matter of temperament and conscience — in a way, a matter of honour."

"What has honour got to do with it?" asked Oliver.

"I'll try to explain. It's somehow this way. When I came to my senses after being chucked for incompetence — that was the worst hell I ever went through in my life — and I enlisted, I swore that I would stick to it a Tommy without anybody's sympathy, least of all that of the folks here. And then I swore I'd make good to myself as a Tommy. I was just beginning to feel happier when that infernal Boche sniper knocked me out for a time. So Peggy or no Peggy, I'm going through with it. I suppose I'm telling you all this because I should like you to know."

He passed his hand, in the familiar gesture, from back to front of his short-cropped hair. Oliver smiled at the reminiscence of the old disturbed Doggie; but he said very gravely:

"I'm glad you've told me, old man. I appreciate it very much. I've been through the ranks my-

self and know what it is — the bad and the good.
Many a man has found his soul that way —"

"Good God!" cried Doggie, starting to his feet.
"Do you say that too?"

"Who else said it?"

The quick question caused the blood to rush to
Doggie's face. Oliver's keen, half-mocking gaze
held him. He cursed himself for an impulsive
idiot. The true answer to the question would be a
confession of Jeanne. The scene in the kitchen
of Frélus swam before his eyes. He dropped into
his chair again with a laugh.

"Oh, someone out there — in another heart-to-
heart talk. As a matter of fact, I think I said it
myself. It's odd you should have used the same
words. Anyhow, you're the only other person who
has hit on the truth as far as I'm concerned. Finding one's soul is a bit high-falutin' — but that's
about the size of it."

"Peggy hasn't hit on the truth, then?" Oliver
asked, with curious earnestness, the shade of
mockery gone.

"The war has scarcely touched her yet, you see,"
said Doggie. He rose, shrinking from discussion.
"Shall we go in?"

In the drawing room they played bridge till the
ladies' bedtime. The Dean coming in, played the
last rubber.

"I hope you'll be able to sleep in a common or
garden bed, Marmaduke," said Peggy, and kissed
him a perfunctory good-night.

"I have heard," remarked the Dean, "that it
takes quite a time to grow accustomed to the little
amenities of civilisation."

"That's quite true, Uncle Edward," laughed
Doggie. "I'm terrified at the thought of the silk
pyjamas Peddle has prescribed for me."

"Why?" Peggy asked bluntly.

Oliver interposed laughing, his hand on Doggie's shoulder.

"Tommy's accustomed to go to bed in his day-shirt."

"How perfectly disgusting!" cried Peggy, and swept from the room.

Oliver dropped his hand and looked somewhat abashed.

"I'm afraid I've been and gone and done it. I'm sorry. I'm still a barbarian South Sea Islander."

"I wish I were a young man," said the Dean, moving from the door, and with his courtly gesture inviting them to sit, "and could take part in these strange hardships. This question of night attire, for instance, has never struck me before. The whole thing is of amazing interest. Ah! what it is to be old! If I were young, I should be with you, cloth or no cloth, in the trenches. I hope both of you know that I vehemently dissent from the bishops who prohibit the younger clergy from taking their place in the fighting line. If God's archangels and angels themselves took up the sword against the Powers of Darkness, surely a stalwart young curate of the Church of England would find his vocation in warring with rifle and bayonet against the proclaimed enemies of God and mankind?"

"The influence of the twenty thousand or so of priests fighting in the French army is said to be enormous," Oliver remarked.

The Dean sighed. "I'm afraid we're losing a big chance."

"Why don't you take up the Fiery Cross, Uncle Edward, and run a new Crusade?"

The Dean sighed. Five-and-thirty years ago, when he had set all Durdlebury by the ears, he might have preached glorious heresy and heroic schism; but now at seventy the immutability of the great grey fabric had become part of his being.

"I've done my best, my boy," he replied, "with the result that I am held in high disfavour."

"But that doesn't matter a little bit."

"Not a little bit," said the Dean. "A man can only do his duty according to the dictates of his conscience. I have publicly deplored the attitude of the Church of England. I have written to the *Times*. I have published a pamphlet — I sent you each a copy — which has brought a hornet's nest about my ears. I have warned those in high places that what they are doing is not in the best interests of the Church. But they won't listen."

Oliver lit a pipe. "I'm afraid, Uncle Edward," he said, "that though I come of a clerical family, I know no more of religion than a Hun Bishop; but it has always struck me that the Church's job is to look after the people, whereas, as far as I can make out, the Church is now squealing because the people won't look after the Church."

The Dean rose. "I won't go as far as that," said he with a smile. "But there is, I fear, some justification for such a criticism from the laity. As soon as the war began, the Church should have gathered the people together and said, 'Onward, Christian soldiers. Go and fight like — er —'"

"Like Hell," suggested Oliver, greatly daring.

"Or words to that effect," smiled the old Dean. He looked at his watch. "Dear, dear! past eleven. I wish I could sit up talking to you boys — But I start my day's work at eight o'clock. If you want anything, you've only got to ring. Good-night. It is one of the proudest days of my life to have you both here together."

His courtly charm seemed to linger in the room after he had left.

"He's a dear old chap," said Oliver.

"One of the best," said Doggie.

"It's rather pathetic," said Oliver. "In his

heart he would like to play the devil with the Bishops
and kick every able-bodied parson into the trenches
— and there are thousands of them that don't need
any kicking and, on the contrary, have been kicked
back; but he has become half petrified in the atmosphere of this place. It's lovely to come to as a
sort of funk-hole of peace — but my holy Aunt! —
What the blazes are you laughing at?"

"I'm only thinking of a beast of a boy here who
used to say that," replied Doggie.

"Oh!" said Oliver, and he grinned. "Anyway,
I was only going to remark that if I thought I was
going to spend the rest of my life here, I'd paint the
town vermillion for a week and then cut my throat."

"I quite agree with you," said Doggie.

"What are you going to do when the war's over?"

"Who knows what he's going to do? What are
you going to do? Fly back to your little Robinson
Crusoe Durdlebury of a Pacific Island? I don't
think so."

Oliver stuck his pipe on the mantelpiece and his
hands on his hips, and made a stride towards Doggie.

"Damn you, Doggie! Damn you to little bits!
How the Hades did you guess what I've scarcely
told myself, much less another human being?"

"You yourself said it was a good old war, and it
has taught us a lot of things."

"It has," said Oliver. "But I never expected
to hear Huaheine called Durdlebury by you, Doggie.
Oh, Lord! I must have another drink. Where's
your glass? Say when?"

They parted for the night the best of friends.

Doggie, in spite of the silk pyjamas and the soft
bed and the blazing fire in his room — he stripped
back the light excluding curtains forgetful of
Defence of the Realm Acts, and opened all the
windows wide, to the horror of Peddle in the morning — slept like an unperturbed dormouse. When

Peddle woke him, he lay drowsily while the old butler filled his bath and fiddled about the drawers. At last aroused, he cried out:

"What the dickens are you doing?"

Peddle turned with an injured air. "I am matching your ties and socks for your bottle-green suit, sir."

Doggie leaped out of bed. "You dear old idiot, I can't go about the streets in bottle-green suits. I've got to wear my uniform." He looked around the room. "Where the devil is it?"

Peddle's injured air deepened almost into resentment. "Where the devil —!" Never had Mr. Marmaduke, or his father, the Canon, used such language. He drew himself up.

"I have given orders, sir, for the uniform suit you wore yesterday to be sent to the cleaners."

"Oh, Hell!" said Doggie — And Peddle, unaccustomed to the vernacular of the British Army, gaped with horror. "Oh, Hell! Look here, Peddle, just you get on a bicycle, or a motorcar, or an express train at once and retrieve that uniform. Don't you understand? I'm a private soldier. I've got to wear uniform all the time, and I'll have to stay in this beastly bed until you get it for me."

Peddle fled. The picture that he left on Doggie's mind was that of the faithful steward with dismayed, uplifted hands, retiring from the room in one of the great scenes of Hogarth's "Rake's Progress." The similitude made him laugh — for Doggie always had a saving sense of humour — but he was very angry with Peddle, while he stamped around the room in his silk pyjamas. What the deuce was he going to do? Even if he committed the military crime (and there was a far more serious crime already against him) of appearing in public in mufti, did that old ass think he was going to swagger about Durdlebury in bottle-green suits, as though he were ashamed of the King's uniform? He dipped his shaving brush into the hot water. Then he threw it, anyhow, across the room. Instead of shaving, he would be gloating over the idea of cutting that old fool, Peddle's throat, and therefore would slash his own face to bits.

Things, however, were not done at lightning speed in the Deanery of Durdlebury. The first steps had not even been taken to send the uniform to the cleaners, and soon Peddle reappeared carrying it over his arm, and the heavy pair of munition boots in his hand.

"These too, sir?" he asked exhibiting the latter resignedly, and casting a sad glance at the neat pair of brown shoes exquisitely polished and beautifully treed which he had put out for his master's wear.

"These, too," said Doggie. "And where's my grey flannel shirt?"

This time Peddle triumphed. "I've given that away, sir, to the gardener's boy."

"Well, you can just go and buy me half-a-dozen more like it," said Doggie.

He dismissed the old man, dressed, and went downstairs. The Dean had breakfasted at seven. Peggy and Oliver were not yet down for the nine o'clock meal. Doggie strolled about the garden and sauntered round to the stable-yard. There he encountered Chipmunk in his shirt-sleeves, sitting on a packing case and polishing Oliver's leggings. He raised an ugly, clean-shaven mug and scowled beneath his bushy eyebrows at the newcomer.

"Morning, mate!" said Doggie pleasantly.

"Morning," said Chipmunk, resuming his work.

Doggie turned over a stable bucket and sat down on it and lit a cigarette.

"Glad to be back?"

Chipmunk poised the cloth on which he had poured some brown dressing: "Not if I has to be worried with private soljers," he replied. "I came 'ere to get away from 'em."

"What's wrong with private soldiers? They're good enough for you, aren't they?" asked Doggie with a laugh.

"Naow," snarled Chipmunk, "especially when they ought to be orficers. Go to 'ell!"

Doggie, who had suffered much in the army, but had never before been taunted with being a dilettante gentleman private, still less been consigned to hell on that account, leapt to his feet shaken by one of his rare sudden gusts of anger.

"If you don't say I'm as good a private soldier as any in your rotten, mangy regiment, I'll knock your blinking head off!"

An insult to a soldier's regiment can only be wiped out in blood. Chipmunk threw cloth and legging to the winds and, springing from his seat like a monkey, went for Doggie.

"You just try."

Doggie tried, and had not Chipmunk's head been very firmly secured to his shoulders, he would have succeeded. Chipmunk went down as if he had been bombed. It was his unguarded and unscientific rush that did it. Doggie regarded his prostrate figure in gratified surprise.

"What the devil's all this about?" cried a sharp, imperious voice.

Doggie instinctively stood at attention and saluted, and Chipmunk, picking himself up in a dazed sort of way, did likewise.

"You two men shake hands and make friends at once," Oliver commanded.

"Yes, sir," said Doggie. He extended his hand and Chipmunk, with the nautical shamble, which in moments of stress defied a couple of years' military discipline, advanced and shook it. Oliver strode hurriedly away.

"I'm sorry I said that about the regiment, mate. I didn't mean it," said Doggie.

Chipmunk looked uncertainly into Doggie's eyes for what Doggie felt to be a very long time. Chipmunk's dull brain was slowly realising the situation. The man opposite to him was his master's cousin. When he had last seen him, he had no title to be called a man at all. His vocabulary volcanically rich, but otherwise limited, had not been able to express him in adequate terms of contempt and derision. Now behold him masquerading as a private. Wounded. But any fool could get wounded. Behold him further coming down from the social heights whereon his master dwelt, to take a rise out of him, Chipmunk. In self-defence he had taken the obvious course. He had told him to go to hell. Then the important things had happened. Not the effeminate gentleman but someone very much like the common Tommy of his acquaintance, had responded. And he had further responded with the familiar vigour but unwonted science of the rank and file. He had also stood at attention and saluted and obeyed like any common Tommy, when the Major appeared. The last fact appealed to him, perhaps, as much as the one more invested in violence.

"'Ere," said he at last, jerking his head and rubbing his jaw, "how the 'ell did you do it?"

"We'll get some gloves and I'll show you," said Doggie.

So peace and firm friendship were made. Doggie went into the house, and in the dining room found Oliver in convulsive laughter.

"Oh, my holy Aunt! you'll be the death of me, Doggie. 'Yes, sir!'" He mimicked him. "The perfect Tommy. After doing in old Chipmunk. Chipmunk with the strength of a gorilla and the courage of a lion. I just happened round to see him go down. How the blazes did you manage it, Doggie?"

"That's what Chipmunk's just asked me," Doggie replied. "I belong to a regiment where boxing is taught. Really a good regiment," he grinned. "There's a sergeant instructor, a chap called Ballinghall — "

"Not Joe Ballinghall, the well-known amateur heavy-weight?"

"That's him right enough," said Doggie.

"My dear old chap," said Oliver, "this is the funniest war that ever was."

Peggy sailed in full of apologies and began to pour out coffee.

"Do help yourselves with dishes and things. I'm so sorry to have kept you poor hungry things waiting."

"We've filled up the time amazingly," cried Oliver, waving a silver dish-cover. "What do you think? Doggie's had a fight with Chipmunk and knocked him out."

Peggy splashed the milk over the brim of Doggie's cup and into the saucer. There came a sudden flush on her cheek and a sudden hard look into her eyes.

"Fighting? Do you mean to say you've been fighting with a common man like Chipmunk?"

"We're the best of friends now," said Doggie. "We understand each other."

"I can't quite see the necessity," said Peggy.

"I'm afraid it's rather hard to explain," he replied with a rueful knitting of the brows, for he realised her disgust at the vulgar brawl.

"I think the less said, the better," she remarked acidly.

The meal proceeded in ominous gloom, and as soon as Peggy had finished she left the room.

"It seems, old chap, that I can never do right,"

said Oliver. "Long ago, when I used to crab you, she gave it to me in the neck; and now when I try to boost you, you seem to get it."

"I'm afraid I've got on Peggy's nerves," said Doggie. "You see, we've only met once before during the last two years, and I suppose I've changed."

"There's no doubt about that, old son," said Oliver. "But all the same, Peggy has stood by you like a brick, hasn't she?"

"That's the devil of it," replied Doggie, rubbing up his hair.

"Why the devil of it?" Oliver asked quickly.

"Oh, I don't know," replied Doggie. "As you have once or twice observed, it's a funny old war."

He rose, went to the door.

"Where are you off to?" asked Oliver.

"I'm going to Denby Hall to take a look round."

"Like me to come with you? We can borrow the two-seater."

Doggie advanced a pace. "You're an awfully good sort, Oliver," he said, touched, "but would you mind — I feel rather a beast —".

"All right, you silly old ass," cried Oliver cheerily. "You want, of course, to root about there by yourself. Go ahead."

"If you'll take a spin with me this afternoon, or to-morrow —" said Doggie in his sensitive way.

"Oh, clear out!" laughed Oliver.

And Doggie cleared.

CHAPTER XXI

ALL right, Peddle, I can find my way about,"
said Doggie, dismissing the old butler and
his wife after a little colloquy in the hall.

"Everything's in perfect order, sir, just as it
was when you left; and there are the keys," said
Mrs. Peddle.

The Peddles retired. Doggie eyed the heavy
bunch of keys with an air of distaste. For two
years he had not seen a key. What on earth could
be the good of all this locking and unlocking?
He stuffed the bunch in his tunic pocket, and
looked around him. It seemed difficult to realise
that everything he saw was his own. Those trees
visible from the hall windows were his own, and the
land on which they grew. This spacious, beautiful house was his own. He had only to wave a
hand, as it were, and it would be filled with serving
men and serving maids ready to do his bidding.
His foot was on his native heath, and his name was
James Marmaduke Trevor.

Did he ever actually live here, have his being
here? Was he ever part and parcel of it all —
the oriental rugs, the soft stair-carpet on the noble
oak staircase leading to the gallery, the oil paint-
ings, the impressive statuary, the solid historical
oak hall furniture? Were it not so acutely remembered, he would have felt like a man accustomed
all his life to barns and tents and hedgerows and
fetid holes in the ground, who had wandered into
some ill-guarded palace. He entered the drawing
room. The faithful Peddles, with pathetic zeal
to give him a true home-coming, had set it out

fresh and clean and polished; the windows were
like crystal, and flowers welcomed him from every
available vase. And so in the dining room. The
Chippendale dining table gleamed like a sombre
translucent pool. On the sideboard, amid the
array of shining silver, the very best old Water-
ford decanters filled with whisky and brandy, and
old cut glass goblets invited him to refreshment.
The precious mezzotint portraits, mostly of his own
collecting, regarded him urbanely from the walls.
The *Times* and the *Morning Post* were laid out on
the little table by his accustomed chair near the
massive marble mantelpiece.

"The dear old idiots," said Doggie, and he sat
down for a moment and unfolded the newspapers
and strewed them around, to give the impression
that he had read and enjoyed them.

And then he went into his own private and particular den, the peacock and ivory room, which
had been the supreme expression of himself and
for which he had ached during many nights of
misery. He looked round and his heart sank.
He seemed to come face to face with the ineffectual,
effeminate creature who had brought upon him
the disgrace of his man's life. But for the creator
and sybarite enjoyer of this sickening boudoir,
he would now be in honoured command of men.
He conceived a sudden violent hatred of the room.
The only thing in the place worth a man's consideration, save a few water-colours, was the honest
grand piano, which, because it did not aestheti-
cally harmonise with his squeaky, pot-bellied theor-
bos and tinkling spinet, he had hidden in an alcove
behind a curtain. He turned an eye of disgust
on the vellum backs of his books in the closed
Chippendale cases, on the drawers containing his
collection of wall-papers, on the footling peacocks,
on the curtains and cushions, on the veined ivory

paper which, beginning to fade two years ago, now looked mean and meaningless. It was an abominable room. It ought to be smelling of musk or pastilles or joss-sticks. It might have done so, for once he had tried something of the sort, and did not renew the experiment only because the smell happened to make him sick.

There was one feature of the room at which for a long time he avoided looking: but wherever he turned, it impressed itself on his consciousness as the miserable genius of the despicable place. And that was his collection of little china dogs.

At last he planted himself in front of the great glass cabinet, whence thousands of little dogs looked at him out of little black dots of eyes. There were dogs of all nationalities, all breeds, all twisted enormities of human invention. There were monstrous dogs of China and Japan; Aztec dogs; dogs in Sèvres and Dresden and Chelsea; sixpenny dogs from Austria and Switzerland; everything in the way of a little dog that man had made. He stood in front of it with almost a doggish snarl on his lips. He had spent hundreds and hundreds of pounds over these futile dogs. Yet never a flesh and blood, real, lusty *canis futilis* had he possessed. He used to dislike real dogs. He had wasted his heart over these contemptible counterfeits. To add to his collection, catalogue it, describe it, correspond about it with the semi-imbecile Russian prince, his only rival collector, had once ranked with his history of wall-papers as the serious and absorbing pursuit of his life.

Then suddenly Doggie's hatred reached the crisis of ferocity. He saw red. He seized the first instrument of destruction that came to his hand, a little gilt Louis XV music stool, and bashed the cabinet full in front. The glass flew into a thousand splinters. He bashed again. The woodwork of

the cabinet stoutly resisting, worked hideous dam-
age on the gilt stool.   But Doggie went on bashing
till the cabinet sank in ruins and the little dogs,
headless, tail-less, rent in twain, strewed the floor.
Then Doggie stamped on them with his heavy
munition boots until dogs and glass were reduced
to powder and the Aubusson carpet cut to pieces.

"Damn the whole infernal place!" cried Doggie,
and he heaved a mandolin tied up with disgusting
peacock-blue ribbons at the bookcase, and fled
from the room.

He stood for a while in the hall shaken with his
anger; then mounted the staircase and went into
his own bedroom, with the satinwood furniture
and Nattier blue hangings. God! what a bed-
chamber for a man! He would have liked to throw
bombs into the nest of effeminacy.   But his mother
had arranged it, so in a way it was immune from
his iconoclastic rage.   He went down to the dining
room, helped himself to a whisky and soda from the
sideboard, and sat down in the armchair amidst
the scattered newspapers, and held his head in his
hands and thought.

The house was hateful; all its associations were
hateful. If he lived there until he was ninety,
the abhorred ghost of the pre-war little Doggie
Trevor would always haunt every nook and cranny
of the place, mouthing the quarter of a century's
shame that had culminated in the Great Disgrace.
At last he brought his hand down with a bang
on the arm of the chair. He would never live
in this House of Dishonour again. Never. He
would sell it.

"By God!" he cried, starting to his feet, as the
inspiration came.

He would sell it, as it stood, lock, stock and
barrel, with everything in it. He would wipe
out at one stroke the whole of his unedifying his-

tory. Denby Hall gone, what could tie him to Durdlebury? He would be freed for ever from the petrifaction of the grey, cramping little city. If Peggy didn't like it, that was Peggy's affair. In material things he was master of his destiny. Peggy would have to follow him in his career, whatever it was, not he Peggy. He saw clearly that which had been mapped out for him, the silly little social ambitions, the useless existence, little Doggie Trevor for ever trailing obediently behind the lady of Denby Hall. Doggie threw himself back in his chair and laughed. No one had ever heard him laugh like that. After a while he was even surprised at himself.

He was perfectly ready to marry Peggy. It was almost a pre-ordained thing. A rupture of the engagement was unthinkable. Her undeviating loyalty bound him by every fibre of gratitude and honour. But it was essential that Peggy should know whom and what she was marrying. The Doggie trailing in her wake no longer existed. If she were prepared to follow the new Doggie, well and good. If not, there would be conflict. For that he was prepared.

He strode, this time contemptuously, into his wrecked peacock and ivory room, where his telephone (blatant and hideous thing) was ingeniously concealed behind a screen, and rang up Spooner and Smithson, the leading firm of Auctioneers and Estate Agents in the town. At the mention of his name, Mr. Spooner, the senior partner, came to the telephone.

"Yes, I'm back, Mr. Spooner, and I'm quite well," said Doggie. "I want to see you on very important business. When can you fix it up? Any time? Can you come along now to Denby Hall?"

Mr. Spooner would be pleased to wait upon Mr.

Trevor immediately. He would start at once. Doggie went out and sat on the front doorstep and smoked cigarettes till he came.

"Mr. Spooner," said he, as soon as the elderly auctioneer descended from his little car, "I'm going to sell the whole of the Denby Hall estate, and, with the exception of a few odds and ends, family relics and so forth, which I'll pick out, all the contents of the house, furniture, pictures, sheets, towels and kitchen clutter. I've only got six days' leave, and I want all the worries, as far as I am concerned, settled and done with before I go. So you'll have to buck up, Mr. Spooner. If you say you can't do it, I'll put the business by telephone into the hands of a London agent."

It took Mr. Spooner nearly a quarter of an hour to recover his breath, gain a grasp of the situation, and assemble his business wits.

"Of course I'll carry out your instructions, Mr. Trevor," he said at last. "You can safely leave the matter in our hands. But, although it is against my business interests, pray let me beg you to reconsider your decision. It is such a beautiful home, your grandfather, the Bishop's, before you."

"He bought it pretty cheap, didn't he, somewhere in the seventies?"

"I forget the price he paid for it, but I could look it up. Of course we were the agents."

"And then it was let to some dismal people until my father died and my mother took it over. I'm sorry I can't get sentimental about it, as if it were an ancestral hall, Mr. Spooner. I want to get rid of the place, because I hate the sight of it."

"It would be presumptuous of me to say anything more," answered the old-fashioned country auctioneer.

"Say what you like, Mr. Spooner," laughed Doggie in his disarming way. "We're old friends. But send in your people this afternoon to start on inventories and measuring up, or whatever they do, and I'll look round to-morrow and select the bits I may want to keep. You'll see after the storing of them, won't you?"

"Of course, Mr. Trevor."

Mr. Spooner drove away in his little car, a much dazed man. Like the rest of Durdlebury and the circumjacent county, he had assumed that when the war was over Mr. James Marmaduke Trevor would lead his bride from the Deanery into Denby Hall, where the latter, in her own words, would proceed to make things hum.

"My dear," said he to his wife at luncheon, "you could have knocked me over with a feather. What he's doing it for, goodness knows. I can only assume that he has grown so accustomed to the destruction of property in France, that he has got bitten by the fever."

"Perhaps Peggy Conover has turned him down," suggested his wife, who, much younger than he, employed more modern turns of speech. "And I shouldn't wonder if she has. Since the war girls aren't on the lookout for pretty monkeys."

"If Miss Conover thinks she has got hold of a pretty monkey in that young man, she is very much mistaken," replied Mr. Spooner.

Meanwhile Doggie summoned Peddle to the hall. He knew that his announcement would be a blow to the old man; but this was a world of blows; and, after all, one could not organise one's life to suit the sentiments of old family idiots of retainers, served they never so faithfully.

"Peddle," said he, "I'm sorry to say I'm going to sell Denby Hall. Messrs. Spooner and Smithson's people are coming in this afternoon. So give them every facility. Also tea, or beer, or whisky, or whatever they want. About what's going to happen to you and Mrs. Peddle, don't worry a bit. I'll look after that. You've been jolly good friends of mine all my life, and I'll see that everything's as right as rain.'

He turned, before the amazed old butler could reply, and marched away. Peddle gaped at his retreating figure. If those were the ways which Mr. Marmaduke had learned in the Army, the lower sank the Army in Peddle's estimation. To sell Denby Hall over his head! Why, the place and all about it was *his!* So deeply are squatters' rights implanted in the human instinct.

Doggie marched along the familiar high road, strangely exhilarated. What was to be his future he neither knew nor cared. At any rate, it would not lie in Durdlebury. He had cut out Durdlebury for ever from his scheme of existence. If he got through the war, he and Peggy would go out somewhere into the great world where there was man's work to do. Parliament! Peggy had suggested it as a sort of country-gentleman's hobby that would keep him amused during the autumn and summer London seasons — so might prospective bride have talked to prospective husband fifty years ago. Parliament! God help him and God help Peggy if ever he got into Parliament. He would speak the most unpopular truths about the race of politicians if ever he got into Parliament. Peggy would wish that neither of them had ever been born. He held the trenches' views on politicians. No fear. No muddy politics as an elegant amusement for him. He laughed as he had laughed in the dining room at Denby Hall.

He would have a bad quarter of an hour with Peggy. Naturally. She would say, and with every right: "What about me? Am I not to be considered?" Yes, of course she would be considered. The position his fortune assured him would always be hers. He had no notion of asking her to share a log cabin in the wilds of Canada, or to bury herself in Oliver's dud island of Huaheine. The great world would be before them. "But give me some sort of an idea of what you propose to do," she would with perfect propriety demand. And there Doggie was stuck. He had not the ghost of a programme. All he had was faith in the war, faith in the British spirit and genius that would bring it to a perfect end, in which there would be unimagined opportunities for a man to fling himself into a new life, amid new conditions, and begin the new work of a new civilisation.

"If she'll only understand," said he, "that I can't go back to those blasted little dogs, all will be well."

Not quite all. Although his future was as nebulous as the planetary system in the Milky Way, at the back of his mind was a vague conviction that it would be connected somehow with the welfare of those men whom he had learned to know and love; the men to whom reading was little pleasure, writing a schoolchild's laborious task, the glories of the earth as interpreted through art a sealed book; the men whose daily speech was foul metaphor; the men, hemi-demi-semi-educated, whose crude socialistic opinions the open lessons of history and the eternal facts of human nature derisively refuted; the men who had sweated and slaved in factory and in field to no other purpose than to obey the biological laws of the perpetuation of the species; yet the men with the sweet minds of children, the gushing tenderness of women, the hearts of lions; the men compared to whom the rotten squealing heroes of Homer were a horde of cowardly savages. They were men, these comrades of his, swift with all that there can be of divine glory in man.

And when they came home and the high gods sounded the false trumpet of peace?

There would be men's work in England for all the Doggies in England to do.

Again, if Peggy could understand this, all would be well. If she missed the point altogether, and tauntingly advised him to go and join his friend Mr. Ramsay Macdonald at once — then — he shoved his cap to the back of his head and wrinkled his forehead — then —

"Everything will be in the soup," said he.

These reflections brought him to the Deanery. The nearest way of entrance was the stable yard gate, which was always open. He strode in, waved a hand to Chipmunk, who was sitting on the ground with his back against the garage, smoking a pipe, and entered the house by the French window of the dining room. Where should he find Peggy? His whole mind was set on the immediate interview. Obviously the drawing room was the first place of search. He opened the drawing room door, the hinges and lock oily, noiseless, perfectly ordained, like everything in that perfectly ordained English Deanery, and strode in.

His entrance was so swift, so protected from sound, that the pair had no time to start apart before he was there, with his amazed eyes full upon them. Peggy's hands were on Oliver's shoulders, tears were streaming down her face, as her head was thrown back from him, and Oliver's arm was around her. Her back was to the door. Oliver withdrew his arm and retired a pace or two.

"Lord Almighty," he whispered, "here's Doggie!"

Then Peggy, realising what had happened, wheeled round and stared tragically at Doggie who, preoccupied with the search for her, had not removed his cap. He drew himself up and saluted.

"I beg your pardon, sir," he said with imperturbable irony, and turned.

Oliver rushed across the room.

"Stop, you silly fool!"

He slammed the open door, caught Doggie by the arm and dragged him away from the threshold. His blue eyes blazed, and the lips beneath the short-cropped moustache quivered.

"It's all my fault, Doggie. I'm a beast and a cad and anything you like to call me. But for things you said last night — well — no, hang it all, there's no excuse. Everything's on me. Peggy's as true as gold."

Peggy, red-eyed, pale-cheeked, stood a little way back, silent, on the defensive. Doggie, looking from one to the other, said quietly:

"A triangular explanation is scarcely decent. Perhaps you might let me have a word or two with Peggy."

"Yes. It would be best," she whispered.

"I'll be in the dining room if you want me," said Oliver, and went out.

Doggie took her hand and very gently led her to a chair.

"Let us sit down. There," said he, "now we can talk more comfortably. First, before we touch on this situation, let me say something to you. It may ease things."

Peggy, humiliated, did not look at him. She nodded.

"All right."

"I made up my mind this morning to sell Denby Hall and its contents. I've given old Spooner instructions."

She glanced at him involuntarily. "Sell Denby Hall?"

"Yes, dear. You see, I had made up my mind definitely, if I'm spared, not to live in Durdlebury after the war."

"What were you thinking of doing?" she asked, in a low voice.

"That would depend on after war circumstances. Anyhow, I was coming to you, when I entered the room, with my decision. I knew of course that it wouldn't please you — that you would have something to say to it — perhaps something very serious."

"What do you mean by something very serious?"

"Our little contract, dear," said Doggie, "was based on the understanding that you would not be uprooted from the place in which are all your life's associations. If I broke that understanding it would leave you a free agent to determine the contract, as the lawyers say. So perhaps, Peggy dear, we might dismiss — well — other considerations, and just discuss this."

Peggy twisted a rag of a handkerchief and wavered for a moment. Then she broke out, with fresh tears on her cheek.

"You're a dear of dears to put it that way. Only you could do it. I've been a brute, old boy; but I couldn't help it. I *did* try to play the game."

"You did, Peggy dear. You've been wonderful."

"And although it didn't look like it, I was trying to play the game when you came in. I really was. And so was he." She rose and threw the handkerchief away from her. "I'm not going to step out of the engagement by the side door you've left open for me, you dear, old simple thing. It stands if you like. We're all honourable people, and Oliver —" she drew a sharp little breath — "Oliver will go out of our lives."

Doggie smiled — he had risen — and taking her hands, kissed them.

"I've never known what a splendid Peggy it is, until I lose her. Look here, dear, here's the whole thing in a nutshell. While I've been morbidly occupied with myself and my grievances and my disgrace and my efforts to pull through, and have gradually developed into a sort of half-breed between a Tommy and a gentleman, with every mortal thing in me warped and changed, you've stuck to the original rotten ass you lashed into the semblance of a man, in this very room, goodness knows how many months, or years, or centuries ago. In my infernal selfishness, I've treated you awfully badly."

"No, you haven't," she declared stoutly.

"Yes, I have. The ordinary girl would have told a living experiment like me to go hang long before this. But you didn't. And now you see a totally different sort of Doggie, and you're making yourself miserable because he's a queer, unsympathetic, unfamiliar stranger."

"All that may be so," she said, meeting his eyes bravely. "But if the unfamiliar Doggie still cares for me, it doesn't matter."

Here was a delicate situation. Two very tender-skinned vanities opposed to each other. The smart of seeing one's affianced bride in the arms of another man hurts grievously sore. It's a primitive sex affair, independent of love in its modern sense. If the savage's abandoned squaw runs off with another fellow, he pursues him with clubs and tomahawks until he has avenged the insult. Having known ME, to decline to Spotted Crocodile! So the finest flower of civilisation cannot surrender the lady who once was his to the more favoured male without a primitive pang. On the other hand, Doggie knew very well that he did not love Peggy, that he had never loved Peggy. But how in common decency could a man tell a girl who had wasted

a couple of years of her life over him, that he
had never loved her? Instead of replying to her
question, he walked about the room in a worried
way.

"I take it," said Peggy incisively, after a while,
"that you don't care for me any longer."

He turned and halted at the challenge. He
snapped his fingers. What was the good of all
this beating of the bush?

"Look here, Peggy, let's face it out. If you'll
confess that you and Oliver are in love with each
other, I'll confess to a girl in France."

"Oh?" said Peggy, with a swift change to coolness. "There's a girl in France, is there? How
long has this been going on?"

"The last four days in billets before I got
wounded," said Doggie.

"What is she like?"

Then Doggie suddenly laughed out loud, and
took her by the shoulders in a grasp rougher than
she had ever dreamed to lie in the strength or
nature of Marmaduke Trevor, and kissed her the
heartiest, honestest kiss she had ever had from
man, and rushed out of the room.

Presently he returned, dragging with him a
disconsolate Major.

"Here," said he, "fix it up between you. I've
told Peggy about a girl in France, and she wants
to know what she's like."

Peggy, shaken by the rude grip and the kiss,
flashed, and cried rebelliously:

"I'm not quite so sure that I want to fix it up
with Oliver."

"Oh, yes, you do," cried Oliver.

He snatched up Doggie's cap and jammed it on
Doggie's head and cried:

"Doggie, you're the best and truest and finest
of dear old chaps in the whole wide world!"

Doggie settled his cap, grinned and moved to the door.

"Anything else, sir?"

Oliver roared, delighted: "No, Private Trevor; you can go."

"Very good, sir."

Doggie saluted smartly and went out. He passed through the French window of the dining room into the mellow autumn sunshine. Found himself standing in front of Chipmunk, who still smoked the pipe of elegant leisure by the door of the garage.

"This is a dam' good old world, all the same. Isn't it?" said he.

"If it was always like this, it would have its points," replied the unworried Chipmunk.

Doggie had an inspiration. He looked at his watch. It was nearly one o'clock.

"Hungry?"

"Always 'ungry. Specially about dinner time."

"Come along of me to the Downshire Arms and have a bite of dinner."

Chipmunk rose slowly to his feet, and put his pipe into his tunic pocket, and jerked a slow thumb backwards.

"Ain't yer having yer meals 'ere?"

"Only now and then, as sort of treats," said Doggie. "Come along."

"Ker-ist!" said Chipmunk. "Can yer wait a bit until I've cleaned me buttons?"

"Oh, bust your old buttons!" laughed Doggie. "I'm hungry."

So the pair of privates marched through the old city to the Downshire Arms, the select, old-world Hotel of Durdlebury, where Doggie was known since babyhood; and there, sitting at a window table with Chipmunk, he gave Durdlebury the great sensation of its life. If the Dean himself, clad in tights and spangles, had juggled for pence by the West door of the cathedral, tongues could scarcely have wagged faster. But Doggie worried his head about gossip not one jot. He was in joyous mood, and ordered a Gargantuan feast for Chipmunk and bottles of the strongest old Burgundy, such as he thought would get a grip on Chipmunk's whiskyfied throat; and under the genial influence of food and drink, Chipmunk told him tales of far lands and strange adventures; and when they emerged much later into the quiet streets, it was the great good fortune of Chipmunk's life that there was not the ghost of an Assistant Provost Marshal in Durdlebury.

"Doggie, old man," said Oliver afterwards, "my wonder and reverence for you increases hour by hour. You are the only man in the whole wide world who has ever made Chipmunk drunk."

"You see," said Doggie modestly, "I don't think he ever really loved anyone who fed him before."

CHAPTER XXII

DOGGIE, the lightest-hearted private in the British Army, danced, in a metaphorical sense, back to London, where he stayed for the rest of his leave at his rooms in Woburn Place; took his wholesome fill of theatres and music-halls, going to those parts of the house where Tommies congregate; and bought an old Crown Derby dinner service as a wedding present for Peggy and Oliver, a tortoise-shell-fitted dressing-case for Peggy, and for Oliver a magnificent gold watch that was an encyclopaedia of current information. He had never felt so happy in his life, so enchanted with the grimly smiling old world. Were it not for the Boche, it could hold its own as a brave place with any planet going. He blessed Oliver, who, in turn, had blessed him as though he had displayed heroic magnanimity. He blessed Peggy, who, flushed with love and happiness and gratitude, had shown him, for the first time, what a really adorable young woman she could be. He thanked Heaven for making three people happy, instead of three people miserable.

He marched along the wet pavements with a new light in his eyes, with a new exhilarating breath in his nostrils. He was free. The war over, he could do exactly what he liked. An untrammelled future lay before him. During the war he could hop about trenches and shell-holes with the freedom of a bird. . . .

Those awful duty letters to Peggy! Only now he fully realised their never-ending strain. Now he could write to her spontaneously, whenever the mood suited, write to her from his heart: *"Dear old Peggy, I'm so glad you're happy. Oliver's a splendid chap. Et cetera, et cetera, et cetera."* He had lost a dreaded bride; but he had found a dear and devoted friend. Nay, more: he had found two devoted friends. When he drew up his account with humanity, he found himself passing rich in love.

His furlough expired, he reported at his depôt and was put on light duty. He went about it the cheeriest soul alive, and laughed at the memory of his former miseries as a recruit. This camp life in England, after the mud and blood of France — like the African gentleman in Mr. Addison's "Cato," he blessed his stars and thought it luxury. He was not sorry that the exigences of service prevented him from being present at the wedding of Oliver and Peggy. For it was the most sudden of phenomena, like the fight of two rams, as Shakespeare hath it. In war-time people marry in haste; and often, dear God, they have not the leisure to repent. Since the beginning of the war there are many, many women twice widowed. . . . But that is by the way. Doggie was grateful to an ungrateful military system. If he had attended — in the capacity of best man, so please you — so violent and unreasoning had Oliver's affection become, Durdlebury would have gaped and whispered behind its hand and made things uncomfortable for everybody. Doggie from the security of his regiment wished them joy by letter and telegram, and sent them the wedding presents aforesaid.

Then, for a season, there were three happy people, at least, in this war-wilderness of suffering. The newly wedded pair went off for a honeymoon whose promise of indefinite length was eventually cut short by an unromantic War Office. Oliver returned to his regiment in France and Peggy to the Deanery, where she sat among her wedding presents and her hopes for the future.

"I never realised, my dear," said the Dean to his wife, "what a remarkably pretty girl Peggy has grown into."

"It's because she has got the man she loves," said Mrs. Conover.

"Do you think that's the reason?"

"I've known the plainest of women become quite good-looking. In the early days of our married life" — she smiled — "even I was not quite unattractive."

The old Dean bent down — she was sitting and he standing — and lifted her chin with his forefinger.

"You, my dear, have always been by far the most beautiful woman of my acquaintance."

"We're talking of Peggy," smiled Mrs. Conover.

"Ah!" said the Dean. "So we were. I was saying that the child's happiness was reflected in her face —"

"I rather thought I said it, dear," replied Mrs. Conover.

"It doesn't matter," said her husband, who was first a man and then a Dean. He waved a hand in benign dismissal of the argument. "It's a great mercy," said he, "that she has married the man she loves instead of — well . . . Marmaduke has turned out a capital fellow, and a credit to the family — but I never was quite easy in my mind over the engagement. . . . And yet," he continued, after a turn or two about the room, "I'm rather conscience-stricken about Marmaduke, poor chap. He has taken it like a brick. Yes, my dear, like a brick. Like a gentleman. But all the same, no man likes to see another fellow walk off with his sweetheart."

"I don't think Marmaduke was ever so bucked in his life," said Mrs. Conover placidly.

"So —?"

The Dean gasped. His wife's smile playing ironically among her wrinkles was rather beautiful.

"Peggy's word, Edward, not mine. The modern vocabulary. It means —"

"Oh, I know what the hideous word means. It was your using it that caused a shiver down my spine. But why bucked?"

"It appears there's a girl in France."

"Oho!" said the Dean. "Who is she?"

"That's what Peggy, even now, would give a good deal to find out."

For Doggie had told Peggy nothing more about the girl in France. Jeanne was his own precious secret. That it was shared by Phineas and Mo didn't matter. To discuss her with Peggy, besides being irrelevant, in the circumstances, was quite another affair. Indeed, when he had avowed the girl in France, it was not so much a confession as a gallant desire to help Peggy out of her predicament. For, after all, what was Jeanne but a beloved war-wraith that had passed through his life and disappeared?

"The development of Marmaduke," said the Dean, "is not the least extraordinary phenomenon of the war."

Now that Doggie had gained his freedom, Jeanne ceased to be a wraith. She became once again a wonderful thing of flesh and blood towards whom all his young, fresh instinct yearned tremendously. One day it struck his ingenuous mind that, if Jeanne were willing, there could be no possible reason why he should not marry her. Who was to say him nay? Convention? He had put all the conventions of his life under the auctioneer's hammer.

The family? He pictured a meeting between
Jeanne and the kind and courteous old Dean. It
could not be other than an episode of beauty.
All he had to do was to seek out Jeanne and begin
his wooing in earnest. The simplest adventure
in the world for a well-to-do and unattached young
man — if only that young man had not been a
private soldier on active service.

That was the rub. Doggie passed his hand over
his hair ruefully. How on earth could he get
to Frélus again? Not till the end of the war, at
any rate, which might be years hence. There
was nothing for it but a resumption of intimacy
by letter. So he wrote to Jeanne the letter which
loyalty to Peggy had made him destroy weeks
ago. But no answer came. Then he wrote another,
telling her of Peggy and his freedom, and his love
and his hopes, and to that there came no reply.

A prepaid telegram produced no result.

Doggie began to despair. What had happened
to Jeanne? Why did she persist in ruling him out
of her existence? Was it because, in spite of her
gratitude, she wanted none of his love? He sat
on the railing on the sea front of the South coast
town where he was quartered, and looked across
the Channel in dismayed apprehension. He was
a fool. What could there possibly be in little
Doggie Trevor to inspire a romantic passion in
any woman's heart? Take Peggy's case. As soon
as a real, genuine fellow like Oliver came along,
Peggy's heart flew out to him like needle to magnet.
Even had he been of Oliver's Paladin mould, what
right had he to expect Jeanne to give him all the
wonder of herself after a four days' acquaintance?
Being what he was, just little Doggie Trevor, the
assumption was an impertinence. She had sheltered herself from it behind a barrier of silence.

A girl, a thing of low cut blouse, truncated skirts

and cheap silk stockings, who had been leaning unnoticed for some time on the rails by his side, spoke.

"You seem to be pretty lonely."

Doggie swerved round. "Yes, I am, darned lonely."

"Come for a walk, or take me to the pictures."

"And then?" asked Doggie, swinging to his feet.

"If we get on all right, we can fix up something for to-morrow."

She was pretty, with a fair, frizzy, insolent prettiness. She might have been any age from fourteen to four-and-twenty.

Doggie smiled, tempted to while away a dark hour. But he said, honestly:

"I'm afraid I should be a dull companion."

"What's the matter?" she laughed. "Lost your best girl?"

"Something like it." He waved a hand across the sea. "Over there."

"French? Oh!" She drew herself up. "Aren't English girls good enough for you?"

"When they're sympathetic, they're delightful," said he.

"Oh, you make me tired! Good-bye," she snapped and stalked away.

After a few yards she glanced over her shoulder to see whether he was following. But Doggie remained by the railings and presently went off to a picture palace by himself and thought wistfully of Jeanne.

And Jeanne? Well, Jeanne was no longer at Frélus; for there came a morning when Aunt Morin was found dead in her bed. The old doctor came and spread out his thin hands and said "*Eh bien*" and "*Que voulez-vous?*" and "It was bound to happen sooner or later," and murmured learned words. The old Curé came and a neighbour or two, and candles were put round the coffin, and the *pompes funèbres* draped the front steps and entrance and vestibule in heavy black. And as soon as was possible Aunt Morin was laid to rest in the little cemetery adjoining the church, and Jeanne went back to the house with Toinette, alone in the wide world. And because there had been a death in the place the billeted soldiers went about the courtyard very quietly.

Since Phineas and Mo and Doggie's regiment had gone away, she had devoted, with a new passionate zeal, all the time she could spare from the sick woman to the comforts of the men. No longer restrained by the tightly drawn purse-strings of Aunt Morin, but with money of her own to spend — and money restored to her by these men's dear and heroic comrade— she could give them unexpected treats of rich coffee and milk, fresh eggs, fruit. . . . She mended and darned for them and suborned old women to help her. She conspired with the Town Major to render the granary more habitable; and the Town Major, who had not to issue a return for a centime's expense, received all her suggestions with courteous enthusiasm. Toinette, taking good care to impress upon every British soldier who could understand her, the fact that to Mademoiselle personally and individually he was indebted for all these luxuries, the fame of Jeanne began to spread through that sector of the Front behind which lay Frélus. Concurrently spread the story of Doggie Trevor's exploit. Jeanne became a legendary figure, save to those thrice fortunate who were billeted on *Veuve Morin et Fils, Marchands des Foins en Gros et Détail*, and these, according to their several stolid British ways, bowed down and worshipped before the slim French girl with the tragic eyes, and when

they departed, confirmed the legend and made
things nasty for the sceptically superior private.

So, on the day of the funeral of Aunt Morin, the
whole of the billet sent in a wreath to the house,
and the whole of the billet attended the service
in the little church, and they marched back and
drew up by the front door — a guard of honour
extending a little distance down the road. The
other men billeted in the village hung around,
together with the remnant of the inhabitants, old
men, women and children; but kept quite clear
of the guarded path through which Jeanne was
to pass. One or two officers looked on curiously.
But they stood in the background. It was none
of their business. If the men, in their free time,
chose to put themselves on parade, without arms,
of course, so much the better for the army.

Then Jeanne and the old Curé, in his time-
scarred shovel-hat and his rusty soutane, followed
by Toinette, turned round the corner of the lane
and emerged into the main street. A sergeant
gave a word of command. The guard stood at
attention. Jeanne and her companions proceeded
up the street, unaware of the unusual, until they
entered between the first two files. Then for the
first time the tears welled into Jeanne's eyes. She
could only stretch out her hands and cry somewhat
wildly to the bronzed statues on each side of her,
"*Merci, mes amis, merci, merci*," and flee into the
house.

The next day Maître Pépineau, the notary,
summoned her to his *cabinet*. Maître Pépineau
was very old. His partner had gone off to the
war. "One of the necessities of the present situation," he would say, "is that I should go on living
in spite of myself; for if I died the whole of the
affairs of Frélus would be in the soup." Now,
a fortnight back, Maître Pépineau and four neigh-

bours — the four witnesses required by French law when there is only one notary to draw up the *instrument public* — had visited Aunt Morin; so Jeanne knew that she had made a fresh will.

"*Mon enfant,*" said the old man, unfolding the document, "in a previous will your Aunt had left you a little heritage out of the half of her fortune which she was free to dispose of by the code. You having come into possession of your own money, she has revoked that will, and left everything to her only surviving son, Gaspard Morin in Madagascar."

"It is only just and right," said Jeanne.

"The unfortunate part of the matter," said Maître Pépineau, "is that Madame Morin has appointed official trustees to carry on the estate until Monsieur Gaspard Morin can make his own arrangements. The result is that you have no *locus standi* as a resident in the house. I pointed this out to her. But you know, in spite of her good qualities, she was obstinate. . . . It pains me greatly, my dear child, to have to state your position."

"I am then," said Jeanne, "*sans asile* — homeless?"

"As far as the house of Monsieur Gaspard Morin is concerned — yes."

"And my English soldiers?" asked Jeanne.

"Alas, my child," replied the old man, "you will find them everywhere."

Which was cold consolation. For, however much inspired by patriotic gratitude a French girl may be, she cannot settle down in a strange place where British troops are billeted, and proceed straightway to minister to their comforts. Misunderstandings are apt to arise even in the best regulated British regiments. In the house of Aunt Morin, in Frélus, her position was unassailable. Anywhere else. . . .

"So, my good Toinette," said Jeanne, after having explained the situation to the indignant old woman, "I can only go back to my friend in Paris and reconstitute my life. *Si tu veux m'accompagner —?*"

But no. Toinette had the peasant's awful dread of Paris. She had heard about Paris; there were thieves, ruffians that they called *apaches*, who murdered you if you went outside your door —

"The *apaches*," laughed Jeanne, "were swept into the army on the outbreak of war, and they've nearly all been killed, fighting like heroes."

"There are the old ones left, who are worse than the young," retorted Toinette.

No. Mademoiselle could teach her nothing about Paris. You could not even cross a street without risk of life, so many were the omnibuses and automobiles. In every shop you were a stranger to be robbed. There was no air in Paris. You could not sleep for the noise. And then — to live in a city of a hundred million people and not know one living soul! It was a mad-house matter. Again, no. It grieved her to part from Mademoiselle, but she had made her little economies — a difficult achievement, considering how regardful of her pence Madame Morin had been — and she would return to her Breton town, which forty years ago she had left to enter the service of Madame Morin.

"But after forty years, Toinette, who in Paimpol will remember you?"

"It is I who remember Paimpol," said Toinette. She remained for a few moments in thought. Then she said: "*C'est drôle, tout de même.* I haven't seen the sea for forty years, and now I can't sleep of nights thinking of it. The first man I loved was a fisherman of Paimpol. We were to be married after he returned from an Iceland voyage, with a

gros bénéfice. When the time came for his return,
I would stand on the shore and watch and watch
the sea. But he never came. The sea swallowed
him up. And then — you can understand quite
well — the child was born dead. And I thought
I would never want to look at the sea again. So
I came here to your Aunt Morin, the daughter of
Doctor Kersadec, your grandfather, and I married
Jules Dagnant, the foreman of the carters of the
hay . . . and he died a long time ago . . . and now
I have forgotten him, and I want to go and look
at the sea where my man was drowned."

"But your grandson, who is fighting in the
Argonne?"

"What difference can it make to him whether
I am in Frélus or Paimpol?"

"*C'est vrai,*" said Jeanne.

Toinette bustled about the kitchen. Folks had
to eat, whatever happened. But she went on
talking. Madame Morin. One must not speak
evil of the dead. They have their work cut out
to extricate themselves from Purgatory. But all
the same — after forty years' faithful service —
and not a mention in the will — *même pour une
Bretonne, c'était raide.* Jeanne agreed. She had
no reason to love her Aunt Morin. Her father's
people came from Agen on the confines of Gascony,
he had been a man of great gestures and vehement
speech; her mother, gentle, reserved, *un peu dévote.*
Jeanne drew her character from both sources;
but her sympathies were rather Southern than
Northern. For some reason or the other, perhaps
for his expansive ways — who knows? — Aunt
Morin had held the late Monsieur Boissière in
detestation. She had no love for Jeanne, whom
she made eat the bitter bread of servitude. Jeanne,
who before her good fortune had expected nothing
from Aunt Morin, regarded the will with feelings

316 THE ROUGH ROAD

of indifference. Except as far as it concerned
Toinette. Forty years' faithful service deserved
recognition.   But what was the use of talking
about it?

"So we must separate, Toinette?"

"Alas, yes, Mademoiselle — unless Mademoiselle
would come with me to Paimpol."

Jeanne laughed. What should she do in Paimpol? There wasn't even a fisherman left there to
fall in love with.

"Mademoiselle," said Toinette later, "do you
think you will meet the little English soldier, Monsieur Trevor, in Paris?"

"*Dans la guerre on ne se revoit jamais,*" said
Jeanne.

But there was more of personal decision than of
fatalism in her tone.

So Jeanne waited for a day or two until the regiment marched away, and then, with heavy heart,
set out for Paris. She wrote, indeed, to Phineas,
and weeks afterwards Phineas, who was in the thick
of the Somme fighting, wrote to Doggie telling him
of her departure from Frélus; but regretted that
as he had lost her letter he could not give him her
Paris address.

And in the meantime the house of Gaspard Morin
was shuttered and locked and sealed; and the
bureaucratically minded old Postmaster of Frélus,
who had received no instructions from Jeanne to
forward her correspondence, handed Doggie's letters
and telegrams to the aged postman, a superan-
nuated herdsman, who stuck them into the letter
box of the deserted house, and went away conscious
of duty perfectly accomplished.

Then, at last, Doggie, fit again for active service,
went out with a draft to France, and joined Phineas
and Mo, almost the only survivors of the cheery,
familiar crowd that he had loved, and the grimness

of battles such as he had never conceived possible took him in its inexorable grip, and he lost sense of everything save that he was the least important thing on God's earth struggling desperately for animal existence.

Yet there were rare times of relief from stress, when he could gropingly string together the facts of a pre-Somme existence. And then he would curse Phineas lustily for losing the precious letter.

"Man," Phineas once replied, "don't you see that you are breaking a heart which, in spite of its apparent rugosity and callosity, is as tender as a new-made mother's? Tell me to do it, and I'll desert and make my way to Paris and —"

"And the military police will see that you make your way to hell via a stone wall. And serve you right. Don't be a blithering fool," said Doggie.

"Then I don't know what I can do for you, laddie, except die of remorse at your feet."

"We're all going to die of rheumatic fever," said Doggie, shivering in his sodden uniform. "Blast this rain!"

Phineas thrust his hand beneath his clothing and produced a long, amorphous, and repulsive substance, like a painted tallow candle overcome by intense heat, from which he gravely bit an inch or two.

"What's that?" asked Doggie.

"It's a stick of peppermint," said Phineas. "I've still an Aunt in Galashiels who remembers my existence."

Doggie stuck out his hand like a monkey in the Zoo.

"You selfish beast!" said he.

CHAPTER XXIII

THE fighting went on, and to Doggie the inhabitants of the outside world became almost as phantasmagorical as Phineas's providential Aunt in Galashiels. Immediate existence held him. In an historic battle, Mo Shendish fell with a machine bullet through his heart. Doggie, staggering with the rest of the company to the attack over the muddy, shell-torn ground, saw him go down, a few yards away. It was not till later that he knew he had gone West with many other great souls. Doggie and Phineas mourned for him as a brother. Without him, France was a muddier and a bloodier place, and the outside world more unreal than ever.

Then to Doggie came a heart-broken letter from the Dean. Oliver had gone the same road as Mo. Peggy was frantic with grief. Vividly Doggie saw the peaceful deanery, on which all the calamity of all the war had crashed with sudden violence.

"Why I should thank God we parted as friends, I don't quite know," said Doggie, "but I do."

"I suppose, laddie," said Phineas, "it's good to feel that smiling eyes and hearty hands will greet us when we too pass over the Border. My God, man," he added reflectively, after a pause, "have you ever considered what a goodly company it will be? When you come to look at it that way, it makes Death quite a trivial affair."

"I suppose it does to us while we're here," said Doggie. "We've seen such a lot of it. But to those who haven't — my poor Peggy — it's the end of her universe."

Yes, it was all very well to take death philo-

sophically, or fatalistically, or callously, or whatever
you liked to call it, out there, where such an attitude was the only stand against raving madness;
but at home, beneath the grey mass of the Cathedral,
hitherto untouched by tragedy, folks met Death
as a strange and cruel horror. The new glory of
life that Peggy had found, he had blackened out
in an instant. Doggie looked again at the old
man's letter — his handwriting was growing shaky
— and forgot for a while the familiar things around
him, and lived with Peggy in her sorrow..

Then, as far as Doggie's sorely tried Division was
affected, came the end of the great autumn fighting. He found himself well behind the lines in
reserve, and so continued during the cold, dreary
winter months. And the more the weeks that
crept by, and the more remote seemed Jeanne,
the more Doggie hungered for the sight of her.
But all this period of his life was but a dun-coloured
monotony, with but few happenings to distinguish
week from week. Most of the company that had
marched with him into Frélus were dead or wounded.
Nearly all the officers had gone. Captain Willoughby, who had interrogated Jeanne with regard
to the restored packet, and, on Doggie's return,
had informed him with a friendly smile that they
were a damned sight too busy then to worry about
defaulters or the likes of him, but that he was going
to be court-martialled and shot as soon as peace
was declared, when they would have time to think
of serious matters — Captain Willoughby had gone
to Blighty with a leg so mauled that never would
he command again a company in the field. Sergeant Ballinghall, who had taught Doggie to use
his fists, had retired, minus a hand, into civil life.
A scientific and sporting helper at Roehampton,
he informed Doggie by letter, was busily engaged

on the invention of a boxing glove which would enable him to carry on his pugilistic career. "So, in future times," said he, "if any of your friends among the nobility and gentry want lessons in the noble art, don't forget your old friend Ballinghall." Whereat — incidentally — Doggie wondered. Never, for a fraction of a second, during their common military association, had Ballinghall given him to understand that he regarded him otherwise than as a mere Tommy, without any pretensions to gentility. There had been times when Ballinghall had cursed him — perhaps justifiably and perhaps lovingly — as though he had been the scum of the earth. Doggie would no more have dared address him in terms of familiarity than he would have dared slap the Brigadier-General on the back. And now the honest warrior sought Doggie's patronage. Of the original crowd in England who had transformed Doggie's military existence by making him penny-whistler to the Company, only Phineas and himself were left. There were others, of course, good and gallant fellows, with whom he became bound in the rough intimacy of the Army; but the first friends, those under whose protecting kindliness his manhood had developed, were the dearest. And their ghosts remained dear.

At last the Division was moved up, and there was more fighting.

One day, after a successful raid, Doggie tumbled back with the rest of the men into the trench and, looking about, missed Phineas. Presently the word went round that "Mac" had been hit, and later the rumour was confirmed by the passage down the trench of Phineas on a stretcher, his weather-battered face a ghastly ivory.

"I'm alive all right, laddie," he gasped, contorting his lips into a smile. "I've got it clean through the chest like a gentleman. But it gars me greet I canna look after you any longer."

He made an attempt at waving a hand, and the stretcher-bearers carried him away, out of the army for ever.

Thereafter Doggie felt the loneliest thing on earth, like Shelley's cloud, or the Last Man in Tom Hood's grim poem. For was he not the last man of the original Company, as he had joined it, hundreds of years ago, in England? It was only then that he realised fully the merits of the wastrel, Phineas McPhail. Not once or twice, but a thousand times had the man's vigilant affection, veiled under cynical humour, saved him from despair. Not once, but a thousand times had the gaunt, tireless Scotchman saved him from physical exhaustion. At every turn of his career, since his enlistment, Phineas had been there, watchful, helpful, devoted. There he had been, always ready and willing to be cursed. To curse him had been the great comfort of Doggie's life. Whom could he curse now? Not a soul — no one, at any rate, against whom he could launch an anathema with any real heart in it. Than curse vainly and superficially, far better not to curse at all. He missed Phineas beyond all his conception of the blankness of bereavement. Like himself, Phineas had found salvation in the army. Doggie realised how he had striven in his own queer way to redeem the villainy of his tutorship. No woman could have been more gentle, more unselfish.

"What the devil am I going to do?" said Doggie.

Meanwhile Phineas, lying in a London hospital with a bullet through his body, thought much and earnestly of his friend, and one morning Peggy got a letter.

"Dear Madam,

" *Time was when I could not have addressed you without incurring your not unjustifiable disapproval.
But I take the liberty of doing so now, trusting to
your generous acquiescence in the proposition that
the war has purged many offences. If this has not
happened, to some extent, in my case, I do not see
how it has been possible for me to have regained and
retained the trust and friendship of so sensitive and
honourable a gentleman as Mr. Marmaduke Trevor.*

"*If I ask you to come and see me here, where I am
lying severely wounded, it is not with an intention to
solicit a favour for myself personally — although
I'll not deny that the sight of a kind and familiar
face would not be a boon to a lonely and friendless
man — but with a deep desire to advance Mr. Trevor's
happiness. Lest you may imagine I am committing
an unpardonable impertinence, and thereby totally
misunderstand me, I may say that this happiness
can only be achieved by the aid of powerful friends
both in London and Paris.*

"*It is only because the lad is the one thing dear to
me left in the world, that I venture to intrude on your
privacy at such a time.*

I am,
Dear Madam,
Yours very faithfully,
Phineas McPhail."

Peggy came down to breakfast, and having duti-
fully kissed her parents, announced her intention
of going to London by the eleven o'clock train.

"Why, how can you, my dear?" asked Mrs. Conover.

"I've nothing particular to do here for the next
few days."

"But your father and I have. Neither of us can
start off to London at a moment's notice."

Peggy replied with a wan smile: "But, dearest
mother, you forget. I'm an old, old married
woman."

"Besides, my dear," said the Dean, "Peggy has
often gone away by herself."

"But never to London," said Mrs. Conover.

"Anyhow, I've got to go, dearest." Peggy turned
to the old butler. "Ring up Sturrocks' and tell
them I'm coming."

"Yes, Miss," said Burford.

"He's as bad as you are, mother," said Peggy.

So she went up to London, and stayed the night
at Sturrocks' alone, for the first time in her life.
She half ate a lonely, execrable war dinner in the
stuffy, old-fashioned dining room, served cere-
moniously by the ancient head-waiter, the friend
of her childhood, who, in view of her recent widowhood, addressed her in the muffled tones of the
sympathetic undertaker. Peggy nearly cried. She
wished she had chosen another hotel. But where
else could she have gone? She had stayed at few
hotels in London; once at the Savoy; once at
Claridge's; every other time at Sturrocks'. The
Savoy? Its vastness frightened her. And Claridge's? — no; that was sanctified for ever. Oliver
in his lordly way had snapped his fingers at Sturrocks'. Only the best was good enough for Peggy.

Now, only Sturrocks' remained.

She sought her room immediately after the dreary
meal and sat before the fire — it was a damp, chill
February night — and thought miserable and aching
thoughts. It happened to be the same room which
she had occupied, oh — thousands of years ago —
on the night when Doggie, point-device in new
Savile Row uniform, had taken her to dinner at
the Carlton. And she had sat, in the same imita-
tion Charles the Second brocaded chair, looking
into the same generous, old-fashioned fire, thinking

— thinking. . . . And she remembered clenching her fist and apostrophising the fire and crying out aloud: "Oh, my God! if only he makes good!"

Oceans of years lay between then and now. Doggie had made good; every man who came home wounded must have made good. Poor old Doggie. But how in the name of all that was meant by the word Love she could ever have contemplated — as she had contemplated, with an obstinate, virginal loyalty — marriage with Doggie, she could not understand.

She undressed, brought the straight-backed chair close to the fire, and, in her dainty nightgown, part of her trousseau, sat elbow on knee, face in thin, clutching hands, slippered feet on fender, thinking, thinking once again. Thinking now of the gates of Paradise that had opened to her for a few brief weeks. Of the man who never had to make good, being the wonder of wonders of men, the delicious companion, the incomparable lover, the all-compelling revealer, the great, gay, scarcely, to her woman's limited power of vision, comprehended, heroic soldier. Of the terrifying meaninglessness of life, now that her God of Very God, in human form, had been swept, on an instant, off the earth into the Unknown.

Yet was life meaningless after all? There must be some significance, some inner truth veiled in mystery, behind even the casually accepted and never probed religion to which she had been born, and in which she had found poor refuge. For, like many of her thoughtless, unquestioning class, she had looked at Christ through stained-glass windows, and now the windows were darkened. . . . For the first time in her life her soul groped intensely towards eternal verities. The fire burned low, and she shivered. She became again the bit of human flotsam cruelly buffeted by the waves, forgotten of God. Yet, after she had risen and crept into bed, and while she was staring into the darkness, her heart became filled with a vast pity for the thousands and thousands of women, her sisters, who at that moment were staring, hopeless, like her, into the unrelenting night.

She did not fall asleep till early morning. She rose late. About half past eleven as she was preparing to walk abroad on a dreary shopping excursion — the hospital visiting hour was in the afternoon — a telegram arrived from the Dean.

"*Just heard that Marmaduke is severely wounded.*"

She scarcely recognised the young private tutor of Denby Hall in the elderly man with the deeply-furrowed face, who smiled as she approached his bed. She had brought him flowers, cigarettes of the exquisite kind that Doggie used to smoke, chocolates . . .

She sat down by his bedside.

"All this is more than gracious, Mrs. Manning-tree," said Phineas. "To a *vieux routier* like me, it is a wee bit overwhelming."

"It's very little to do for Doggie's best friend."

Phineas's eyes twinkled. "If you call him Doggie, like that, maybe it won't be so difficult for me to talk to you."

"Why should it be difficult at all?" she asked. "We both love him."

"Ay," said Phineas. "He's a lovable lad, and it is because others besides you and me find him lovable, that I took the liberty of writing to you."

"The girl in France?"

"Eh?" He put out a bony hand and regarded her in some disappointment. "Has he told you? Perhaps you know all about it."

"I know nothing except that — 'A girl in France,' was all he told me. But — first about yourself.

How badly are you wounded — and what can we do for you?"

She dragged from a reluctant Phineas the history of his wound, and obtained confirmation of his statement from a nurse who happened to pass up the gangway of the pleasant ward and lingered by the bedside. McPhail was doing splendidly. Of course, a man with a hole through his body must be expected to go back to the régime of babyhood. So long as he behaved himself like a well-conducted baby all would be well. Peggy drew the nurse a few yards away.

"I've just heard that his dearest friend out there, a boy whom he loves dearly and has been through the whole thing with him in the same company — it's odd, but he was his private tutor years ago — both gentlemen, you know — in fact, I'm here just to talk about the boy —" Peggy grew somewhat incoherent — "Well — I've just heard that the boy has been seriously wounded. Shall I tell him?"

"I think it would be better to wait for a few days. Any shock like that sends up their temperatures, — we hate temperatures — and we're getting his down so nicely."

"All right," said Peggy, and she went back smiling to Phineas. "She says you're getting on amazingly, Mr. McPhail."

Said Phineas: "I'm grateful to you, Mrs. Manningtree, for concerning yourself about my entirely unimportant carcass. Now, as Virgil says, 'paullo majora canemus.'"

"You have me there, Mr. McPhail," said Peggy.

"Let us sing of somewhat greater things. That is the bald translation. Let us talk of Doggie — if so be it is agreeable to you."

"Carry on," said Peggy.

"Well," said Phineas, "to begin at the beginning, we marched into a place called Frélus —"

In his pedantic way he began to tell her the story of Jeanne, so far as he knew it. He told her of the girl standing in the night wind and rain on the bluff by the turning of the road. He told her of Doggie's insane adventure across No Man's Land to the Farm of La Folette. Tears rolled down Peggy's cheeks. She cried, incredulous:

"Doggie did that? Doggie?"

"It was child's play to what he had to do at Guedecourt."

But Peggy waved away the vague heroism of Guedecourt.

"Doggie did that? For a woman?"

The whole elaborate structure of her conception of Doggie tumbled down like a house of cards.

"Ay," said Phineas.

"He did that — " Phineas had given an imaginative and picturesque account of the episode — "for this girl Jeanne?"

"It is a strange coincidence, Mrs. Manningtree," replied Phineas, with a flicker of his lips elusively suggestive of unctuousness, "that almost those identical words were used by Mademoiselle Boissière in my presence. '*Il a fait cela pour moi!*' But — you will pardon me for saying it — with a difference of intonation, which, as a woman, no doubt you will be able to divine and appreciate."

"I know," said Peggy. She bent forward and picked with finger and thumb at the fluff of the blanket. Then she said, intent on the fluff: "If a man had done a thing like that for me, I should have crawled after him to the ends of the earth." Presently she looked up with a flash of the eyes. "Why isn't this girl doing it?"

"You must listen to the end of the story," said Phineas. "I may tell you that I always regarded myself, with my Scot's caution, as a model of tact and discretion; but after many conversations with

Doggie, I'm beginning to have my doubts. I also imagined that I was very careful of my personal belongings; but facts have convicted me of criminal laxity."

Peggy smiled. "That sounds like a confession, Mr. McPhail."

"Maybe it's in the nature of one," he assented. "But, by your leave, Mrs. Manningtree, I'll resume my narrative."

He continued the story of Jeanne; how she had learned through him of Doggie's wealth and position and early upbringing; of the memorable dinner party with poor Mo; of Doggie's sensitive interpretation of her French *bourgeoise* attitude; and finally of the loss of the letter containing her address in Paris.

After he had finished, Peggy sat for a long while thinking. This romance in Doggie's life had moved her as she thought she could never be moved since the death of Oliver. Her thoughts winged themselves back to an afternoon, remote almost as her socked and sashed childhood, when Doggie, immaculately attired in grey and pearl harmonies, had declared, with his little effeminate drawl, that tennis made one so terribly hot. The scene in the Deanery garden flashed before her. It was succeeded by a scene in the Deanery drawing room, when to herself indignant he had pleaded his delicacy of constitution. And the same Doggie, besides braving death a thousand times in the ordinary execution of his soldier's duties, had performed this queer deed of heroism for a girl. Then his return to Durdlebury —

"I'm afraid," she said suddenly, "I was dreadfully unkind to him when he came home the last time. I didn't understand. Did he tell you?"

Phineas stretched out a hand and with the tips of his fingers touched her sleeve.

"Mrs. Manningtree," he said, softly, "don't you know that Doggie's a very wonderful gentleman?"

Again her eyes grew moist. "Yes. I know. Of course he never would have mentioned it. . . . I thought, Mr. McPhail, he had deteriorated — God forgive me! I thought he had coarsened, and got into the ways of an ordinary Tommy — and I was snobbish and uncomprehending and horrible. It seems as if I am making a confession now."

"Ay. Why not? If it were not for the soul's good, the ancient Church wouldn't have instituted the practice."

She regarded him shrewdly for a second. "You've changed, too."

"Maybe." said Phineas. "It's an ill war that blows nobody good, and I'm not complaining of this one. But you were talking of your miscomprehension of Doggie."

"I behaved very badly to him," she said, picking again at the blanket. "I misjudged him altogether — because I was ignorant of everything — everything that matters in life. But I've learned better since then."

"Ay," remarked Phineas, gravely.

"Mr. McPhail," she said, after a pause, "it wasn't those rotten ideas that prevented me from marrying him —"

"I know, my dear little lady," said Phineas, grasping the plucking hand. "You just loved the other man as you never could have loved Doggie, and there's an end to it. Love just happens. It's the holiest thing in the world."

She turned her hand, so as to meet his in a mutual clasp, and withdrew it.

"You're very kind — and sympathetic — and understanding —" her voice broke. "I seem to have been going about misjudging everybody and everything. I'm beginning to see a little bit — a little bit further — I can't express myself —"

"Never mind, Mrs. Manningtree," said Phineas soothingly, "if you cannot express yourself in words. Leave that to the politicians and the philosophers and the theologians, and other such windy expositors of the useless. But you can express yourself in deeds."

"How?"

"Find Jeanne for Doggie."

Peggy bent forward with a queer light in her eyes.

"Does she love him — really love him as he deserves to be loved?"

"It is not often, Mrs. Manningtree, that I commit myself to a definite statement. But, to my certain knowledge, these two are breaking their hearts for each other. Couldn't you find her, before the poor laddie is killed?"

"He's not killed yet, thank God!" said Peggy, with an odd thrill in her voice.

He was alive. Only severely wounded. He would be coming home soon, carried, according to convoy, to any unfriendly hospital dumping-ground in the United Kingdom. If only she could bring this French girl to him! She yearned to make reparation for the past, to act according to the new knowledge that love and sorrow had brought her.

"But how can I find her — just a girl — an unknown Mademoiselle Boissière — among the millions of Paris?"

"I've been racking my brains all the morning," replied Phineas, "to recall the address, and out of the darkness there emerges just two words, *Port Royal*. If you know Paris, does that help you at all?"

"I don't know Paris," replied Peggy humbly. "I don't know anything. I'm utterly ignorant."

"I beg entirely to differ from you, Mrs. Manning-tree," said Phineas. "You have come through much heavy travail to a correct appreciation of the meaning of human love between man and woman, and so you have in you the wisdom of all the ages."

"Yes, yes," said Peggy, becoming practical. "But *Port Royal* —?"

"The clue to the labyrinth," replied Phineas.

CHAPTER XXIV

THE Dean of an English cathedral is a personage. He has power. He can stand with folded arms at its door and forbid entrance to anyone, save perhaps the King in person. He can tell not only the Bishop of the Diocese, but the very Archbishop of the Province, to run away and play. Having power, and using it benignly and graciously, he can exert its subtler form known as influence. In the course of his distinguished career he is bound to make many queer friends in high places.

"My dear Field Marshal, could you do me a little favour . . .?"

"My dear Ambassador, my daughter, etc., etc...."

Deans, discreet, dignified gentlemen, who would not demand the impossible, can generally get what they ask for.

When Peggy returned to Durdlebury and put Doggie's case before her father, and with unusual fervour roused him from his first stupefaction at the idea of her mad project, he said mildly:

"Let me understand clearly what you want to do. You want to go to Paris by yourself, discover a girl called Jeanne Boissière, concerning whose address you know nothing but two words — Port Royal — of course there is a Boulevard Port Royal somewhere south of the Luxembourg Gardens —"

"Then we've found her," cried Peggy. "We only want the number."

"Please don't interrupt," said the Dean. "You confuse me, my dear. You want to find this girl and re-establish communication between her and Marmaduke, and — er — generally play Fairy Godmother."

"If you like to put it that way," said Peggy.

"Are you quite certain you would be acting wisely? From Marmaduke's point of view —"

"Don't call him Marmaduke —" She bent forward and touched his knee caressingly — "Marmaduke could never have risked his life for a woman. It was Doggie who did it. She thinks of him as Doggie. Everyone thinks of him now and loves him as Doggie. It was Oliver's name for him, don't you see? And he has stuck it out, and made it a sort of title of honour and affection — and it was as Doggie that Oliver learned to love him, and in his last letter to Oliver he signed himself '*Your devoted Doggie.*'"

"My dear," smiled the Dean and quoted: "'What's in a name? A rose —'"

"Would be unendurable if it were called a — a bug-squash. The poetry would be knocked out of it."

The Dean said indulgently: "So the name Doggie connotes something poetic and romantic?"

"You ask the girl Jeanne."

The Dean tapped the back of his daughter's hand that rested on his knee.

"There's no fool like an old fool, my dear. Do you know why?"

She shook her head.

"Because the old fool has learned to understand the young fool, whereas the young fool doesn't understand anybody."

She laughed and threw herself on her knees by his side.

"Daddy, you're immense!"

He took the tribute complacently. "What was I saying, before you interrupted me? Oh, yes.

About the wisdom of your proposed action. Are you sure they want each other?"

"As sure as I'm sitting here," said Peggy.

"Then, my dear," said he, "I'll do what I can."

Whether he wrote to Field Marshals and Ambassadors or to lesser luminaries, Peggy did not know. The Dean observed an old-world punctilio about such matters. At the first reply or two to his letters he frowned; at the second or two he smiled in the way any elderly gentleman may smile when he finds himself recognised by high-and-mightinesses as a person of importance.

"I think, my dear," said he at last, "I've arranged everything for you."

So it came to pass that while Doggie, with a shattered shoulder and a touched left lung, was being transported from a base hospital in France to a hospital in England, Peggy, armed with all kinds of passports and recommendations, and a very fixed, personal sanctified idea, was crossing the Channel on her way to Paris and Jeanne.

And, after all, it was no wild goose chase, but a very simple matter. An urbane, elderly person at the British Embassy performed certain telephonic gymnastics. At the end:

"*Merci, merci. Adieu!*"

He turned to her.

"A representative from the Prefecture of Police will wait on you at your hotel at ten o'clock to-morrow morning."

The official called, took notes, and confidently assured her that he would obtain the address of Mademoiselle Jeanne Boissière within twelve hours.

"But how, Monsieur, are you going to do it?" asked Peggy.

"Madame," said he, "in spite of the war, the

telegraphic, telephonic, and municipal systems of France work in perfect order — to say nothing of that of the police. Frélus, I think, is the name of the place she started from?"

At seven o'clock in the evening, after her lonely dinner in the great hotel, the polite official called again.   She met him in the lounge.

"Madame," said he, "I have the pleasure to inform you that Mademoiselle Jeanne Boissière, late of Frélus, is living in Paris at 743bis Boulevard Port Royal, and spends all her days at the succursale of the French Red Cross in the Rue Vaugirard."

"Have you seen her and told her?"

"No, Madame; that did not come within my instructions."

"I am infinitely grateful to you," said Peggy.

"*Il n'y a pas de quoi, Madame.* I perform the tasks assigned to me, and am only too happy, in this case, to have been successful."

"But, Monsieur," said Peggy, feeling desperately lonely in Paris, and pathetically eager to talk to a human being, even in her rusty Vévey school French, "haven't you wondered why I've been so anxious to find this young lady?"

"If we began to wonder," he replied with a laugh, "at the things which happen during the war, we should be so bewildered that we shouldn't be able to carry on our work.   Madame," said he, handing her his card, "if you should have further need of me in the matter, I am always at your service."

He bowed profoundly and left her.

Peggy stayed at the Ritz because, long ago, when her parents had fetched her from Vévey, and had given her the one wonderful fortnight in Paris she had ever known, they had chosen this dignified and not inexpensive hostelry. To her girlish mind, it had breathed the last word of splen-

dour, movement, gaiety — all that was connoted
by the magical name of the City of Light. But
now the glamour had departed. She wondered
whether it had ever been. Oliver had laughed
at her experiences. Sandwiched between dear old
Uncle Edward and Aunt Sophia, what in the sacred
name of France could she have seen of Paris? Wait
till they could turn round. He would take her to
Paris. She would have the unimagined time of
her life. They dreamed dreams of the Rue de la
Paix — he had five hundred pounds laid by, which
he had ear-marked for an orgy of shopping in that
Temptation Avenue of a thoroughfare; of Mont-
martre, the citadel of delectable wickedness and
laughter; of funny little restaurants in dark streets
where you are delighted to pay twenty francs
for a mussel, so exquisitely is it cooked; of dainty
and crazy theatres; of long drives, folded in each
other's arms, when moonlight touches dawn,
through the wonders of the enchanted city.

Her brief dreams had eclipsed her girlish memories.
Now the dreams had become blurred. She strove
to bring them back till her soul ached, till she broke
down into miserable weeping. She was alone in
a strange, unedifying town; in a strange, vast,
commonplace hotel. The cold, moonlit Place de
la Vendôme, with its memorable column, just opposite her bedroom window, meant nothing to her.
She had the desolating sense that nothing in the
world would ever matter to her again — nothing
as far as she, Peggy Manningtree, was concerned.
Her life was over. Altruism alone gave sanction
to continued existence. Hence her present adventure. Paris might have been Burslem for all the
interest it afforded.

Jeanne worked from morning to night in the
succursale of the Croix Rouge in the Rue Vaugirard.

She had tried, after the establishment of her affairs, to enter, in no matter what capacity, a British base hospital. It would be a consolation for her surrender of Doggie to work for his wounded comrades. Besides, twice in her life she owed everything to the English, and the repayment of the debt was a matter of conscience. But she found that the gates of English hospitals were thronged with English girls; and she could not even speak the language. So, guided by the Paris friend with whom she lodged, she made her way to the Rue Vaugirard, where, in the packing-room, she found hard and unemotional employment. Yet the work had to be done: and it was done for France, which, after all, was dearer to her than England, and among her fellow-workers, women of all classes, she found pleasant companionship.

When, one day, the old concierge, be-medalled from the war of 1870, appeared to her in the packing-room, with the announcement that a *dame anglaise* desired to speak to her, she was at first bewildered. She knew no English ladies — had never met one in her life. It took a second or two for the thought to flash that the visit might concern Doggie. Then came conviction. In blue overall and cap, she followed the concierge to the ante-room, her heart beating. At the sight of the young English woman in black, with a crêpe hat and little white band beneath the veil, it nearly stopped altogether.

Peggy advanced with outstretched hand.

"You are Mademoiselle Jeanne Boissière?"

"Yes, Madame."

"I am a cousin of Monsieur Trevor —"

"Ah, Madame —" Jeanne pointed to the mourning — "you do not come to tell me he is dead?"

Peggy smiled. "No. I hope not."

"Ah!" Jeanne sighed in relief, "I thought —"

"This is for my husband," said Peggy quietly.

"*Ah, Madame! je demande bien pardon. J'ai dû vous faire de la peine. Je n'y pensais pas—*"

Jeanne was in great distress. Peggy smiled again. "Widows dress differently in England and France." She looked around and her eyes fell upon a bench by the wall. "Could we sit down and have a little talk?"

"*Pardon, Madame, c'est que je suis un peu émue. . .*" said Jeanne.

She led the way to the bench. They sat down together, and for a feminine second or two took stock of each other. Jeanne's first rebellious instinct said "I was right." In her furs and perfect millinery and perfect shoes and perfect black silk stockings that appeared below the short skirt, Peggy, blue-eyed, fine-featured, the fine product of many generations of scholarly English gentlefolk, seemed to incarnate her vague conjectures of the social atmosphere in which Doggie had his being. Her peasant blood impelled her to suspicion, to a half-grudging admiration, to self-protective jealousy. The Englishwoman's ease of manner, in spite of her helter-skelter French, oppressed her with an angry sense of inferiority. She was also conscious of the blue overall and close-fitting cap. Yet the Englishwoman's smile was kind and she had lost her husband. . . . And Peggy, looking at this girl with the dark, tragic eyes and refined, pale face and graceful gestures, in the funny instinctive British way tried to place her socially. Was she a lady? It made such a difference. This was the girl for whom Doggie had performed his deed of knight-errantry; the girl whom she proposed to take back to Doggie. For the moment, discounting the uniform which might have hidden a midinette or a duchess, she had nothing but the face and the gestures and the beautifully modulated voice to go upon; and between the accent of the midinette and the duchess — both being equally charming to her English ear — Peggy could not discriminate. She had, however, beautiful, capable hands and took care of her finger-nails.

Jeanne broke the tiny spell of embarrassed silence.

"I am at your disposal, Madame."

Peggy plunged at once into facts.

"It may seem strange, my coming to you; but the fact is that my cousin, Monsieur Trevor, is severely wounded . . ."

"*Mon Dieu!*" said Jeanne.

"And his friend, Mr. McPhail, who is also wounded, thinks that if you — well —"

Her French failed her — to carry off a very delicate situation one must have command of language — she could only blurt out —"*Il faut comprendre, Mademoiselle. Il a fait beaucoup pour vous.*"

She met Jeanne's dark eyes. Jeanne said:

"*Oui, Madame, vous avez raison. Il a beaucoup fait pour moi.*"

Peggy flushed at the unconscious correction — "*beaucoup fait,*" for "*fait beaucoup.*"

"He has done not only much, but everything for me, Madame," Jeanne continued. "And you who have come from England expressly to tell me that he is wounded, what do you wish me to do?"

"Accompany me back to London. I had a telegram this morning to say that he had arrived at a hospital there."

"Then you have not seen him?"

"Not yet."

"Then how, Madame, do you know that he desires my presence?"

Peggy glanced at the girl's hands clasped on her lap, and saw that the knuckles were white.

"I am sure of it."

"He would have written, Madame. I only

received one letter from him, and that was while
I still lived at Frélus."

"He wrote many letters and telegraphed to
Frélus, and received no answers."

"Madame," cried Jeanne. "I implore you to
believe what I say; but not one of those letters
has ever reached me."

"Not one?"

At first Peggy was incredulous. Phineas McPhail
had told her of Doggie's despair at the lack of response from Frélus, and, after all, Frélus had a
properly constituted post office in working order,
which might be expected to forward letters.
She had therefore come prepared to reproach the
girl. But . . .

"*Je le jure, Madame*," said Jeanne.

And Peggy believed her.

"But I wrote to Monsieur McPhail, giving him
my address in Paris."

"He lost the letter before he saw Doggie again"
— the name slipped out — "and forgot the address."

"But how did you find me?"

"I had a lot of difficulty. The British Embassy
— the Prefecture of Police —"

"*Mon Dieu!*" cried Jeanne again. "Did you
do all that for me?"

"For my cousin."

"You called him 'Doggie.' That is how I know
him and think of him."

"All right," smiled Peggy. "For Doggie then."

Jeanne's brain for a moment or two was in a
whirl. Embassies and Prefectures of Police!

"Madame, to do this, you must love him very
much."

"I loved him so much — I hope you will understand me — my French I know is terrible — but
I loved him so much that until he came home
wounded we were *fiancés*."

Jeanne drew a short breath. "I felt it, Madame. An English gentleman of great estate would naturally marry an English lady of his own social class. That is why, Madame, I acted as I have done."

Then something of what Jeanne really was became obvious to Peggy. Lady or no lady, in the conventional British sense, Jeanne appealed to her, in her quiet dignity and restraint, as a type of Frenchwoman whom she had never met before. She suddenly conceived an enormous respect for Jeanne. Also for Phineas McPhail, whose eulogistic character sketch she had accepted with feminine reservations subconsciously derisive.

"My dear," she said. "*Vous êtes digne de toute dame anglaise!*" — which wasn't an elegant way of putting it in the French tongue — but Jeanne, with her odd smile of the lips, showed that she understood her meaning — she had served her apprenticeship in the interpretation of Anglo-Gallic. "But I want to tell you. Doggie and I were engaged. A family matter. Then, when he came home wounded — you know how — I found that I loved someone — *aimais d'amour*, as you say — and he found the same. I loved the man whom I married. He loved you. He confessed it. We parted more affectionate friends than we had ever been. I married. He searched for you. My husband has been killed. Doggie, although wounded, is alive. That is why I am here."

They were sitting in a corner of the ante-room, and before them passed a continuous stream of the busy life of the war, civilians, officers, badged workers, elderly orderlies in pathetic bits of uniform that might have dated from 1870, wheeling packages in and out, groups talking of the business of the organisation, here and there a blue-vested young lieutenant and a blue-overalled packer,

talking — it did not need God to know of what.
But neither of the two women heeded this multi-
tude.

Jeanne said: "Madame, I am profoundly moved
by what you have told me. If I show little emotion,
it is because I have suffered greatly from the war.
One learns self-restraint, Madame, or one goes
mad. But as you have spoken to me in your noble
English frankness — I have only to confess that
I love Doggie with all my heart, with all my soul —"
with her two clenched hands she smote her breast
— and Peggy noted it was the first gesture that she
had made. "I feel the infinite need, Madame —
you will understand me, — to care for him, to protect him —"

Peggy raised a beautifully gloved hand.

"Protect him?" she interrupted. "Why, hasn't
he shown himself to be a hero?"

Jeanne leant forward and grasped the protesting
hand by the wrist; and there was a wonderful
light behind her eyes and a curious vibration in
her voice.

"It is only *les petits héros tout faits* — the little
ready-made heroes — ready-made by the bon Dieu
— who have no need of a woman's protection.
But it is a different thing with the great heroes who
have made themselves without the aid of a bon
Dieu, from little dogs of no account (*des petits chiens
de rien du tout*) to what Dog-gie is at the moment.
The woman then takes her place. She fixes things
for ever. She alone can understand."

Peggy gasped as at a new Revelation. The
terms in which this French girl expressed herself
were far beyond the bounds of her philosophy.
The varying aspects in which Doggie had presented
himself to her, in the past few months, had been
bewildering. Now she saw him, in a fresh light,
though as in a glass darkly, as reflected by Jeanne.

Still, she protested again, in order to see more clearly.

"But what would you protect him from?"

"From want of faith in himself; from want of faith in his destiny, Madame. Once he told me he had come to France to fight for his soul. It is necessary that he should be victorious. It is necessary that the woman who loves him should make him victorious."

Peggy put out her hand and touched Jeanne's wrist.

"I'm glad I didn't marry Doggie, Mademoiselle," she said simply. "I couldn't have done that." She paused. "Well?" she resumed. "Will you now come with me to London?"

A faint smile crept into Jeanne's eyes.

"*Mais oui, Madame.*"

Doggie lay in the long, pleasant ward of the great London hospital, the upper left side of his body a mass of bandaged pain. Neck and shoulder, front and back and arm, had been shattered and torn by a high explosive shell. The top of his lung had been grazed. Only the remorseless pressure at the base hospital had justified the sending of him, after a week, to England. Youth and the splendid constitution which Dr. Murdoch had proclaimed in the far off days of the war's beginning, and the toughening training of the war itself, carried him through. No more fighting for Doggie this side of the grave. But the grave was as far distant as it is from any young man in his twenties who avoids abnormal peril.

Till to-day he had not been allowed to see visitors, or to receive letters. They told him that the Dean of Durdlebury had called; had brought flowers and fruit and had left a card "From your Aunt, Peggy, and myself." But to-day he felt wonderfully

strong, in spite of the unrelenting pain, and the
nurse had said: "I shouldn't wonder if you had
some visitors this afternoon." Peggy, of course.
He followed the hands of his wrist watch until they
marked the visiting hour. And sure enough, a
minute afterwards, amid the stream of men and
women — chiefly women — of all grades and kinds,
he caught sight of Peggy's face smiling beneath
her widow's hat. She had a great bunch of violets
in her bodice.

"My dear old Doggie!" She bent down and
kissed him. "These rotten people wouldn't let
me come before."

"I know," said Doggie. He pointed to his
shoulder. "I'm afraid I'm in a hell of a mess. It's
lovely to see you."

She unpinned the violets and thrust them towards
his face.

"From home. I've brought 'em for you."

"My God!" said Doggie, burying his nose in the
huge bunch. "I never knew violets could smell
like this." He laid them down with a sigh. "How's
everybody?"

"Quite fit."

There was a span of silence. Then he stretched
out his hand and she gave him hers and he gripped
it tight.

"Poor old Peggy dear!"

"Oh, that's all right," she said bravely. "I
know you care, dear Doggie. That's enough.
I've just got to stick it like the rest." She with-
drew her hand after a little squeeze. "Bless you.
Don't worry about me. I'm contemptibly healthy.
But you —?"

"Getting on splendidly. I say, Peggy, what
kind of people are the Pullingers who have taken
Denby Hall?"

"They're all right, I believe. He's something in

the Government — Controller of Feeding-bottles —
I don't know. But, oh, Doggie, what an ass you
were to sell the place up!"

"I wasn't."

"You were."

Doggie laughed. "If you've come here to argue
with me, I shall cry, and then you'll be turned out
neck and crop."

Peggy looked at him shrewdly. "You seem to
be going pretty strong."

"Never stronger in my life," lied Doggie.

"Would you like to see somebody you are very
fond of?"

"Somebody I'm fond of? Uncle Edward?"

"No, no." She waved the Very Reverend the
Dean to the empyrean.

"Dear old Phineas? Has he come through?
I've not had time to ask whether you've heard
anything about him."

"Yes, he's flourishing. He wrote to me. I've
seen him."

"Praise the Lord!" cried Doggie. "My dear,
there's no one on earth, save you, whom I should
so much love to see as Phineas. If he's there,
fetch him along."

Peggy nodded and smiled mysteriously and went
away down the ward. And Doggie thought:
"Thank God, Peggy has the strength to face the
world — and thank God, Phineas has come
through." He closed his eyes, feeling rather tired,
thinking of Phineas. Of his last words as he passed
him stretcher-borne in the trench. Of the devotion
of the man. Of his future. Well, never mind his
future. In all his vague post-war schemes for
reorganisation of the social system, Phineas had
his place. No further need for dear old Phineas
to stand in mulberry and gold outside a Picture
Palace. He had thought it out long ago, although

he had never said a word to Phineas.   Now he could
set the poor chap's mind at rest for ever.

He looked round contentedly, and saw Peggy
and a companion coming down the ward, together.
And it was not Phineas.   It was a girl in black.

He raised himself, forgetful of exquisite pain,
on his right elbow, and stared in a thrill of amazement.

And Jeanne came to him, and there were no longer
ghosts behind her eyes, for they shone like stars.

www.ingramcontent.com/pod-product-compliance
Lightning Source LLC
Chambersburg PA
CBHW022207010726
47493CB00002B/451